Judge #1, 29th Annual Writer's Digest Self-Published Book Awards:

Myrica Moss's love of science fiction and fantasy comes through loud and clear in this novel. The concept is wild, promising and full of potential. The most striking aspect of this book probably comes in the form of conviction and how well integrated everything is in this world that Moss has created. The many characters are all intriguing to follow – my favorites being Twila and Rowan, for whatever reason. The structure, too, was very well done, and it felt like we held an excellent pace that goes naturally with this genre story. Overall, Moss's novel is a captivating read with a lot of entertainment value for the fantasy lover.

The Dragon's Tear Chronicles
Of Dark Ones and Dragons

By Myrica Moss

Myrica Moss'

The Dragon's Tear Chronicles

Book One:
Of Dark Ones and Dragons

Book Two:
Saressa's Child

Book Three:
Lunaria

Book Four (The Final in this Series):
Valeskas*

*Coming soon in 2023

Cover illustration by JL Alfaro

ISBN-13: 979-8581381816

US Library of Congress Registration Number: TXu 2-222-292

I dedicate this book to Gary, who sadly did not get to see it published.

My thanks to family and friends who encouraged me along the way. Randy, for letting me write in his Lincoln during lunch breaks. Mandy, Graeme, and Kris for believing in me. Jake, Hoss, and Rick, for letting me talk endlessly about my progress. Jace, Vicky, Sally, Holli, Janet and Karen, for being my readers.

Special thanks to Joshua and Logsdon Publishing.

The Main Characters in The Dragon's Tear Chronicles – Of Dark Ones And Dragons

Twila – A light magic user, wronged by the Gypsy and seeks revenge

Amani – A Darpelian (half Dark One and half-human) who is the dragon's guardian, a shapeshifter, and a magic-user

Shayla – A bard, skilled with daggers, who serves the goddess in another of her worlds and joins the quest

Devon – A Lunarian from the unfinished world where the Dark Ones are trapped, his powers include the ability to meld with natural elements as it suits his purpose and spell casting

Raven – A mercenary, skilled with all weapons, predicts the future with Telling Cards and seeks to avenge the death of his old teacher

Motomo – A young wolf who communicates mentally with the group, joins them to avenge the death of one of his pack members

CHAPTER ONE

Prologue

Danior shuddered as a glimmer crashed into his head and slithered icily down his spine. This warning from the seal after all these years took him entirely by surprise. He almost cried out in alarm when he sensed it. Danior knew that if his heart were still capable of beating, it would be pounding away at his chest wall in response. He fought with an impulse to run out into the street and not stop running until he reached the seal, but if Danior left now, though, he would lose his place in the line. After waiting for more than an hour already with this torturous pain of burning hunger steadily increasing within him, Danior knew he could not leave right now. Investigating what may be wrong with the seal would have to wait.

It had been more than thirty-five years ago when Ramos, a dark magic user, had approached the Gypsy clan leaders requesting their assistance to end the invasion of the Dark Ones in their world of Sheukhawn. Danior had been one of the Gypsies that had offered to help him in this quest. Ramos created a magic seal and used the blood of a young Gypsy girl. The seal closed a rift between Sheukhawn and Lunaria's shadow world that imprisoned the Dark Ones. Danior and the other Gypsies who accompanied Ramos slew the few Dark Ones that became trapped in Sheukhawn when he placed the seal. Danior sighed as he clearly remembered being attacked and bitten by one of those remaining Dark Ones and became infected with the blood hunger himself. Danior had begged Ramos to slay him, but he refused. Instead, he asked that Danior become a guardian of the seal and report back to him should it ever fail. Danior knew how devastating the Dark Ones' invasion had been to the peaceful Sheukhawn's inhabitants, so he had agreed. The only condition that he asked of Ramos was to cast a spell on him preventing him from satisfying his blood hunger in Sheukhawn. The only place that Danior could satisfy his blood hunger was on the Lunaria side of the seal, although he could freely travel across the seal and back again.

Danior tried to concentrate on what remained of the warning from the seal in his mind. But the noise from the crowd around him, in addition to his blood hunger, made it impossible. Danior had felt nothing from the seal since its creation. He attempted to guess what kind of warning it could be. It hadn't felt like a crossing. He would have instantly recognized that, after all, his role was to protect his native world from the creatures in this world. Danior's eyes narrowed as he tried to determine what else could have generated such a powerful glimmer, but he had no idea.

Stop it, Danior thought hurriedly. Why torture yourself like this. I must wait until the blood hunger is satisfied, and then I can investigate the seal.

Impatiently he shuffled a little closer to this evening's offering when the crowd moved slightly forward. As was usual, Danior avoided looking directly at the victim's glazed expression, especially now as he was close enough to see the Feeder's face. He quickly hung his head down so their eyes would not accidentally meet. Danior felt that the Feeder's eyes burned into his mind, seeking him out amongst the others, accusing him of not trying to stop this atrocity. He continued to move forward as, one by one, the trail of Dark Ones ahead of him drank blood from a young woman, tonight's Feeder. Danior could sense the increasing excitement oozing from the pores of the shabbily dressed Dark One in front of him. He turned away in disgust and found himself gazing longingly at the young Feeder. Horrified by the reality of what he had become, Danior quickly dropped his head again.

It wasn't always a woman Feeder. Men, too, were often part of an establishment's stock. They weren't always young, either. Danior hated this nightly ritual, but like the rest of the Dark Ones, the hunger gave him no choice. He irritably brushed his icy cold fingers through his thick long black hair. Danior fought against a mixture of disgust and excitement that continually stirred within him the closer he got to the Feeder. There was a forbidding-looking guard at the front of the line keeping the patrons in check. The guard was a lieutenant in Stefan's dark army. Danior recognized the uniform.

As Danior's hunger grew, it became increasingly more difficult to notice anything else except the over-powering, delicious smell of blood. The jostling impatient crowd behind Danior no longer disturbed him either. He raised his head and found himself looking directly at the Feeder's face. Her eyes were no longer accusing. They were inviting, encouraging him forward from deep within their tantalizing, liquid brown depths. The Feeder being drained of blood before it was his turn now concerned him. Changing Feeders often took a long time, and he would have to wait with this unbearable hunger until they brought out another one.

Danior knew this was a well-established house with strict rules and good stock, but to have to wait while they changed the Feeder was unthinkable now that he was so close. Each evening he got here early to leave town quickly and head for the seal, but when a Feeder was still usable from the previous night, they would bring them out. So that resulted in a changeover. Although everyone in line was only allowed enough blood to take the edge off their hunger, and no more, a previous night's Feeder did not last long.

Controlling the blood hunger was even more challenging than dealing with the pain it created. This pain could cause a Dark One to lose their reason and disobey a Feeding house's rules. Danior suddenly found himself fighting against an urge to leap across the room and fall upon the woman. He imagined himself sinking his teeth deeply into the pale beauty of her neck, drinking her blood until he experienced the last faltering beats of her heart, betraying her imminent death. Danior almost groaned aloud with desire and also the impossibility of such a desire. He had no choice but to control his instincts. To break the rules in these places brought swift and irreversible consequences to the offender. A Dark One attempting to drink more deeply than they had purchased or to try and drink without paying at all would get them cast out into the street. To be thrown out of a Feeding house was not something that Danior dared even to contemplate.

Danior finally reached the front of the line, and with trembling fingers, he dropped his token into the guard's massive hand. The Lieutenant peered closely at the smooth round stone, looking for the mark that identified it as belonging to this particular establishment. Danior could smell the fresh blood on him. I see he has taken his fill before we get a chance to, he thought miserably.

3

Many warriors from Stefan's army worked as guards when they were not patrolling the border or sending slaves out on raids to the light side. All of Stefan's warriors were full-bloods. He tolerated nothing less. Danior shifted his weight from one foot to the other as he watched the warrior inspect his token. The Lieutenant studied it carefully, turning the token over in the dim light of a lantern balanced on the sturdy wooden table where he sat. A sizeable bladed sword rested on the table by the lantern, and Danior noticed that the Lieutenant's right hand never strayed more than a few inches away from its handle. Satisfied that the token was genuine, the guard flapped his hand impatiently, indicating to Danior that he could finally ease the pain of his hunger.

Danior gratefully headed towards the small-enclosed area beyond the guard. A young woman lounged on a scantily padded straw-stuffed mattress. She lay on her right side, gazing out into the smoky mist of the crowded room. The only access to her from the public area was walking past the guard. There was, however, an entrance in the floor behind the mattress, secured with a solid metal chain, attached to a massive lock. They brought the Feeders in and out through the floor entrance. Walking them through a room crowded with hungry Dark Ones was no way to stay in business. From the back of the public area, it was impossible to see the Feeder at all. Only when you got close to the head of the line could the Feeder finally be seen. This practice allowed the guard to quickly end the occasional fight or stop an attack on the Feeder by a hunger-crazed Dark One.

Occasionally, despite all the precautions, a Feeder would be slain by an out-of-control customer. However, the rest of an establishment's stock remained safe because the floor entrance stayed locked until they brought up a new Feeder. Another guard always hovered in the shadows at the rear of the enclosure. He waited for a signal to step forward by the owner, who kept the key to the floor entrance, should a Feeder need changing out.

Danior took a deep breath and finally sank his teeth into an inner portion of the woman's bony arm, just above the place where the last person had drunk. The Feeder attendants marked the vein sites for the customers. Rotating the sites was how these places delayed the inevitable destruction of a Feeder's veins. This practice extended the length of life of the veins. Once the veins were rendered useless, the owner decided their fate. They would either be breeders or given to Stefan to use as he saw fit. Feeders that an owner may deem to be beneficial to them may even become servants. They remained prisoners within the Feeder compound. To wander around the streets would result in death from a hungry Dark One.

The scar tissue along this woman's veins betrayed many months of being a Feeder, and it forced Danior to push his teeth in deeper than he liked. The woman slightly moaned as he penetrated through the rigid surface and into the blood vessel beneath.

"Hey, be careful with the merchandise," yelled the Lieutenant in response to the woman's moan, "Feeders are hard to come by."

Danior barely heard this caution as the sweet-tasting blood flowed into his mouth. He drank quickly, lost in the exquisite sensation of satisfying his hunger. All too soon, he felt a resounding slap across his shoulders from the broad side of the Lieutenant's sword, indicating that his time was up. Reluctantly Danior released the woman's arm, quickly licking the last few drops of blood that welled up in the fresh holes that his teeth had made. The Feeder's attendant, a girl of perhaps six years, quickly pressed on the wound to stop the blood while the Lieutenant at the desk was checking the next person's token in line.

It hadn't always been this way on Lunaria. Prey to feed the Dark One's hunger had never indeed been in abundance, but when Danior first came to this world, it hadn't been this bad. As he hurriedly made his way through the crowd of impatient blood-hungry Dark Ones towards the exit, a woman grabbed his arm, pulling him close to her.

"How about sharing a little blood with a girl down on her luck," she crooned, flicking her tongue quickly across his throat.

Danior pulled himself from her grasp and continued towards the door. He knew that she would not step out of line to pursue him. Her screeching laughter echoed after him into the street, but he ignored it. Danior breathed a sigh of relief as the bitter cold air greeted him. The ordeal was over until the blood hunger forced him once again to return. He also began to feel the effects of the calming herbs given to the Feeders in their meals. It concerned Danior that his craving for this calming effect gradually became as urgent as his need for blood.

A Forlorn scuttled along the ground towards Danior and clamped its bony fingers around his ankle.

"Help me, half-breed," the Forlorn rasped miserably.

"You are too wasted," Danior responded, noticing the mortified state of the Forlorn's outstretched arm. It reminded him of a lightning-struck tree. "My blood cannot help you now."

"Don't you think I know that?" The creature croaked weakly, "it is not your blood I ask for."

"Then what is it that you ask of me?" Danior asked.

The Forlorn released its grip on Danior's leg. "I have been watching you head into the mountains every evening since I have been here," he said. "The border of the light side lies just beyond those mountains."

"Yes," confirmed Danior growing impatient, "I see the border every day."

"I want you to help me get there," the Forlorn whispered urgently. "I can pay you."

Danior understood why the Forlorn wanted to go there. The wretched creature could end his suffering by stepping into Lunaria's light side and allowing the sun's rays to destroy him. What Danior didn't understand was the offer of payment.

"What could you offer as a payment?" Danior asked curiously, "you surely became what you are because you could no longer afford to pay for blood?"

"Not in my case," replied the Forlorn. "If you take the pouch from around my neck, you will find at least a year's supply of tokens in it. They are yours if you help me get to the light side."

Danior dropped to one knee and removed a well-stuffed pouch from around the neck of the Forlorn. He peered into the top of the bag and saw the many coins and tokens crammed in there.

"There is a good sum here," said Danior curiously, "why are you here in the gutter with all this money and tokens?"

"I angered Stefan," the Forlorn replied, "he cast me out and made sure everyone knew it."

"There are many places that will sell you blood if you have the means to pay for it," said Danior.

"Stefan chained me to the floor," explained the Forlorn, pointing a blackened finger towards his left leg. "No one would willingly bring a Feeder here in plain view for fear of Stefan."

Danior moved the damp stinking mud away from the Forlorn's leg. A shudder of revulsion ran down his spine when he saw a rusty black bolt rammed through the lower leg just above the ankle. The thick chain of the same metal, secured by a series of bolts driven deep into the rain gully's stone foundation, held the Forlorn prisoner. Danior tugged experimentally on the chain and realized that the only way the Forlorn could get free was to cut off his lower leg. He dug further down into the mud, and suddenly, a hand or at least the mortified remains of one weakly grabbed at his wrist. Danior reeled back in horror, watching the hand, grasping the empty air where he had just been.

"I thought her body had finally become one with the earth," mumbled the Forlorn sadly. "Does this living death never end?"

Danior and the Forlorn watched as the hand flopped back into the mud and gradually disappeared.

"I can't help you," said Danior fighting the urge to dive into the mud and rescue whatever was down there. "You didn't say that Stefan had put a bolt through your leg. The only way to release you is to cut off your leg."

"I know that," responded the Forlorn weakly, "that is why I asked for your help."

"I don't think I can do that," said Danior fighting a sudden wave of nausea.

"I only ask that you bring me an ax or sharp sword," pleaded the Forlorn. "I can do it myself then."

Danior looked down thoughtfully at the portion of mud where the hand had disappeared.   "Is she secured in the same fashion?" Asked Danior slowly.

"We all are," responded the Forlorn.

"How many more are there?" Asked Danior, appalled.

"In this stinking pit, there were five of us," he responded. "I am the last one not to join the earth with my fallen brothers and sisters, although it seems Junor still lives."

"I will find something so you can free yourself," said Danior firmly, "I just have something to attend to first."

"Thank you," said the Forlorn, relief evident in his voice, "just bring me a tool, and I will trouble you no more."

Danior hurried away from the Forlorn towards the edge of town. The Forlorn watched Danior until he disappeared from his sight, hoping that someone would help him this time. It was difficult not to become hopeful.   The half-breed sounded sincere about his promise to bring a tool. The Forlorn relaxed back into the mud and thought pleasantly of death while waiting for Danior to return.

* * *

Danior reached the mound of rocks and boulders that marked the position of the seal. He ran his fingers over the stones and sensed the familiar tingle of the power, maintaining it. Danior concentrated on the crossing spell and then pushed his way through the seal. It felt intact, but there was a change in its power. It had grown weaker. Danior stood on the Sheukhawn side of the seal and looked at the rocks, puzzled. Is it failing? He thought alarmed, I need to know if all is well with Netta. She was the Gypsy whose blood Ramos had used to create it.

Danior placed one hand on the seal and the other on his forehead. A warm sensation ran down his arm, through his body, and up into his head. In his mind, a vision appeared to him of a group of Gypsies camped four days south from where he stood. Danior needed them to be closer to the seal to see if he could determine why it seemed to be weakening.

He took his hand off his forehead and aimed it in the direction of where the gypsies camped. A powerful flash of yellow light exploded from his outstretched fingers as he cast a beckon spell. He breathed deeply for a moment as the vision of the Gypsies faded. Now he would continue to monitor the seal's strength from the Lunarian side as he waited for the Gypsies to come into the area.

Satisfied, Danior then headed towards the nearest farm to find something the Forlorn could use to free himself with and take it back to him.

CHAPTER TWO

The Divano

The woman slit the rabbit open from chin to tail, thanking it for its sacrifice, and then removed the skin. She began gutting the creature, tossing to one side the parts she would not be using. The two drooling dogs that watched her every movement darted forward. They snarled and snapped at each other as they fought for the prize.

A rustle in the bushes to the woman's left caused the dogs to lift their heads and sniff the air. Satisfied with a familiar scent, they did not investigate the noise. Instead, they returned to their vigil of watching the woman as she worked.

The woman also heard the sound and raised her head to glance in that direction. A young woman walked into view carrying a small woven basket filled with potatoes and beans.

"Marla sent these over, Mother," she announced, pausing to place the basket beside the woman. "Young Cal found them growing wild, or so he said." she grinned as she headed for the caravan at the rear of the clearing.

The older woman stopped what she was doing long enough to inspect the contents of the basket. She nodded, satisfied with the gift, and went back to work.

"You should hurry and get ready, Twila," she said. "Your father will be coming for you soon."

Her mother tossed chunks of flesh from the rabbit into a large cooking pot hanging over a glowing fire. Liquid splashed out of the pot in response, hissing as it landed on the rocks that contained the fire.

She raised her head in time to see Twila disappear into the caravan. The woman peered at the bones of the rabbit, and finding not a scrap of flesh left, put them to one side with the skin. She would cure the fur later and grind the bones to enrich future meals. She swished her knife in a wooden bowl filled with murky water and pulled out the first potato from the basket. The dogs now lost interest. They sniffed the air once more before settling down beneath the caravan.

Her mother brushed a strand of gray hair from her eyes and continued peeling and slicing the vegetables. Standing up stiffly, she gave the pot contents a brief stir with a large wooden spoon. Her free hand rubbed unconsciously at the nagging pain in her hip.

Her hair, once wild and flowing like Twila's, was now sparse and gray, woven into a knot at the back. It framed her lined, weather-beaten face, carved by the harshness of life on the road. There was no bitterness in her heart at the premature aging of her body; she was a Gypsy and valued her freedom.

A faint jingling heralded Twila's appearance in the caravan's doorway. She wore a white shirt, fashioned off the shoulders, decorated in colorful embroidery. Gaudy trinkets, made from beads and gold, embellished the fabric of her flowing black skirt. Gold chains shimmered around her neck, arms, and ankles. Each chain had many different charms attached. All passed down through generations. Twila had fashioned small braids in her long black wavy hair, as was the custom. A bright red ribbon secured each one, the ends of which she left loose. The braids in her hair waved around with each movement of her head as she intended. Twila was five feet in height, petite in stature, and had an olive complexion, tanned darker by the sun from living outdoors, as was typical of her kin. The most startling thing about Twila was her bright blue eyes. She was finishing the final lace of the black leather vest that completed her outfit as her father stepped into the clearing of their camp accompanied by her cousin Jo.

When she went into town to dance in the local tavern, her father and another male member of their group would always accompany her. They would watch for trouble from the drunken men in the bar and make sure that whatever Twila earned was not stolen by thieves on the way home.

Twila started down the caravan's steps, each movement creating a tinkling melody all of its own. She checked that her large gold hoop earrings were secure as she reached the ground. Then she grabbed a small sack that contained her tambourine and dancing slippers from a storage hook beneath the steps of the caravan and then followed her father and Jo into the woods. Her mother watched as they left, wistfully remembering the days that she, too, had been accompanied by her father and brother into the taverns to dance for money. Twila had now come of age and would soon marry the young leader of another group. At the first Gypsy gathering that followed her birth, her father had promised her to him. It was an excellent family that Twila would be marrying into, and her mother clearly remembered how thrilled she had been when Stavos, her husband, had told her of the marriage promise. Now she wasn't too sure how she felt about it.

The years had gone by so fast, and soon her daughter would be gone. Twila would join her new husband to live with his group after the wedding, and her mother would only get to see her once a year at the annual gathering. She sighed slowly, suddenly realizing how her mother must have felt when she had left her group to marry Stavos. Suddenly Netta felt in need of some company. Quickly, she stirred the rabbit stew with the big wooden spoon and then returned it to a hook on the caravan wall. She grabbed her shawl as she muttered a simple Gypsy protection spell, which would alert her should anyone enter their home in her absence.

Netta followed the same path that Twila and her father had gone, but turned right instead of left and entered another, a much larger area. This area was where the rest of their group camped. She made her way to where the women were seated together, preparing their family meals.

"Hey, Netta!" called out one of the women as she noticed Twila's mother approach the group. "Has Twila left already then?" she asked.

Netta nodded her head in response as she sat down with the women.

"Well, when she marries young Morry, there'll be no more tavern dancing for her then, that's for sure," another woman chuckled in response to this comment.

The rest of the women joined in with laughter, but Netta remained silent, nodding her head thoughtfully.

It took Twila, her father, and Jo almost an hour to reach the village's outskirts. She knew that she always slowed the men's regular walking pace down, but they never complained. Mostly they just talked between themselves as she trailed along behind them, trying to listen in on their conversation.

She watched her father stride forward at a leisurely pace; his back was broad and straight. He was an influential and respected leader of their group. As many of the other men did to their women, he had never raised his hand to her mother. He wouldn't stand by and watch a man beat a woman either; he would intervene.

Her thoughts wandered to her fast-approaching wedding day, and she found herself shuddering a little, despite the lingering warmth of the early evening air. Morry was a handsome man, and she knew that her father had done very well for her by arranging this marriage. She just hoped that Morry would be as kind and gentle with her as her father always was to her mother. Twila did not love Morry, but love did not matter with a marriage promise created at their first gathering following birth. All the women in their group kept telling her that she would grow to love him, and she presumed that in time she would.

Her father and their group had been working on her caravan now for almost a year. It was the tradition for the bride's father to provide the first home. He was doing an excellent job, too, and had spent many hours adding detail to the intricate carvings that decorated it. It was unusual to stay this long in one place, but her father had decided to finish her caravan, which had meant staying here. This expression of his love for her filled her heart with pride, and she hated the thought that soon she would have to leave him and her mother to live in Morry's group.

As they reached the village, Twila forcefully pushed her wedding thoughts to the back of her mind. She loved to dance and needed her mind clear to enjoy it. It made the chore of dancing in the taverns more fun if Twila enjoyed it. The place where she had been dancing every night since they arrived here a few weeks ago was better than most. The patrons of this particular tavern weren't too boisterous, and not many had tried to pull at her or make lewd suggestions as was common in other places.

Her father and Jo grew silent as they snaked their way through the small side streets towards the tavern. They paused briefly before entering the place so Twila could put on her dancing slippers and retrieve the tambourine from the sack. Her father took the empty sack from her and tucked it into the wide leather sash around his waist. The light was fading now, and there was a slight chill to the air.

Twila realized that she should have brought her shawl for the walk home. Slightly irritated with herself for forgetting it, she pushed open the heavy oak door of the tavern. Laughter and noise greeted her from inside. The air, thick with pipe smoke, and the rancid smell of stale beer assaulted her nose as she pushed her way through the crowd. She managed to attract the attention of the tavern keeper, who grinned widely when he finally noticed her.

"Hey, Twila," his voice boomed out across the bar. "About time. I thought you must have lost your way tonight. Quiet everyone." he yelled at the crowd, banging a solid wooden club on the nearest support beam in an attempt to attract attention to what he was saying.

With the crowd somewhat hushed, the tavern keeper glanced at his regular musician, who, in turn, grinned and lifted his fiddle to his chin.

Haney liked to play for this Gypsy girl, and he just wished that he could watch for a change. He knew that she was excellent by the response from the crowd, but he wanted to see for himself instead of just catching glimpses as she spun round and round.

Straining his ears, he listened for the sound of her tambourine, which signaled to him that she was ready to start. The tavern keeper announced her name, and when the loud cheers and the racket created by people banging their mugs on the tables finally faded and died, an expectant hush filled the room. Haney heard her shake and clap the tambourine and his bow scraped across the strings of his fiddle in response. He played while she danced, following the rhythm and pace that she set.

Twila wove her way around the small space made available to perform in, twisting and turning, spinning faster and faster. Faces of the tavern men became a blur. Music and the dances captured all of her attention. The fiddle player easily kept up with the pace that she set, and it made it so much easier for her. She wished there was a fiddle player like Haney at every place she danced.

It was towards the end of her second dance that a strange feeling washed over her. She shared her mother's natural ability of the Gypsy Gift, except that her mother could direct it, Twila could not. Experience had taught her though not to ignore it, and suddenly Twila's senses were keenly alert. She located where Jo and her father were as she whirled around. Nothing seemed amiss there. Her father, as usual, was comfortably leaning against a beam by the door. By his stance and slight movement of his head, she knew he was watching the crowd intently, ready to act if anyone got close to her. Jo was watching everyone as well, but he stood stiffly and looked ill at ease. Twila knew, however, that he was also ready to protect her if needed.

She swirled faster, searching the sea of faces watching her, and nothing looked out of place. As usual, the tavern's patrons were shouting and cheering her on, grinning and clapping as she danced. Then something caught her eye near a low beam beside the large fireplace at the far end of the lantern-lit room. When she turned to look more closely, she saw only shadows. Her eyes strained to peer into the gloom as the strange feeling within her grew in intensity. On the final part of her dance, she was spinning faster and faster, causing the crowd to roar in excitement, and then suddenly, she saw him.

He had stepped from the shadows and was closely watching as her dance came to an end. Twila stood for a moment after she had finished dancing to catch her breath. She was reluctant to face this stranger for some reason and did not know why. Their eyes suddenly met, and Twila felt herself being drawn inexplicably towards him, and the noise from the crowd faded far into the background.

Twila felt as though she was floating over their heads, and maybe she was until finally, she was face to face with the most handsome man she had ever seen in her life. Her breath caught in her throat as his eyes held hers, drawing her closer and closer. She sensed rather than heard his words as quietly he told her that she was beautiful. His kiss on her lips felt like a small breeze on her face. She trembled as a rush of excitement coursed through her body, and she found herself gasping for air. For a moment, she began to wonder if she was sick and had fainted or something. None of this was making sense. Then just as suddenly as the strange encounter had begun, she found herself back in the center of the dancing space in front of the loudly cheering crowd.

The crowd showed their appreciation by tossing coins into the sack that she held out in front of her. Glancing down at the bag in her hands, she realized that she couldn't remember getting it back from her father. The sack grew heavy with coins as she made her way around the crowd. Her mind was still racing, trying to make sense of what had just occurred. Assuming it had occurred at all. She found herself in the shadows of the fireplace beam where the man stood. A little cautiously but very curious now, she peered into the gloom that even the nearest lantern could not seem to penetrate.

The man leaned against the beam, watching her approach, and he sensed her caution and curiosity. As she reached him, she looked up, catching her breath as she did so. Her eyes grew wider as she tried to adjust to the shadows. He wore a long black travel cloak. The folded back hood allowed Twila to see his long black hair, loose and flowing around his shoulders. He was tall and slim, but his facial features were in the shadows and hard for Twila to see.

Her eyes were startling to him. A Gypsy with blue eyes was so unusual, and he was captivated by them. She was still slightly flushed from her dancing, and it added to her beauty. Smiling gently at her, he purposefully brushed her hand as he deposited a few coins into her sack. Her breathing was still heavy, maybe from the dancing or perhaps from her memory of the event on the dance floor.

He knew he should not have drawn her to him like that, Danior had alarmed her, but he just could not help himself. It had been so easy too. He had taken her deeper than was usual for him because of the raw and undeveloped power she had. Danior had not expected that. He would have to go more slowly and more carefully the next time they met, and they would meet again, and it had to be soon because time was growing short.

As she flashed him a quick smile in response to his coins, he smiled in return, his eyes never leaving hers. Then she was out of the shadows and back into the better lit area of the tavern, swiftly picking up any coins thrown and missed rather than placed into her sack.

"Yes, she is the one," he thought to himself as he silently watched her from the shadows.

Twila's fear had faded when he had dropped the coins into her sack, and other emotions replaced that she tried hard to understand. She wasn't sure what exactly had happened. The one thing she was sure of, though, this man strongly attracted her, and for one so soon to be married, that was not the right way to feel at all.

"I must be tired or something tonight," she thought to herself as she grabbed some coins out of the sack and gave them to Haney.

As always, he protested, but she forced them on him anyway. Walking towards her father and Jo waiting for her by the door, she glanced once more into the shadows. Twila, however, saw nothing, and the strange feeling that she had experienced earlier was gone.

Her father left the tavern first, and Twila followed him still deep in thought. Jo took one last look around the bar to make sure no one appeared interested in them. He hesitated for just a moment and then followed them out of the tavern.

Haney watched them leave. He drank deeply from the foaming mug of ale that the tavern keeper had sent his way. Carefully he put his fiddle and bow into a shabby-looking leather sack. His gnarled brown fingers swiftly laced up the top. He then secured a thin strip of leather through a loop at the bottom and top of the sack, allowing him to carry the bag slung over his shoulder. He sighed as he finished his ale, the sight of Twila with the Gatekeeper had disturbed him deeply, and he wasn't sure what that encounter meant. One thing he was sure of, though, something was very wrong.

"I am too old for this now," he thought sadly.

For a few moments, his mind raced to try to make sense of what he had just witnessed and what he must do next. A flash thought of Raven crossed his mind painfully, and he abruptly forced that name from his mind.

"I have to find Amani," he decided suddenly, and he quickly downed the dregs of his ale.

The cold fresh air greeted her as she stepped outside, and Twila breathed it in eagerly. It was as if by doing so, she could clear her head of the strange event. They stopped for a moment while she took off her dancing slippers and returned them and her tambourine to the coin filled sack. Her father always carried the bag for the journey home. She walked between her father and Jo on the return journey, and they were silent and alert for any trouble. In this village so far, though, they had not had any problems, but it didn't hurt to be cautious. The further away from the town they got, the more relaxed they all became.

As they started to approach the camp, Twila had a fleeting feeling that someone was watching them from the shadows. She turned and scanned the area as they walked but saw nothing. Her father followed Jo towards the camp's central location, but she headed towards her parent's caravan site. It was the custom to have the leader's caravan away from the rest of the group, and Twila liked the privacy it afforded.

It was very dark now, and although there was a moon

tonight, its rays could not penetrate the thick leaves and branches as she headed towards the clearing. Suddenly he was there before her. She almost stumbled into him. Initially, she thought it was her mother, who would occasionally walk out to meet her, but then quickly realized it was the stranger from the tavern.

Twila was startled but not alarmed as he stood before her smiling. Strangely she did not feel threatened by him, and it never occurred to her to call for help. Once more, his eyes captivated her, though Twila couldn't see them in the darkness, just sensed them. Twila also sensed a deep power within him, much more prominent than she had ever felt before. Silently she cursed herself for not trying to develop her Gypsy Gift as her mother had nagged her to do for as long as she remembered.

"Who are you?" she finally breathed, afraid that if she raised her voice, her mother would hear her. "What do you want with me?"

"My name is Danior," he said softly. "I have searched for you for some time."

A noise a few feet away caused the two of them to turn in its direction.

"Meet me here when everyone is sleeping," he whispered.

She turned to answer him, but he was gone.

"Twila, is that you?" A warm glow from the lantern that her mother held high filtered through to where Twila stood.

"Yes, mother, it's me," she called back. Her voice sounded strange to her, but her mother didn't appear to notice.

"Is your father not with you then?" Her mother peered into the gloom of the woods behind Twila as she stepped into the clearing.

"No, he went with Jo. They are sharing out the money before eating tonight. I earned a good sum, too; the sack was heavy."

Twila's heart was racing as she glanced behind her before heading towards the caravan to change her clothes.

"What is wrong with me?" she thought, "I should be screaming and calling for my father, not planning to meet a stranger."

Netta was still peering into the woods holding the lantern high to direct the light better.

"I thought for a moment there...." her voice trailed off as she turned to see Twila climbing the steps of the caravan.

Netta had been jumpy all night. "Something is coming," she muttered to herself as she wandered over to the campfire.

She stirred the rabbit stew absent-mindedly and waited for

17

Stavos and Twila to come and get their meal. Her eyes sought out the dogs, both of which were pacing around the perimeter of the camp. They were behaving very strangely tonight too. If there were strangers anywhere near their campsite, they would let her know by loudly barking and would chase off in that direction, but that hadn't happened. She didn't quite know what to think as she watched them circling the camp. They seemed reluctant to leave the glow of light from the fire and the lanterns. She shivered suddenly and pulled her shawl more closely around herself.

"The last time I saw dogs behave like that," she thought slowly to herself, "was when the Dark Ones plagued the lands."

Her thoughts wandered back to those days when, as a child, she would hear her mother and the other women whispering together. She was always a curious child, and when the women got together like that, Netta would find an excellent place to hide beneath one of the caravans. Once in position beneath a van, she could just hear what the women were saying without being seen. Eavesdropping in this fashion, Netta had learned all about the creatures of the night. The whispered tales of butchered men and women, their necks broken, blood drained, would cause her to have dreadful nightmares, but she would still listen breathlessly, despite the fear it instilled in her.

Victims had been found occasionally around an area where they had camped, and that had resulted in the group immediately packing up and moving to a safer spot. Netta didn't remember anyone attacked from within their camp. She did remember a particular night, however, when there had been trouble with the dogs.

Netta's job was to tend to the dogs because she was the youngest child in the group. This particular night she had to search for them, as they hadn't come to her call, and she had found them pacing around the far edge of the camp. They weren't barking or growling, just staring out intently into the woods as they slowly padded back and forth. At first, she had called them and then became curious about what they may be sensing out there that she could not see. As she reached the very edge of the woods, she suddenly found herself being dragged to the ground by one of the dogs. He tugged at her shift, tearing it but not injuring her, as he pulled her back to where the other dogs were. It was as if she had crossed some unseen forbidden line.

She remembered bursting into tears from the shock of being pulled to the ground and expected swift retribution from her mother for the torn shift. Netta ran to their caravan and discovered that her mother was packing up their belongings, and it was apparent to her they were on the move again.

Her mother had distractedly listened to Netta's story, then instructed her to prepare to leave quickly. She remembered thinking how strange it was that her mother hadn't questioned her further. Netta asked her why they were moving again so soon. Her mother, in response, had whispered that there was a Dark One amongst them. Netta had tried many times after that night to get her mother to tell her more about the Dark Ones, but she had always refused, and finally, Netta stopped asking about them.

She now glanced over at her dogs, they had settled down somewhat, but their eyes remained fixed on the woods, their ears up alert for any sound. Netta relaxed a little and added some wood to the fire, causing sparks to cascade from its glowing heart. Some caught the breeze and danced before her for a moment until they cooled and fell as charred black remnants of their brief splendor. She absent-mindedly brushed some from her skirt and briefly wondered why she was suddenly thinking about the Dark Ones again after all these years.

She remembered that they had continuously moved during the time of the Dark Ones. Everyone in the towns and villages was fearful. There had even been a few instances where the villagers had threatened and attacked members of their groups, blaming them for bringing the Dark Ones into their villages. The villagers ranted and raved like madmen as they charged into their camps at night, threatening to burn them out if they did not leave. Netta clearly remembered the frightened children's cries, herself included, as they stumbled around trying to gather their belongings quickly. The men of the group armed themselves, ready to defend their women, children, and possessions, and the dogs snarled and barked madly. It became so bad at one point that even the villages that had once welcomed them also turned them away.

Netta clearly remembered that the Dark One's reign of terror ended around the Divano or vital gathering when she was about ten years old.

The message to come together, delivered to the various groups by placing secret Gypsy messages on the roadways, old campsites, and commonly used Gypsy forest trails. Gypsy messages were a simple but effective way of passing on information of importance to the various groups. Simply created from multiple natural objects, for example, carefully positioned stones at the side of roads, twigs, and branches that had been broken and then placed in a certain way. Some leaders sent messengers to track down any of the groups known to stay in little traveled areas, to make them aware that the Elders had called a Divano gathering. They were all camped in a glen surrounded by the Lian Mountains' majestic peaks within the month.

At the annual gatherings, the children had total freedom to roam around the individual camps. It was fun for them to find their old friends that they had not seen since the last annual gathering. This gathering, however, was very different right from the start. The parents had forbidden the children to roam from their family's campsite and beaten if they set one foot outside of it. The usual festive mood of a gathering was not present, and even the smallest child sensed the somber atmosphere.

Daily, the men gathered at the Elder's campsite, huddled together, their faces stern and troubled, while the women tended to the animals and the meals. Netta's mother told her that they were waiting for the arrival of a man of great magic. Netta's interest grew at this revelation, and it spawned many questions, but her mother offered no more information about him.

She had learned later that the man of magic's name was Ramos, and he arrived quietly without any ceremony. Netta hadn't been sure at first if this was the man that they had all been expecting. When she saw some of the men approach him as he entered the campsite area and escorted him to the Elder's campfire, she knew it was him. Netta remembered feeling disappointed that the man appeared so ordinary. She had expected something far more splendid. He was a young man too, which had surprised her. Netta had expected a much older man. He wore a black travel cloak with the hood down, the folds of which blew behind him as he walked into the area. Beneath his cloak, he wore a white shirt, tucked into his black leather pants, and boots fashioned from the same black leather.

The only surprising things about him were his vivid blue eyes and how he had styled his very dark black hair. His hair was long and reached his shoulders, trimmed back to the center of his left ear, but kept long on the right side. He wore an earring made from gold in that ear, fashioned as a small-sized loop with a long dangling ornament threaded through it. Netta learned later that the decoration was a magic symbol.

Daylight had been rapidly fading when he had casually walked through the center of the enormous gathering of people and their animals and caravans and headed towards the Elder's campsite. His features had displayed no emotion, but the way he held himself portrayed confidence and purpose. Netta had watched with curiosity as the Elders, and the male leaders that had gathered greeted him.

The leader's wives took food and wine to them, and the men had spoken with Ramos well into the early hours of the morning. Netta had longed to be able to get closer somehow and hear what they were discussing, but she knew she didn't dare to try. She had watched them quietly until their meeting had ended, and the men started to return to their family's campsites, then she had crept into her bed.

Netta had held herself rigid, straining her ears to hear what her father and mother whispered together about the discussion at the meeting. Netta hadn't understood all that she did hear but was rewarded amply for her patience. She discovered that Ramos was her uncle, banished from the Gypsy clan years before her birth. He was her father's elder brother. It was no surprise that she had never heard of Ramos until that night, though, because once banished, no one is allowed to speak that person's name again.

It was many years later before Netta discovered the reason for his banishment. It was because of his involvement with dark magic, in particular Necromancy. Even had Netta heard the details of his exile back then, she was just a young girl and would not have understood it.

As she had laid quietly listening to what her father told her mother, she learned that the Elders had agreed to meet with Ramos after they had received a message from him. He had sent word that he had found a way to rid the lands of the Dark Ones, but to do so, he needed their help. Netta clearly remembered how the excitement had grown in her at hearing her father's words. The gypsies had been badly affected by the Dark Ones' plague, and it was clear why the Elders had agreed to meet with him. Everyone would be very anxious to assist anyone who made such a claim, even if banished from their midst as he had.

She remembered hearing the tension in her father's voice as he told her mother that Ramos had stated that he had located the Dark One's lair. He had tracked them over many months and had almost become infected himself when one had attacked him. Only because of his magic and powerful spells had Ramos managed to escape this fate and successfully killed the Dark One that had charged at him. He had taken the body back with him to study it, and he claimed that this was how he had discovered a way to end their reign of terror and, in particular, avoid becoming one of them.

She had barely been able to control herself as her father related all this. Her body had ached from holding herself so stiffly. In a way, she was proud that her uncle was brave enough to defeat the Dark Ones. Neither Netta nor her mother had understood what her father had said next.

Her mother had asked her father to repeat himself, and he confessed that he didn't understand what Ramos was planning to do either. Ramos had told them that he planned to force the Dark Ones' leader back through a tear in the fabric between worlds where his kind had entered. Then he proposed to trap him there, sealing the entrance with powerful dark magic.

What Ramos had needed from them was strong willing men to help him do this. After they trapped the leader, the men would need to assist Ramos in slaying the Dark Ones left behind on this side of the rift. Netta's mother had then asked why Ramos had come to them for men. She had remarked it seemed odd to her that a man of such powerful magic could not have found for himself strong and willing men anywhere to assist him.

"What else other than the men has he come to us for?" Her mother had persisted. "There must be something else."

Netta had strained to hear her father's response to her mother's question. When he had spoken, his whispered words were so low that she had held her breath, trying to hear what he had said. Her mother must not have heard him either, for she asked him to repeat himself.

"He says he needs blood," her father had repeated.

Her father's voice had sounded weary and possibly even fearful. However, her mother's voice became raised, and her father had begged her to speak quietly.

"Blood?" her mother had repeated.

"Ramos says he needs the blood of an innocent Gypsy girl, who has the Gift," her father had said quietly.

Netta remembered the long silence that had followed this statement. She had sensed the great tension in the darkness as she waited for them to continue.

"Who has been chosen to give the blood?" Her mother had

finally asked.

"He will choose tomorrow," her father had said quickly. "The blood, freely given and offered, I think, was Ramos's exact words." His voice had been so quiet by the end of this that Netta had barely heard him.

"Is he to be trusted?" Her mother had asked slowly.

"I don't know," her father had whispered, "I just don't know."

Netta had stayed awake long after she was sure her parents were asleep, thinking about everything she had overheard. Finally, convinced that she would never fall asleep, she had got up quietly, and, pulling her blanket around her, she had crept outside. Netta had wandered over to the dying embers of the fire, adding some more wood to rekindle the flames, then had sat as close to it for warmth as the wood began to burn. Netta remembered that she had sensed his presence before she had seen him. He was leaning against a tree quietly, watching her. As he stepped towards her, one of the dogs ran up to Ramos, greeting him like a long-lost friend. She had not been afraid but was very surprised by the dogs; they never greeted anyone, even her father, in this manner. Ramos had sat beside her, and the two of them watched the growing flames of the campfire in silence.

She had sensed his power as she probed him carefully with her raw Gypsy Gift. He turned to look at her and smiled gently. She remembered clearly how his features relaxed, and then his hand reached out to tenderly stroke her hair. It was then that Netta had suddenly realized that she was the one he was seeking to provide the blood he needed to complete the magic seal. Thinking back now, she wasn't quite sure if it had been his power, or just a child's need to feel important, that had made her do what she had done next. She had held out her arms towards him, letting the blanket fall from her shoulders, and she had firmly stated that she offered her blood willingly to help him rid the world of the Dark Ones. Ramos had only nodded in response and asked her to wait until he returned.

Netta had sat huddled in her blanket, waiting for him, her mind racing with a mixture of fear and excitement. Ramos had returned relatively quickly, but to her, it had felt like an eternity as she had waited. Nervously Netta watched as he spread out a sheet of linen, intricately embroidered with strange symbols. She found herself gasping a little, her teeth almost chattering with fear, as he carefully removed and then unwrapped a knife from his pack. The blade was curved and decorated with more strange symbols. The handle, crafted

23

from what Netta assumed must be bone, and even though a child, she could see what expert artistry had gone into its making.

Ramos must have sensed her fear. At times, he would smile at her or rest his hand on her head as if to comfort her. At no time, though, had her conviction to offer her blood fade. She knew that this was what she had to do. He had started mumbling strange words, waving his hands in gestures that were uniform and precise. The slight breeze increased, tugging at her hair and blanket. She had shivered as the wind cut through her clothing, chilling her to the bone.

Ramos had finally reached down for her. Gently taking her hands, he brought her to her feet. The blanket had fallen from her shoulders into a crumpled heap, her teeth had chattered, and she trembled from head to foot. The cold had been bitter now that only her shift protected her from the biting wind. He had led her by the hand to the strip of linen and instructed her to kneel. His eyes closed, he began chanting, she had heard him call on forces with names unknown to her, his hand gestures grew faster. She had knelt as still as she could, trying to fight the involuntary movements of her body's response to the cold, and possibly a mixture of fear and excitement, she hadn't known which.

Netta watched as he had carved out a perfect circle around them, sealing it with a strange-looking rock taken from his pack. Finally, his chanting stopped. He had reached once more into his bag and brought forth a flask, fashioned from leather. The flask's main body also had symbols burnt onto it, one of which matched his earring. Carefully he had removed the stopper, and then he had kneeled before her. He had set the flask down between them. She had heard the wind raging through the trees, but within their circle, everything had been perfectly still. There was not even a breeze. Ramos had smiled at her then, and there was so much warmth within that smile that she no longer felt afraid, and her shaking stopped. Smiling broadly back at him, she once more had offered him her arms, her chin held up, and her eyes held his. He had nodded and started chanting once more as he had swiftly grabbed her wrists, so small that he easily held both in one hand, and in his other hand, he had held up the knife, and she had sucked in her breath waiting.

She had barely felt the knife cut her wrists; the blade was so sharp. Ramos squeezed had her wrists encouraging her blood to flow as he skillfully collected it in the flask. The expected pain from the cuts had started as a dull ache then increased as nerve endings finally responded to their assault. Netta had grown alarmed by the amount of blood that had flowed profusely from the cuts in her wrists. Her heart had started to pound, and she had suddenly felt dizzy and lightheaded. Netta had gasped for breath as waves of nausea swept over her, and she had thought she was about to collapse. At that very moment, he thrust her wrists high above her head. Ramos had swiftly begun binding first one of her wrists and then the other with soft strips of linen, chanting again as he did so. The waves of nausea had stopped, and she had felt her heart rate slowly return to normal, and the pounding in her chest had ceased.

Netta had watched in silence as he carefully sealed the flask, still chanting as he did so. Then suddenly, he had ceased chanting and had quickly returned everything to his pack in silence. Only then had Netta noticed that Ramos, too, was bleeding. She had assumed he had combined his blood with hers in the flask. Netta had seen that there was one more strip of linen carefully draped between them. She had known that this was for his wound, and Netta had picked it up. Her hands had been trembling, but Ramos had allowed her to bind his cut in the same fashion. Netta had sensed a great sadness in him that she could not define, and she had been too nervous to question it. She had finished and then smiled shyly at him, hoping that maybe the gesture would alleviate his sadness somehow.

He had then placed both his hands on her head firmly but gently and mumbled what she assumed was a spell. Ramos had then lifted her chin and held her gaze with his vivid blue eyes.

"You have been a brave child," he had told her, "your father should be very proud to have a daughter like you. Work on your Gypsy Gift, for it is your birthright and will protect and serve you at all times. Now you must rest, and my work can begin."

He had then stood up and walked to the stone that had sealed the circle, chanting once more as he had picked it up. The wind had once more become a gusty breeze, and Netta had shivered again. Ramos had grabbed her blanket, draped it around her shoulders, and then carried her to the caravan steps. She had felt his grip tighten briefly in a sort of an awkward hug, and in response, she had put her arms around his neck, hugged him back, and kissed him briefly on his cheek.

Ramos had set her down gently on the top step of the caravan. Netta had been surprised to see a sparkle of tears in his eyes. Exhausted now, she had clung to her blanket as she had watched him

25

pick up his pack from beside the fire. He had turned once more, blew her a kiss, and then disappeared into the night. Netta had crept carefully back to her bed, climbed in, and had fallen instantly asleep.

Netta remembered that it was almost noon by the time she had finally woken up. Netta's mother had told her that many men had left with Ramos, but they still were confined to their campfire. The mood of the gathering had changed somewhat after Ramos had left. They were all concerned for the men that had gone with him. It had been almost three weeks before they did return, but it had been a success. The story of how Ramos's spell had worked and the Dark One's leader was now banished to his world circled the campfires.

Ramos and two of the men had not returned to the camp with the rest of them. She had heard her father telling her mother that one of the men had been slain by a Dark One before they could help him. The other was a young man who was to have been married at the next annual gathering. Ramos and the young man had left together the night he placed the seal, but Ramos had returned alone. He had spoken of the young man's courage but had not the details of his fate. The other men all assumed that a Dark One had slain him also.

Twila sat down beside Netta and looked at her, a little concerned when she hadn't seemed to notice her approach.

"Are you all right, mother?" she asked, "is it your hip bothering you again or something? You seemed far away just then?"

Netta still caught up in her memories, hadn't even noticed when Twila approached the campfire.

"No, my hip is not bothering me too much today," she finally answered, "I was just thinking back to when I was a girl, that's all."

She was relieved because she was concerned that her mother might have sensed a difference in her behavior. Twila began telling her mother all about the fiddle player at the tavern. She could not sit in silence because of her excitement about the meeting later. Tonight thankfully, her mother was unusually talkative as well. Had this been a typical evening, Twila would have been surprised by this because her mother was a quiet woman who spoke very little except when something needed to be said. Tonight, both of them, however, had other things on their mind.

Netta was only half listening to Twila as the girl chatted away about the fiddle player. Suddenly, Netta decided to share with her daughter, something never shared with anyone before, and she couldn't stop herself. Netta told her all about the encounter with Ramos so many years ago.

She saw Twila's eyes widen with interest as Netta told her all about the terrorizing plague of the Dark Ones, the Divano, and the role Ramos had played in ending their reign. Breathless now, unaccustomed to speaking for so long, Netta glanced over at her silent daughter, attempting to judge how Twila had received all this information. She still had no idea what had compelled her to share this with Twila. The girl now looked quite pale.

Twila was not only pale; she was stunned by what her mother had just told her. Her mind was reeling with so many questions; she had no idea where to start with them. Instead, Twila stayed silent and tried to process it all.

"This has been an extraordinary evening." She thought slowly to herself. "Mother, did you ever see Ramos again?" She finally asked curiously.

"No, I never did see or hear of him again," Netta answered truthfully.

"I want to develop my Gypsy Gift, mother," Twila said suddenly.

Now it was Netta's turn to look stunned. She had been trying to encourage the girl to develop her Gypsy Gift ever since she was a toddler. However, Twila was always impatient with things that took time and concentration, so she had no time for it. Dancing had come naturally to her, though, and she hadn't needed to try too hard to get good at it.

"Well, you are going to have to start by using it more," Netta stated. "I can teach you some basic spells because that is all I know myself, but you have a natural Gypsy Gift that you will have to develop yourself. Start by letting it speak to you, direct you, pay attention to what it is saying, and use your intuition. As you become more accustomed to the impressions shown to you, then you can begin to direct it".

Twila thought about this for a while, staring into the flames of the campfire. She had always assumed that there must have been more to it than that.

"It doesn't get stronger overnight, though, Twila," her mother cautioned, "so don't be discouraged if you don't feel anything at first. Just keep working at it."

Twila nodded in response to her mother's words. She realized that this was the first time she had felt close to her mother and resolved to spend more time talking with her before the wedding.

That realization suddenly saddened her, and her thoughts returned to her future marriage.

Her father came into the clearing, and they ate their evening meal together in silence, each of them wrapped up in their thoughts. After they had eaten supper, her father told them both about one of the children in their group. The child had apparently leaped forward in the middle of them sharing out the money, grabbed a coin, and then hid it beneath his caravan behind one of the support struts. Her father roared with laughter as he shared with them how a pail of slops had spilled onto the child's father as he had tried to catch him. This one child was always up to something. Twila smiled as she envisioned the scrawny little three-year-old, with his wild shock of dark hair. Always giggling and very free with hugs and kisses for everyone he met.

She helped her mother clear away the dinner bowls, and then they all retired to bed. It usually wasn't very long before her mother and father fell asleep, but tonight, they talked for a while before everything finally grew silent. Twila grew restless as she waited for the familiar snore of her father and the soft, deep breathing of her mother. Even after she was confident that they had fallen asleep, Twila remained a little while longer to be sure.

When she did finally leave the caravan, Twila noticed the dog's strange behavior. They were pacing back and forth at the edge of the camp, staring silently into the woods.

"What's gotten into them tonight," she thought, "are they perhaps sensing Danior is nearby? If that is the case, then why are they not barking?"

Twila was suddenly relieved that the dogs were not barking and needed to leave here quickly if she planned to meet Danior. If the dogs did start barking, they would wake up her father. She would be in real trouble then. Gypsy fathers guard their daughters very well and especially before their marriages. It was common practice and quite acceptable for a father to kill his daughter if the girl shamed the family name. Twila was beginning to have second thoughts on whether she should risk meeting this man. The attraction, experienced earlier, was hard to remember now, and she was about to go back to bed when he stepped into the clearing.

Twila found herself standing in front of him without realizing that she had moved. The dogs stopped pacing and watched Twila and

28

the stranger with interest.

Danior smiled down at Twila, his deep dark eyes holding her captive once more. Breathlessly she smiled back at him; he was very handsome.

"Come," he said softly, taking her hand.

She hesitated a moment before willingly following the stranger from the safety of her campsite and into the woods. One of the dogs whined then howled softly as they both disappeared into the night.

CHAPTER THREE

The Seal

Haney made his way to the tavern's rear and opened a door that led to the kitchen. The tavern keeper's wife Liffy greeted him.

"You played well tonight," she said as she bustled around the huge kitchen, "that young gypsy girl fires everyone up." She wiped her hands on the front of her apron and then reached up to grab a wooden bowl on the nearby shelf.

"Here," Liffy said as she filled the bowl with a thick meaty stew from a big pot hanging on a hook over the fireplace grate that safely contained the burning logs. "You earned your supper tonight."

Liffy smiled warmly at him as she placed the bowl and a clean spoon in front of him on the recently scrubbed wooden kitchen table. Haney quickly made himself comfortable at the table; the stew, as always, smelled and looked delicious.

"I wish I could get out there and watch the entertainment some nights instead of being stuck back here." She said wistfully, "Ned needs to get me some help, and then maybe I can have a night off once in a while. Don't you agree, Haney?"

She burst into laughter at the thought of her husband Ned's reaction should she suggest such an audacious thing. She turned to Haney, who was quietly enjoying his meal, obviously looking for some kind of response to this suggestion. Haney kept his head down, enjoying the stew. He knew better than to get mixed up in these types of conversations.

"I'll tell Ned to get right on it first thing tomorrow." Liffy chuckled to herself as she started to make the dough for tomorrow's bread.

Haney had to hold his bowl with one hand to secure it and eat with the other now because Liffy's bread-making activities caused the whole table to jolt each time she slammed the dough down on the other end of the table. She was a heavy-set woman, but her actions were quick and agile as she expertly kneaded the dough. The flour went up around her in a big dusty cloud as she sprinkled it over the dough to stop it from sticking to the table.

He smiled as Liffy chuckled happily to herself at her joke. He knew she had a heart of gold, and for all her complaining about Ned, she loved him dearly. He remembered how Liffy and Ned had taken him in when they had found him badly injured on the road. It had been years ago now, and he was still here with them. They had given him a room at the rear of the tavern, tiny but clean and dry, and in return, he played every night in the bar and helped out around the place during the day.

"I need to leave for a while," Haney said suddenly, in between mouthfuls of food. "I have to see someone."

Liffy stopped what she was doing and stared at him, shocked. "What do you mean?" She asked. She looked like she was about to burst into tears. "Where would you go?"

"I have to see someone." He repeated firmly. Leaving here was going to be more challenging than he thought.

"Why now, after all this time?" She asked, her eyes bright with threatened tears. "Is it Ned? Has he said something to you?" She wiped her hands irritably on her apron. "Well, if he has, we will settle it right now." She pushed a few stray hairs back inside her clean starched bonnet and began stomping her way towards the door leading to the bar.

"Wait, Liffy," Haney said quickly. "Ned has nothing to do with this."

Liffy stopped in her tracks, and as she turned to face Haney, she fumbled into her apron pocket for a big white handkerchief. She began dabbing at her eyes with it as the tears tumbled down her plump red cheeks.

Haney stood up quickly and put his skinny but strong arms around her ample shoulders.

"Please, Liffy, don't take on so. I will be gone just for a little while. Why I owe you and Ned everything, without your kindness, I would have been in the ground long ago."

Liffy sniffed loudly and began blowing her nose.

"You're like my own father," she sniffled miserably. "Where do you need to go? You said you had no family, and in all the years you've been here, the only friends I've known you to have are right here."

He sighed deeply. "Liffy, I can't tell you everything, but I owe you something, after all you have done for me. There's trouble coming lass, and I have to find an old friend and warn him."

Haney wearily smoothed his long gray hair back from his face as he saw the questions start to form on Liffy's face.

"That's all I can tell you, Liffy," his pale blue eyes searched her face imploringly, "please leave it at that lass," he begged.

Liffy nodded sadly. "I'll respect your wishes." She said quietly. "I'll pack you some food to take with you. You're so skinny as it is. You'll just wither away if I don't see to it that you have something to eat."

She began cutting chunks of cheese and cold roasted beef, carefully wrapping them in clean muslin strips of cloth.

Haney thankfully sat back down to finish his supper, quietly watching Liffy as she gathered enough food together to feed him for a month. He knew it was useless to try and stop her.

"Why now?" Haney thought. "After all these years had the Gatekeeper suddenly arrived here, and what was his interest in the gypsy girl." He had to seek out Amani; he had no choice.

"I'm an old fool," Haney muttered, not realizing that he had spoken out loud.

"I agree," Liffy said loudly; she stood with her hands on her hips and smiled at him. "How far do you have to travel? Can you tell me that much?" she asked.

He looked up at her; his appetite was gone now despite the delicious food before him.

"My friend lives near the coast of Edenberry. That's as much as I can tell you, Liffy."

Haney got up and walked over to the pig slop pail by the rear door and scooped the last of his meal into it.

"That's where he was when I saw him last." He added quietly.

"What?" Liffy screeched when she heard where he was going. "That's a long way from here, Haney," she fussed, "you are in your 50's, and as spry as you are for your age, you'll never make it."

She pulled out her handkerchief again, dabbed at her eyes

with it, and blew her nose hard.

"There's nothing else for it," she said firmly, "you will have to take Apple. It will still take you at least four days there and four back on the horse, but I'll feel better about it."

Haney started to protest, but she had disappeared through the door leading to the bar. He shook his head sadly. Liffy was right; his age was against him. The more Haney thought about the Gatekeeper's appearance, the more convinced he was to find Amani.

He unconsciously felt for the pendant that he always wore around his neck. The knowledge that it was there, securely attached to the leather cord, was comforting to him. He clutched it for a moment; the familiar smooth coolness of the metal was like an old friend. Had his presence been discovered after all these years, he wondered? He didn't think so but couldn't take the chance. Haney had always known that this day could come. He had just hoped to have died of old age long before it did. Sudden unwelcome thoughts of Raven pushed their way into his head.

"Raven made his choice," he thought bitterly.

When Haney had last seen Raven, he had been young and spirited.

"What young man craving adventure the way that Raven had would want to stay with an old man like me?" Haney thought. "Maybe if I had told him everything, been truthful with him, then things might have gone differently."

He almost had been truthful with Raven a few times, but it just never seemed to be the right moment to do it.

"I was foolish; now, there is trouble. I have no other choice but to find Amani," Haney grumbled to himself as he started to prepare for the journey.

Ned had reacted to the news that Haney was leaving worse than his wife had done. After he had closed the bar for the night, Ned found Haney packing a few things needed for his journey.

"Are you sure about this here journey?" Ned asked the old fiddle player.

"Yes, Ned, I am more certain about this than I am about the notes I play." Haney promptly answered.

Then good luck to you, my old friend," Ned said sadly. "Just take care of yourself and bring Apple back home." He smiled warmly and slapped Haney gently on the back.

Liffy started sobbing again when at the last moment, Haney

pressed a small leather pouch into her hand.

"If I don't make it back here," he said quietly, "then someone will come that this belongs to. Please give it to them for me."

"How will I know who that will be?" She asked, still sniffing.

"You will know," Haney said firmly.

Ned could see that Haney had decided to make this journey and would be wasting his breath, trying to talk him out of it. He was comforted, knowing that it was nothing that they had said or done to cause him to leave. Ned liked him.

An hour later, Haney was on his way to Edenberry, his heart still heavy from the difficult task of saying goodbye to his old friends. Apple was a sure-footed old mare, and the rhythmic clip-clop of her feet on the dark, desolate road echoed the sound of the lonely beat in his heart. A dog howled in the distance as the last twinkling light from the village disappeared from Haney's sight.

Twila sat on a grassy mound by the side of the river. The moon was high, and it bathed the area in a pale luminous glow. She could hear the river lapping at its banks, the ripples sparkling in the moon's rays. Danior sat quietly next to her.

"Will you please tell me what you want with me?" Twila asked finally, unable to contain herself any longer. "I have willingly come here at your bidding, at great risk to myself, and now you are silent."

She turned her gaze from the dancing lights on the water to face him. His features were more evident now, the moon's glow creating an almost eerie paleness to his skin. Twila saw that his hair was past his shoulders and as dark as her own. His eyes were so dark they intrigued her. As her mother had suggested earlier, Twila directed her power, attempting to discover anything at all about this man.

Danior felt her strength gaining as she directed her mind towards him, and he slowly smiled.

"That is what you must do, Twila, use your gift, and you will develop it. This gift you have can also protect you against the powers of others."

Twila was suddenly thrust from him mentally, with such a force, she became lightheaded for a moment. She felt or sensed him rush into her mind and weakly tried to resist him. Twila sensed a darkness within him as she fought to clear her mind of his presence.

Then Danior was gone from her head as suddenly as he had arrived. A little breathless now, she lifted her head and once more looked into his eyes.

"Are you here to help me develop my gift then?" She asked, feeling a little excited at that prospect because he was powerful.

"It is because of your power that I am here, Twila, but it is up to you to start using it. I am not here to help you with that," he finished softly. "Your mother has told you something tonight that I willed her to relate to you. Did you understand the importance of what occurred all those years ago?"

Danior had leaned towards her stressing his every word, closely monitoring her response.

Twila was alarmed now. How had he willed her mother to do something like that? Her mother's power was strong, and she also wondered why her mother had not detected his presence either? It was very unusual for her mother to speak that much too. Her mother had never been one to tell stories or even gossip with the other women. Twila knew that she went to the other women in the group to hear all the news or even a bedtime story.

"My mother's gift is very intuitive. How was it that she didn't detect you and stopped you from putting suggestions in her mind?" She asked curiously.

"She grows old," he said quietly, "her power weakens, she is no longer able to protect herself against a power like mine."

He glanced at Twila, trying to judge how she was taking this.

Danior's words suddenly saddened Twila because she knew he was right. Her mother had seemed very pale tonight. The pain in her hip had been bothering her, and recently she had been coughing far more often than was usual. She had suspected that her mother might be sick and hidden it from her and her father for some time.

"Your mother was important in creating the seal that prevents the return of the Dark Ones," he said, "as she weakens, so does the seal's strength."

"What has this got to do with me?" She asked quickly, "I only learned of the seal this evening, and Ramos created it many years ago."

"It has everything to do with you," he sighed, realizing that this was a lot for her to understand in such a short time.

Danior had initially thought that he could have just asked Netta if she knew why the seal was weakening. It was after he had mentally commanded Netta's group to come to this area, and he had found her, that he realized why. She had grown old, and because of this, her strength, that had once kept the seal intact, was weakening.

Initially, when Danior discovered that the reason why the seal was failing was Netta's health, he wasn't sure what to do about it. Then he had accidentally found that Twila's power was even more intuitive than Netta's had been when Ramos created the seal. She seemed to be the only hope in preventing the seal from failing and providing the Dark Ones access to this peaceful world once again. He had searched the rest of her group just in case, and although one or two had a suggestion of the power, Twila's was the strongest.

"Your mother's gift grows old as she does," Danior said gently, "and although you have not attempted to develop the gift that was your birthright, it does have the strength that the seal needs to be restored and maintained."

Twila was having a hard time understanding all that he was telling her. She remembered what her mother earlier had said about a man of magic using some of her blood to create a seal.

"Is this why Danior has brought me here," she thought, "to ask for my blood?"

Then she remembered that her mother had stressed that the blood had to be offered freely and not requested. Twila had felt a rush of pride when her mother had said what she had done as a child. The brief account of how things were when the Dark Ones had plagued the lands made it clear why her mother had wanted to help.

Twila looked across at Danior, who was quietly watching her. She sighed deeply as she finally understood what he wanted; it was to help replace the seal. Twila realized that she had been born with the same Gypsy gift as her mother. She should, therefore, do what her mother had done. Before she had second thoughts, Twila held her arms out in front of her and repeated the words her mother had said all those years ago.

This time it was Danior that sighed. He smiled at Twila's outstretched arms and her statement to willingly offer her blood. Danior nodded in response to this gesture, and she smiled stiffly back at him.

"There is much to do," he quickly said, "you must find Ramos. He created the seal. I am not a man of magic. You must leave quickly tell him that I sent you."

Twila's eyes widened as he spoke, and she wondered if she

was hearing him correctly. He was telling her that she needed to find Ramos. How could she do that? Her father would never allow her to leave the camp alone and incredibly so close to her wedding.

"How?" She began, but Danior held up his hand to stop her from continuing.

"I will see to all that," he said hurriedly, realizing what she was about to say. "I will suggest that your mother sends you to another group to assist you in developing your power."

"My father would never allow it," she responded, "I am to be married at the next gathering, and he is guarding me well, as any father would."

Danior nodded at her words. "I will see to it that he agrees," he said firmly, "I know this will be challenging for you, Twila, but there is no other way. Tomorrow after you have danced at the tavern, you must leave in search of Ramos. I will give you a map so that you will be able to find him. It will perhaps take you two days to get there, so be sure to take the things that you will need with you to the tavern."

"Are you not coming with me?" She had never traveled alone before, and that thought alone alarmed her.

"I cannot leave this area," he said gently, "I wish I could accompany you, but I must stay here. I watch the seal; I am the Gatekeeper if you prefer. I cannot prevent the crossing of the Dark Ones if the seal does fail. I can only warn Ramos."

Danior looked away, unwilling to meet Twila's gaze as he finished because he knew what Ramos had done to him, and she might have seen the pain within his eyes.

"Why can't you leave." She persisted, deeply fearful now.

"I am the Gatekeeper," he reinforced, "I do not have a choice but to stay within a mile of the seal." He was about to explain further but then changed his mind.

"I will protect you as much as I can, Twila, but the further you are away from this place, the less I can help. You have to find Ramos alone; there is no one else."

He watched her as she thought about what he had said. This time he could not use his power of suggestion to get her to go; she had to do it freely. He would use it on her parents, though after taking her home, that would be easy.

Twila was about to question him further about why he could not leave the seal but stopped. Instead, she thought about Ramos. He must be old now, and Twila hoped that his power was not fading also.

Slowly she nodded her head.

"I will go." She stated firmly.

Danior was by her side before she realized he had moved. He gathered her up and firmly held her arms while looking into her eyes. Her stomach lurched once more as she met his gaze. Vaguely she could hear the gentle lapping of the water in the river. She was lost, however, in his eyes.

He smiled gently at her and then held her closely, whispering words of comfort and encouragement that she barely heard. Stepping back once more, Danior was scarcely able to contain himself, and finally, he kissed her. At first hesitant, she found herself responding to his kiss, as wave after wave of emotion flooded through her.

They were both breathless when he finally pulled back. For a long time, Danior could not speak, but he continued to explore every aspect of Twila's face with his eyes. That kiss was very dangerous, and he knew it. It was taking every ounce of control that he had not to sweep her up into his arms again. She was so pretty, and it had been so long, and he was trying to make this moment last.

"Come," Danior eventually said, his voice was barely audible, "I will take you home, rest well tonight. Tomorrow your journey begins."

Twila barely heard him over the pounding of her heart. Neither of them said anything as he led the way through the forest back to her camp. Before she realized it, they were at the edge of the clearing. Danior held her again but briefly this time and raised her chin so he could see her face.

"Sleep well, Twila, and be courageous, for we must not fail."

He kissed her quickly, and she smiled at him.

"Go now," he whispered hoarsely, fighting for control once more. "I will find you at the tavern tomorrow night."

Twila flashed him another smile, and a little reluctantly, she turned and headed for the caravan. She looked back just once more as she reached the steps, but he was gone. The dogs had resumed their pacing along the edge of the campsite. Twila noticed them but was too exhausted to question it. She crept into her bed, falling instantly asleep as her head touched the pillow.

Danior watched her from the shadows until she had disappeared inside. He stepped once more into the clearing, mentally commanding the dogs to ignore him. They stopped pacing instantly and sought out their usual sleeping spots. Swiftly Danior entered the caravan, waves of nostalgia flooding through him as he scanned the interior. It had been many years since he had lived like this.

Reluctantly he forced the memories to the back of his mind and concentrated on Twila's father. Danior smiled when he detected no resistance and easily implanted the suggestion to allow Twila to leave on a journey tomorrow.

Danior used more caution when he entered the sleeping mind of Twila's mother. There was some resistance, but he was surprised to discover that her power appeared to be even weaker than it had been earlier that evening. It was as if something was draining the strength from her. He puzzled on this a moment and then suggested sending Twila to another group to develop her power into her thoughts.

Before he left the caravan, Danior found himself drawn once more to Twila. He watched her for a moment as she slept. This girl was affecting him in a way that he was finding hard to control. His desire for her grew as Danior watched her sleeping.

Danior had not fed yet tonight and thought for a moment that this could be causing his weakness. Reluctantly he turned and left, striding purposefully into the forest.

He quickly reached the mound of boulders that housed the seal, and as Danior crossed through it, his mind became focused on his search for prey.

Haney tried desperately to stay awake, but the gentle swaying of Apple's body as she plodded forward was like being rocked in a baby's cradle. He shifted his weight in an attempt to wake himself up, and it worked for a little while, but then he felt himself drifting again. It had been many years since Haney had ridden a horse, and a dull throbbing ache that had started at the bottom of his back reminded him of that fact. He gritted his teeth against the increasing discomfort and shifted his position again to gain some relief.

Haney had envisioned this night many times in the beginning. As the years had passed uneventfully, however, he had assumed he was safe. Haney had been recently thinking that it was a good time to talk to Amani anyway. Haney knew that he was getting too old to protect the key successfully anymore. The sight of the guardian of the seal had convinced him that now was time. The Gatekeeper had no interest in the key, as far as Haney knew, but there must have been a reason for him to be at the tavern tonight. A shudder went down his spine, and he pulled his cloak more securely around him.

"I hope there is nothing amiss with the seal." He thought grimly.

Haney smiled to himself as he thought of how he would have enjoyed this challenge when he was younger. He wouldn't have been running to Amani. Haney would have been seeking out the Gatekeeper and questioning him about the seal's status.

The long hours tending his father's farm as a boy had made him strong. Haney had worked in the fields from dawn to dusk by his father's side since being a young boy. He tried hard to remember his father's facial features but couldn't recall them. The only thing he could recall when Haney thought of his father was the gentle way he would swing him up onto his broad shoulders for the walk home every evening from the fields. After supper, his father would play the fiddle, and his mother would clap and sing along to the music.

Haney barely remembered his mother at all, but that dark winter, when the sickness took them both, Haney remembered that time as clearly as if it was yesterday. He was just a young child and had no one. His mother had died first, and both Haney and his father sobbed as they dug her a grave beneath the great oak tree at the rear of the house, right next to his baby sister that he had never seen.

His father had never really recovered from his mother's death, but within the same month, the sickness had taken him too. Not knowing what else to do, Haney had buried his father by the side of his mother. It had taken him two days to dig the grave, and if the holy man from the next village hadn't stopped by and helped him, he doubted if he would have ever managed to get his father into the ground at all.

The holy man refused to let Haney stay there by himself. He had forced him to pack his few meager belongings and then had promptly taken him to the next village. The blacksmith Jeb and his wife, Hanna, had agreed to take him in. They treated him kindly enough, but Haney was always running back to his old home every chance he got.

Jeb and Hanna were very patient with him, and Haney felt a pang of guilt recalling how he had been nothing but trouble to them at first. Hanna's mother, Lizzie, lived with them too, and she had slowly become Haney's best friend. The happiest times he remembered from his childhood was being with Lizzie. She would tell exciting stories and show him treasures that she kept in the small wooden box beneath her bed. In return, Haney would play her the tunes that he was learning on his father's fiddle, and she had clapped along and encouraged him.

Haney had worked long days with Jeb learning the blacksmith trade. The hard work and the heat of the smithy was not a problem to him, but his heart had not been in it, and Jeb knew that.

Life had abruptly changed again for Haney the day that Hanna ran into the smithy, sobbing and carrying on dreadfully, so much so that neither of them could understand what was wrong.

Jeb had grabbed her gently in his arms, and his coal dirtied hands created black streaks on her flax colored gown as he had held her and attempted to calm her down. Hanna had finally got control of herself, and in between sobs, she had told them that Lizzie was sick.

Haney had run back to the house, the minute he heard about Lizzie. Haney burst into tears on reaching her room and saw how sick she was. Lizzy had looked so pale lying on the bed, clutching her chest. Lizzy had tried to get up when she had seen him, and he had quickly dropped to his knees by the side of the bed to stop her.

"Get my treasure box and open it," she had gasped, trying to get her breath.

Haney had pulled it out from under her bed and had held it open for her with shaking hands. He guided her flailing hand until she could reach the contents. Lizzie's breathing had gotten worse, and Haney had been alarmed at her increasingly pale face that was now glistening with droplets of sweat.

"Lizzy," he had begged, his voice shaking with emotion. "Lay still, for now, your treasures are safe, and I will protect them for you if that's your concern."

"I'll be laying still soon enough," she had said, pushing the contents of the box around trying to find something.

Haney had offered to help her find what it was that she searched for, but Lizzy shook her head. Then he had heard a loud click.

"There," she had said satisfied, "take this," Lizzie had said, pointing into the box, her face grimaced from the increasing pain in her chest.

"You must Protect it now and show no one," she had then fallen back on the pillows gasping for breath.

41

Lizzie watched him anxiously as he peered into the box. A small panel in the bottom of the box had opened to reveal a secret compartment. Haney had looked at Lizzie, who nodded to him, so breathless now that she could no longer speak. An involuntary groan escaped from her blue, tinged lips.

Haney remembered carefully feeling around in the secret compartment and finally pulling out a metal object. As he did so, Lizzie had smiled, satisfied, and had indicated that Haney should put her treasure box back underneath the bed. Haney had clumsily closed the panel to the secret compartment and replaced the box just as they had heard Jeb and Hannah climbing the stairs to Lizzie's room. Lizzie put a finger to her lips to indicate that he was to say nothing as Jeb and Hanna entered. Haney had carefully put the object in his pocket, and as instructed, never mentioned it to Jeb or Hanna.

He had stayed by Lizzie's side and held her hand until she died, as Hanna had sobbed uncontrollably in her husband's arms. Haney had touched Hanna's arm briefly in a clumsy attempt to comfort her because she had been so distraught. He had been devastated by Lizzie's death as well; after all, she had been like a second mother to him.

It was much later that evening after everyone had retired to bed that Haney had finally got to examine what Lizzie had given to him. He had carefully brought it out of his pocket, noticing how strangely cold the metal was in his hand. At his first look at the sculpted figure, Haney had not known that it was a dragon. It looked to him like a strange kind of serpent fashioned from a metal he had not seen before.

It was the size of the palm of his hand and exquisitely detailed. The dragon, captured in flight, its front legs curled as if attempting to gallop upwards to the sky. Muscular back legs portrayed the strength needed to propel the immense body from the ground, and its long tail curled beneath them. The dragon's wings extended, its fearsome looking head held upwards, mouth open, rows of teeth visible. Haney gently followed the fine details with his finger, tracing over the scales, tensed muscles, and the claws at the end of the toes on each foot. The red stones set in the place of the creature's eyes had flashed and glowed in the light from the lantern. Symbols, not recognized by Haney, encircled the dragon. He had thought it was the most beautiful thing he had ever seen. Carefully Haney had attached a braided strip of leather threading it through the circle of symbols containing the dragon. The leather strip was long enough to keep the dragon hidden beneath his shirt. He fastened it securely around his neck and had finally fallen asleep, clutching the pendant in his hand.

That night he had dreamt of the dragon for the first time. It had spoken to him in a melodious raspy voice, telling him that he was of the dragon species, and his name was Radon. Radon said to him that he must protect the pendant and that it was a key. The dragon had also spoken about a man named Amani, who would soon come to find him and explain everything. Haney remembered how he had jolted awake from that first dream encounter with Radon, fearfully looking around the room, expecting him to be there.

Amani had found him as Radon had predicted, two days after Lizzie's death. Jeb was putting the last of the earth on top of her grave when he arrived. Haney had known that this must be the man that Radon had spoken of in his dream, and it also confirmed that it had been a real experience and not imagination.

His first impression of Amani was that he must be a holy man. Amani wore a long dark travel cloak, the hood of which pulled up against the increasing wind. Beneath the coat, Haney could see that he wore a simple gray-colored robe secured at the waist with a braided brown leather rope. The man was tall, slim, and the visible wisps of hair beneath the hood were pure white. Amani had offered his condolences to Jeb as he reached them, stating that he knew Lizzie some years ago and had just heard of her passing. Not recognizing the man, Jeb had looked a little surprised by this statement. He had just mumbled his thanks and headed back to the house with his shovel. Haney had not followed him. He had instead looked at the man curiously, waiting to see what Amani would say. Suddenly the pendant resting against his chest had grown warmer. Alarmed, he touched it through his shirt.

Amani had smiled when he saw this gesture that confirmed that this was indeed the key's new keeper.

"Hello," Amani had said, "I see that Lizzie chose you to keep the key before she died. She chose well. You look strong and fit enough for the task. Meet me after the sun has set tonight at the edge of the village, and bring your belongings, you are no longer safe here."

Amani had then turned and strode off towards the road, back the way he had come, not waiting for Haney to respond.

Haney remembered being filled with a mixture of emotions as he watched him walk away, but despite his love for Jeb and Hanna, he knew he had to leave to meet Amani. The pendant against his chest had pulsed as if to confirm his decision had been the right one.

Amani had been waiting for him at the edge of the village at sunset. Haney left with him that night without question and had never returned home again, not even for a visit.

Haney shifted his weight on Apple once more, bringing his attention back to the present; he had to stop and sleep for a while. Afraid of falling off the horse and breaking his leg or something if he continued, Haney led the horse off the path and into the forest that edged it.

He chose a spot that seemed secluded enough and then gratefully and somewhat stiffly, climbed down from Apple's back. Haney tied the end of the horse's rein to a low bush and gave her some feed and water. Then using bracken and moss as a bed, and covering himself with his travel rug, he drifted off into an exhausted sleep, thinking wistfully about his comfortable bed back at the tavern.

Twila followed her father and Marcus, another group member, as they made their way into the village. She could not believe that all this was happening. Her mother had told her at breakfast that she must leave today to develop her power and had even helped her gather the things needed for the journey. Netta had firmly told her father that Twila must take the young mare Fen, and he had agreed without question.

She watched her father chatting with Marcus as they headed into town. Twila led Fen, who carried her travel pack secured to a hand-woven blanket that served as a saddle. Stavos's reaction to Twila leaving the camp had significantly surprised her too. Danior had said that there would be no problem with either parent allowing her to go, but she had not believed him. Marcus had raised his eyebrows when he learned that Twila would not be returning to the camp with them after she had danced, but Stavos was their leader, and Marcus had not questioned him. Unless the group was adversely affected by what Stavos had decided for his daughter, no one would speak against him.

Twila was aware of Danior's presence the instant she stepped into the tavern. Ned told her that Haney was out of town for a few days, so Twila danced to just her tambourine's music. Danior didn't show himself while she danced, and all too quickly, her dances finished, and Twila left the tavern with her father and Marcus.

Her heart was beating rapidly by the time the three of them reached the edge of the village. Twila was unsure what she should do next when Danior suddenly approached them.

Stavos greeted Danior as an old friend, introducing him to Marcus as a remote nephew. Her father smiled warmly at Danior and told him to take good care of his daughter. He then turned, hugged Twila briefly, and quickly pressed a pouch of coins into her hand. Her father had never been one to show his affection for her openly. That was just the way he was. But she saw that his eyes sparkled with tears before he blinked them quickly away. Twila's heart went out to him in a sudden rush of emotion, and for a moment, she almost changed her mind about the whole thing. Her father and Marcus left for the campsite, and she thoughtfully watched them until they disappeared.

Now that she was alone with Danior, Twila wanted to unleash her anger at seeing Stavos so upset. Without thinking about it, she suddenly thrust herself into his mind, and he physically reeled from the force. Twila found no resistance, this was an unexpected assault, and she pushed deeper into the shadows of his mind.

Danior recovered instantly, surprised at the increase of her power. He realized that she was angry, and Twila's anger had boosted her power tremendously. Irritated with himself for his lack of caution, he decided to allow Twila to explore, and it would be a good lesson for her. In the future, she may use more caution before bursting into the thoughts of others like that.

Twila felt an initial suggestion of resistance at the force of her entry. She expected to be thrown out of his thoughts again. However, surprisingly this time, she wasn't. Looking into his eyes, Twila felt his words enter her mind, inviting her in, giving her free access to his thoughts.

"You will see all that I have seen," his mind somehow whispered to her, "and be joined with me mentally."

He somehow pulled Twila deeper and deeper into his memories and held her there. Danior watched Twila's face grow pale, her eyes widening in fear. Twila's attempt to pull out failed because he trapped her there. More images and sensations flooded her mind, and none of them good ones.

When Danior saw Twila begin to sway a little and appear to be on the verge of collapse, he thrust her out forcefully, and she collapsed in a heap at his feet. Initially, he thought Twila was gasping for breath, and then he realized she was sobbing.

Danior knelt beside Twila, absent-mindedly stroking her hair. He gave Twila the time she needed to recover and gently whispered words of comfort to her, using his mind and not his voice. Danior did not need to use his voice now; Danior's actions had linked them telepathically. Twila's breathing became quieter, and she laid her head on his chest.

"Perhaps I should have kept a grip on my anger," he thought to himself, "but I cannot change it now. The girl has no knowledge of the potential power she possesses."

His feelings had strengthened towards her too, and this was not the way it should be. It was dangerous to be feeling like this for her. It weakened him. He shifted Twila's weight and lifted her head until she faced him. Her face was still awash with tears, and he gently brushed them away, but they continued to fall slowly.

"I am sorry that I caused you so much pain," Danior whispered, "I did it in anger, and that was wrong of me. Linking us like this was the way I had planned to offer some protection for you on your journey to find Ramos, but I should have been more careful. Will you forgive me for what I have done?"

Twila was surprised by what he said.

"You ask for forgiveness when I am crying at the pain you have suffered," she told him hesitantly, her voice hoarse with emotion. "You had to sacrifice everything to guard that seal," Twila finished sadly.

Tears continued to slowly trickle down her face as Twila remembered all that he had shown her. She had seen him bravely volunteer to go with Ramos and the others to track the Dark One's leader. Twila shuddered as she experienced the pain of the bite in his neck when the leader had pounced on him as he tried to escape. The others had managed to pull the leader off him, but it was too late; he was by then infected. Danior had begged them to slay him, knowing full well what he would become.

Ramos had stopped them and explained that he would do it. But Ramos had lied to them, and instead, he had let Danior live. Ramos had explained to Danior that should the seal weaken, he needed to know immediately, and there had to be a Gatekeeper. Danior had agreed to be the Gatekeeper on the condition that Ramos created a way to prevent him from taking others' lives like the rest of the Dark Ones had done in this world. If the seal's strength failed, he instructed Danior to mentally command an owl, a night bird, to seek out Ramos and screech to him until he recognized it was a message.

Twila had also felt that hunger and the satisfaction Danior felt after feeding. She took a deep breath and pushed his memories to the back of her mind; it was too overwhelming. Twila needed to be courageous now and find Ramos.

"Why do you cry for someone who is already lost?" Danior asked gently, deeply moved by what she had just said.

"You are not lost now, Danior," Twila stated firmly. "No longer will you carry this pain alone, with no one ever knowing that you sacrificed yourself in this way, I am now with you."

He didn't know what to say to this, or if she realized what her statement implied to him. Twila might be saying this now, but how strong would her convictions be to maintain this link between them after Ramos replaced the seal? It was very tempting to allow her into his heart, how deeply he longed for someone after all these years.

Twila sensed his confusion but respected his private thoughts.

"Please, Danior, enter my thoughts too, and you will see what I say is the truth."

He smiled at her, and gently he entered her thoughts. A chill ran through his body as she held onto him, taking him deeper and deeper. Her power was continuing to grow, and once more, it surprised him. So innocent and loving were her thoughts that they brought a light to his darkness. When Twila released him, Danior felt a peace inside him that he had not experienced for a long time. The last ounce of his resistance dissipated; the girl was in his heart. Danior lowered his head sadly because he knew that Twila had allowed him into her heart also.

Twila reached out her hand and pushed his hair back from his face. His arms were suddenly around her, and she relaxed in his grasp, enjoying the closeness it afforded. His kisses on her hair, her face, and finally her mouth, releasing emotions she had not experienced before. It seemed too soon when Danior released her, but Twila knew he was reluctant to let go.

"You must leave now, Twila; we must finish this and replace the seal," his voice broke with emotion.

Danior assisted her in getting on the back of Fen. Then he pulled a roll of cloth from inside his robe.

"Here is a map that I made for you," Danior told her,

47

handing it to her as he spoke. "Head for those hills over there," he said, pointing north of them. "When you reach them, follow the stream's path to its source, and he will find you."

"How will he know that I am there?" Twila asked, puzzled.

"He will know," Danior responded. "Call me from here if you need me," he told her firmly, touching her head with his hand. "Do not speak of this link between us to Ramos and take great care with your thoughts while you are with him," he added, not sure why he felt a sudden need to caution her in this way.

"The link between us mentally will fade the further apart we are, but be brave, Twila," he said encouragingly.

Danior walked alongside her as she rode on Fen until they reached the point where he could go no further. Twila smiled briefly at him and then used her knees and the reins to encourage the pony to follow the path that led to the hills.

CHAPTER FOUR

Preparation

Every bone in Haney's body ached, and no matter what position he shifted himself into, it afforded him no relief.

"What a blessing that Apple is such a docile horse," he thought, "a younger spirited mount would probably have thrown me off already and bolted for home."

It was late afternoon, and he'd been on the road since the first light of morning. Haney had seen only a few people, but each encounter had made him all the more anxious to reach the coast. The solitude of the day's long journey had allowed him to contemplate on how Lizzie's gift had forever changed his life.

First, there had been the arrival of Amani. Many times, he had questioned his decision to become the protector of the key. It was a free choice that Amani had given to him when they had first met. His grief for Lizzie was so fresh, old wounds that had taken years to heal after his parents' death opened wide again, bleeding tears like spring rain. Haney would not have considered parting with the pendant. Lizzie had fought so hard to stay alive long enough to give it to him. When Amani had given him the choice of protecting it or handing it over, of course, he had agreed to guard it.

Haney smiled warmly at the memory of his younger self. What an aggressive young man he had been when he had met Amani that day. Back then, he had a lean muscular frame from his early years doing farm work with his father, followed by the grueling hours in the smithy working with Jeb. The young Haney had feared nothing back then, despite Amani's cautionary words about what protecting the key meant. Haney swore to keep it safe. Haney had never regretted that decision to keep the key safe, but he acknowledged that it had prevented him from leading an everyday life.

"It's not been a bad life though," he muttered to himself, as he painfully changed position once again.

Apple continued to plod forward at the same leisurely pace, paying no attention to her restless passenger.

The first few years after, he decided to assume the key's keeper role was the toughest. He was a young lad alone in the world, with nothing to offer except his pure strength and hard work to earn a bed and food. After his initial concern that everyone was out to take the key from him, Haney learned over time that its existence was almost unknown. It's previous protectors, and there had been many, according to Amani, had chosen to live their lives quietly. Haney had decided from the start to be a worthy opponent should someone discover its existence and come searching for it.

Amani had told him that the key's significance was to maintain balance across all worlds and dimensions, but it also provided access to them. Haney had instantly seen the danger of the dragon key falling into the wrong hands. Amani had been satisfied by Haney's conviction to keep the key safe and had promptly left him to get on with it.

The sun was setting now, and Haney decided it was time to find a secluded spot to spend the night, as he encouraged Apple to leave the path and head into the gloom of the forest.

Twila reached the foot of the hills at sunset on the second day. In the fading light, it took her some time to locate the stream. Twila heard it before she saw it and decided to rest for a short time before going on. The water was sweet-tasting, and she gulped it down. Fen appreciatively sank her muzzle into cold water, also drinking deeply. This short break revived her somewhat, and slowly she began the trek up into the hills. Her pace was much slower now because, at times, it was almost impossible to see. Finally, Twila gave up and decided she would camp for the night and then set out again in the morning.

As she was on the verge of sleep, Twila suddenly felt a dark foreboding wash over her that was so intense she sat upright in alarm. Fen snorted and skittishly stamped her feet, unable to bolt because of being tethered to a tree. Breathing rapidly, Twila peered into the gloom beyond the dying embers of the small fire that she had made, but it was too dark to see anything. The canopy of trees she camped beneath prevented any light from the moon or the stars.

Twila added some wood to the fire and blew it until the crackling flames satisfied her, then she went over to calm Fen. Sure that something had been close to them, Twila listened carefully, looking around once more, but saw or sensed nothing. When Fen had calmed down, she wearily lay back down beside the fire, wrapping herself tightly in her thick travel blanket. Despite the comfort that the light from the new flames provided, it still took her some time to drift off to sleep.

At first light, Haney was back on the road to Edenberry. He didn't feel as stiff this morning, and his mood felt lighter, knowing that he had little more than a day's ride left before he reached the coast. Haney had tried to contact Amani before falling asleep, but his exhaustion intervened and had fallen asleep before he was successful.

Following his first encounter with Amani, after Lizzie had passed on the key to him, Haney had traveled everywhere, seeking out the best fighters he could find. He had worked very hard to master every combat skill that anyone was willing to teach him. Haney had become an expert in the sword and also the staff. The next time Amani met him, he had grown into a strong and skilled fighter. Haney remembered his surprise when Amani had found him because he had moved around so often since Lizzie's death.

Amani had appeared suddenly out of the woods when Haney had been on his way to meet a monk who had agreed to teach him more skills with the staff. They had sat together, and Amani told him that now Haney had proved himself to be more than worthy of keeping the key safe, he needed to share more information about what exactly it was that needed protecting.

Haney had also learned that day a lot more about Amani. He had also discovered that Amani guarded the dragon Radon. The dragon Radon spoke to Haney the night he had received the key from Lizzie, and he still occasionally heard him. Amani also monitored any potential threats to passageways between the many worlds that the key, Haney kept, could unlock. It hadn't been a long encounter, and after Amani had finished what he had come to tell him, they had both gone their separate ways once again.

The next time he encountered Amani, it had been late in

the afternoon when he was walking towards the village of Landston. He had been on the road all day and was more than ready to find somewhere to stay for the night. Haney had visited the sleepy hamlet of Landston many times and always slept at the same local tavern, the owner of which had become a good friend. Just before he had reached the edge of the village, a man suddenly stepped out of the woods and started to walk towards him. Haney, not immediately recognizing who it was, had instantly drawn his sword. Amani had stopped in his tracks when Haney had drawn his sword so swiftly, with his stance readied for battle. Haney's sword had blazed in orange light from the reflection of the setting sun's rays, as he had held it aloft, ready to strike in an instant.

"You have come a long way, Haney," Amani had called to the young warrior he now saw before him. When Haney heard Amani's voice, he had recognized who it was, and had swiftly sheathed his sword, then dropped to one knee in respect before Amani.

"I am sorry, Amani, you startled me, and the sun was in my eyes. I did not recognize you." He said quickly.

He had laughed softly and indicated that Haney should follow him as Amani led the way deep into the forest.

Amani had sat down on a cushion of luscious moss in a small clearing and leaned comfortably against a large tree and indicated to Haney also to sit. Haney had settled himself on the remnants of one of the tall tree's neighbors. He remembered how Amani had studied him for a moment before speaking as if deciding on how best to deliver his news.

"I came to warn you that someone has discovered the existence of the key." Amani had said slowly.

Haney had studied him as he spoke. Amani's hood was down this time, and he had long white hair, worn loose except for a braid fashioned on either side of his face. Haney also had noticed that his eyes were startling, and although they were dark, they contained specks of light, as golden as the color of the setting sun they had just left behind them on the roadway. His dress had been as simple as the last time they met, but it had also been just as strange. A simple white shirt was visible beneath his black cloak's ample folds, which had flowed down over his black leather trousers and the black boots he wore.

"There is a man named Ramos," Amani had said slowly, "and his meddling has resulted in a break in the passageways between two worlds."

His voice had risen slightly, indicating a wave of anger deep within him.

"Ramos has invited a dark demon named Stefan to cross into his world so that he can become a blood drinker, a Dark One, and therefore immortal. I know this is a strange concept for you to grasp Haney, but I need you to understand only this, Ramos has discovered the existence of the key."

"Then, he will not find taking it from me to be easy," Haney had growled nastily. "I have spent many hours learning fighting skills to prevent the key from falling into the wrong hands. I pledged to fight to the death to protect it, and I meant that."

Haney's fingers had unconsciously traced the smooth molded handle of his sword, secured safely now, but readied quickly should the need arise.

Amani had smiled grimly. "I can see that the key has an admirable protector," he had said. "I have come to find you and show you how to use the key. Moving the key to another world has always been the best way to keep it safe. Even though Ramos knows it exists, finding which world it is in should prove to be an almost impossible task." He had finished firmly.

Haney had agreed with this concept, although somewhat disappointed that he could not use his fighting skills to end this Ramos. There had been something about how Amani had finished his explanation that made Haney feel there must be something more to Ramos' discovery of the key.

"I believe that this man Ramos disturbs you for other reasons." Haney had commented.

Amani had nodded slowly in response.

"Yes, you are correct. Ramos is becoming a strong magic user, and now that Stefan has made him into a blood drinker, he will no longer age or die naturally. He has an infinite amount of time now to seek out the key. Already he has caused a breach between two worlds, and although it has created many problems for him, Ramos has managed to correct the damage it caused, at least for now."

"Then take me to him." Haney had said firmly. "Let us end this right now, and I will slay this Ramos, just tell me how best to accomplish it, if as you say, he is now a Dark One."

Amani had slowly shaken his head at Haney's statement.

"Radon knows and sees everything. Ramos and fiends

like him have a purpose in the fabric of all things. Now is not the right time to destroy him. Some events have not occurred yet, and to deal with Ramos now would create a ripple effect throughout time and across worlds. It would also prevent things that are to come, known only to Radon, that must occur. If Radon wants Ramos left alone, then it has to be so." Amani had finished firmly.

He had then gazed intently at Haney, analyzing how he had received all this information.

Haney had grown uncomfortable under Amani's intense scrutiny. He remembered turning his back to him to avoid those eyes while trying desperately to make sense of his words. It had sounded like he wanted him to leave this world and start again in a new one. As incredible as it had seemed, the thought of that excited him. Haney had no family ties in the world where he had grown up. In truth, Haney had never returned to see Jeb and Hanna after he left with the key.

"And if I don't agree, or refuse to follow you, then what?" Haney had asked, turning to face Amani once more.

"Then I will find another." Amani calmly answered.

"You would slay me?" Haney challenged, as his fingertips once again brushed the handle of his sword reassuringly.

Amani had sighed deeply.

"No, Haney," he had said firmly.

As Amani finished his statement, Haney had become aware of a warm sensation on his chest where the pendant rested. It had alarmed him, and he had suddenly clutched the dragon key through the fabric of his shirt, afraid that it may no longer be there.

Haney had known that he had to continue to protect it. Lizzy had entrusted it to him in her final moments. He was not about to fail her now or fail Radon either for that matter.

"Tell me what I need to do," he had said firmly, "I will continue to protect the key and do whatever that takes."

Amani had nodded in response at this statement; a look of relief had washed over his face.   "Come." He had said and quickly got to his feet to lead the way, and of course, Haney had followed him.

That was the only time Amani had taken Haney to Vesta to meet Radon. Haney would never forget that experience.

Looking back on that moment now, as Haney shifted his weight once more to ease yet another dull ache at the base of his spine, he realized that point in time was probably one of the most significant crossroads of his life. Haney didn't regret choosing to follow Amani for a second time all those years ago but realized there were some things he could have experienced in his life, and had not, because of that decision.

Unconsciously his fingers sought out the comforting and very familiar shape of the pendant beneath his shirt. The sun was high now, and Haney nostalgically realized that it would all be over by this time tomorrow.

Twila reached the stream's source well into the afternoon of the second day. The last few feet had been challenging, and at times she had to crawl over rocks and boulders in her path. Twila found it much easier to allow the surefooted Fen to find her own way up to the top.

Completely out of breath, she gratefully rested once more. Unsure of what would occur now, Twila grew anxious. It didn't help her nerves any when an hour later, Twila was still waiting, and doubt crept into her mind as to whether she was actually in the correct place. As more time went by and there was still no sign of Ramos, Twila started to wonder what on earth she was doing here at all.

Twila, exhausted, finally drifted off to sleep, and by the time she woke up, the sun was starting to set. Hungry again, Twila ate some more of her dwindling food supply, made a fire, and then fed and watered Fen.

"If Ramos does not come by morning," Twila resolved, "then I will just make the journey home." She wrapped herself in the warm blanket and gazed wearily into the dancing flames of the fire.

Twila sensed Ramos before she saw him. Fen also grew restless and suddenly snorted, and as Twila got to her feet to calm the pony, a man stepped into the clearing.

He was beside her before she had time to react, and fear blazed through her veins. Twila caught her breath as she saw his hair trimmed to the ear on the left and the earring with a magic symbol. This person couldn't possibly be Ramos, though. This man looked to be in his twenties. She wondered if perhaps this was Ramos's son, and if so, then it also occurred to her that if Ramos himself hadn't come to meet her, then maybe his power weakened with age too, just like her mother's had.

Twila felt her thoughts cautiously entered, and she resisted instantly, pushing him back. His eyes narrowed slightly, and then he slowly smiled. In that brief moment, she had sensed his presence, had also allowed her to detect the strength of his power and just how dark it was. Twila shuddered, suddenly unable to control this involuntary response.

"Who sent you?" He asked slowly. His voice had a soft but commanding tone to it.

"Danior," Twila answered simply, unsure if she should offer more than that. "I seek Ramos." She finally added after the man had not responded.

"The seal is threatened?" He asked quickly.

Twila just nodded in response.

"Come," he commanded, "there is no time to lose."

He grabbed her travel pack, and she followed him, leading a reluctant Fen.

As Twila trailed after him and saw how well hidden his place was, she realized she would never have found his home by herself. It had taken them perhaps thirty minutes from the source of the stream, to get there. Ramos lived on the uppermost point of the hill, which afforded a clear view in all directions. She was impressed with the vista because she could see for miles. Accustomed all her life to living mostly in the forests, Twila stopped, enthralled. She felt a gentle touch on her arm and turned to find the man smiling at her.

"Captivating, is it not?" He asked her softly.

"Yes," she replied, "yes, it is."

He smiled again, then turned and beckoned her to follow him into a small cabin that nestled into the side of the hill.

The interior of the cabin was clean and very basic. There was nothing in the place that made Twila feel anyone out of the ordinary lived here. He invited her to sit at a large wooden table that dominated the small room. Then he offered her some wine that she accepted gratefully. It was a deep red wine, and she savored its delicious taste. The man produced a dark loaf of bread and a large chunk of creamy cheese, which he placed before her. Then sitting down opposite her at the table, the man slowly sipped his wine, quietly watching her eat.

"Tell me what has happened to the seal?" He asked.

Twila told him what Danior had explained to her in between mouthfuls of the food he had provided.

"Is Ramos here?" Twila asked curiously, for she had not detected any other presence nearby since her arrival.

"I am Ramos." He quietly stated.

Twila's stopped eating and stared at him wide-eyed.

"How can you possibly be Ramos?' Twila exclaimed before she could stop herself, "you look so young."

He smiled at her response, clearly remembering Twila's mother all those years ago, bravely offering her small arms to him. It saddened him to learn that she had now grown old. A lot of this young woman's features reminded him of her mother. Ramos found her vivid blue eyes very appealing, despite being still wide with curiosity and disbelief.

"I remember your mother very well," he said with an element of sadness, "when I discovered the way to create a seal, I did not suspect that its power might eventually fade in this fashion."

His eyes, Twila noticed, were blue like her own.

"I came to offer my blood as my mother did, to help recreate the seal," she said, her voice almost a whisper, "if you need it that is."

Ramos nodded in response.

"You must rest now," he instructed, "I have much to prepare, come," Ramos said as he led the way through a doorway at the rear of the cabin.

She followed him out of the room and gasped at the sight before her. Beyond the humble space of the cabin was an immense cavern, the height of which appeared to go on forever. Twila realized that the house stood at the mouth of a natural cave. She also noticed smaller caves, and many tunnels were branching off from the main cavern. It was impossible to guess what the actual size of the cave was as a whole.

The air was thick with the odor of strange incenses. Twila also sensed foreboding darkness in the atmosphere that she found very disturbing. She allowed her senses to probe this atmosphere, drinking in the impressions received in response. Twila also detected something else in there that was entirely beyond her understanding and reason. The sensations that she felt were such that Twila grew a little alarmed at the thought of Ramos's true nature.

Twila cautiously directed herself into his thoughts and found complete silence. Ramos turned, alerted by her presence, then smiled slowly and allowed her access. Twila found that she couldn't sense much; however, Ramos was carefully controlling what he allowed her to feel. It confirmed that he was indeed Ramos, and that was all she could detect.

Ramos stopped and pointed to a room off to one side, created from a small niche in the main cavern's walls.

"Rest in there for now," he instructed, "I will wake you when it is time."

Twila nodded and climbed gratefully into a small cot at the far end of the room.

Several times, while she was sleeping Ramos, had checked on her. The sleeping draft that he had put in the wine had worked well. Ramos was irritated that he had not foreseen the seal's strength could diminish as Netta grew older.

"I must find a way to stop this happening again," he thought to himself, "this young woman that Danior has sent to me has a powerful gift. It is still in its infancy, but it is much more potent than Netta's had been when I created the seal.

"I need that key." Ramos thought angrily to himself.

Twice he had seen the key's glimmer when it crossed through worlds, but both times the flash had been far too brief for him to locate where it was. What he did know, though, was that it was still in Sheukhawn, this world. Ramos had waited many years for the key to be used again without any luck. Now he had to deal with this business of the seal failing. Ramos frowned impatiently and then started to gather the things that he needed to replace the seal.

Twila woke suddenly and found Ramos standing over her. Ramos had prepared the basics of the spells that he would use, and the only component left to complete it was their blood.

"It is time." He said as he turned to walk out of the room and back into the main cavern.

She followed him, still half asleep. The wine had relaxed her more than she had expected it would. Twila knew she had slept very deeply, but did not realize, however, that he had drugged it. Ramos led the way deeper into the cave. He took many turns down passages that ran in different directions, and Twila realized that she would not be able to find her way back by herself. The air also had grown cold and damp the deeper they got, and she was shivering a little by the time he finally stopped.

Twila immediately saw a strip of embroidered linen spread out on the top of a low table fashioned from a rock on the cave floor. Ramos had placed a knife with an intricately carved handle and a brown leather flask on top of the linen strip. Ramos turned to her silently waiting, and for a moment, Twila was unsure what he was waiting for, and then she remembered what her mother had said.

She went over to the table and knelt. Twila held out her arms palms up and then stated clearly that she freely offered her blood. Her voice echoed eerily inside the cave. Ramos smiled briefly at her and nodded. He began chanting now, words unknown to her, Ramos's voice rose and fell, his hands performed precise gestures. He chanted faster and faster, his voice creating echoes because of the cave's acoustics until it sounded like many other voices chanted with him.

She watched him draw a circle around them, placing a carved rock at the most northern point. Twila heard a sudden roar of the wind, and she watched in alarm as the dust began to swirl around them in the cave. Within the circle that Ramos had created to protect them, there was no wind, only a chill to the air and the strange melody of his chants.

Then suddenly, his chanting stopped, and he knelt before her on the opposite side of the table. She held her arms out to him once again, and Ramos smiled in response. His movements were swift as he grasped both her wrists with one hand, and Twila flinched as she saw the knife descend. When the blade sliced open her flesh Twila felt no pain, but she did gasp at the sight of her blood gushing from the wounds. Twila did not experience any nausea or a light-headed feeling that her mother had described experiencing, but then Netta had been just a child. However, Twila did feel her heart rate start to increase, and slowly she became aware of a painful throb developing at the site of her wounds.

Suddenly she felt her arms thrust upward, and he quickly bound first one wound and then the other. Twila watched as he carefully placed a stopper into the top of the flask. She noticed that he was bleeding too from his left wrist, and Twila picked the remaining cloth strip from the table and wrapped it around his wound, as her mother had done.

Ramos gazed into her eyes at this gesture. He smiled sadly at this reincarnation of the young girl that her mother had once been. Emotions stirred within him long since buried. Ramos fought hard to keep his mind focused on what he had earlier decided to do.

The wind suddenly died as Ramos began chanting again,

59

and at the same time, he removed the rock that had completed the circle. All was now quiet once more within the cavern, and Twila allowed herself to relax. She watched him as he began to place items into a large leather sack. Occasionally he would glance over at her and smile reassuringly but remained concentrated on the preparations for his spells.

Twila eventually lost track of time as she patiently waited. Still not free from the effects of the drugged wine, she quietly fell asleep again, uncomfortably slumped against the table of rock.

Ramos smiled when he saw her sleeping.

"She will be well-rested by the time we leave." He thought to himself.

The last task he had to do before they could leave was to prepare the potion that allowed him to go outside in the daylight. It had been many years since he had found a need for it, and it took him some time to find the ingredients. He began chanting as he blended the powders in a carved wooden bowl. For the final component, he carefully added a small amount of their combined blood. Ramos poured this newly created potion into a separate small black leather flask.

The power generated into the air that his spell created crept its way into Twila's sleeping thoughts, and it slowly roused her. She opened her eyes in time to see Ramos drinking from a small black flask that he then tucked into a pocket within the ample folds of his cloak. Twila also noticed that the dressing to his wound was gone, but she couldn't see that area of his wrist from her line of vision.

Ramos realized that she was awake and knelt beside her. Stroking her hair gently, he told Twila that they must leave. Twila saw instantly that the wound on his wrist was gone.

The sun was just beginning to rise as they left the cabin to begin their journey back. They traveled mostly in silence, and Ramos allowed her to set the pace on the back of Fen. It was evening before he suggested that they rest for a while. Twila agreed instantly; she was exhausted. Fen too had started to slow her pace the farther they went. Twila noticed that Ramos appeared tired also. His face looked ashen and drained of energy. She fed and watered Fen then wrapped herself in the travel rug. Twila quickly fell asleep, too exhausted even to eat.

Ramos sat watching her, his back leaning comfortably

against a tree. When he was sure she was asleep, Ramos mumbled the words of a protection spell and cast it over her sleeping form. Ramos had to feed; the hunger had been growing within him for the last couple of hours, and it was becoming unbearable. The scent of blood from her wounds was irresistible, and he was fighting to control himself. Ramos had located a potential victim not too far from here. His senses were so keenly alert now, enhanced because of his blood hunger. It would take him about an hour to reach his prey and return, but he was confident that Twila would be safe until then.

Twila bolted upright from a deep sleep, panting feverishly.

"Has something happened to the seal?" She frantically whispered in terror to Ramos. "I can sense it," she said, scrambling over to him.

"Yes." He said quietly, stroking her hair as if to calm her. "I have been aware of it for some time now. Are you rested enough to continue?" He asked.

She nodded. There was now a peaceful manner about Ramos that she had not detected earlier, and he appeared slightly flushed. Twila wondered if he had been drinking more of the wine that they had shared at his place.

"Yes, I am rested enough." She whispered hastily, her senses tingling with indefinable dread.

Twila gathered her things quickly and became increasingly curious by the change in Ramos. He appeared to be in a dream-like state and was moving and speaking in a maddeningly slow way.

"Perhaps he is tired." She thought as they set out once more.

As the sun began to rise, the powerful sense of evil that had stayed with her all night suddenly flickered and died like a snuffed-out candle flame.

"It's gone." She thought in surprise, pulling Fen to a stop. She turned to see Ramos drinking deeply from the black leather flask.

"I don't feel it now." She called to him.

"I know," he responded, "we need to press on." He said as he put the flask back into his pocket.

By mid-afternoon, they finally arrived at what Twila assumed was the site of the seal situated about a mile from her campsite. It was a serene sort of place located at the side of a river. The steep banks gave way to gently rolling mounds, covered in lush green grass, rising in height until they formed a hill. There was a curious mound of boulders and rocks on the uppermost point of the peak. The stack of boulders appeared out of place to her.

"This must be it," she thought. "How innocent it appears."

"What must we do now?" She asked Ramos quietly.

"We wait." He stated simply, his eyes seemed fixed on the ripples of the water, flashing in golden light from the sun's rays.

CHAPTER FIVE

Betrayal

Haney's weariness lifted a little as he approached the fork in the road. Soon he would find Amani and be back on his way home. The right fork in the road led to the bustling port of Edenberry. The left fork twisted its way up into the cliffs that surrounded the bay of Dove. Haney longed to take the road into Edenberry.

"I'd find myself a clean tavern, a few mugs of ale, and then sleep for a week." He chuckled.

Somewhat reluctantly, he nudged Apple to follow the fork to the left. The road eventually ended, and it became little more than a sandy track between the rocks and boulders that had fallen from the cliffs' jagged peaks rising above him. As they climbed higher, Haney finally got off Apple, and he traveled the rest of the way on foot, with Apple following him. He was very relieved when the two of them reached the top of the cliffs without any serious injury. Apple, who was more sure-footed than Haney, had stumbled dangerously more than once. Despite the fading light, Haney quickly found the cave where he had last seen Amani.

The cave was well hidden from view by rubble and gorse bushes. It was doubtful that anyone would find it other than by accident. Haney secured Apple to a weather-tortured tree, then scanned the immediate area to make sure they were indeed alone, and no one had followed them. He even backtracked down the trail for a short distance just to be sure. When he was fully satisfied that they were alone, Haney brought Apple into the shelter of the mouth of the cave out of the bitterly cold wind.

Haney gathered wood and dried gorse and then started a fire just inside the cave's entrance. He doubted that the fire was visible from the trail, and it took the chill out of the air. Apple was munching quietly on some of the grain that Liffy had packed for their journey. Haney found a dry sandy spot in one corner and set out his bedroll. He lay there watching the flickering shadows on the walls and roof created by the fire's flames. Now all Haney had to do was wait until Amani came, and suddenly, he found himself thinking again about Raven.

Amani had shown Haney how to cross between worlds using the key, but he had done so only twice. The first time he had crossed, he had found himself in a very different world from this one. Trained armies were fighting under the orders of their leaders to capture each other's land. Continents and rulers had changed hands so frequently while he had lived there; it had been hard to stay informed of the current King or Queen. However, that world had given Haney plenty of opportunities to use and improve his fighting skills. In fact, for a time, he had even been a King's champion.

Haney smiled wistfully at the memory of his younger self. He had earned reasonable sums of coinage selling his mercenary skills to first one leader's cause, and then the next. As age started to take its toll on his speed and stamina, Haney had become a teacher and mentor to young lads wanting to be fighters like himself, and more importantly, willing to pay him for the privilege. That was how he had met Raven. He added more wood to the fire, the memory of Raven painfully flooding his heart with a mix of emotions.

Haney remembered that he had first noticed Raven at the end of an incredibly frustrating training session with a very stupid pupil. The lad he was trying to train was just not cut out to be a fighter. His student was downright dangerous to himself when he was attempting to handle his sword. But the lad had paid for his lesson, and Haney had tried to teach him at least something useful.

When Haney saw Raven, who was closely watching what he was teaching without his permission, it made him angry. There had been observers of his lessons in the past, but that came with a fee. When Raven realized that Haney had seen him, he turned and ran off amongst the trees, but Haney had chased him down. He caught up to him quickly and dropped him to the floor, pinning him down, the point of his drawn sword dangerously pressing into the soft flesh of his arm.

"Let me go." Raven had yelled, attempting to shuffle away without causing the sword to dig in any deeper.

Haney planted his foot in the middle of Raven's back to hold him still, and then he noticed a small trickle of blood, making its way to the lad's right arm. Haney's anger waned somewhat when he saw the blood because it was not his intention to wound him.

"You'd do well to keep still lad and tell me who you are. My lessons aren't free, and maybe I need to make a visit to your father and get my fee."

Haney had leaned more of his weight on the leg that pinned Raven to the ground to stress his point.

"My father's gone, left us years ago," Raven said, stifling a moan.

Haney felt the fight going out of Raven and eased up on the pressure a little. He did not want to kill the lad just stop him from bolting away.

"Where is your mother then," Haney asked.

"My mother's dead, killed," Raven said. "You're the best trainer for miles around here, everyone says so. I came to learn so that I can avenge my mother's death." Raven's words broke off in what was almost a sob.

"I have no money, so I thought I could maybe just pick up a few tips by watching you."

Haney had listened to this; his anger gone now as he saw the flush of anger in Raven's cheeks as he once again struggled to get free. Something about this lad reminded Haney of his younger self, and then he did something that was really out of character for him back then.

"Then, the first rule you need to learn is never to lose your temper in battle," Haney said quietly and took his foot off Raven's back. "If I teach you all I know, I expect something in return."

Raven got to his knees, turned, and eyed Haney suspiciously.

"What would I have to do?" He asked slowly.

Although Haney had let the lad up off the floor, he had kept his sword drawn.

"My weapons need to be kept clean and sharp. I need to train someone to spar with my pupils for practice, and my horse needs feeding and grooming. In return, I will teach you all I know, and I will see to it that you are clothed and fed. How does that sound to you?"

Haney returned his sword to its sheath because he knew that Raven was not a threat.

Raven slowly got to his feet, a mixture of relief and perhaps hope had crossed his face.

"Is that all?" He asked quietly.

"That's it." Haney had answered, his heart was warming up even more to the lad. "If you decide to accept my offer, then meet me here tomorrow after my student has left for the day."

Haney had smiled at the look of surprise on the lad's face. Raven had quickly nodded in agreement, and Haney nodded back in return, then turned and walked back towards his waiting pupil. Haney suddenly stopped and turned to face him again.

"What's your name, lad? He asked kindly.

"You don't need to know my name. I don't have one." The lad had said quietly, backing his way into the bushes, his eyes never leaving Haney.

Suddenly a large Raven burst forth from the undergrowth. It's sleek black wings gracefully carried the bird up into a tree high above their heads, where it squawked angrily at being disturbed from its nest.

Haney squinted up into the branches where the large bird sat, eying them both with first one side of its head and then the other. It cawed once more in response to Haney's scrutiny, and then effortlessly swooped down and landed on a rotten stump of a long since fallen tree. The bird perched fearlessly just feet away from Haney and then cawed again. He laughed and turned to see what the lad thought of the bird's antics, but he was already gone. He turned back to the bird.

"Raven then," Haney thought to himself. "I'll call the lad Raven."

Haney, suddenly brought back to the present when he felt exhaustion sweep over him. The wind outside had increased. The heat from the fire and his soft, warm bedroll were beginning to affect him. His eyes grew heavier and finally closed, as he remembered how pleased he had been when Raven was there waiting for him the following day. The lad had brought everything he owned with him, all wrapped up into a tiny bundle. Haney had never regretted giving Raven that opportunity, and as a result, what a skilled fighter the lad had turned out to be. A deep sigh escaped Haney's lips as he fell into a deep sleep.

Danior strode towards them the very moment the sun went down. Emotions flooded through her unexpectedly when she saw him approach. Twila quickly tried to suppress her feelings so that Ramos did not detect their attraction for each other. Danior, however, pulled

Twila into his arms and held her tightly.

"I am glad you made it back safely," Danior said, and Twila smiled in response.

Ramos watched with cold amusement at their embrace.

"This might complicate the situation," he thought.

A sense of foreboding suddenly crashed into Twila's mind. It held such a dark element that it caused her to break away from Danior's embrace.

"Someone comes," she whispered fearfully but saw that Ramos was already on his feet, closely looking in the direction of the mound.

A tall figure suddenly stepped into view and purposefully made his way towards them. His long black cloak flowed behind him in the breeze as he came. When he reached them, the man turned to face Ramos. Twila noticed that his long blonde hair flowed well past his shoulders, and the man's brilliant green eyes flashed with anger.

"We meet again, Stefan," Ramos said tonelessly, no emotion displayed on his face.

He appeared relaxed, but Twila sensed the tension between them.

"I grow tired of these games, Ramos." Stefan snarled.

The guttural depth of Stefan's voice betrayed the extent of his anger.

"You must return," commanded Ramos. "This is not your place, and you are no match for me."

"It was you that first invited me here, and now that I have returned, and intend to stay." Stefan spat back sarcastically.

He turned as he finally noticed Twila, and her blood chilled at the pure evil in his eyes.

Ramos's eyes narrowed at this statement, and Danior stepped towards Stefan, shielding Twila as he did so.

"What lies do you speak now, Stefan?" Danior snapped. "Ramos banished you from here, and you were not invited, perhaps you forget." He finished.

"Ramos?" Questioned Stefan tauntingly. "You appear not to have been completely truthful with the Gatekeeper here, have you?" He sneered, wagging his finger at him.

"This matter is no concern of his," Ramos responded quickly.

Danior was puzzled. Stefan had spoken in a manner that

made him feel there was an element of truth in his words.

"He didn't tell you," Stefan continued, his face getting closer and closer to Danior's enjoying the confusion he was creating. "That because of his desire to become a blood drinker, he made this breach between our worlds." Stefan continued, "I am surprised at you, Ramos, forgetting to mention a little thing like that."

"Quiet," snarled Ramos, "enough of this. You couldn't live quietly. While you were here in Sheukhawn, you created blood drinkers indiscriminately. Feeding upon, but not slaying, all in your path. You risked my detection, putting me at risk of being hunted down as you were."

"I threatened your source of power is what you mean." Stefan spat back.

"You were never a threat to me." Boomed Ramos, his arms were rising from his sides, palms outwards facing Stefan.

Twila heard Ramos start mumbling, but Stefan was too enraged to notice as the winds around them increased.

Stefan suddenly realized what Ramos was doing and lunged at him, only to be cast back against the mound of boulders. With a swift movement of Ramos's hands, a bright blue light burst from his fingers and hit Stefan squarely in the chest. He was unable to move from the rocks, held there by an invisible force. Stefan became enraged, snarling, and spitting as he fought to get free.

"Release me." He demanded, his voice barely audible over the roaring winds.

Ramos's eyes were closed, his voice becoming louder until he screamed the words of his spell. Then he suddenly stopped chanting and knelt before the mound. Ramos removed the small wooden bowl and several leather pouches from his pack, the contents of which he emptied into it.

His chanting began again as he ignored Stefan's shouts and threats. Finally, he removed the flask that contained their combined blood from his pack. Twila recognized it by the symbols burned into its leather. He emptied the flask's contents into the bowl and then rose to his feet again, holding it up before him. Ramos faced Stefan, who was now literally frothing at the mouth with rage.

"You were never a threat to my power." Ramos restated coldly, "you served my purpose and then grew too greedy. Because of your greed and anger, Stefan, you have been careless, allowing me to trap you for a second time, and so very easily too." Ramos's words were dripping with contempt. "Now, you will return, and the seal will not fail a second time," he added firmly and began chanting again as red smoke started to pour out of the wooden bowl.

"You are not the only one with such power," screamed Stefan. "There is another more powerful than you. When you are also cast out of Sheukhawn, Ramos, know that I will be waiting for you."

Twila watched almost breathlessly as the red smoke thickened into a fog. It crept it's way up the mound of rocks and boulders until finally, she could no longer see Stefan at all.

His shouts were growing fainter too. A low rumbling began deep beneath their feet, and the hill appeared to lurch and roll. Twila dropped to her knees in pure terror. Danior knelt beside Twila and wrapping his arms protectively around her.

They saw the thick red smoke continue to spread until it reached the top of the mound. Then there was a tremendous boom, and the fog was instantly gone. So too was Stefan. Only the pile of boulders and rocks remained. Nothing appeared to have been disturbed. It was as innocent-looking as before.

Ramos, on his knees now, eyes closed, arms still outstretched, with the wooden bowl on the floor in front of him stopped chanting.

Danior had questions for Ramos. Stefan's words had disturbed him. Everything suddenly made sense. Banishment had not been done lightly by the Gypsies for his meddling with the dark magic. The council had met for many hours. Once banished, Ramos must have discovered a way to cause a breach between their two worlds. It now seems that he had invited Stefan to cross from his world as a reward for making him into a blood drinker.

"Why had Ramos not closed the breach some other way instead of a spell to create a seal? Did he want to have easy access between the worlds? It seems that I have sacrificed my life to guard this seal for Ramos's evil purposes only, and not to protect Sheukhawn?" Danior angrily realized.

Danior assisted Twila to her feet. The winds had died, and the moonlit up the area with an eerie glow. Ramos had repacked his things, and then he turned to face them both.

"There is just one more thing to do now to ensure the seal's strength never weakens again," Ramos said and stepped quickly towards Twila, with no emotion on his face.

Danior suddenly realized what he was about to do.

"Run, Twila." He screamed into her thoughts.

Twila hesitated for a moment and then turned to run, even though she had no idea why. Ramos quickly blocked her path, and as she turned to run in the other direction away from him, he grabbed Twila's arms, dragging her to her knees. His strength was immense, and Twila weakly struggled to break free of his grasp.

Danior leaped at him, and the surprise attack caused Ramos to release her in response, and she quickly scrambled away from them as they fought. Ramos threw Danior away from him with one mighty blow to the head and started to chant. Twila knew she should have got far away from them but just sat there sobbing in fear.

As Danior got back to his feet and lunged again, Ramos cast another ensnarement spell in response. Blue lights once again streamed from his outstretched fingers. Danior found himself pinned to a tree with invisible bonds.

"No." He screamed, struggling uselessly, "you cannot condemn her like this." His voice broke with emotion.

Twila, not knowing what else to do, ran to Danior, knelt beside him, and clung to his legs. She could not feel the bonds that held him, and Twila still had no idea what was going on. She wondered if Ramos intended to kill her.

"There is no other way," Ramos stated coldly. "If the seal's strength fades when she grows old, as it did with her mother, then the rift will open once more. The next time Stefan gets through, it will be harder to trap him. His anger made him careless this time. He will be ready for me next time.

Ramos's face was incredibly pale and drained as he reached down for Twila's sobbing, shaking form at Danior's feet.

"Come, Twila," he said softly to her, "let us finish this."

"Get away from him, Twila." Yelled Danior. "Please don't do this, Ramos." He begged.

"Quiet." Snapped Ramos, there was anger in his voice now. "It must be so."

"Then let me be the one," pleaded Danior. "It should be me that brings her over."

"You cannot feed this side, you know that," said Ramos. "Besides," he added, a touch of malice creeping into his voice, "it seems I need to teach you to respect my power."

"I'm sorry, Ramos," said Danior, appearing almost to choke on the words. "Let me take Twila across the seal and then return here when done." He begged.

"Ha!" Ramos retorted, "and I am supposed to trust you?"

"Yes." Answered Danior quietly.

Ramos appeared thoughtful for a moment. "You can revive her then." He finally stated. "I don't trust you, and besides that, I hunger."

Danior's head dropped in defeat at these words, and Twila saw the resignation in his face. Twila hadn't understood any of this conversation at all, and she had no idea what Ramos planned to do. She tried to go back to Danior's side, but Ramos turned her to face him. Gently he brushed away her tears, softly telling her that this was the only way. Then suddenly she knew what he was planning to do, but it was too late to save herself by then.

Ramos's hunger grew as he dropped to his knees, taking Twila gently down with him, his eyes never leaving hers. His voice was almost a melody. Murmuring words of comfort, soothing, and calming her fear. Twila's resistance and anxiety melted away as she relaxed into his arms.

Twila was now barely aware of her surroundings. Ramos's eyes never left hers, drawing her closer and closer into their vivid blue depths. He began to kiss and caress her hair, and as Twila felt herself start to respond, she feebly tried to fight against it. The sensations that his caresses were creating coursed through her body in waves of exquisite unbearable pleasure. No longer able to resist, Twila responded to him, willingly, begging hungrily for more.

Ramos was out of control now. When he felt her begin to respond, his excitement and hunger grew to unimaginable heights. His kisses and caresses became feverish, and in response, a small groan escaped her lips. He swiftly ran his tongue over the elongated fangs that had descended smoothly from their sockets, lubricating them with the increasing saliva that threatened to escape from his hungry mouth. Unable to contain himself any longer, Ramos grabbed the back of Twila's hair, pulling her head backward, which extended the neck. Pausing only for a moment, he plunged his fangs deeply into her taut flesh. She cried out weakly and gasped. He sighed in anticipation as the blood began to flow from her punctured vein. He suckled the warm sweet harvest greedily, encouraging its flow with his tongue and lips.

Danior was distraught as he observed the passionate, deadly assault on Twila. He hadn't wanted to watch but was unable to tear his eyes away. Hatred for Ramos coursed menacingly through every fiber of his being. Danior didn't know how yet, but silently he resolved to avenge her.

Ramos drank until Twila became limp in his arms. His heightened senses heard Twila's heartbeat increase and then become erratic as he drained her blood. As her heartbeat became faint, indicating that she was moments now from dearth, he reluctantly tore himself away, savoring the last drops of blood as he did so.

As a wondrous feeling of satisfaction flooded through him, he eased her to the floor. Twila was barely breathing now, and Ramos knew she was on the brink of death. He had to act soon because as Twila's life faded, so did the seal's strength. Ramos leaned back on his heels and mumbled a release spell, waving his hand in the direction of Danior, who, once released, fell to his knees.

Ramos pulled a knife from his pack and handed it to Danior.

"Do it quickly." He commanded.

Danior needed no prompting. He pushed up his sleeve of the shirt he wore and, using Ramos's knife, sliced open his wrist.

Twila lay still between them both, barely alive. She vaguely became aware of someone pushing her face into cold soft flesh. A warm sweet-tasting liquid, with a salty metallic flavor to it, trickled into her mouth. Danior's thoughts rushed into Twila's mind begging her to drink. At first, hesitant, coughing, and spluttering as the increasing flow of Danior's blood filled Twila's mouth and trickled down the back of her throat. More words of encouragement filled her thoughts, and she found herself starting to suck greedily at the liquid's source, in an attempt to increase its flow.

Twila felt her strength begin to return as someone pushed her mouth away from the source of the delicious tasting liquid. She finally opened her eyes and found herself kneeling before Danior. The gash on his left wrist was still trickling slightly. Twila reached out with an unsteady hand and carefully traced the edge of his wound with her fingers, collecting the last few drops of blood. Hesitating only for a moment, she slowly licked them clean, savoring the taste.

"Am I like you now?" She asked, and Danior nodded sadly in reply.

Twila suddenly felt her stomach explode with pain. The incredible pain grew and spread throughout her body, coursing through her veins, and she began to shake violently. Her eye's stared widely in fear at Danior.

"Help me." She gasped between waves of intense pain.

"You are crossing over, my dear," Danior said softly, unable to bear the fear and pain he saw in her eyes. "It will quickly pass," he explained and eased her twitching body to the floor.

The light of life faded from Twila's eyes, and then they glazed over. Danior turned his head away, no longer able to watch.

Danior glared over at Ramos, who was casually leaning against the tree. His angry expression coldly amused Ramos.

"You can do nothing to me." Ramos stated icily, "to do so would destroy the seal forever, giving both Stefan and his demons free access to Sheukhawn."

He knew Ramos's words were valid, defeat and weariness washed over him. His heart once more went out to Twila, still in the grips of her human death.

"It will take some time," said Ramos quietly. "She has drained you. You need to feed," he added, observing Danior's pale features. "I will watch over her."

Danior glanced over at him with suspicion but knew that Ramos had no choice but to protect Twila, for the sake of the seal. The hunger was screaming within him now, and he desperately needed to feed. Danior nodded and headed towards the mound. There was an expression on Ramos's face that Danior could not define, but the hunger made it impossible for him to think now.

Ramos noticed the look of suspicion cross Danior's face as he hesitated briefly before crossing the seal. He watched as Danior appeared to meld with the rocks and the mound's boulders and then disappear. Ramos smiled after Danior was gone and then got to his feet. He began to chant, his eyes closed, his arms outstretched. Bolts of brilliant green fire exploded from his fingers that he aimed towards the mound. The mound began to glow with luminous green light and appeared to pulsate as Ramos's voice grew louder and louder. Then he stopped, everything returned to normal again, and an eerie silence filled the air.

"I no longer need a Gatekeeper," Ramos stated simply, as he sat back down again by the tree. Content now, he resumed his vigil over Twila, who appeared to be sleeping.

Faintly Twila became aware of Danior pushing his way into her thoughts. The distress he was expressing didn't make any sense to her. Lazily Twila stretched and opened her eyes. She lay for a moment, totally disorientated. Her eyes immediately noticed that the moon's features were incredibly focused. She could see landmasses and what appeared to be vast canyons stretching across its illuminated surface.

Curiously Twila sat up and looked around. Every blade of grass, each leaf on the tree, was sharp and well defined. Then she saw Ramos, who was quietly watching her. He smiled at her puzzled but delighted expressions. Twila's reaction to her improved vision was like a child discovering something for the first time.

"Your senses are much sharper now, are they not?" Ramos asked Twila quietly, enjoying her reaction to the sound of his voice.

"I can see and hear for miles," she whispered. "I can hear small insects in the grass over there." Twila told him excitedly, "it's wonderful."

Ramos rose to his feet slowly.

"I must go," he announced. "Remember your new gifts will fade to less than that of a human, during daylight hours. Find somewhere safe and protected during that time and rest. Feed carefully. Choose prey that no one misses. Do not feed in one area for long, or people will detect your presence and hunt you down.

"Most importantly, remember this," he leaned forward his face inches from Twila's. "Never feed after the heart stops, and be sure to break the neck. I do not want blood drinkers everywhere, as it was when Stefan was here. If you get greedy or stupid, I will hunt you down and imprison you in my cavern," he threatened. "You know where I am if you run into trouble."

Ramos then turned and started walking down the hill.

"Wait!" Twila shouted after him as she scrambled to her feet. She caught up to him and grabbed his arm in panic. "You can't just leave me like this."

Ramos appeared surprised by Twila's statement and smiled as he looked down at her.

"Leave you like what?" He asked.

"I have nowhere to go," Twila whispered, her voice husky with unshed tears. "I cannot return home. That's gone now. I don't even know how to feed. You cannot be this cruel just to walk away and abandon me here."

Twila had continued to grip his arm tightly while she spoke, and he firmly removed it.

"Twila, your new instincts will be your guide; you need no

other. You survive, that is all there is to it," Ramos stated abruptly. "Do you wish to come with me?"

Twila looked up at him, not knowing what she should do. Danior's thoughts suddenly crept into her head again, but they were so faint that she couldn't understand his words.

"Where is Danior?" Twila asked Ramos suddenly, her head turning as she frantically scanned the area.

"Do you wish to come with me or not?" Asked Ramos once again impatiently.

Twila concentrated on Danior's thoughts, and she faintly heard him tell her what Ramos had done. Ramos had been watching her expressions and became suddenly suspicious. He crashed into her mind, and she instantly thrust him back.

Twila faced him immediately, physically shaking with anger.

"What have we done to you to deserve this?" Twila's voice was barely audible.

Ramos was surprised at the increase in her power and very curious. In the brief moment he had been in her thoughts, Ramos had sensed another's presence. It could only have been Danior because Twila somehow knew that he had reversed the spell, preventing him from crossing back over the seal. Ramos didn't feel threatened by the revelation that Danior had reached into her thoughts. It angered him, however, that he couldn't prevent it.

"You have to let him cross again," Twila demanded. "We did everything that you asked."

Ramos grabbed the front of Twila's dress and lifted her effortlessly until their faces were only inches apart.

"I don't have to do anything, but you will continue to do all I ask." Ramos snarled as he flung her away from him, and she landed in a heap a few feet away. "Now, I will ask you for the last time," Ramos boomed at her. "Are you coming with me or not?" He scowled impatiently, waiting for her reply.

Twila got to her feet again and faced him, anger coursing through her every fiber, ignoring Danior's frantic pleas to use caution flooding her mind.

"Well?" Ramos demanded impatiently.

"Never." She finally spat at him.

Ramos paused for a second about to speak, but then decided against it and set out down the hill once more.

She didn't stop Ramos this time. Twila just watched until he disappeared into the forest. Sobbing now, she collapsed by the side of the mound, placing her head and hands upon the smooth surface of the rocks. Twila allowed Danior's thoughts to flow through her mind because this was all they both had left now.

As Ramos entered the forest, a sudden shudder flooded through him. He stopped in his tracks, puzzled. There was something familiar about the sensation that initially Ramos could not define. His eyes flashed with delight when he realized what he had felt.

"The key," Ramos thought excitedly, "and not too far from here, either."

He concentrated hard on the fading sensation, and then slowly, he smiled. Abruptly changing direction, at speed only Dark Ones can achieve, he ran towards the coast of Edenberry.

CHAPTER SIX

Decisions

Haney wasn't sure what had disturbed him from his exhausted sleep. The fire was out, and the cold, damp air within the cave had found its way into his bones. He was painfully aware of a dull ache throughout his body that reminded him he was too old to be traveling for days on a horse.

Stiffly he sat up and began fumbling around searching for the kindling. It was so dark in the cave now that the fire was out. It was impossible to see anything. He found what he was looking for, and blindly he sparked the two pieces of flint together onto the dried gorse bush to create a flame.

Once the fire took hold and had started to consume the gorse, he slowly added the larger pieces of wood that he had found. He wondered what had disturbed his sleep. He was wide awake now.

Apple suddenly snorted and restlessly tugged against her tether. Haney glanced over at her to see what was wrong, and then he saw Amani stood by her side, patting her neck to calm her. Haney's heart lurched in his chest with surprise.

"You will be the death of me one day Amani." Haney chuckled. "In my youth, I would have sliced you in half sneaking up on me like that."

"And I would have deserved it," laughed Amani, "how are you, my old friend?" He asked, noting how the passage of time had aged Haney.

"I am as well as any old man who has traveled a long way, only to be scared almost to death by the very man he seeks, would expect to be." Haney laughed. "How goes it with you, Amani?"

"It was going well until Ramos reared his head again," Amani answered, sitting down opposite Haney.

"That is why I am here," Haney stated quietly. "There must be something wrong with the seal. I saw the Gatekeeper showing great interest in a young gypsy girl who has been dancing recently at Ned and Liffy's tavern."

Amani nodded. "The seal had weakened, and Ramos has already used the young gypsy girl's blood to reinforce it. Ramos's desire for the key now grows like a vine within his black heart," he finished solemnly.

"That is the other reason why I came to find you," Haney said, looking across the smoke and flames of the fire that separated them. "I sense that the key is in danger of being discovered. How I would have loved this to have happened when I was much younger Amani, as it is, I have grown too old to protect it safely. It breaks my heart to have to say this, but you must take the key and give it back to Radon until you have found another keeper." He sighed deeply.

When Amani did not respond, Haney grew uncomfortable in the silence. He sadly removed the key from around his neck and held it tightly for a moment before offering it to Amani.

"I cannot take the key," Amani stated quietly. I am unable even to touch it. To fully protect Radon, no one can access both his realm and the key to all things. To do so would give them the total power that Ramos is seeking."

"But can you not take it to pass it to another?" Haney asked desperately.

Amani shook his head slowly. "If I so much as touch it, then I shall be instantly destroyed by its magic. I took an oath in the beginning when I agreed to protect Radon's realm, and I accepted this condition just in case I became greedy for that power."

Haney dropped his hand, holding the key wearily into his lap. "Then what must I do?"

"There is no one that you feel worthy of protecting it, that you can pass the key to?" Amani asked, raising his head until his eyes met Haney's over the dancing flames.

Haney shook his head. "No, there is no one."

Amani quietly watched Haney's expression at his response and knew the internal turmoil he was going through.

"Then, if you are sure that there is no other that you wish to pass the key to, I must try to find someone," Amani said.

"And until you find someone, what must I do?" Haney asked wearily, knowing full well what the response would likely be. He would ask him to keep it until another he found another person.

Amani looked around the cave for a few minutes. "This is a good place to leave it," Amani said calmly.

"What do you mean by that?" Haney asked, astonished. "I might as well just deliver the key myself to Ramos rather than leave it here for any mad man to find." He unconsciously clutched the key tighter in his hand.

Amani laughed. "You misunderstand me, Haney. I may not touch the key, but I can cast a powerful concealment spell over it. Hiding it will give me time to find a worthy keeper, just as you have been." He smiled warmly at Haney, who still eyed him suspiciously. "My only concern is that when I use magic to hide the key, that will cause it to glimmer. It will be only slight, but if Ramos has grown to be as powerful as I suspect he has, he may sense it.

"He will not find the key once my spell is in place but likely be attracted to this cave. Hopefully, he will think the key has left this world, but I feel sure he will still come here. "

"So, what if he does come here?" Haney asked. "The key will not be visible by the time he gets here, and both of us will be gone." He finished firmly.

"I am not so sure about that," Amani said slowly. "Ramos has grown in power in the years since he became a blood drinker. He will likely have the speed to get here within hours, not days."

"Blood drinkers lose their powers during the day, though, don't they?" Haney asked, an idea forming in his mind.

"Yes." Amani agreed, slowly understanding what Haney was planning.

"Then, if we hide the key just before dawn, I should be almost a day's ride away from here before he arrives. Maybe I will just lay low in Edenberry for a couple of days, so I won't be on the open road while Ramos is in the area. Ramos will soon lose interest in this place when he thinks the key has left this world. Then when you have found a new keeper, Ramos will be long gone." Haney chuckled at the simplicity of it.

"You're a wily old goat Haney," Amani said warmly. "The sun will rise in about four more hours, so we should wait for a little longer than that and then conceal it." Amani got up and wandered around the cave, looking for a suitable spot.

Haney was satisfied with the plan. However, he hated to part with the key. Hiding the key had not been the way Haney had visualized his last act of keeping it safe. After he had met Raven and taken him in, Haney assumed that he would eventually pass the key on to him, just as Lizzy chose him when Jeb and Hanna had taken him in. Amani had initially told him that Lizzy had sought him out to tell him all about the young scrawny lad's arrival, and how she knew he would be the next keeper when it was time to pass the key on.

Haney painfully thought back to that day when Raven had shown up with his meager belongings the morning after their first meeting. Over time he had grown to be the son that he never had. During the eight years that Raven had stayed with Haney, the lad had spent every waking moment learning everything he could about weapons and fighting. Many times, Haney had to caution Raven not to be so hard on himself. The lad would be battered and bloody to the point of exhaustion and still get back on his feet to fight. Over the years, Raven became muscular and more skilled. When he saw Haney begin to weaken in a battle between them, it always inspired Raven to fight even more forcefully to beat him.

Towards the end of their time together, there had been more than one occasion that Raven had very nearly beat Haney. The frustration in Raven's face when Haney rallied and was once more fighting back would set Haney off laughing fit to burst, and the battle would end.

Haney realized that up until their last meeting, he had never really known anything more about Raven than what the lad had told him on the first day. Raven had a gift with the cards, though. Surprisingly accurate, he could sometimes be with his predictions too. Haney had never seen what cards Raven would refer to when the lad occasionally mentioned that there was trouble coming because it was in the cards. He had never even seen Raven using any cards in a predictive manner, but Haney accepted any warning without question after the first couple of times they had proved to be so accurate it had shocked him.

When Raven came of age, he became restless. That was the main reason that Haney had held off passing the key on to him. Haney had accepted Raven's drinking and the nights that he failed to come home as a natural part of growing up. Raven no longer spent all his time learning to fight; he was already extremely skilled. Then Raven had met a group of young men, who like himself, were fighters. They were mercenaries, hiring themselves out to anyone with a battle to win and plenty of gold to pay them. Not one of them was anywhere near as skilled as Raven was, and Haney told him this. They had many heated arguments as Haney tried desperately to get Raven to see where he and his new friends would likely end up.

Haney shook his head sadly at the memory of their arguments.

"Maybe if I had not argued against it, he would have outgrown those mercenaries," Haney thought.

As it was, Haney had always felt that his arguments against those mercenaries probably pushed Raven away from him.

Raven had started coming home less and less. Even weeks would sometimes pass before Haney suddenly saw him again, usually disheveled with some injury or another. He would stay for a couple of days and then be gone once more. Then came the day that Haney found him packing his belongings. Haney had watched him quietly, knowing in his heart that Raven would not be coming back this time. They said very little to each other when Raven had left, and as suspected, he never returned.

It was almost two years later that Haney met up with Raven again. A young rebel king of a nearby continent declared war on the province that Haney lived. The defending king asked Haney to join him in the battle against the invaders, and despite his advancing years, he had agreed.

The fighting eventually led to a final confrontation of the opposing troops on the defending province's shores. It was one of the bloodiest battles Haney could remember. The rebel King had employed troops to increase his numbers, and the fight was going in his favor. By late afternoon it was just a matter of time before the rebel king raised his flag in victory, and that's when Haney found himself facing Raven in the fight.

It had been a fight to the death. They ignored their past life together as each of them strove to slay the other. Despite Haney's experience and skill, Raven's youth and strength took the upper hand. Haney, exhausted and bloody, was finally knocked to the ground by a massive blow to the side of his head from the broad side of Raven's sword. He lay gasping for breath on his back, trying to focus on Raven, who stood over him, his sword raised ready to finish the job. Instead, Raven had grabbed Haney by his arm. He had then dragged him into some bushes at the edge of the clearing where the battle still raged.

"Get out of here, old man," Raven said, catching his breath. "I should kill you where you lay, but I won't. I have just discovered that you trained the butcher who killed my mother, and you deserve to die for that, but you took me in and taught me all I know. For that, I will spare you this one time. Should we ever meet again in battle, I'll finish this."

Raven then turned back to the battle, leaving a severely wounded Haney hidden in the bushes. Not knowing what else to do, he tore the key from his neck and slammed it into the ground.

When he regained his senses, Haney found himself in the back of a cart, headed for Ned and Liffy's tavern.

Haney suddenly realized that Amani was speaking to him. Thankfully Haney pushed his memories of Raven to the back of his mind as he listened to what Amani was telling him.

"It is time, Haney, are you ready?" Amani asked for the second time. He could see that Haney was deep in thought.

"Yes, I'm sorry, Amani, I was reminiscing. Where shall I place the key?"

Haney struggled to his feet as he waited for Amani to show him the place he had chosen.

Amani went to the rear of the cave carrying a burning branch to illuminate the way. He stopped in front of a niche in the wall of the farthest recess from the entrance. Haney probed it with his fingers and found it went deep within the wall's structure.

"This will be a good place." Haney agreed. He then removed the key from around his neck and pushed it as far as it would go into the niche. Haney felt a slight shudder in his fingers as the key melded itself into the rock's structure.

"Stand back," Amani instructed Haney.

His eyes closed, and Amani touched his forehead with the fingers of one hand.

Haney watched him curiously. Suddenly Amani dropped his hand slowly, and a brilliant red flare shot from his fingers and surrounded the niche in the rock where the dragon key lay. For a moment, the whole wall glowed red, and then it was gone. The appearance of the rockface returned to normal. Haney squinted in the gloom, trying to see where the niche was, but it was gone.

Amani smiled at Haney's expression.

"Run your hands over the place where you placed the key."

Haney gently ran his hand over the place, and he was alarmed when his fingers appeared to disappear into the rock. He pulled them back quickly and turned to face Amani with a big grin on his face.

"That's amazing." Haney stated, "It is just a trick to the eye."

Amani laughed. "A minor spell, but it suits our purpose very well."

They made their way back to the fire, and Haney threw the remnants of the branch into the flames.

"I must go now and seek a new keeper. Take care not to linger here, old friend; do not underestimate Ramos. We will meet again soon."

Amani smiled warmly as he quickly left the cave and disappeared into the night.

Haney was in no hurry as he ate breakfast and fed Apple before beginning to pack up his things. He left the cave and made his way to the edge of the cliffs just as the sun rose. Haney stood for a few moments thoughtfully, looking out across the bay.

"I have plenty of time before Ramos reaches this place." He thought to himself as he turned back to the cave to retrieve Apple, grab his things, and then extinguish the fire.

Twila finally pulled herself reluctantly from the mound, knowing what she had to do. It was almost dawn when she left the hill and headed home, leading Fen instead of riding because the horse became too skittish when she had tried to mount her. The farther away from the seal Twila got, the harder it became to sense Danior. By the time she reached the edge of the clearing of her parent's campsite, Twila no longer felt his presence.

She had fed on two rabbits on the way back, and as Ramos had said, Twila had known what to do. As Twila stepped into the clearing of her parent's camp, the dogs began to snarl at her. Without realizing what she was doing, Twila mentally commanded them to ignore her. They did so instantly. Twila's mother was already up, building a fire and preparing their breakfast.

Netta took one look at her daughter and knew what she had become. Her heart lurched dangerously, and the erratic beating that had come and gone over the last few weeks returned. Netta drew in a deep breath and tried to calm herself, hoping that the beat of her heart would return to normal.

Twila saw how deathly pale her mother's face suddenly was and realized that she knew. She rushed to Netta's side, and they held each other tightly as Twila whispered everything that had happened to her.

"What must I do, mother?" Twila sobbed.

Tears were trickling down Netta's chin too.

"Go and rest now," Netta whispered to Twila between her sobs. "I will think of something. If you can command the dogs not to see you, then do the same with your father. Let me think about this first."

Netta appeared to have somewhat regained control of her emotions.

Twila nodded and blindly made her way into the caravan. Her father was still sleeping, and she could not bear the thought of having to tell him what had happened. Twila crept into his mind and commanded him not to see her. It was painful for her to do this to her father, but knew she had no choice. Still sobbing softly, Twila climbed quickly into her bed and fell deeply asleep.

Netta watched Stavos closely as she painfully related what had happened to Twila. Netta knew it was the hardest thing that she had ever had to do. Stavos was usually so controlled in any situation, which made him such a good leader. When Netta had finished, Stavos just sat there quietly. She noticed the tears sparkling in his eyes and how flushed his face had become.

Stavos finally stood up and, for a moment, gazed in the direction of the caravan, and then without saying a word, he turned and walked off into the forest. Netta's heart went out to him, and she was about to follow but understood his need to be alone. When she could no longer hear the rustling of the undergrowth that betrayed his passage, Netta no longer fought to hide her grief. Great heaving sobs racked through her until she sat slumped in an exhausted heap, unable to cry anymore.

Wearily, Netta eventually got to her feet and went to get Fen from where she had hidden her until after discussing Twila's dilemma with Stavos. It helped to be busy doing something practical because she did not know what to do next with Twila and her situation.

Netta took the travel rug off Fen, and a sudden gasp of emotion rushed through her. Gently she brushed off the travel dust from Fen's coat, and the repetitive movements calmed them both.

Stavos was gone for more than an hour. When Stavos did return, Netta knew that he would never recover from this. He appeared years older somehow, his shoulders drooped, and the spark that always seemed to blaze from those kindly eyes was gone.

"I have called a meeting with the group," Stavos announced, his voice breaking up so severely that Netta barely understood him.

She nodded slowly, feeling the tears welling up inside of her once more.

"I must banish Twila because of what she has become. It puts the safety of the group at risk..." Stavos stopped, unable to go on, and Netta saw his shoulders begin to heave.

She went up to Stavos and, in an unusual display of affection, circled her arms around him. His body stiffened at first, ashamed of his weakness. The memories of his little girl and the pretty young woman that she had become were suddenly just too much for him to bear alone. Stavos's knees buckled, and Netta followed him to the floor. The two of them held onto each other tightly as they fought through the pain of their loss together.

When his senses returned, Haney couldn't understand where he was. His whole body felt numb. He slowly opened his eyes and saw the deep blue sky above him. Amani's face suddenly blocked his view of the sky.

"I must warn him about Ramos." Haney thought, suddenly remembering the encounter."

However, Haney discovered that he couldn't speak, and he couldn't understand why.

"Lie still, Haney." Amani's gentle voice eased its way into Haney's mind.

"Ramos came." Haney thought, hoping Amani could hear him.

"Yes, I know." Amani's voice once more came to Haney.

"I am dying, aren't I?" Haney asked mentally.

"Yes," Amani replied sadly. "But know this, my old friend, I will avenge your death."

Haney was having difficulty breathing now, desperately he tried to drag in air, but it was useless.

"Find Raven, Amani. The key should be his, "Haney suddenly said.

"I will find him, Haney, be certain of that," Amani said firmly.

Haney sighed as he heard the truth of this statement in his voice.

Amani's face shimmered slightly, and Haney watched as the face above him changed into a black bird, a Raven. He watched as the large black raven soared into the blue sky above him.

"It was you, that day, you were that raven in the bushes." Haney thought suddenly.

"Yes, Haney, it was me," Amani answered.

Haney smiled, comforted now, now knew it was alright to let go, and he closed his eyes and took his last shuddering breath.

It was mid-afternoon when Stavos felt strong enough emotionally to cope with what he must do next. He had thought about telling the group the truth about Twila but had changed his mind and decided against it. They would hunt her down and kill her. He just couldn't bring himself to do that. The reason he would give for Twila's banishment would have to be something else.

Stavos sought out Marcus just before the meeting. Marcus had always been like a son to him. Stavos had already decided that he would pass the group's leadership to him when the time came. Stavos decided to tell Marcus the truth about Twila. He had to just in case she did cause problems for the group in the future. Marcus would know what he was up against and address it.

Marcus was distraught and also angry by what Stavos had haltingly told him. He saw the pain in Stavos's eyes and knew that his leader had spoken the truth. For the first time in his life, Marcus silently questioned his leader's decision on what Stavos planned to tell the rest of the group. Marcus also recognized that in the same situation, he might have done the same thing.

He reached out and rested his hand on Stavos's shoulder. No words passed between them at this point, but Stavos nodded gratefully in response to this apparent gesture of support. The two sat down together beneath the trees and quietly discussed the plan to tell the others.

It was an hour later when Stavos finally faced the group. Most of them knew that something was wrong even before he had arranged this meeting. They all listened in stunned silence as painfully Stavos told them that someone had raped Twila while out on the road. His voice rose with emotion, which was unusual for their normally quiet-spoken leader. They all understood the pain Stavos must be feeling that he was trying so hard to conceal.

One woman groaned and pulled her young daughter closer. Some of the children who were old enough to understand began to weep for their lost friend quietly. In particular, one ran and dropped at Stavos's feet, begging him not to banish Twila. The girl's father hurried forward and carried her back to his wife.

"I have no choice but to banish her. These are the rules that we live by."

Stavos was using every ounce of strength he had left to prevent himself from breaking down in front of his group. They all nodded in agreement at his words, knowing how much courage it must take to banish your child. Respect for his leadership grew within them all.

"Marcus and I have discussed who we might offer in place of Twila," continued Stavos. "Morry's father will expect us to do that at the next gathering. We both feel that Karla is the best choice, and although a little younger than a girl would typically marry, it's close enough."

Karla's father nodded appreciatively at this announcement, as his daughter's eyes grew wide with astonishment.

"We will all help prepare her caravan," Marcus announced quickly, and the entire group nodded in agreement.

"Then we leave at first light," Stavos said. "If we head for the site of the gathering, we can complete the work on the caravan in time for the wedding. Marcus has volunteered to track down Morry's father and explain about Karla. He has also agreed to destroy Twila's van, as is the custom. We will not speak of Twila again." His voice broke a little at this statement fighting for the strength to finish this.

The group slowly and quietly dispersed; they wandered back to their caravans to make preparations to leave. An eerie silence had descended on them all, as they all pondered over Twila's fate.

CHAPTER SEVEN

The Raven and the Wolf

Raven groaned as he slowly opened his eyes. The bright morning sun blinded him painfully as it streamed through the window, and he closed his eyes again quickly. Raven sat up on the edge of the bed, whose bed it was he didn't know. The act of sitting up caused the painful throbbing in his head to increase immensely. Raven kept his eyes closed for a few moments longer waiting for the pain in his head to subside.

"I am never drinking again." He resolved.

Carefully he opened his eyes again and took in his surroundings. It appeared to be a small lodging room, but Raven had no recollection of how he had gotten here. Flashes of the previous evening came to him as Raven tried to remember where he was.

A slight movement behind him on the bed caused him to stand up quickly and turn in that direction. The sudden movement caused the room to tilt alarmingly, and he almost lost his balance. The pounding in his head increased, and a wave of nausea swept over him.

Raven saw the sleeping form of a young woman in the bed. Her back was towards him, and blonde curls spilled out from the blanket wrapped around her. Raven struggled to remember who the woman was. He realized that the room belonged to her because all the female articles and trinkets strewn around the place.

Fighting the waves of nausea and the pounding in his head, he hastily dressed. His clothes spread out all over the floor, but the travel pack he noticed, that contained yesterday's earnings, had been placed carefully on a chair by the door. After Raven had assured himself that the gold was still safe in the concealed pocket within the pack, he poured some water from the pitcher into an ornate washbowl on a table by the window. Quickly he splashed some of the cold water over his face hoping that it would clear his head.

Raven decided he did not want to be around when the woman woke up. He placed a gold coin on the table by the side of the bowl, then quietly left the room, and found himself in a dimly lit narrow hallway. Raven noticed stairs leading down to the lower level at the far end and heard a cheerfully singing woman in the distance.

He made his way to the stairs, desperate now to get out of this place. Raven descended the creaking staircase and found himself in the main room of a tavern. An overwhelming stench of stale ale mixed with the smell of freshly baked bread caused another wave of nausea, and Raven's stomach lurched dangerously.

A small round woman bustled out of the kitchen as he entered the room.

"Good morning, sir," the woman chirped. "I trust you slept well. Can I get you some breakfast?

Her face was covered with flour and flushed from the heat in the kitchen. Raven waved her away, still struggling to control his nausea.

"No, thank you," he said quickly. "I need to be on my way. Do I owe you anything for the room?"

He staggered a little and gripped the edge of the bar for balance.

"No, sir, you would have had to pay in advance for a room here. My husband insists on it," the woman said politely.

"I'll be on my way then," Raven said thankfully and headed for the door.

He almost groaned out loud as the sunlight blazed into his eyes when he opened the tavern door and stepped outside. As he headed out of the village through the winding streets, Raven became aware of all kinds of aches and pains throughout his body. To be expected after a battle like the one he had fought in yesterday. By the time he reached the lake just outside the town, Raven was feeling slightly better.

A few minutes later, he was swimming lazily in the refreshingly cold water. The aches and pains from yesterday's battle and last night's celebrations faded into just another memory. Raven floated on his back for a while, reluctant to leave the water. He saw a large bird fly across the sky above his head, and he watched its graceful movements as it hovered above him for a moment before flying off into the branches of a nearby tree.

A few moments later, the bird reappeared and flew around the lake again. This time it flew in the direction of the bushes concealing Raven's belongings. Raven was curious now and started swimming towards the shore. He recognized the bird as a Raven, and Ravens were notorious for stealing trinkets that they found appealing. The bird was perched on a nearby rock, now watching him approach. Raven reached the shore, and the bird flew up into the trees' tops again then disappeared from view.

"That was odd," he thought, as he dried off and got dressed.

Raven stretched his aching muscles as he ran through parts of yesterday's battle in his mind to identify any weaknesses in his technique that he could improve on for next time. Haney had taught him to do that, so he would never grow complacent in battle. He sighed at the memory of Haney, as time had moved on, the anger had faded away in Raven's heart against his old teacher.

He leaned himself against a large maple tree and closed his eyes, enjoying the peaceful sounds of the water lapping against the shore. He pushed out all thoughts of yesterday away and allowed the tree's thoughts to enter his mind. Raven became one with the maple tree, and he experienced the joy the tree felt of the sun on its uppermost branches. He shuddered in pleasure as the cool breezes ruffled the leaves and caressed the tree's bark. The primitive voice of the maple tree filtered into his mind, telling him how happy she was to be in this place of sun, breeze, and water that seeped into her roots, quenching her thirst.

Suddenly sadness flowed through the tree into Raven. He felt the leaves rustle as the tree tried to understand what the wind had carried to her. The tree felt the sadness but could not discern the cause, and Raven broke his connection with the tree and stood up puzzled.

He retrieved the cards of telling from his travel pack, closed his eyes, and shuffled the cards slowly, the sadness sensed by the tree had disturbed him. Raven cut the deck and then turned over the first card and laid it face up before him. The detailed hand-painted picture of a raven stared up at him. A shudder went through him as he saw the card; it was the Raven card. Rarely had he drawn the Raven card. Each of the times that it had appeared in his hand, there had been trouble.

His mother had made the cards and had taught him how to read them. She also taught him the tree magic known as Ogham. His mother had instructed him on becoming one with the trees and letting them speak to him. Trees had their roots deep within the earth and their branches high up in the air. They knew many things from the sensations carried to them from above and below. Whenever possible, Raven would connect with a tree, allowing its thoughts to wash over him.

He looked at the card in front of him and turned over a second card. This time, the wolf card, the teacher, and the card that Raven had always identified as Haney's card. Thoughts of Haney once again flowed into his mind. The last time he had seen his old teacher was a painful memory. Raven had been so angry with him.

"What a fool I was." Raven thought as he remembered how their last fight had almost ended.

Raven had been furious because earlier that day, as the battle raged, he had found himself fighting the man responsible for his mother's death. The man had taunted Raven throughout their fight. He had told Raven as they fought that Haney had been his teacher, and how ironic they both had the same teacher. Raven had swiftly ended the man's life with a blow from his sword so powerful it had severed the head. He smiled grimly at the memory of the grinning fool's head rolling away from his twitching body. Raven had stomped on that grinning face until it no longer looked human, and it had felt good to avenge his mother's death in that way.

Later that day, to make matters worse, he had found himself waged against Haney in battle. His anger had grown again, remembering that his old teacher taught the man who had slain mother. Raven decided to spare Haney's life at the last moment, somehow finding the strength to hold back on what would have been a fatal blow had he used the blade of his sword.

Raven, no longer angry, had tried many times to find Haney since that day, but without success. It was as if he had disappeared from the face of the earth.

Raven gathered up the two cards, returned them to the deck, and put them back in his travel pack.

"Maybe I will try once more to find Haney." He thought. "I do not need to fight someone else's battles for a while with the gold I received yesterday."

He decided to go back into the village and prepare for the journey. A sense of urgency and purpose washed over him as he headed back to the town.

As the sun went down, Twila slowly opened her eyes. Instantly all the previous night's events came flooding back to her. She was also aware of the blood hunger that rapidly became her only thought. Twila stepped out of the caravan and found Netta waiting for her.

"You must leave," her mother told her quickly.

Twila saw her father sat slumped by the campfire. He knew she was there but did not acknowledge her.

"You have been banished." Her mother responded when Twila turned to her for an explanation. "I have moved most of your things over to your van. Marcus moved it further down the river for you, and your father bought that horse over there."

She noticed her mother's hand was trembling as Netta pointed to a sturdy brown horse with an unruly shaggy mane tied to a tree. Twila knew that her father should not provide her with these things if she had been banished and understood that it was impossible to stay with her group. Twila was not even sure how much of a potential risk she could become to the group, and this blood hunger was so intense. It screamed within her. What if she lost control and fed on a member of their group by accident?

"Has a replacement for me been decided?" Twila asked quietly.

"Karla will take your place," Netta responded.

Twila nodded approvingly.

"Morry will be pleased, Karla has grown into a pretty young woman. What did he say the reason for my banishment is?"

Twila looked across at her father as she said this; tears filled her eyes, blurring his image.

"He told them someone attacked and raped you on the road," Netta said quietly.

"That is not a reason for a gypsy girl to be banished. Didn't the group question this?" Twila asked, astonished.

"The group would never question your father's decision on a matter so close to his heart. A gypsy leader is not required to give a reason for a banishment." Netta replied sadly. "The group is aware of his love for you. They all know that whatever the real reason for your banishment was, it must be serious enough to warrant it."

Twila fought back the tears again as she retrieved the last of her things. When she had finished, Twila hugged her mother long and hard. Neither one of them dared to speak, so great was their grief. Twila then went over to her father and kneeled beside him, laying her head in his lap. For a moment, it brought back childhood memories of the nights when he would tell her stories. She felt his hand gently stroke her hair, just as he had done all those years ago. Twila hugged her father tightly and thanked him for not sending her away with nothing. He briefly nodded in response, too heartbroken to speak.

Twila got to her feet, and after kissing Stavos gently on the cheek, she walked towards the horse, commanding it to be calm. Its nostrils flared, and it became skittish the closer she got. Twila crept into its primitive but surprisingly intelligent mind. She mentally murmured comforting thoughts to him as Twila loaded two sacks containing the rest of her things onto his back. Twila turned around just one more time before she led the horse into the forest. Netta was now sitting by Twila's father, and his arm was protectively around her.

Hatred for Ramos continued to grow deep within Twila. She would revenge both Danior and her parents for what he had done. Stefan had spoken of one with more powerful magic than Ramos, and Twila decided she would try to find him.

As she led the horse into the forest, her thoughts reluctantly returned to her hunger.

"First, I must feed." Twila thought to herself as she left her human life behind forever

Amani stood in the shadows quietly, watching Twila leave the camp. His eyes blazed for a moment with anger at Ramos because he had caused this young girl's plight and killed Haney. It had been a long time since he had visited Sheukhawn. There had been no need. This world was a simple place, still in its infancy, destined to progress in culture and technology.

Amani frowned, inwardly cursing himself for ignoring his instincts when they had concealed the key. He should have stayed with Haney until sure of his safety before leaving him. Amani had known that Ramos would likely sense the small glimmer as the key buried itself into the rock. He had not suspected that Ramos's magic had grown powerful enough for him to be out in the daylight, though.

Radon had told Amani that he suspected Ramos had somehow attracted the key into this world because when Haney had

93

used it to escape from the battle, it had brought him right here to the world where he lived. When the key, if used urgently like that, transported the keeper randomly to another world. It seemed too much of a coincidence that the key brought Haney to this world by accident.

The dragon key itself had its special magic, and at times it made its own choice of what world it went to next. Radon had also told Amani that Ramos had cast a spell on the key shortly after Haney first arrived. Ramos's magic now prevented the dragon key from leaving Sheukhawn. Amani at the time saw no need to alarm the old keeper when Radon had told him all this. The key was not detectable unless it glimmered. So, instead, Amani told Haney that the dragon key would be much safer here, right under Ramos's nose.

"If Ramos ever does succeed in finding the key and starts meddling with the delicate weave of things, any change he causes can ripple through the intricate strands of all that is." Amani thought angrily. "Especially if he ever manages to reach Radon."

He stopped suddenly, unable to even contemplate that notion. A cold shudder ran through him.

Amani turned his attention to the distraught image of Twila's parents, holding each other, attempting to gain what little comfort and strength they could by their closeness. Almost without thinking, he concentrated on them.

"Forget," Amani commanded silently, gently forcing his way deep within the minds of Netta and Stavos.

He realized in that brief moment how very little time Netta had left. Amani, now satisfied, turned, and then silently went deeper into the shadows of the forest.

Netta and Stavos sat bewildered for a moment, unsure of where they were. Suddenly both remembered that they were about to break camp and leave. Netta grinned foolishly at Stavos, who was still looking a little bewildered, as he went to attach the horse to the caravan. Memories of Twila now gone from each of their thoughts. Replaced by an emptiness that neither of them would ever define.

Amani followed Twila until she reached where Marcus had concealed her caravan; he sensed the pain of her grief but could not allow her to forget. He needed time to bring Raven to the key.

Amani had found Raven quickly enough, but persuading him to become a new keeper of the dragon key might not be easy.

Twila's back suddenly stiffened, as if she sensed his presence, turning quickly, she looked straight at him. Raven cloaked himself swiftly with a shadow spell and watched her cautiously. Twila hesitated for a moment before securing the horse to a tree and then ran off into the woods to search for prey.

The strength of Twila's perception had surprised Amani, but he had no doubts that Ramos had chosen her for that very reason. Amani knew he must plan this carefully, and the first thing to do was make sure she remained safe. Then he would speak to Raven.

His cloak appeared to swallow him up with a decisive gesture of his arm, and Amani was gone.

Amani quickly sensed the pack of wolves that he sought. They were less than 10 miles away from where Twila was greedily feeding on the blood from her first kill of the night.

"Ah, the one that leads," Amani said to the large brown timber wolf that stalked towards him. "How goes it with you, my friend?" Amani bowed his head, respectively, as the wolf grew closer.

"It has been a long time, Amani; it is good to see you." The wolf's words crept into Amani's thoughts with a deep guttural tone.

"I have missed you, my friend, Kamots." Replied Amani, using the birth given name of the wolf.

At the sound of his name, Kamots's eyes glowed warmly.

"I sense that this is not a chance encounter." The wolf said as he sat down before Amani.

Kamots's deep amber eyes gazed fondly at Amani as he also sat down to join him. Amani smiled as he pushed back the hood of his black robe. His pure white hair fell around his shoulders now that it was free from the confines of the heavy material.

"I have a great favor to ask of you and your family, Kamots. It is of great importance, or I would not ask this of you."

Amani turned and smiled as the rest of Kamots' pack slowly began entering the small clearing.

"Ask your favor Amani; our pack owes you a lot of favors." Stated Kamots firmly.

"Ramos has become a danger again, Kamots," began Amani.

A deep growl from one of the other wolves caused him to turn in its direction. A piercing glance from Kamots towards the offender sent the young gray male slinking off to the pack's rear with the women.

"We all know from our ancestors the legend of Ramos," acknowledged Kamots.

He flashed another threatening glance at the young gray wolf moving forward again, and it stopped him instantly in his tracks.

"You will have to forgive my son, Amani. He is what his birth name means, he who goes first", Kamots said apologetically.

"Ah, yes, a good name," replied Amani and smiled at the proud yet embarrassed look in Kamots's eyes. "Motomo will no doubt follow in his father's steps honorably, my friend."

Kamots ears flexed a little in pleasure at Amani's compliment.

"Motomo is young and impetuous, but his heart is good." Said Kamots. "One of our kin was killed in the hills to the north of here two nights ago, a meal for the Dark One Ramos. When we heard that he replaced the seal, even though Ramos treated the Gatekeeper and the Gypsy girl so cruelly, we assumed that was its end. Ramos does not normally walk amongst us to feed, so we felt that it was a small sacrifice compared to the alternative had the seal not been replaced."

"Yes, and that should have ended it." Replied Amani quietly. "Ramos now seeks the dragon key. If successful, then not only could he cross between all worlds, but also the power of Radon will then be accessible to him."

"How can we help?" Motomo's mellow but forceful voice pushed its way into Amani's thoughts.

Amani turned and smiled as he saw Kamots's son at the front of the pack again.

"Motomo," snarled Kamots, causing the young wolf to cringe almost to the ground.

Amani rested his hand on the lean, powerful shoulders of Kamots to calm him.

"Kamots, Motomo, is just the one who can help me with what I need to do."

Kamots eyed Amani suspiciously, while Motomo crept closer, continually glancing at his father out of the corner of his eye.

"Watch Twila until I return. She grows powerful, and I am afraid she will seek out Ramos in revenge before it is the right time to do so." Amani said. "I need to bring the new key keeper, Raven, here first, and it might not be an easy task to persuade him to come. Haney chose him, and I agree that he is the best option we have for the job."

He looked from Kamots to Motomo, patiently awaiting a response.

Motomo was so excited by this prospect that he began panting, his tongue falling out to one side of his mouth. He betrayed his youth by this gesture and restlessly began pacing again. Kamots was a fierce and respected leader, and choosing his son for this task was one of the hardest decisions he had to make.

"Will my son be safe from the Gypsy girl's hunger?" Kamots asked slowly.

Amani nodded quickly.

"Motomo will befriend the girl, speak with her, make it known he has come to help. She is feeling alone right now and will have no cause to harm him. Twila will welcome his friendship. I can be there in an instant if Motomo signals me. I will teach him how to do that before I leave." Amani finished.

Kamots nodded slowly.

"You are surely more powerful than Ramos is. Why is it that you need the Gypsy girl? Can you not just destroy him yourself and put an end to this?"

Amani's features hardened for a moment, causing Motomo to stop in his tracks and Kamots to stiffen slightly.

"I cannot destroy him," Amani said slowly, "I only wish that I could. I can, however, assist in his destruction, and that is what I plan to do. I would have liked to release the Gatekeeper to watch Twila, then I would not be here before you to ask for your help Kamots, but I cannot destroy a spell cast by another."

Amani's eyes met Kamots, and the wolf knew that he had spoken the truth.

"Then, if Motomo wants to go, so be it," Kamots said quietly and firmly.

He looked over to where Motomo was impatiently waiting.

"Motomo?" Asked Kamots. "Are you willing to watch over this girl until Amani returns with the new keeper of the key?"

Motomo was ecstatic that his father would agree to this request. Desperately, he sought to control himself, and he looked directly into his father's eyes and gave his answer.

"Yes, father, I will go with Amani and protect the girl," Motomo stated firmly, he was amazed at how controlled his voice had sounded.

Amani once more rested his hand on Kamots's shoulders.

"Thank you, old friend," Amani said. "I will leave you two alone for a few moments."

Kamots nodded in appreciation as Amani left the clearing, and the rest of the pack followed, affording him the last private moments with his son.

Motomo was overwhelmed as Kamots nuzzled him in an unusual display of affection. Kamots could see so much of Motomo's mother, Kaoni, in his son.

"My son, go proudly and protect the girl as Amani asks," Kamots said.

Motomo raised his head proudly.

"With my life Father." He firmly answered.

Kamots nodded and then raised his head and howled softly to signal to the rest of the pack and Amani that they could return.

Motomo loped easily by Amani's side as the two of them ran through the forest searching for Twila, but what Amani did next stopped Motomo in his tracks. One second, Amani was a man, and the next, he had shapeshifted into a large white wolf.

"Be calm little brother." Amani's soft voice said into Motomo's mind. "This is a much faster way for me to travel."

Motomo recovered from the surprise and then quickly followed Amani's wolf form as they sped onward towards Twila's camp.

Amani and Motomo watched Twila as she returned to her caravan. Motomo walked into the clearing carefully. He knew Amani was watching him and would intervene if necessary. Twila's horse became restless as the wolf approached. When Twila finally noticed him, Motomo sat down in the center of her camp and mentally introduced himself.

"My name is Motomo." He announced. "I know how you have been abandoned by all you have known, and that is why I am here. You must head for the coast of Edenberry; there is someone there who can help. I will lead you to him."

Motomo looked at Twila, waiting for some kind of response. His ears were alert, and he was ready to run in an instant if Twila should attack him. What he didn't expect was for Twila to burst into tears the way she did.

"Thank you, Motomo." Blurted Twila as she dropped into a crumpled heap by Motomo and flung her arms around his neck.

"She means to feed on me." Motomo initially thought alarmed, expecting to feel pain from her teeth.

Twila, however, was hugging him tightly, her cheek against the back of his shoulders. The only damage Twila caused was an increasingly damp patch on his fur from her tears.

"You fear me," Twila said and released him as she caught his thoughts.

Tears trickled down her cheeks as she looked into Motomo's darting gray eyes.

"Is this what I have now become, something to be detested and feared?"

Motomo was both ashamed and concerned by his initial reaction to her embrace. He moved to a position where he could lick away her tears; it was the only way he knew how to comfort her. His mother had done the same thing to him when he needed consoling as a pup. There was an unmistakable blood flavor amongst the expected saltiness in her tears, but Motomo wanted to ease the pain he had caused and chose to ignore it.

Amani smiled from the shadows. He could now go to find Raven. Motomo had been the perfect solution to watch over Twila.

"Kamots has every right to be proud of his son." Amani thought as he quietly left the campsite.

Amani sadly glanced at the mound that marked Haney's grave, as he made his way to the cave. He wanted to make sure that Apple had food and water before he crossed into Raven's world. Amani planned to bring Raven to this place and retrieve the key. Ramos will undoubtedly be heading back this way too, for he must have sensed the key hidden in the cave.

"He cannot retrieve it, though," Amani thought angrily. "Let him try all the spells he knows. Nothing can break the concealment spell unless I reverse it myself."

Amani stopped as he reached the entrance to the cave; there was someone other than Apple inside. Initially, he thought it might be Ramos but discounted this notion immediately when the vibrations from within the cave were human and female. Amani hesitated for a moment. If someone found Apple, they would take care of her, but he needed Haney's fiddle to help persuade Raven to follow him back here.

His decision made, he stepped into the cave and saw a young woman who jumped to her feet as he entered. Her long dark hair tied back in a loose braid, and some strands had escaped and framed her determined face. Dark brown eyes blazed at him fearlessly. The girl wore a brown suede leather tunic fringed at the bottom, leggings, and boots, more befitting a man.

Amani realized with surprise that she had drawn a small dagger from a hidden pocket in one of her long sleeves. The way the girl held the small knife left no doubt in Amani's mind that she knew how to use it.

"Who are you?" The girl snarled.

"I mean, you no harm," Amani said calmly. "I came to collect some things that belonged to a friend of mine."

He glanced over in the direction of Haney's travel pack, and it was apparent she had been searching through it.

"I've been here hours, and no one has come looking for these things, or the horse." The girl clutched her dagger dangerously. "Finders keepers, that's what I say."

She stepped closer to Haney's pack.

Amani inwardly groaned. He had no time for this.

"I came only for the fiddle. You are welcome to keep the rest, except for the horse. The horse must go back to the rightful owners." Amani said firmly, stepping towards Haney's fiddle placed by the side of the rest of his things.

"Stay right where you are." Demanded the girl.

Amani decided he had no choice but to mentally influence the girl, and he turned to face her. The girl felt this movement towards her threatening and threw the dagger skillfully at him. It buried itself deep into the front of Amani's shoulder, stopping him dead in his tracks. In a flash, another blade dropped into her hand from beneath her sleeve. She appeared on the point of throwing that one too.

"Stop," Amani commanded, rushing into the girl's mind.

She instantly stopped. The hand holding the weapon dropped to her side, the dagger fell to the floor with a resounding clatter.

Amani pulled the dagger from his shoulder, and blood seeped out from the resulting wound. He threw it to the floor in front of the girl who now stood silently, her eyes wide with alarm. Amani closed his eyes for a moment in concentration. A white glow grew around the wound and covered his shoulder, and then instantly, it was gone. He opened his eyes and inspected the place where the dagger had entered his shoulder. The only visible trace was a dark stain and the tear in his shirt.

"You had no cause to attack me," Amani grumbled irritably. "I meant you no harm."

He waved his hand in her direction, and the girl retrieved the daggers the instant she could move again.

"What are you?" The girl said breathlessly, wiping her blade clean on the side of her leggings. "Are you a blood drinker?"

Amani eyed her suspiciously.

"Is she some sort of slave to Ramos like the Gatekeeper is?" He thought. "What is your name, girl?" He asked abruptly.

"Shayla." The girl replied, afraid of what Amani would do next if she didn't answer him.

"Well, Shayla, you are in great danger if you stay here," Amani said, quietly.

"From you?" The girl asked hesitating.

"No, not from me," Amani said firmly. "What do you know of blood drinkers? He asked, knowing that there had been none in this world for some time, so it surprised him that she spoke of them.

"I know that you are one," Shayla said quickly. "I can sense them, but you are something else too that I can't understand."

She looked at him with a puzzled look on her face.

"You are wrong; I am not a blood drinker. I am Darpelian." Amani answered.

There was something strange about this girl. The vibrations and aura that she emitted like a beacon were human, but there was also something else. Amani wanted to pursue this but knew that time was growing short, and he must get her out of here to collect Raven.

"A Darpelian," Shayla whispered. "I have heard stories, but thought they were just myths. I find it difficult to believe that a human and a Dark One could produce an offspring."

Shayla relaxed her guard as she spoke and slipped the daggers back into their custom-made sheath in her sleeve. She straightened her sleeve again, and they were once more concealed.

"I wish to find more about you, Darpelian. What name do

you go by?" She asked.

"My name is Amani." He answered. "But this is not the time to talk, because if you do not leave this place now, then a blood drinker named Ramos will slay you where you stand."

Shayla's eyes narrowed when she heard the name, Ramos.

"A famous legend indeed. I have heard of that Gypsy." She said.

"Well, you know the potential danger you are in then," Amani said firmly, a sudden thought was forming in his mind. "Would you be willing to do something for me and save your life in the process? He asked.

"What is it you wish me to do?" Shayla asked, suspicion crossing her face.

"I need to bring someone here to this place, but I know Ramos will also be coming back here. If I give you the money to stay at the Black Wolf inn until I return, we will talk then. The inn is in Edenberry, and you should be safe there. Take the horse with you and have it stabled.

"Will you be willing to do this small thing to satisfy your curiosity about what I am?" Amani asked her quietly.

Shayla thought about what he had said. She made a good portion of her living by telling stories at inns and taverns, and Shayla knew there was a story to be had here. Amani could have slain her by now had he chosen to, so Shayla decided that he did not plan to harm her. The thirst for a new and unusual story captured her. Without another thought, she agreed to his proposal.

"I'll do it," Shayla said firmly. "Give me the money, and I will leave now." She held out her hand, waiting.

Amani sighed profoundly and handed her a small pouch of gold coins that he retrieved from the folds of his cloak. He thought that if he had problems with Raven, maybe this Shayla could potentially be the next protector of the key.   There was something about this girl that piqued his interest.

"Do you know where the inn is?" He asked as she took the gold.

"Yes, I know it well," Shayla replied. "How long am I to wait there?"

She examined the bag of coins and then looked up satisfied. There was enough here for her and the horse to live very well and for a long time.

"One maybe two days, and I will come and find you in the bar at the inn," Amani answered quickly.

He bent down and retrieved Haney's fiddle and put it carefully back into the specially made sack that usually held it.

Shayla, now caught up in this new adventure, was already formulating a tale about the Darpelian in her head. Quickly she gathered the rest of Haney's belongings and her own. Apple went calmly with Shayla as she led her outside. Luckily it was a full moon, and the path back down to Edenberry was well lit. Amani led the way until he was sure that Shayla was well away from the cave and Ramos.

She hurried towards the welcoming glow emitted from the windows of the Black Wolf inn. Shayla turned about to tell Amani goodbye and found that he was gone already. As Shayla entered the inn's courtyard where the stable lad hurried to greet her, she smiled.

"I want to know everything about this, Darpelian Amani." She thought excitedly. "I hope he comes back soon."

CHAPTER EIGHT

Vesta

Raven headed towards the sleepy hamlet where he'd first encountered Haney. He had no idea where to start looking for him, but maybe someone there could help. It was late in the afternoon, and the sun was hot on his back, and as he walked, it became more uncomfortable. Raven knew this area very well and finally decided to leave the road and travel on a forest trail instead. It was the right decision because he made faster progress in the cool shade of the trees.

When the light began to fade, Raven decided he would travel for another hour then camp for the night. Raven enjoyed the peace and solitude after his recent battles, but he never let his guard drop for even a second. Haney had taught him that.

Raven smiled fondly at a memory of Haney pushing him in a stream one time to prove the point. That was the last time his old teacher had ever caught him off guard, though. Raven always expected to be attacked and had managed to stay alive that way. He had made many enemies in his chosen career as a mercenary. There was always someone with a grudge to settle looking for him, but Raven quickly sent them away defeated. If they were still alive, that was.

When the tall figure stepped from the shadows, Raven was ready. He dropped his pack, threw his cloak back to expose his sword, and drew it smoothly. It was such a practiced series of moves that he was ready to fight in an instant.

"State your business," Raven said coldly.

He was surprised that the man had suddenly appeared in front of him like that. His enemies usually attacked him from the rear.

"I came to speak to you, Raven, that is all," replied Amani carefully. "I have a proposition for you."

Raven smiled grimly, "I am not currently for hire, but I can give you the name of a good fighter that is."

He lowered his sword slightly but stayed prepared for trouble.

"You misunderstand me," Amani replied slowly. "If you will allow me to explain, it may change your mind. You can sheath your sword for I am unarmed."

Raven eyed him suspiciously. "Then tell me quickly," he growled. "I have no time for this.   Amani smiled. Haney had been correct. Raven was indeed an excellent choice to keep the key safely.

"Perhaps if I show you this." Amani held out the sack that contained Haney's fiddle. "You will allow me to tell you why I am here?"

Raven's eyes grew wide when he saw what Amani was holding. It was Haney's, he was sure of it. "Open it up." He demanded, raising his sword again.

Raven felt a sense of dread at the sight of the sack. Haney would not have let the fiddle out of his sight unless he was very sick, or even worse, dead.

Amani opened the sack carefully and pulled out Haney's fiddle. He held the fiddle high before him so that Raven could see it. Raven, in response, lowered his sword.

"Where is he?" Raven asked quietly.

The telling cards that he had drawn earlier in the day, and now the stranger before him holding Haney's fiddle gave Raven a deep sense of foreboding.

Amani sighed deeply. "Killed, I'm afraid," he answered carefully.

A burning flash of anger rushed through Raven as he heard these words.

"Who is responsible for his death? He snarled. "If the work you offer me is to avenge Haney's death, then consider it done, and for free." His voice broke a little with emotion.

"The man who killed Haney is named Ramos, but there is more to it than that," Amani stated. He could sense the emotions rushing through Raven. "If you are about to make camp for the night, then we could discuss my proposition more thoroughly."

Raven just nodded in reply; he could not trust himself to speak. He sheathed his sword and then led the way deeper into the forest until they came to a small clearing. Mechanically he searched for suitable wood for a fire, not speaking a word to Amani, who was quietly watching him.

When the fire blazed, Raven sat beside it, waving his hand at Amani to indicate that he should join him. Amani accepted the offer without words and sat down by the fire.

"Tell me what happened," Raven said quietly.

Amani took a deep breath and then slowly, and carefully he told Raven why he had come.

Motomo slept under Twila's caravan during the daylight hours; this spot suited him perfectly. It was sheltered and warm. He could also observe the clearing without being seen should anyone approach the caravan. Motomo no longer feared Twila and liked the fact that she was a hunter too. Shortly after he walked into her camp last night, they had gone hunting together. She drank the blood, and Motomo ate what was left.

He watched the shadows of the trees grow longer within the small clearing of the camp. Soon the sun would set, and Motomo would lead Twila to the coast as Amani had instructed. He felt Twila enter his thoughts, alerting him that she was awake. Stretching lazily, he crawled from his shelter and was waiting patiently by the steps of the caravan when Twila finally opened the door.

"Motomo." Twila greeted the wolf as she saw him waiting for her by the steps. "I trust you rested well."

He stepped forward to meet her. "Very much so." Motomo gently replied, his mellow voice finding its way into her thoughts.

He could sense her blood hunger and felt disturbed by its intensity as it screamed through Twila's whole being.

"So, this is what drives a blood drinker to hunt so ferociously." He thought.

Motomo had never sensed a hunger so intense, even in the harshest snow of both the winters since his birth, when food had been scarce, he had not been that hungry. The longest he had ever gone without food was four days, and Motomo remembered that his hunger had felt like a throbbing ache in his stomach. The pain had even woken him from his sleep.

He sadly watched Twila prepare the caravan for the journey to the coast, now condemned to suffer that hunger for eternity. His loyalty to Twila grew, and she became a pack member to him in his heart. Motomo silently vowed to give up his life to protect her if needed.

Twila attached the horse that she had named Reed, to her caravan, speaking quietly into his ear to calm him. She had solved the wolf's presence, causing Reed to be skittish, by influencing him to think that Motomo was also a horse. It was a simple solution and was working well. The wolf sat patiently, waiting for her to finish. Twila had been to Edenberry many years ago and was sure she could find it quite easily by herself. She was growing fond of the wolf, though, and was pleased he would be with her. Twila had to speak to Danior before they set out, and she couldn't talk to him from here.

"Motomo." Twila began slowly. "I must visit the seal before we leave. I know it is in the wrong direction, but Danior needs to hear that someone has come to help us." She said firmly.

"Then leave the caravan here. It will be faster if we take the forest path." Motomo said as he padded towards Twila.

"It won't take long," Twila promised, and after securing Reed to a tree, she headed purposefully into the forest.

Motomo and Twila traveled side by side. When they reached a large open meadow that led to the hills that housed the seal, they ran through the tall stems of sleeping wildflowers. Twila stumbled on some tangled grasses and rolled over as she hit the ground, taking Motomo with her. Motomo yipped in surprise, and Twila giggled at the tangled mess they were now in, and the two of them ended up wrestling around like a pair of yearling cubs in the chilly evening air. Both of them enjoyed this brief moment of childish abandonment, and it bonded them even closer together.

When they reached the mound of rocks, Twila knelt before the seal sadly, her eyes closed, concentrating on Danior. Motomo sat, looking out over the moon-speckled water of the river. He was close enough if Twila needed him, but at a respectful distance to afford her some privacy.

Danior crept into her mind just as Twila began to think that he would never sense her call. His thoughts were full of shadows, which she could not penetrate. Danior was masking the real horrors of the place where he was, and Twila knew it. Excitedly she told him about Motomo and the one who had offered to help them. Twila felt his mood lighten at this revelation, but he still cautioned her not to trust anyone until she knew more about them.

"You need to feed Twila," Danior told her firmly. "Your hunger screams through my senses like a thousand sorrows."

"I hate to kill Danior," Twila answered sadly. "The small animals taste so earthy, and there is so little blood that it barely takes the edge off my hunger, nothing like it was when I drank from you."

"Nothing will truly satisfy your hunger except human blood," Danior said cautiously. "Choose carefully, Twila, if the hunger does become so great that you need human blood. Choose someone who will not be missed and remember to break their neck or sever the head afterward."

"I cannot kill another just to feed this hunger, Danior," Twila answered quickly, but her voice lacked conviction. "That would make me no better than Ramos." Twila took a deep breath to clear her mind of the exciting possibility that she could taste human blood again.

"I know how it feels," Danior said urgently. "It will grow worse, more painful. I tried not to drink human blood at first, and animals worked for a while. The bigger the animal, the better it took the worst of the pain away. What you don't realize is that your body craves the human element of the blood. You will starve without it.

"The blood hunger will drive you into a crazed state, and you will be unable to control your actions. No one will be safe from you until the hunger is satisfied by human blood. Twila, you are heading for Edenberry. That town is large because of the trading ships that sail there. There are many places by the docks that harbor the worst kind of thieves and murderers you could imagine. If you notice that your hunger is becoming unbearable, then visit the back streets of the docks. That can control the hunger for some time before you need to drink human blood again. Think of it only as removing the town of its rats."

Twila felt confident that she could never take a human life to satisfy the need, but the thought of human blood had stirred unknown darkness within her.

Motomo's ears pricked up as he sensed a stranger enter his thoughts.

"Watch over Twila for me," Danior said into Motomo's mind. "Her blood hunger grows, and soon nothing will quench it until she has drunk human blood. When you get to Edenberry, encourage her to find a human that no longer deserves to live. Make sure she finishes the job by breaking the neck or removing the head. If Twila is too hungry, she may forget to do this."

He mentally assured Danior that he would break the neck himself if need be, and Danior thanked the wolf for his loyalty.

Motomo could hear his pack's calls in the far distance as Twila was saying goodbye to Danior. He suddenly felt a little homesick for his old life.

He followed Twila back to the caravan and struggled to control the urge to howl a reply to his family's night calls.

Ramos looked around the cave and saw that the horse and Haney's belongings were gone. The ashes from the fire were still warm, though, and he grew curious. Ramos realized that a thief could have happened on the cave and helped himself to Haney's things, but maybe there was more to it than that. Alarmed, Ramos wondered if the key was still here, but felt sure he would have detected its glimmer had it moved. Ramos closed his eyes and concentrated in an attempt to sense the key's presence. Then sighed with relief when he felt the key's power close to him.

He searched the back of the cave where the vibrations were most powerful but could see nothing. Ramos then opened his pack and began removing an assortment of flasks and pouches. Carefully he emptied each of them into a small wooden bowl that he used for his spells.

Ramos began chanting, adding the flasks' and bags' contents, one by one, into the bowl. With his words, he invited demons to work with him and help create the spell that would expose the key.

Shayla had watched Ramos enter the cave and was becoming restless. She felt sure that he would have discovered the things were gone and come outside again.

She had paid for her room at the inn and then returned here almost immediately. It was hours before Ramos rewarded her patience with his return, but she couldn't see what he was doing inside the cave. Finally, Shayla couldn't stand it any longer and crept her way to the entrance of the cave. She only hesitated a moment before slipping inside and quietly hid behind a mass of rubble to the right of the cave access.

Shayla could see only shadows at the rear of the cave, but Ramos had started another fire that did give some light to the front portion of the cave where he was. Shayla could hear Ramos chanting strange words over and over, none of which she recognized. His voice grew louder, and the speed of his chanting increased. A gust of wind blasted its way through the entrance of the cave that chilled her to the bone. The fire appeared to flicker and die for a moment, and the cave plunged into darkness. Shayla almost panicked and was about to dart for the entrance, but she took a deep breath and stayed hidden.

The fire suddenly burst into life again, and she watched with interest as smoke began to rise from the rear of the cave. Ramos held his arms out as smoke billowed from the bowl at his feet, his cloak flapped around his legs as the wind increased. A sudden flash of white light spewed from his outstretched fingers and illuminated every corner of the cave. The smoke continued to billow from the bowl and appeared to be forming into a shape.

Shayla watched in the unnatural bright light and saw the smoke change into the shape of a monstrous demon. Horror washed over her as she saw red eyes develop within the smoke, followed by contorted facial features. The mouth seemed to froth with deep red spittle as it worked to form words. Shayla suddenly decided that she had seen enough and very carefully crept out of the cave.

Once safely outside, Shayla ran back towards the inn and didn't once look back, grateful for the simple shadow spell that she had cast. At least Ramos had not discovered her. She decided that she would just wait for Amani to return before venturing back to that cave again.

Shayla decided to include the spell casting that she had just witnessed into one of her tales at some point. It was the type of thing her audiences loved to hear.

Ramos concentrated the spell on summoning Valeskas, the demon lord, and as usual, he had answered his call for help. Valeskas told him that the key was there but hidden by another's spell, and he grew angry when Valeskas told him this.

"The no one can retrieve the key unless the person who cast it removes the magic," said Ramos, with an edge of frustration in his voice.

"Then, let's seal the cave with a spell of our own." Sneered Valeskas, as dark red foam sprayed from his smoke mouth.

"An excellent idea," responded Ramos. "Then, the spell caster will have to seek me out to remove it, and of course, it will be on my terms." His laugh eerily echoed around the cave. "Then, consider it done."

Ramos turned in the direction of the cave's entrance, and a blue flash exploded from his fingers. The craggy exit glowed for a second and then was plunged into shadows once more.

"Now, only I can enter or leave this cave," said Ramos, satisfied.

He watched Valeskas's features start to lose their definition as his summoning spell wore off. Moments later, the demon was nothing more than a few wisps of smoke emitting from the bowl.

"I have waited so long for the key," Ramos thought to himself as he repacked his things. "Waiting a little longer is not such a hardship, and I am very interested in meeting the spell caster, very interested indeed."

Ramos left the cave and smiled as a brief tingle rushed through him as he crossed the barrier spell. He casually slung his pack over his shoulder and headed back home.

Amani closely watched Raven as he finished telling him about Haney and the key. He had sat rigid as Amani spoke, his eyes never leaving his for a moment. Raven's eyes were blue, but with rings of brown and green within their depths and depending on the fire's light, they changed colors. Raven was solidly built but not exceptionally tall. His long dark wavy hair was pulled off his face and tied back neatly.

Without a word, Raven got up and walked to the edge of the clearing. Amani watched him struggle with his emotions, and he patiently waited for Raven's decision. He added another branch to the fire and looked over towards Raven again. Raven sat down on the ground beneath one of the enormous oak trees that edged the clearing. He was leaning heavily against the trunk of the tree, and his eyes appeared closed, but it was difficult to judge in the gloom beyond the fire's light.

Amani grew curious and carefully concentrated on Raven's thoughts. He entered them unnoticed and was surprised to find another's presence joined with Raven. Amani realized that Raven must be communicating with the tree's spirit. He had heard of this magic but never encountered anyone who practiced it. Amani turned his attention to the fire once more and tried to remember as much as he could about this ancient practice.

Raven was beside himself with anger at how Haney had died, and even the oak tree's calming voice was doing little to help it. He wanted to avenge Haney's death desperately, but after listening to Amani's proposal, Raven realized that it would not be that simple.

He remembered seeing a pendant around Haney's neck, but never realized that it was some kind of key. Raven wondered why Haney had never told him about it, but then the two of them had grown apart during their last year together.

Raven wished that Haney had entrusted him with the key. He would have agreed to take over the role as its keeper, and Raven would have sworn to protect it with his life just as Haney had. Raven liked his current lifestyle; there were no rules, and that thought caused him to question the sense in taking over the dragon key's keeper job. Currently, he had nothing else to consider when taking his next job. The freedom aspect was one of the reasons that made him part ways with Haney.

Haney had been both a mother and father to him, fussing and worrying over every move he made. The band of mercenaries that he joined up with eventually became like his new family. Raven fought by their sides and celebrated each victory at any inn or tavern that had the ale and the women to entertain them. Raven had lived each day like it was his last. He was a formidable warrior that feared nothing, his friends admired him, and the women loved him. Raven realized that Haney had been wise not to give him the key back then because he was not responsible enough at that time to make any commitment to anything.

It had only been since his last meeting with Haney that Raven had changed. He no longer fought recklessly, not respecting the skills of his many opponents. Raven fought with his brain as well as his body now, calculating his moves. His victories were no longer down to pure strength and, in some cases, luck. They were the result of an experienced calculating fighter who knew how to win a battle and win it well. Raven had seen two of his old friends die in fights, and a third injured so severely that he ran himself through with his sword, preferring death with dignity than a life begging for alms.

Raven now only took jobs when his money was low and chose to concentrate on what he remembered of his mother's lessons of the Ogham faith.

He took out his telling cards from his pack. "This will decide it." He thought.

A card slipped out from the deck as he shuffled them and fluttered to the ground at his feet, face up. It was the tree of life card. The tree branches reaching up into the sky, its roots beneath the ground displayed and surrounded by a circle of limbs and roots intertwined.

He had always associated this card with his mother for some reason. When Raven had drawn this card before a battle, he knew it would be a good fight and a successful one, therefore a good omen for accepting Amani's proposal.

Raven cut the deck and then turned over the top card. It was the spider card, indicating a storyteller, or of fates entwined as in spiders web. This card also was a good omen for joining forces in a battle or cautioning against being fooled by a storyteller, perhaps. He glanced over at Amani; he had been truthful with him; he knew that. Just to be sure, he pulled one more card, and it was the owl card. Owls were wise, trustworthy, and also night hunters. Raven liked this card too.

He thought deeply for a moment and then decided that he would follow Amani and take Haney's place as the key's keeper. There was nothing for him in this world now that he could not find in another. Without a second thought, Raven put away his telling cards, then stood up and walked back towards Amani, who still waited patiently by the fire.

"I will come with you, Amani," Raven stated firmly. "I will protect the key to the death if need be, for as long as I am physically able. But know this, Amani, I will not rest until Haney's murderer has paid for what he has done. You tell me that it is the key that this murderer Ramos seeks and if that is the case, let him come and try to take it from me. I cannot confess to caring about what Ramos did to the Gypsy girl and the Gatekeeper because I don't know them, but they are two more reasons why I need to deal with him. However, retaliation for Haney's murder is the most important thing I care about."

Amani nodded in response. "Then we have no time to lose Raven." He stood up and kicked some of the moist earth over the campfire, plunging them both into darkness.

Raven grabbed his pack, and as his eyes adjusted to the sudden darkness, he followed Amani to the edge of the clearing. Amani gripped Raven's shoulder firmly with one hand and placed the palm of his other hand on his forehead.

"Do not be alarmed.' Amani said as he felt Raven stiffen at his touch, "you must see what it is that you are willing to give your life to protect."

Raven was about to state that he feared nothing but held his tongue. A green glow was illuminating them both, and Raven noticed for the first time how remarkably pale Amani skin tone was. The glow grew brighter and lit up the trees with an eerie mixture of shadows and brilliant green light. Raven felt his knees weaken, and he staggered slightly, attempting to shift his weight to regain balance. Amani's grip tightened in response, and Raven was glad of his support.

The ground suddenly shifted alarmingly beneath his feet, and Raven realized that Amani was holding him up now. Raven balked at the strength Amani must possess to enable him to do this with just one hand. He could no longer see the trees; the light surrounding them was too bright, blinding him, as Amani's grip on his shoulder grew tighter. Suddenly the light around them seemed to explode into a million stars, cascading upward and outward until they finally disappeared into a darkness beyond.

Amani released Raven's aching shoulder and removed the other hand from his forehead. This sudden release almost caused Raven to fall to his knees, but he managed to stay upright. Raven looked around them in awe. The forest was gone, and Raven saw that he was at the entrance of a vast hallway.

The hallway was so long that Raven could not see where it ended. On either side of the hallway were massive carved marble pillars that went upwards into oblivion. If they supported anything above them, Raven could not see what it was. He grew dizzy, looking upwards, trying to see where they ended.

The carvings on the pillars were intricate and detailed; each one was depicting a different dragon. The dragons wrapped around their columns; some had their mouths open wide, spewing flames of marble at unseen foes. Others looked down on him with frozen expressions of curiosity or surprise that he had dared disturb them. Many wrought iron braziers placed in between the pillars lit the hallway. The glowing red coals were flickering like millions of eyes watching them. The floor made up of huge slabs of slate were all uniform and perfectly level. Raven noticed that Amani was quietly watching his reactions.

"Come," Amani said, his calm voice echoing eerily. "Radon wishes to meet you."

Amani began walking down the hallway; the noise he created sounded like an army marching into battle. Raven followed him, trying to do so quietly but failing miserably. They walked in silence because it was impossible to hear anything over the loud echoes from their footsteps.

The hallway finally ended at a pair of enormous oak doors. Another carved dragon created from what Raven presumed was gold lounged comfortably across the top of the door's frame. Large red gems, possibly rubies but Raven wasn't sure, depicted the dragon's eyes. As he drew closer to the doors, they opened invitingly. Raven stopped in his tracks, not sure if he should continue or not. Amani smiled at him.

"You have nothing to fear here, Raven." He turned and went through the open doors, and Raven, without hesitation, followed him.

The room that Raven found himself in was immense. More pillars edged the room's circular shape, but these were fashioned from the same gold ore as the dragon above the entrance was. Each of these columns also had carvings but not of dragons. These carvings were of different animals. The ones closest to the door were of wolves. The next ones were of giant bears. The animals were in pairs; on Raven's left, a wolf and a second wolf on his right. The next couple were the bears and then birds, Ravens. He was intrigued by the detail of the carvings, each hair or feather intricately defined.

Torches lit the room from ornate holders attached to the walls in between the pillars. Raven looked up to see that the pillars supported a ceiling, painted to depict a night sky. Stars filled every available space in formations that were unknown to Raven. As he looked up in admiration of the artistry, he saw a shooting star flash its way across his line of vision. Raven gasped in surprise, attempting to follow the star's path, but it was gone. He searched for it but then began to doubt that it was real. Raven finally returned his attention to the center of the room. He decided that his eyes had played tricks on him with the shooting star, and if they hadn't, then the alternative was too terrifying even to contemplate.

In the center of the room was a massive dragon statue, again carved from a golden metal. The dragon stood on its hind legs, the muscles and tendons clearly defined. One scaled foot with long claws supported the rest of the body, and the other foot raised, the toes curled. The dragon's wings spread wide, ready for flight. The mouth was open, showing rows of golden teeth. The eyes were looking upwards towards the stars, its nostrils flared. One of the dragon's front legs reached imploringly upwards. The other held a large globe securely in its curved clawed foot.

Raven stepped towards the statue to study it further. It was more than three times his height. He noticed that the globe's interior shifted and swirled as if it contained a liquid. The color of which varied from the darkest purple to the brightest red. Small flashes of silvery-white light sparked from within the globe's center that reminded Raven of lightning during a summer storm. The dragon statue was so realistic that Raven expected it to rise in flight at any moment. Reluctantly he tore his eyes away from the golden dragon and noticed that Amani was continuing forward to the far shadows at the back of the room. Raven cautiously followed, his fingers brushing the handle of the sword secured in its sheath on his right side. The smooth, familiar feel of his sword was comforting to him in comparison to all that currently surrounded him.

At the far end of the room was a large stone platform with graduated steps leading up. Raven followed Amani into the shadows, and when his eyes adjusted to the gloom, he finally came face to face with Radon.

CHAPTER NINE

Radon

Raven involuntarily took a step backward when Radon appeared from the shadows at the rear of the room.

"Welcome, Raven, Radon said as he approached the two of them. His deep resounding voice rumbled around the room. "I have been expecting you."

Raven was struggling to reply but was overwhelmed by the massive creature looming above him. Radon's long talons clattered on the slate floor as he advanced.

"Thank you, Lord Radon." Raven finally said, dropping to one knee, with his head bowed as a sign of respect before him.

Radon lowered his massive head until it was level with Raven's.

"Do not fear me, Raven, you are amongst friends here." The dragon said kindly.

A soft rush of warm air washed over Raven, and as the dragon spoke, an acrid smell of burnt wood stung his eyes. He managed to smile weakly in response to Radon's words. The situation that he now found himself was so ridiculous he almost laughed.

"Forgive me, Lord Radon, for my clumsy ignorance, I have never seen a dragon before, and you are truly a magnificent sight." Raven finished.

Radon laughed deeply in response to this comment, causing the whole room to vibrate with the sound.

"We have much to discuss, so make yourself comfortable."

Radon sat down on the floor gracefully, causing a large

cloud of dust to rise in response to his weight, and he curled his huge tail around him. The way Radon positioned himself reminded Raven of an enormous dog settled in front of a fireplace. At Amani's invitation, he removed his pack and made himself comfortable on one of the many pillows around the room's rear. Raven was fascinated by the dragon, his eyes drinking in as much detail as they possibly could.

The dragon was covered from head to tail in varying sizes of scales, and the largest covered his back and his wings. The tips of the veins on his wings ended in long curved plates, and at the end of the tail was a plate-sized razor-sharp protrusion. Raven was sure that just a glancing blow from the dragon's tail would be more than enough to kill him. Radon was a silvery green in color. The larger scales were a dark silvery-green, and the smaller scales were varying shades of green and silver depending on how the light from the many torches fell upon them.

Raven found the dragon's head fascinating; many rows of teeth flashed in the light when he spoke. Sharp scales stood upright, ran between his flared nostrils, and continued down his back to the tip of the tail. Two large horns loomed dangerously from the top of his head. His eyes were startling. They were golden in color and glowed with an almost disturbing intelligence. Raven grew uncomfortable under the dragon's gaze and was sure that Radon knew his every thought.

"Amani told me about the key." Raven finally said. "I vow to protect it with my life just as Haney did. The man named Ramos must pay for what he did to Haney, and I intend to see that done." Raven stood up in front of the dragon as he finished speaking as if to reinforce this statement. His anger was evident.

"Yes, I believe you will," Radon said. "You will also die swiftly, just as Haney did unless you listen to what I have to tell you. Ramos is no ordinary man, and therefore his death will not be an easy task. He is a man of magic who has been meddling in dark forces that promise him powers and riches.

"An old adversary of mine named Valeskas has deceived Ramos. He cares nothing of Ramos but uses him to reach me. I have something that he needs. A goddess banished Valeskas many years ago into the Void, and the key would facilitate his freedom."

"Then the key unlocks this Void? Raven asked curiously.

"No," answered Radon. "The key opens the way to me and what I protect with the help of my friend Amani here, and loyal keepers of the key like Haney was. Because of them, what Valeskas seeks has remained safe."

"What exactly is it that Valeskas seeks?" Asked Raven curiously.

"There," Radon said, pointing a long black talon in the direction of the globe that the golden dragon statue held aloft in the center of the room. "It is known as the Dragon's Tear."

Raven turned to look at the Dragon's Tear. "What exactly is it?" He asked curiously.

"It holds enough power to create or destroy anything," Radon said. "It is made from the combined souls of my brothers. All this you see here is a small example of what is achievable with the Dragon's Tears' power. It can also release Valeskas from the Void."

Raven studied the globe with interest, attempting to understand what Radon had said.

"This is too vast for me to understand fully," he said slowly. "Tell me how all this began."

Amani was quietly watching Raven and the dragon. He smiled when he heard Raven's interest in the Dragon's Tear; he was the warrior they had been waiting to arrive. Amani had been concerned that there would not be enough time to prepare for Ramos' battle, but Raven already used simple magic. He would not need much training to control the power that Radon planned to allow him to access.

Radon sighed deeply. "It began with a small wish from a gentle goddess named Saressa. Her name is mostly forgotten now in these worlds that she created."

His voice rose in anger as the memories flooded back to him. The hairs on the back of Raven's neck stood on end in response to the change in Radon's tone of voice. The torches illuminating the room flickered alarmingly, and for a moment, Raven thought they were all about to be plunged into darkness.

"My mother spoke of such a goddess.' Said Raven, suddenly remembering things long forgotten from his childhood. "She told me that Saressa was an earth goddess with beliefs and rituals similar to the Ogham magic."

Radon looked surprised. "Ogham magic is ancient." He said. "I thought it's priests and priestess were all destroyed by Valeska's followers long ago. The word Ogham means earth in the long-forgotten language of my ancestors; its followers were Saressa's faithful. They eventually stopped using Saressa's name to avoid persecution."

"A mercenary like myself slew my mother," Raven said thoughtfully. "I never discovered why someone killed her. I only know that her death was avenged by my hand in the same fashion that Haney's death will be. Do you think that it was because of her beliefs?"

"Possibly." Replied Radon. "If your mother spoke of Saressa, then she would also have known about Valeskas. There are still loyal followers of him out there too, practicing in secret, just waiting for his return from the Void, just as Ramos is.

"Saressa had created peaceful worlds filled with everything her followers needed to flourish under her watchful gaze. She consulted her brothers and sisters, who had already created many worlds, for advice. Saressa carefully chose and crafted every living thing that populated her worlds. She gave magical abilities and powers to all if they chose to use it and presented a wonderful world to my people to live in and grow. We lived peacefully for centuries until the coming of the Dark Ones...." Radon's voice trailed off as if lost for a moment in his memories.

"My mother spoke of Dark Ones too," Raven said, trying to recall what his mother had told him. It was so long ago that he could only remember their name and not the details.

"The Dark Ones are blood drinkers," Radon said quietly. "They are promised immortality then condemned for eternity with a hunger for blood that torments their every moment."

Radon was silent for some time after this revelation, and Raven realized that explaining what had happened in the past was probably opening up old and painful wounds for the dragon. He waited quietly for Radon to continue.

"The dark ones were the hellish creations of the evil god Dra." Radon said slowly. "Unlike Saressa, Dra destroyed worlds because of his love for war and chaos. No one had hunted us before, we were not fighters, and we failed miserably to rid our world of Dra's blood-hungry invaders. One by one, we were bitten and infected with the blood hunger.

"Dra wanted access to the powers given to us by Saressa, and for a short time, he was successful because we had become members of his Dark Ones' army. We gladly followed his command to destroy the peaceful inhabitants of Saressa's worlds. Dra opened doors between her worlds and showed us how to enter them, and then feed on the innocent to satisfy our blood hunger.

"When Saressa discovered what Dra had done, she implored her brothers and sisters to join her in stopping him. A great war of the gods waged, and eventually, Dra was defeated and returned to the far reaches of the Great Barrier."

"The Great Barrier?" Raven asked. "That term is familiar to me also, but I cannot recall why. What exactly is the Great Barrier?"

"The Great Barrier is beyond the edges of Saressa's universe. The worlds there are ruled by war and chaos, Dra had created them, but he had also grown tired of them. His black heart thrives on death and destruction, and when he found these innocent worlds that Saressa had created, he wanted them for himself.

"She tried to restore peace to her worlds after Dra had fled but failed. Her followers had lost faith and turned away from her, feeling that she had failed them in their darkest hour. Saressa then tried to close the paths that Dra had created between the worlds, but nothing worked. Her sisters and brothers could do nothing to help her. Then Saressa finally did the only thing that she was powerful enough to do. She gathered all the dragons that were now blood drinkers. Dra had not known that two hearts beat within our bodies. Although the blood hunger coursed through our bodies with every beat of one heart, the second heart still contained the loyalty and love for Saressa.

"All the dragons that were now blood drinkers willingly allowed Saressa to destroy their physical bodies, capturing their souls as she did so. She then created the Dragon's Tear to hold the released souls of my brothers. Saressa chose the name Dragon's Tear because it was symbolic of the sorrow that Dra had caused us all. She knew that the power of their combined souls would be the protection these worlds needed should Dra ever manage to return."

"And what of Valeskas?" Asked Raven. "Is he a god too?"

Raven now utterly absorbed in what Radon was relating to him, because it brought back more memories of his mother and what she had told him.

"No, not a god." Replied Radon. "Even though he would like to think so. Valeskas was a brother too before the coming of Dra and his dark invaders." He sighed slowly at this last statement.

"Then why did he not become part of the Dragon's Tear also?" Asked Raven.

"Valeskas was the first to be infected by the blood hunger," answered Radon, "because of this, he drank not only from a Dark One but also from Dra himself. Both of his hearts held the darkness, and he became a blood lord for Dra. Valeskas led the onslaught of the Dark Ones while Dra watched.

"When Saressa learned of this, she knew that Valeskas could not become a part of the Dragon's Tear. His dark power was too strong for her to destroy him because of his closeness to Dra. Instead, she cast him into the Void and sealed him there." Radon's massive lip curled as if in a smile as he said this.

"If he was as powerful as you say, then why did he not just return after Saressa had gone?" Raven asked.

"That is what he has been trying to do," said Radon, "Valeskas constantly searched amongst the few followers of Dra that were left, but magic was dying throughout Saressa's worlds. Without Saressa's presence, the people no longer knew how to use the powers they had within themselves. The ones that retained this knowledge passed it down through their families. Eventually, they forgot the name Saressa, and sadly lost their gods." Radon sighed heavily.

"What exactly is the Void?" Asked Raven.

"The Void is deep inside the core of the shadow world. That is why Ramos is involved in all of this. He has the power of Saressa and the greed to succumb to Valeskas's promises. Ramos created the opening between his world and the shadow world. Remnants of Dra's Dark Ones still rule the shadow world, and they were safely confined there. That was until Ramos created the opening. He opened a doorway by developing the natural powers that Saressa had bestowed on all the creatures in her worlds and combined it with a power-infused crystal. Ramos found that the opening was difficult to close after it had served its purpose. He had planned to close it after he had been bitten and infected with the blood hunger.

"Valeskas has no use for the Dark Ones that populate the world of shadows. None of them possess the magic that Saressa had so freely given, and so therefore useless to him in his quest to be free. Ramos already possessed Saressa's gift, and now he had the dark power that came with the blood hunger. Ramos now uses his blood containing the essence of Saressa's love and the evil elements from Dra in his spells. Somehow, he has managed to summon Valeskas with his magic. Valeskas has promised him more powerful magic if he helps to free him.

"We first became aware of Ramos years ago when he combined his tainted blood with the blood of the Gypsy girl's mother, Netta. He created a seal to close the opening to the world of shadows after trapping or killing the Dark Ones that had escaped into his world. We thought about destroying Ramos then, but we would have caused the seal to fail in doing so. So, we have just watched him, and oddly enough, he has not given us much reason for concern until now. Ramos has grown more powerful, creating spells that have brought him closer to the Dragon's Tear, and therefore me, which has always been Valeskas's ultimate goal. Only the power of the Dragon's Tear is powerful enough to break the barrier holding him in the Void, and they both know it."

Raven thought for a moment before asking his next question.

"Why did Saressa spare you?" He finally asked.

"Saressa searched amongst us for one who was strong enough to resist the blood hunger," Radon replied, "I was the last one of us that was infected by the blood hunger. I had resisted the desire to drink blood to the point of rage and was successful. I never drank any blood to satisfy it. So, because of that, Saressa instructed me to drink her blood, and by doing so, she destroyed the darkness coursing through me. The power and magic within her became mine also. With our combined magic and the force generated from within the Dragon's Tear, we banished Valeskas to the Void.

"I am immortal Raven, just as Valeskas is, but unlike him and his followers, I no longer need blood to survive. Once Valeskas was in the Void, Saressa tried desperately to close the doors between her worlds. Dra's magic had created them, and because of that, only he could reverse his spells. We did the only thing we knew possible to close them. By casting a locking spell, we sealed each of the doorways created by Dra. Saressa then constructed this place, and she named it Vesta. Vesta is the word for birthplace or home, in my tongue, and that is what she effectively did, she brought my brother's home.

"Saressa then moved all the entrances to the doorways here." Radon waved a scaly arm in a sweeping gesture around the room. "Each of the pillars that you can see here, and the ones in the outer chamber where you first found yourself, conceal a doorway. Each doorway opens with the key that you have agreed to keep."

Raven looked around at the pillars and remembered how many they had passed on their way to this room. His mind whirled at the thought of just how many worlds Saressa must have created.

"Vesta seems the perfect place to keep the key, though,"

Raven said suddenly. "Isn't it more dangerous to keep it within one of these worlds, out of your sight?"

"That is what we originally thought, too," answered Radon. "The golden statue that holds the Dragon's Tear in one of its hands had initially held the key in the other. When Saressa finally left this place to begin creating new worlds, we both felt that Vesta was secure, and no one would ever find it. She took with her the few remaining dragons not bitten, and I promised her that I would stay here to guard the Dragon's Tear and the key.

"Saressa trusted me completely, but I was still afraid the darkness that had once coursed through my veins might somehow return. So, I asked Saressa to create a spell that would destroy me if I ever touched the key. Saressa felt this was not necessary, but she did as I asked. I was comforted knowing that I could never cross any of the doorways for my gain or be used by anyone for this purpose if I should fail to protect it. I had not forgotten how the blood hunger had driven me to follow Dra.

"All was peaceful for many years after Saressa left. Then one day, I discovered a visitor." Radon turned his attention to Amani. "Luckily, he was on a personal quest against Dra's remaining followers. He is a half-breed known as a Darpelian. His blood hunger infected father violated Amani's mother. In response, the men of his mother's village killed him, and they saved her from being bitten as well. The people of Saressa's worlds by then had learned how to fight back against the remaining Dark Ones and effectively destroy them.

"When the villagers discovered that Amani's mother was pregnant, they realized what the baby would be. As the time for Amani's birth grew closer, his mother fled the village, knowing that they would destroy her baby immediately after the birth. Without the skill of the midwives of her village, she, unfortunately, died giving birth to him. Amani was found and raised by an unsuspecting group of Gypsies who discovered him by his dead mother's side. The only thing the Gypsies found on his mother's body was an armlet fashioned from gold. Because of the armlet, Amani eventually discovered who his mother was and what he was and why."

Raven glanced over at Amani as Radon paused thoughtfully.

"Amani chose to rid his world of the few remaining blood drinkers that had survived. He eventually came across a Dark One that planned, with the assistance of Valeskas, to open a new door to

Vesta. Amani had searched for this Dark One for some time and destroyed him just as he had cast the spell to create the door.

"Thankfully, it was Amani who stepped through that door leading to Vesta that day and not Valeskas's follower." Radon said, "and he also chose to assist me in protecting the doorways and the Dragon's Tear.

"The Dragon's Tear was no longer as safe as I had initially thought. I had no way of contacting Saressa for help, either. After much discussion, Amani and I decided to create a barrier around the Dragon's Tear. We also fashioned a new key and named it the Vesta key. The Vesta key opens all doors, but not the barrier around the Dragon's Tear. Only the dragon key can unlock that.

"We both agreed that the dragon key was no longer safe here, and Amani searched for and found its first keeper. Amani brings each new keeper of the dragon key here to this place, and to meet me. The rest of the keepers have been chosen by the one before them when they were no longer able to protect it. Haney reached out to Amani and asked him to find you when he realized it was time to pass the dragon key to a new keeper.

"Once the original dragon key was safe with its first keeper, Amani then crossed worlds using the Vesta key. The Vesta key allows him to be my watcher, reporting back to me any threat to this place's discovery. We both agreed that I should cast a spell preventing him from touching the dragon's key also.

"Amani fears as I do that, as the darkness is a part of him too, it could one day control his actions. We would be useless to Valeskas or any of his followers if they came here because neither of us can touch the dragon key. If we did, it would instantly destroy us. The dragon key only works for its current keeper too. So, if someone stole it, they could not use it.

"It is not the perfect answer to ensure the key and the Dragon's Tear's safety, but it was the best that we could do."

"The dragon key has crossed worlds a few times, but it glimmers when the magic is activated. The key's glimmer reached Ramos, and somehow, he realized what it was. Since then, he has watched continuously for its brief light," Radon finished slowly.

Raven initially felt overwhelmed by all that the dragon had told him. For the first time in many years, he had to admit that his skills weren't good enough for this battle with Ramos. Emotions raged through him with the strange sensations of fear, inadequacy, and helplessness that was new to him.

He felt their eyes on his back as Raven stood up and walked away from Radon and Amani. Once more, he found himself at the golden dragon statue holding its precious burden up high beneath billions of stars. Raven stared up into the murky depths of the Dragon's Tear for some time, reluctant to return to where Radon and Amani were patiently waiting for him.

Slowly his initial feelings of inadequacy faded and were replaced with a calm acceptance of his mortal capabilities. Raven realized that he could not easily slay Ramos as he had all his other enemies, not without the help from a powerful magic-user or at least some kind of weapon designed for this purpose. Raven's thoughts began to formulate themselves logically again despite the great weariness he was now feeling from the events over the last few hours. His body cried out for sleep, but Raven ignored it as he returned to where Radon and Amani still patiently waited.

"I am a skilled fighter Radon," Raven began quietly, "but it is obvious that I am no match for Ramos. I need something that gives me the ability to finish him." He sighed, not used to be lacking the strength or skill in a fight.

"We know that you are a skilled fighter," Radon said carefully, "and of course, we know that you are no match for Ramos with nothing but your swordsmanship and strength alone. We plan to combine our forces and cast Ramos into the Void with Valeskas. It will not be easy, and the timing must be just right. The Gypsy girl Twila is an important element in Ramos's downfall, and therefore she must be protected at all costs. We think with your assistance, we can do it."

Amani waved his hand, and a massive platter of assorted bread and creamy yellow cheeses appeared on a small table exquisitely fashioned from gold. A large jug and cup appeared by the platter's side, and an ornate knife with a small dish of what appeared to be golden-colored butter rested on a wooden cutting board. "Eat and then rest," Amani said, pointing in the direction of the closest pillow to the table.

Raven's eyes grew wide with surprise at the appearance of the table filled with food and wine. His stomach growled alarmingly at the sight of it.

Gratefully he sat by the table, poured the deep red ruby-colored wine into the cup, and then drank deeply. He broke off a hunk of bread and then coated it with a thick layer of the most delicious butter he had ever tasted. Raven quietly ate as Amani explained where the dragon key's location was and that the young wolf Motomo was leading Twila to that same area.

"When you have rested," said Amani, "I will take you to retrieve the key. Then we can all return here."

Raven was surprised by this revelation. "Why are we returning here with the key?" He asked between mouthfuls. "I thought you had decided that it was not safe here," and broke off another chunk of bread.

"Radon plans to give you access to the Dragon's Tear's power. This power will make the magic you have already, strong enough to assist Twila in casting Ramos into the Void." Answered Amani. "When you have accessed the Dragon's Tear's power, we will return to meet Twila."

Amani stood up and left Raven to finish his meal.

"I will return to collect you when you have slept," Amani said as both he and Radon suddenly disappeared.

Raven gratefully finished his meal, refilling his cup with the delicious wine. He had filled it several times before he realized that the pitcher never emptied.

"Nice." He laughed.

The food and wine settled over him like the softest blanket. His eyes stung with exhaustion. Raven finally nestled himself in one of the larger pillows and lay on his back, gazing up at the stars. The torches in the room flickered, and the light grew dim. Raven could keep his eyes open no longer, his exhaustion and the effects of the food and wine finally overcame him, and he fell into a deep sleep.

CHAPTER TEN

Inn of the Black Wolf

Twila entered the tavern through the main doors. The Inn of the Black Wolf was a little larger than where she typically danced, but it was the same setup. The patron's mood was festive, and it was evident that some of them had been drinking since late afternoon.

"Perfect." She thought and pushed her way to the bar.

Twila immediately spotted the tavern keeper. He was perched on a high stool at the far corner of the bar watching his patrons for any sign of trouble. One hand guarded his frequently filled mug of ale against being knocked over by a drunken reveler, and the other hand toyed with the wooden handle of a large, heavy stick.

Despite his massive ale fed girth, he looked very capable of quelling a fight immediately or evicting a drunk who became too rowdy. His darting brilliant green eyes focused on his patrons, and they also closely monitored the bar staff. He frequently watched them deposit his customer's money correctly into the small metal box on their side of the bar. Twila learned that his name was Tanner when a regular patron called out a greeting to him. The wild shock of red hair and his flushed cheeks betrayed a quick temper.

Twila began to concentrate on Tanner even though the screaming blood hunger, now in her every fiber, made it difficult. The smell of blood in the room from the many patrons filled her hungry senses until she found herself almost drooling in response. Twila entered Tanner's thoughts quickly enough and placed the suggestion that he had been expecting her to dance for his customers tonight. His mind, so occupied with the inn's nightly business that she found no resistance to her suggestion. A brief puzzled look crossed Tanner's face but was quickly replaced with a friendly greeting when his eyes located Twila.

"Welcome, Twila, my customers grow tired of waiting for you to dance," Tanner yelled over the noise.

Twila grinned in response and stood patiently waiting while Tanner heaved his massive frame around the far end of the room and cleared her a space to dance. She noticed a man standing quietly by the large fireplace at the opposite end of the room. He was leaning comfortably against a wooden beam, arms folded across his chest. His face held an expression of bewilderment as he watched Tanner. Twila grew curious despite the chaos Tanner was causing at his end of the room, as he moved tables and customers from their usual places.

A small scuffle that suggested the beginning of a more serious fight broke out in the area where Tanner was. Twila saw the man by the fireplace straighten up, observing the event. When Tanner had swiftly dealt with the offending patrons by grabbing one and yelling loudly at the other, the man relaxed but continued to watch.

Twila realized that he must be employed by Tanner to assist him in keeping the patrons under control. It was not surprising then that the man looked bewildered when he had heard Tanner welcoming her as an old friend. In addition to him reorganizing all the tables so she could dance. The man probably had worked here long enough to know that she was a stranger.

His cold dark brown eyes met Twila's, and a shudder went down her spine. She flashed a smile at him in response to his gaze, but his features did not change. Twila sighed and reluctantly concentrated on him. The man smiled as he felt Twila entering his thoughts.

"No, you don't, girl." He told her firmly and pushed her out of his mind.

Twila reeled from the unexpected attack. Her eye widened as the man almost leaped across the room and was by her side in seconds. He pulled her to one side by the arm; his grip felt like a vice. Twila was too surprised to react.

"I don't know who you are, girl, but I know what you were trying to do." The man snarled into her ear. "You can mess with Tanner's mind all you want but stay out of mine, do you hear me?"

Twila nodded quickly, and the man released his grip on her arm.

"Next time you come to me before you pull any tricks like

this here, okay?" The man said, his face very close to her ear so no one could overhear him. "I am paid well by Tanner to keep this place under control, and the likes of you make my job difficult. The next time you want to dance here, you ask the stable lad at the rear of the inn to fetch Devon."

Twila nodded quickly again, but the closeness of Devon was unbearable. She gazed longingly at the taught vein in his neck as he leaned forward to speak in her ear. Twila watched him as he returned to his position by the fireplace. His long black hair reached the broad shoulders. The way Devon walked reminded Twila of a large animal stalking its prey because graceful power filled his every movement. When he was back in position leaning against the wooden beam, Devon smiled and winked at her. His face was handsome, but Twila noticed a long-jagged scar running down the left cheek. Twila smiled grimly back at Devon and grew annoyed with herself for not planning this better.

Tanner banging on a table turned her thoughts away from Devon. From somewhere in the crowd, Tanner had found a girl who could play a fiddle. Twila ran forward into the space that Tanner had created, shaking her tambourine loudly. The customers roared with approval in response to her appearance. Twila glanced over at the fiddle player and then raised and clapped the tambourine to begin her dance.

Twila danced her way around the edges of the crowd faster than she had ever done before. Her new skills gave every movement incredible speed and grace. Briefly, Twila felt a moment of sadness when she looked towards the main door and could not see her father waiting for her. Twila pushed that thought to the back of her mind as she danced.

As Twila whirled faster and faster around the room, she began to pay closer attention to the customers. The blood hunger roared in Twila's ears as if pleading with her to choose someone quickly. She became aware of a particular man that was grinning stupidly at her. By his dress, the man looked to have money, and Twila realized that he was sober.

His attention was only distracted from Twila when more than one girl approached him and spoke into his ear. The man would nod briefly, and then the girls placed coins on the table in front of him. The girls then returned to their particular corners of the room to collect a man waiting there. Twila smiled to herself when she saw the girls quickly leave the tavern hanging onto the arm of a staggering drunken patron.

Twila decided that this man deserved his fate and began to dance now only for him. She willed him to watch her every movement; the rest of the customers were just a blur now. By the end of her dances, his excitement was evident; he barely acknowledged yet another girl that placed her coins on the table before him.

As she gathered the money thrown to her, Twila purposely lingered at his table. The man eagerly leaned forward, whispering an invitation for her to join him later at the rear of the tavern. He pushed several coins towards her, and she nodded and grinned at him. The smell of his blood was driving her almost wild in anticipation. Twila made her way around the room, collecting coins, but she was not interested in the money. She just wanted to get out of the inn and meet with the man. Twila grabbed a handful of coins from her sack and gave it to the surprised fiddler player. Then she made her way to the door of the inn only to be met by Devon.

"Pay up, girl," Devon demanded.

Twila hurriedly dug into the sack of coins, unsure how much she was supposed to give him. She grabbed a handful and dumped them into his outstretched hand. A big grin appeared on his face as he saw the amount Twila had given him. Devon opened the door wide for Twila and did a sweeping bow to show her the way out. She hurried through the door and out into the cobbled street.

"Come back soon," Devon called as he allowed the door of the inn to swing shut behind her, plunging Twila into darkness.

Twila made her way down the street to the rear of the tavern to meet her prey, and her blood hunger screamed for him.

Shayla quickly pushed Twila's coins deeply into a hidden pouch within the top of her soft leather boot. The cold metal handle of the dagger hidden down inside the same boot was comforting to her. She had watched the Gypsy girl that Tanner had called Twila, encouraging the attention of Nate. Shayla assumed that Twila had a death wish or had friends outside for protection waiting for her. She was puzzled by the whole event. Shayla had been here for four days now and had not seen Twila dancing.

Tanner, however, behaved as if this girl came in every night. She was surprised when he pushed and shoved people around, clearing a space for the Gypsy girl to dance. Shayla grew more curious about Twila when Devon stopped her at the door. This Gypsy girl had no escorts with her that she had seen, and that was not only unusual; it was also foolish in a place like this. Shayla had watched as Devon took the handful of coins from Twila before allowing her to leave the tavern. She saw the confusion on Twila's face before handing some coins over to Devon, and Shayla became a little concerned for the Gypsy girl's safety.

Twila did not look used to being on her own in places like this, and Shayla wondered why she was alone. She knew that sometimes the Gypsies would banish one of their own if they broke the rules, but that was rare. Shayla decided suddenly to follow Twila but wasn't sure why she felt compelled to do so. There was something so wrong about the whole thing that Shayla quickly packed away her fiddle and followed Twila out of the tavern.

Devon watched Shayla leave the inn just after Twila. He frowned as she opened the door just wide enough to slip through it, to avoid casting too much light onto the street beyond. She was up to something out there. Devon had been watching Shayla since she had arrived four days ago. She had come with an old horse and spent money to keep stabled, yet never once checked on it. Shayla had been out of the tavern only once before in the evening, which was the first night. Since then, she had just hung around the bar. Shayla had been paid once by Tanner to tell her stories to his customers. Devon had listened to a couple of them, and although they were well-told, he had no patience for such nonsense.

One of the nights, Shayla had sung songs, and Devon had listened closely; she was excellent. There was something about her though that bothered him. He had tried to enter her thoughts when she had first arrived but found it filled with shadows that prevented him access. Shayla made it clear to him that she knew he had tried, and that had irritated him. There were very few people who could detect him entering their thoughts. Now, this Gypsy girl had shown up, and everything about her was wrong too. She had none of the usual Gypsy escorts and had no idea about the value of money. The girl was now being followed outside by Shayla, who very likely planned to rob her.

Devon shook his head grimly; he knew that Shayla would be trouble from the first moment he saw her. He turned his attention back to the customers and noticed Nate making his way to the door.

Devon groaned as he realized what Nate was planning. It was far too early for him to leave, and three of his girls hadn't returned yet. Devon knew that Nate always stayed until they were all back. He watched as Nate left the tavern and suddenly decided to follow him.

The Gypsy girl was stirring things deep down inside of him buried long ago, and it alarmed him. Devon rationalized that he was losing some easy earned money if anything happened to her. He nodded to Tanner, indicating he was taking a break and followed Nate out of the tavern.

Twila had already left to find her first human prey at the local Tavern when Amani had contacted him. Motomo had been getting nervous about the changes in Twila as her hunger increased. He remembered what Danior had told him and was relieved when they had finally reached Edenberry. Twila had instructed him to stay outside the town for his safety, and Motomo gratefully agreed. He was concerned about her, though. Then Amani had entered his thoughts and asked him to go to this cave and described its location.

Motomo found it quickly and would have gone inside the cave to wait for Amani, but something prevented him when he had tried to enter. He couldn't see or smell anything, but it felt like a wall. Finally, Motomo had given up and chose to wait by the entrance. He assumed Amani had sealed the cave with magic to protect the key.

He sat patiently, waiting by the cave's entrance when Amani and Raven stepped into view.

"Motomo." Called Amani cheerfully as he approached the wolf. "I see you did as I suggested and came alone. Here is Raven, the new keeper of the key," Amani said, waving his hand in Raven's direction. Motomo walked towards them, wagging his tail in greeting.

"I would have waited for you inside the cave, but the barrier stopped me."

"Barrier?" Questioned Amani.

"The barrier you created to protect the entrance. I could not get through," Motomo answered. Amani quickly tried to enter the cave and felt the barrier that Motomo described. He carefully searched around the entrance with his fingertips; a slight tingle confirmed his worst fear.

"This must be the work of Ramos." Amani snarled.

He turned to face Raven and Motomo, who was quietly watching him.

"Is there nothing we can do?" Asked Raven, noticing the anger in Amani's expression.

Amani shook his head slowly and then walked towards the edge of the cliff. He concentrated on Radon and told him that Ramos had sealed the entrance to the cave with magic.

"Then bring Raven and Twila to me." Radon mentally instructed Amani.

"Where is Twila?" Amani asked Motomo.

"She is in Edenberry, searching for her first human prey," Motomo answered, shuddering slightly.

"No." Radon boomed into Amani's mind. "You must stop her. She must not drink human blood, or what I plan to do will not work. Bring her to me quickly."

"Wait here," Amani called to Raven and Motomo.

He began running towards the path that led to Edenberry. As Raven and Motomo watched in fascination, Amani changed into the shape of a large black raven. The raven rose higher and higher until it disappeared into the night in search of Twila.

Twila breathlessly waited in the shadows at the rear of the tavern. She stood in a narrow alley between two shops that had long since closed for the night. One of the shops must have sold butchered meat during the day because animal blood's stale smell was overpowering. Twila's position allowed her to view the narrow-cobbled street that ran behind the inn. She could see a large padlocked gate that must be the entrance to the inn's stables. The road continued down to the harbor to her left, and the cool salty breeze helped to waft away the sickening smell from the butcher's shop. Twila knew that her targeted prey would approach from the right, so she watched closely in that direction.

Shayla had seen Twila approach the street that ran behind the tavern from her right. She immediately went left and carefully wound her way through dark narrow alleys that eventually ended up a short distance away from the tavern's rear. Shayla crouched down in the shadows and peered around the edge of a ramshackle hovel that someone called home.   She could see the whole street from her position, but the only light available was from the two lanterns on either side of the stable gate, and the full moon high in the sky.

Several small buildings were lining the street across from the inn.   Each had small alleys separating them.   They were barely wide enough for a dog to pass through, but Shayla felt that Twila must be waiting down one of them.   She grew a little nervous waiting for Nate to appear, and swiftly with a flick of her right wrist, dropped a concealed dagger into her waiting hand.

Devon followed silently behind Nate as he made his way down the street.   When Nate entered an alley that led to the tavern's stables, Devon silently slipped past the entrance and entered another passage further down.   This maneuver allowed him to approach the tavern's stables without Nate noticing him.   Devon reached his destination faster than Nate had, but he hesitated before stepping into the street.   Instead, Devon carefully edged his way into the street, staying well within the shadows.   He watched Nate striding towards the stable gates.

He could see no one else around until Twila stepped out from an alley near the butcher's shop.   Devon could not hear the conversation between them, but he heard Nate chuckle in response to whatever Twila said.   Nate threw his arm around Twila, and the two of them began walking quickly in the docks' direction.   Devon almost turned back to the inn.   Twila would no doubt be back there tomorrow night employed by her escort.

Devon could not see Shayla anywhere and decided that if she was in the shadows somewhere waiting for Twila, Nate had just ruined any plan of hers to rob the Gypsy girl.   As he turned to leave, Devon saw a slight movement in the shadows beyond the stable gates and watched as Shayla stepped into view behind Twila and Nate. Devon changed his mind when Shayla started to follow them.   His curiosity thoroughly piqued now, and he decided to see what she would do next.

Twila tolerated Nate's arm around her waist, and she giggled at the lewd comments he whispered into her ear.   His breath was hot and clammy as he leaned close to her ear.   Twila led him through the meandering alleys towards the docks. She ignored Nate's whispered suggestions, smiling away his advances.   Nate was starting to become a little impatient by the time they finally reached the docks. Twila encouraged Nate to follow her to a secluded spot beneath one of the piers. The sea lapped against its wooden supports as Nate grabbed for Twila, pulling her roughly towards him. The hunger wailed in Twila's veins as Nate's mouth found hers, the stubble from his unshaven face tearing at her cheek then neck.

Nate's breathing increased as his passion grew, and roughly, he grabbed at Twila's hair, pulling her closer and closer to him. Twila ignored his hands, grabbing and pulling at her clothes. She did not resist when he dragged her down to the sand beneath the pier. Twila's hunger was insatiable now she could bear it no longer. Nate's eyes opened wide with surprise when Twila flung him to one side and leaped on to his chest.

"I like a girl who takes the lead," Nate said huskily.

Twila smiled in response. Her hands caressed his long dirty blonde hair, pushing it back from his neck. She ran her fingers gently down his face, her blood hunger taking away reason. Twila could hear Nate's heartbeat thundering above her own, and she closed her eyes in anticipation. Nate's body stiffened slightly in response to Twila's sudden grip on his hair. He was not alarmed enough to resist, but Twila's sudden strength surprised and excited him.

Nate opened his eyes and looked at Twila's face above him. A sudden flash of alarm rushed through him as he saw the expression on her face. Twila sensed Nate's fear as she pushed her way into his thoughts. She saw how he treated the girls that failed to pay him for their protection or for permission to work in his area.

Twila yanked Nate's head back, exposing the sizable pulsating vein in his neck. Nate finally realized that he was in danger and started to struggle against her, frantically pushing Twila off his chest. She ignored his feeble attempts at freedom. Twila had planned to make this gentle for Nate, but what she had just seen from his memories had convinced her that he deserved the worst death possible.

She smiled. The vein in Nate's neck enticed her. It sang to her, begged her to drink deeply from the river of blood gushing inside. Twila opened her lips slightly as pressure from the growing fangs increased, as she grew more excited. Closing her eyes in anticipation, ignoring Nate's increasing struggles, Twila allowed her tongue to trace a line along his throat slowly. She quivered at the sensation of Nate's pounding pulse against her tongue. Nate was whimpering now, begging for his life.

As Twila's teeth brushed the surface of his skin, there was a sudden flash of light, and she found herself flung away from Nate. She hit the support beams of the pier and was momentarily stunned.

"Stay away from him." Commanded Amani.

A flash of white light streamed from his outstretched fingers and surrounded Twila, pinning her to the beams. Twila was raging with anger and struggled against the invisible bonds. She could barely focus because of the hunger but saw a tall figure in a long flowing cloak standing over her intended victim.

"Who are you?" She screamed at him. "Release me."

Amani ignored Twila and turned his attention to Nate.

"Get out of here." He said.

Nate scrambled to his feet and stumbled across the sand and headed back towards the inn.

"Forget." Commanded Amani, concentrating on Nate's retreating figure.

Nate stopped for a moment as if uncertain where he was and then started to walk at his usual pace back towards the street. When he reached the dockside buildings, Nate stopped to brush sand off his clothes for a moment. Amani watched him until Nate finally disappeared from view down one of the alleys. He now turned his attention back to Twila.

Shayla had watched the whole scene from further down the beach. After Nate had gone, she decided to make her presence known to Amani. Amani saw her approach and smiled in greeting.

"I thought you might need some help," Shayla said.

"As you can see, I am quite capable of dealing with such things without your help but thank you for the offer," Amani replied. "What I would like you to do is to meet me at the cave tomorrow night, and I will explain everything that you have seen here." He said about to return his attention to Twila.

"Will we be leaving the area?' Shayla asked. She glanced at Twila, who had grown quiet at her appearance.

"I am not sure yet." Replied Amani. "Just be there at sundown."

Shayla nodded in reply and left Amani and Twila alone as she made her way back to the tavern.

Devon stayed hidden and watched as Shayla had walked down the beach to where Amani stood. He realized that Shayla and Amani knew each other by the way they had stood talking together beneath the pier. Devon had been surprised by Twila's attack on Nate and was very curious about Shayla's role in all this. When he saw Shayla turn and begin making her way back to town, Devon quickly followed Nate's path down the alley.

He moved more swiftly than Nate and promptly came up behind him. The sight of Twila's foiled attack on Nate had stirred old memories deep within him. As Devon reached Nate, he suddenly grabbed him by the shoulder. Nate spun around in alarm as Devon grabbed him.

"Oh, it's you," Nate said, relief evident on his face when he recognized Devon. "You shouldn't creep up on a man like that. I am just on my way back to the tavern. Let me buy you a drink."

Nate laughed a little nervously when Devon did not reply.

Devon smiled and increased the grip he had on Nate's shoulder. Nate groaned in response, and fear became apparent in his eyes.

"What is it you want, Devon?" Nate asked quickly, "money, is it? I have money, here take it." Nate struggled to pull a pouch of coins from the folds of his cloak. In his haste, he dropped it, and coins spewed over the cobblestones at their feet. The clatter of coins echoed noisily in the quiet alley. The only other sound audible was the heavy breathing of Nate as his fear increased.

"Twila was right," Devon said quietly. "You do deserve to die."

He grabbed Nate's hair and yanked it back, extending his neck. Devon sank his teeth deeply into the now extended vein in Nate's neck. The blood gushed into Devon's eager mouth. He drank greedily, ignoring Nate's weakening moans and feeble struggles. When Devon felt Nate's heartbeat become weaker, reluctantly, he released him. Quickly Devon snapped Nate's neck like a twig and allowed his lifeless body to fall to the floor.

Devon leaned against the wall that was growing damp with the early morning mist. He almost groaned in pleasure as the warmth of Nate's blood coursing through his icy veins. Wave after wave of Nate's memories flashed through Devon. The young boy left alone when his mother died in a bar fight, the street girl who fed and clothed him, and the man who taught him the business. Devon saw the faces of the young girls that Nate had beaten if they failed to earn the coins he demanded from them, and the men he had robbed when they were too drunk to resist.

Devon roughly wiped the spilled drops of blood from his mouth.

He ignored Nate's money and grabbed his body, lifting it easily with one hand. Devon walked quickly in the direction of the 'common pit' where the town deposited its sewage. He smiled nastily, thinking what an appropriate place for scum like Nate to end up. Devon continued to smile as hurried to get rid of the body. Nate's shoes dragged on the floor with a rhythmic thud behind him. He tossed Nate down into the pit like all the others who deserved this fate. Devon chuckled at the familiar scuttling of rats as they rushed towards his gift.

"You are welcome, my hungry friends." He whispered to the rats scrambling beneath him.

By morning they would have stripped Nate's body to the bone. Devon saw the glint of their eager eyes as he mentally bid them farewell. Their simple squeals of delight made him laugh again as he headed back to the tavern, searching for Shayla. She could answer some of his questions.

Devon had not detected that Twila was a blood drinker, and that bothered him, and he also should have sensed the blood hunger in her, and he hadn't done. The sight of Amani disturbed him even more. It had been many years since he had last seen him; his sudden arrival like that must mean trouble was coming. Devon had lived here quietly since Ramos sealed the rift to the shadow world without discovering his presence here. He liked this peaceful world and intended to make sure that no one could ruin it for him.

Amani turned his attention to Twila after Shayla left. He breathed a deep sigh of relief and concentrated on Radon.

"I have her, my friend." He said.

"Well done, Amani," Radon responded into Amani's thoughts.

Amani approached Twila, releasing the binding spell as he did so. Twila immediately leaped at him, her teeth bared.

"Be calm," Amani demanded, rushing into her mind.

He found no resistance to his suggestion. The blood hunger had effectively removed all of Twila's control. She became silent and did not resist when he placed one hand on her head. Amani's other hand gripped her shoulder as his eyes closed in concentration.

Twila became aware of Amani's presence as a bright light surrounded them both. The hunger had weakened somewhat, and she slowly regained control of her actions. His eyes were closed, and the long white hair framing his handsome face was blowing wildly in the increasing wind around them. Her stomach lurched at the similarity between Danior and this man's features as he held her tightly. A sudden rush of despair ran through Twila as the sand beneath their feet shifted, and she almost fell. The stranger's hand gripped Twila's shoulder more firmly, supporting her. Twila wished sincerely that this was death coming to release her.

"End this," Twila said mentally to the man holding her. "I no longer want to live, finish me now." Amani ignored Twila's pleas, but the desperation and sadness of her thoughts wounded him deeply.

When they arrived at Vesta, Amani held Twila gently as she continued to beg him for the blessed release that death would bring to her tortured existence. Twila was too distraught to move. The memory of what had almost occurred to Nate suddenly came to her. Finally, realizing that she was too upset to move, Amani lifted Twila into his arms and carried her as he would a child, to the anxiously waiting Radon.

CHAPTER ELEVEN

Saressa

Shayla slipped back into the inn by the side door, it was well after midnight, and most of the customers had left. She sat by the fireplace, waiting for a server to notice her. When the girl came over, giving the table in front of Shayla a quick wipe, she ordered a glass of mulled ale, hoping it would take the chill from her bones.

The flickering flames from the well-serviced fire in the soot-stained grate felt good as Shayla waited for the ale. She glanced around at the few remaining customers. An older man quietly slept in a far corner, his head on the table. Three men were in the middle of a card game at the back of the room. Shayla saw Tanner dozing quietly on his stool at the end of the bar. He leaned heavily against the wall for support but was awake instantly when her coin chinked into the metal cash box. She searched around the room for Devon, who, surprisingly, was nowhere to be seen.

She clutched the steaming mug of ale in both of her hands and thanked the girl who delivered it. As she sipped the sweet brew, Shayla wondered how sensible her decision to meet with Amani tomorrow evening was. Shayla came to this world searching for a safe, quiet place where the hunted priests and priestesses from her world could escape from invading troops. What she should do was return through the star-passage cavern and find a safer place for them, but Shayla felt compelled to try to help Amani first. The ale was relaxing her, and she decided to go to bed. Shayla drained the last delicious drops from her mug when Devon returned to the inn.

The moment he saw her, Devon was at Shayla's table.

"Still up?" Devon asked sarcastically.

"I was just going to bed." Shayla coldly replied.

She stood up and turned to leave. Devon's icy cold hand encircled her wrist, causing a shiver to flood down Shayla's spine.

"I need to talk with you first," Devon said, firmly pulling Shayla back into her seat.

"Let go of me." Shayla hissed dangerously, and with one quick movement, a dagger dropped into her free hand.

Devon grinned as he swiftly captured Shayla's other wrist, effectively pinning her to the table.

"I followed you tonight," Devon said, ignoring Shayla's protests. "I saw you talking with the one called Amani. What is he to you?"

Shayla's eyes grew wide at Devon's question.

"How do you know Amani?" She asked.

Shayla was curious now, she stopped struggling, and Devon, in response, released her arms. He smiled questioningly at the drawn dagger still in her hand. Shayla nodded and flicked her wrist to return the blade into its sheath.

"Let's have a drink together and discuss this civilly," Devon suggested.

Shayla nodded, and Devon attracted the attention of the server. The girl hurried to serve Devon with a pitcher of a rich, fruity red wine and brought two mugs. The server glanced at Shayla curiously as she took the coins from Devon.

"So, tell me all you know of Amani," Devon said.

He filled the two mugs with wine and pushed one of them across the table to Shayla.

"It sounds to me like you know more about him than I do," Shayla replied, sipping the wine.

It was delicious. Shayla assumed it was kept specially for Devon because none of the inn's usual wine tasted this good.

"Then tell me what you know, and I will explain my interest in Amani." Said Devon.

Shayla thought for a moment before answering Devon. She was unsure about Amani and decided that Devon may have some answers to her questions too. Shayla told Devon how she had met Amani four days ago. Without hesitation, Shayla told Devon all about the strange event in the cave.

"When I saw Amani again tonight, it was because of what

I had seen in the cave that made me approach him," Shayla said. "I have been troubled by the sight of that smoke demon, and I felt a need to tell him. Amani was so preoccupied with Twila tonight though the time was not right to say anything. I agreed to meet him tomorrow evening, and I plan to tell him then." She said as she finished her mug of wine.

Devon ordered another pitcher of wine as the first gray light of dawn eased its way across the sleeping town. He felt his strength wash away as the sun colored the gray.

Shayla noticed that Tanner and the servers were no longer around. However, so engrossed in conversation with Devon, she had not seen the change of staff. Tanner's wife, Sadie, was now up and running things while her husband slept.

Sadie was a bitter woman; she had been married to Tanner for almost thirty years. Sadie's father had arranged the marriage, and her mother, who had ten other children to provide for, gratefully packed up her eldest daughter's meager belongings. Her father had taken Sadie to Tanner's tavern the following day. She knew that money exchanged hands. Sadie's father had left the Black Wolf Inn without even saying goodbye, and his drunken gait told her where most of the cash Tanner paid him had gone already.

It had been a childless marriage. Sadie almost died in childbirth a year after she was married, and there had been no more pregnancies. However, in an unusual display of affection towards her, Tanner brought home a skinny little boy child one day to raise as her own. Sadie's love for Ash was the only solace in her miserable life. She had never asked Tanner where the child had come from; he had probably bought him from one of the street girls down on her luck.

Ash ran the stables and helped Sadie out in the tavern during the day. He was the only person who ever received a kind word from Sadie. She currently had two girls and a boy who cleaned, made beds and helped with the cooking. There had been others over the years. They often ran away or ended up living off the streets, employed by the likes of Nate, or married to a patron who had the money to buy them out of her service.

Sadie gave her orders to the three sleepy children who scrambled to do her bidding. The eldest, a girl, hurried into the kitchen to light the fires that fed the clay ovens. The other girl was younger, and she limped heavily towards one of the large sinks and began washing the mugs and dishes from the previous night. Her next task would be to fetch and start preparing the vegetables for a stew that would feed the hungry patrons throughout the day. The boy was the youngest and hadn't been with Sadie very long. His eyes filled with fear when Sadie turned her attention to him.

"Sweep the floor and clean the tables in here, lad," Sadie yelled at him.

He nodded quickly, ran out of the bar, and returned almost instantly with a broom bigger than he was. The boy began at the end of the room, farthest away from Sadie, hoping her attention would now be elsewhere.

Devon put his foot on a large black roach that scuttled across the floor towards them at the table, disturbed by the boy's broom. Shayla shuddered at the loud crunch that heralded the bug's swift death.
"Come with me," Devon said. "I have rooms here too. We still have much to discuss."

Shayla nodded in agreement and followed Devon out of the bar.

Sadie watched with surprise as she saw the two of them start to head for the rear stairs that led to the boarding rooms.

Devon paused briefly to get the pitcher refilled by her, and he also ordered a breakfast to be brought to his chambers. Sadie agreed to get one of the girls to bring it up when ready and forced a smile when he placed some coins into her outstretched hand. Devon had been here for years, and she had never seen him take a girl back there yet. Sadie felt that a handsome young man like Devon would have had lots of girls, but this was the first.

As she watched them disappear up the stairs together, Sadie wondered about the girl that followed him. Shayla had been hanging around for days. She had a room here and a horse in the stable out back that Shayla had not checked on once. Sadie felt the girl was up to no good, and now seeing her with Devon was convinced nothing good would come of it.

Irritated by the fact that she didn't know what Devon and the girl were up to, Sadie stormed into the kitchen. The two kitchen girls kept their heads down as they worked on their chores to avoid attracting attention, but Sadie thankfully ignored them and began preparing the ingredients to make the bread.

Raven and Motomo sat together, watching the morning arrive. The two of them had spoken together earlier, shortly after Amani had left, but they had just sat side by side quietly since then. They had left the immediate area of the cave's entrance and had made their way to the edge of the cliff. The stars were magnificent. As the morning began to arrive, the white tips of the gentle waves below became visible.

Motomo's thoughts turned to Twila. She should be back now, making her way to the caravan. The sun would be rising at any moment.

Amani found them quickly and rested his hand on Motomo's head as he sat beside him.

"Is Twila with you?" Motomo asked anxiously. He had grown very attached to her.

"No," said Amani, "but she is safe. I want you to return to the caravan and keep it safe for her. Come back here tonight, and Twila will be here." He said.

"Should I take Raven with me to the caravan?" Motomo asked.

"No, Raven must return with me," Amani replied.

Amani and Raven watched Motomo as he turned away from them and walked back towards the cave. Moments later, he disappeared into the undergrowth on his way to the carefully hidden caravan just outside the town of Edenberry.

"Is she safe?" Raven asked.

"Yes." Answered Amani. "Come, let us return to Vesta before the sun weakens my power." He said, placing one hand on Raven's shoulder, the other on his forehead, the green light once again glowed around them.

Twila sat before Radon in quiet awe at his size and appearance. When Amani had first brought her here, she was too distraught to be afraid of him. When Radon had started talking to her gently, his deep but pleasant voice calmed her. She had finally opened her eyes and saw the colossal creature sitting comfortably beside her.

His voice was almost melodic as he told her exactly what it was that Ramos had done. Although Twila had initially felt defeated and hopeless when she had arrived there, after Radon had finished telling her of Ramos's deceit and evil intentions, she had grown angry. Twila wanted to seek Ramos out at that moment and destroy him and the blood lord Valeskas and had demanded to return to seek them out.

Radon had patiently told her that she was not strong enough to stop them, not yet. The last thing he had said intrigued her.

"Not yet?" She asked the dragon.

"No, not yet." He had patiently replied.

Amani had left them earlier, promising to return soon with Raven. Twila learned that Raven was part of the plan to defeat Ramos and Valeskas. She was excited to meet him and wanted to help him.

"What if the hunger controls me again?" Twila asked, suddenly alarmed. "The pain is so great I do not want to feel this way for eternity."

She looked over at the dragon, her eyes filled with fear.

"I believe I can end that hunger in the same way that Saressa ended the hunger for me," Radon said.

Twila looked at Radon curiously.

"How?" She asked, hope starting to rise within her. "I thought Saressa was unable to return here." She said.

"Saressa's blood destroyed the blood hunger and darkness of Dra within me." Said Radon. "I see no reason why it should not destroy it within you too. The only blood you drank was from Danior when he turned you, and the animals. The darkness has not yet penetrated your soul. Come to me and take my blood, and with it, receive the love and the power of Saressa."

Twila was startled by Radon's request. She watched in morbid fascination as he sliced open the soft inner aspect of his wrist with a large talon. Her horror changed to hunger as she watched the blood quickly flood Radon's wound and bubble over onto his wrist.

"Come." Radon said invitingly. "Drink and destroy the darkness and blood hunger forever."

Twila, unable to contain herself any longer, was quickly at his side. Radon lowered his bleeding wrist so Twila's eager mouth could fasten over the flowing wound. She had never known such ecstasy as the blood flowed into her mouth. Twila dug deeper into the wound to encourage the flow as she gulped and swallowed to quench her unbearable thirst.

Radon ignored the painful throbbing and the intense pulling sensation that ran through him as Twila bit deeper and sucked at the flow. He mentally begged for Saressa to hear his plea and make this work. Just for a second, something flickered into and then out of his mind. Radon tried to capture it and analyze it, but it was too brief. The flames on the torches closest to them dimmed slightly simultaneously, and Radon believed that they were a sign from Saressa that all would be well.

Gently he pried Twila's unrelenting mouth from his wrist, and she slumped on the floor before him staring sightlessly up into his face, in a trance-like state. Radon edged his wound once more with a talon, and it closed swiftly, the skin where the cut had been was already returning to normal.

Twila was experiencing a wonderfully warm sensation spreading throughout her body as Radon's blood found its way into her starved veins. The warmth increased until it became unbearably hot. Twila realized something was wrong as every vein in her body burned with fire as Radon's blood forged its way through her body. Twila looked up at Radon in alarm, unable to speak or draw a breath. A flash of light crashed into her head, and she promptly lost consciousness giving her a blessing release from the intense pain.

Radon awkwardly but gently carried Twila in his front claws to the pillow closest to him. She did not respond to his touch. Radon knew that he had to wait now to see if Twila would survive the battle of good and evil as they raged war in her veins and heart.

Amani and Raven approached Twila when they returned. They both stared solemnly at the sprawled out, lifeless figure of Twila on the pillow.

"Is she dead?" Asked Raven.

"Not yet." Replied Radon. "I believe the girl is strong enough to survive this great battle of good and evil. She has survived a mortal death and now must survive this immortal one. I will watch over her until we know who won."

Shayla followed Devon up the darkened stairs to the second floor of the inn. Her room was on the same level as the bar. She guessed that Devon had been given quarters on the same floor as Tanner and his wife because they employed him. At the top of the staircase was a heavily carved oak door that was locked to prevent intruders. Devon used a large iron key to unlock the door and held it open for her. Shayla found herself in a long hallway with several doors leading off it. Lanterns hung on either side and although they were not very bright, they afforded sufficient light for Shayla to notice the rough wooden steps at the far end. She assumed that they must lead to the attic where no doubt, the kitchen staff slept.

Devon locked the stair door and headed towards his

room. Shayla waited while he unlocked the door to his chambers. She could hear resounding snores now coming from the other end of the hall. Shayla looked questioningly at Devon, who grinned.

"Tanner could raise the dead, couldn't he? Devon said.

Shayla suppressed a giggle at Devon's words and nodded in agreement. She followed Devon and found herself in a simple but pleasant room with a newly lit fire crackling in the fireplace on her left. To her right was a heavily draped window, and at the far end was another door. Devon placed the pitcher of wine on a small table, and Shayla placed the mugs by its side. He then returned to the door and locked it. As he turned back to Shayla, he saw a flash of concern on her face.

"I am just cautious," Devon said. "I am at my most vulnerable when the sun rises. You are in no danger from me, Shayla. You are free to leave whenever you say."

Shayla nodded, somewhat relieved, she shouldn't have come here with him at all, but there was something about Devon that was attracting her curiosity. She sensed lots of stories here, and because of that, Shayla abandoned her usual cautious instincts.

She sat down on one side of the braided rug that covered the floor at Devon's invitation. Shayla rested comfortably against a large pillow as Devon handed her a mug of the wine. He sat on the rug by the side of the fireplace and took a drink of his wine.

"Have you heard the story of Ramos?" Devon asked.

"How he freed the world of the Dark Ones?" Shayla said. "Yes, I have heard about him. He returned their leader to his world and sealed the entrance. He destroyed the ones that didn't return with their leader."

"Except me," Devon said.

Shayla sat up, alarmed, almost spilling her wine.

"You are a Dark One, a blood drinker?" She asked incredulously. "How did I not detect that?" She said, beginning to feel a little nervous.

"I am a Lunarian," Devon answered. "I am not like them." He finished firmly.

"I have not heard of a Lunarian," Shayla said, curious now.

Devon refilled his mug and brought the pitcher back with him to the fireplace setting it down between them.

"I was born so long ago that I doubt you could even

comprehend it." He said. "The world of shadows was a peaceful place before Saressa cast Dra's darkness amongst us. My kind does not have the blood hunger like the others. Do you know of the battle between Saressa and Dra?" He asked.

"Yes," Shayla said.

"Then you are not from this world, either are you?" Devon said. "I knew there was something wrong about you. I ask you again, what is your interest in Amani? Do you know what you are getting involved in?"

Devon's voice had risen a little as he spoke, and Shayla once again felt a little nervous.

"I told you I just met Amani four days ago," Shayla said defensively. "I saw the Gypsy girl attack Nate, but Amani dealt with her. Amani is not why I am here in this world. I just decided to meet him tonight, so I could tell him what happened in the cave."

Devon looked at her suspiciously.

"So, what is the real reason you are here, then?" He asked.

"I am seeking a haven for the persecuted followers of Saressa," Shayla replied. "A war is waging in my world because of a battle lord named Saran. For many years my people have held him at bay, but we are now at risk of failing.

"My uncle has a tavern that has become a refuge for the persecuted. They are hiding in the caverns that run beneath it. I begged the goddess Saressa for assistance in finding a safe passage to a haven for them. She appeared in a dream and showed me a star-passage cavern to this world. I found it and came out near the cave. I was about to claim the land there and bring the people here to build a new life when I met Amani."

"This was a quiet place." Said Devon. "I have lived peacefully here since he first placed the seal. Ramos used a Gypsy girl's blood to help create it years ago. It concerns me though that Twila had the blood hunger, and for some reason, I did not detect it."

"Amani said that he had to prevent her from tasting human blood, or all is lost." Said Shayla. "Maybe that is why you couldn't detect it, Twila hadn't drunk any human blood yet."

"I will come with you to the cave tonight. There is something wrong, and if Ramos is involved, then Amani might need my help." Devon said.

A small knock at the door marked the arrival of breakfast.

The young girl delivered it, shyly smiling as Devon placed a coin in her rough hand. He put his finger to his lips to indicate it was for her and to keep it hidden from Sadie. Sara nodded her head quickly and headed back down the hallway as she stuffed the coin deeply into a pocket in her dress.

Shayla and Devon sat quietly together as they ate the simple but satisfying breakfast of fresh bread, hunks of cheese, and juicy red strawberries. They briefly spoke when Shayla questioned Devon about the world of shadows. He told her that it got that name because three-quarters of the world was permanently night. The sun's orbit around it covered only the very southern part. Two moons orbited around the rest, creating a land of shadow illuminated by constant silvery light. Shayla thought that it sounded pretty and told him so.

"It was wonderful and peaceful before they came," Devon said. They slowly destroyed my kind. There were so few of us left when I crossed the seal to escape. I often wonder if any survived. We only need blood when we are born and that we take from our mother.

"The crazed blood hunger of the Dark Ones took us by surprise. We also became infected by the blood hunger when bitten by a Dark One. Our leaders initially encouraged us to destroy the invaders, but there were not enough of us, although we are more powerful than them. Eventually, we hid in the catacombs that ran beneath the great mountain ranges of Silvern."

"Do you drink blood too?" Asked Shayla.

"Yes, I can drink blood," said Devon, "and I am also immortal. The sun weakens my strength as it does with the Dark Ones. The differences between us are subtle. I do not need blood to survive. I can eat and drink like any mortal, and in fact, I prefer it. The only way to be a Lunarian is by birth. I have heard of half breeds like the Darpelian Amani, but none of them are of Lunarian descent."

Shayla ate the rest of her breakfast in silence. She glanced at Devon occasionally and found that he was also watching her. When she got up to leave, he escorted her back to the first floor.

Shayla unlocked the door to her room and stepped inside. Devon touched her shoulder gently. "We both have reasons to help Amani," Devon said. "Meet me in the bar when the sun sets." Shayla nodded. "I welcome your company." She said.

Devon turned and headed for the stairs, and Shayla closed and locked her door. She was tired but knew that there was one last thing to do before sleep. Shayla removed the leather cord that hung around her neck. It had a carving of a young girl attached to it. Shayla clutched the carving willing Saressa to hear her. Silently she poured out her thoughts, hoping that Saressa would listen to her plea. It had disturbed her when Devon had spoken of his people. Shayla could not believe that Saressa would cast the Dark Ones into a world already occupied by the Lunarians.

When Shayla had finished, she removed her outer clothing and climbed gratefully into the simple but clean bed. It took only moments for her to drift into an exhausted sleep.

Raven was alert the instant he heard a small moan from Twila. He saw Amani and Radon watching her closely. They had all kept vigil over her silent form for what seemed like days, but Raven knew it was only a few hours. He had dozed briefly during the wait and heard Radon and Amani murmuring together. They had been speaking of someone that Amani had met. She was to meet them later at the cave. Raven looked at Twila. She was beginning to come around. He stood up and walked over to sit with Amani, who was closer to Twila. Soon they would know whether Twila had lost the blood hunger.

Twila slowly opened her eyes. The first thing she saw was Radon. Twila smiled as she realized the hunger was gone, replaced by a sensation of total peace within her.

"It worked, Radon," Twila said thankfully. "The hunger has gone."

Amani and Raven breathed an audible sigh of relief.

"Then, we must begin the next task." Said Radon, the relief evident in his voice also.

Twila got to her feet a little unsteadily but quickly recovered. "What must we do?" She asked.

"We cannot retrieve the key because Ramos has cast a barrier spell at the entrance of the cave." Said Radon. "This prevents Raven from accessing the Dragon Tear's power to assist us in the fight against Ramos. Raven cannot fight Ramos without assistance from this magic. The new power that you have now, Twila, in addition to Amani's and my own, maybe enough to give Raven a fighting chance. The three of us will empower his chosen weapon with magic. Raven's warrior skills and the power we give to his weapon should give him the best chance of casting Ramos into the world of shadows where he belongs."

"Which weapon do you chose?" Amani asked.

Raven thought for only a moment and then drew his sword.

"This is my weapon of choice." He stated. Raven raised the sword high before him holding it with both hands.

"Then let us do this." Said Radon. "Twila, just concentrate on the weapon, and your new power of light will do the rest."

Amani reached for Twila's hand and held it tightly. Radon's claw carefully held his other hand. The three of them concentrated on the sword held high by Raven before them. The light from the torches flashed on the bright metal of the blade as their flames flickered and blazed.

Twila felt a power growing deep within her as she clung to Amani's hand. It began to forge its way up from the pit of Twila's stomach and into her chest. A second later, the force burst from her chest in a brilliance of white light and blasted into Raven's sword. The beam of light continued as Twila felt the power flowing through her and into the blade.

Almost instantly, another flash of light flashed from Amani's chest. It was a bright red, and it mingled with Twila's white light, and their fingers gripped each other's tightly. The mixture of Amani and Twila's power continued to pour into the sword, and it glowed brightly in response.

Finally, Radon's power flashed across the room. It was brilliant green in color and wove its way amongst the red and white of Amani and Twila's power. This time when their combined powers hit the sword, Raven's knees almost buckled with the impact, and he braced himself as the colorful mixture forced itself into the sword. Then, just as suddenly as it had begun, Twila, Amani, and Radon ceased the power beams. The blade shimmered for a moment, and then the light was gone.

"It is done." Radon boomed his voice, causing the floor beneath them to vibrate.

Amani and Twila stopped the flow of their power at Radon's command. Twila fell to her knees, and Amani dropped his hands, breathing heavily. Raven felt the heat in the handle of his sword start to cool. It throbbed in his grip, almost like a heartbeat as the metal cooled. He lowered the sword, his arms aching from the impact of the force of their combined powers.

"Let us go find Ramos." Raven snarled. He smiled as he felt the sword twitch in his hands. "I am ready."

Shayla found herself in a dark hallway. It reminded her of the one that had led to Devon's room earlier. There was a cold mist swirling around the floor, and she shivered as it touched her bare legs and feet. Shayla realized that she was dressed only in her shift and became alarmed that she was not armed.

"Am I dreaming?" Shayla said aloud. Her voice echoed eerily in the empty hallway.

"Shayla," said a woman's voice. "This way."

Shayla peered into the gloom and saw a figure in the shadows at the far end of the hall.

"Who there?" Shayla whispered.

"Come to me." The voice said. "I cannot come any further."

Shayla slowly walked towards the figure. The mist grew colder and thicker, the closer she got. Finally, the woman's features became more apparent, and Shayla recognized her.

"Saressa," Shayla said, quickly dropping to her knees with respect for her goddess.

"I must tell you this quick child, for the time I can spend here is very short." Said Saressa. "Raise your head Shayla and listen carefully. You must go to Amani and help him finish Ramos's tyranny with the blood lord Valeskas. Take the Lunarian Devon with you. Tell him the sorrow I feel at hearing the fate of his people. I thought the world of shadows was devoid of life. I cannot return to these worlds as part of my agreement with Dra. But what I can do is offer you this."

Shayla accepted a jagged shard of crystal that Saressa handed to her.

"What must I do with it?" She asked, aware of the sharp edges pressing into her tightly closed hand.

"Give it to Amani." Said Saressa. "Help them with this before returning through the star-passage cavern. Their need is more urgent right now than finding a haven for my followers.

"Take Sara to Liffy when you go in search of Ramos. Tell Liffy that Saressa heard her prayers."

Shayla was about to ask who Sara and Liffy was, but

Saressa had almost faded from sight.

"Ramos must be stopped." Said Saressa urgently and then disappeared into the mist.

Shayla suddenly woke, her heart beating rapidly. She sat up in bed and looked around the room. The fire had long since burnt out, and the place, now chilled. The fading light outside told her that the sun would be setting soon.

Shayla scrambled out of bed, and a sharp sensation caused her to stop and open her hand. A large crystal shard lay in her open palm. A small trickle of blood ran down her finger, where the sharp edge of the crystal had cut her skin. Instantly Shayla realized that she had not been dreaming.

"I must hurry and meet Devon." Shayla thought. "Then, on to cave to meet Amani."

CHAPTER TWELVE

The Crystal

Shayla discovered who Sara was when she left her room to meet Devon. A small huddled figure beneath the stairs whispered to Shayla as she was locking her door before heading for the bar.

"Excuse me, Miss, but are you, Shayla?" A child's voice said.

Shayla peered into the gloom beneath the stairs. "Yes." She answered.

"A lady told me that you would help us escape from Ma Sadie and take us to a better place." Said the voice.

"Are you Sara?" Asked Shayla.

"Yes." Said Sara. "And this here is Rudy."

"Rudy?" Said Shayla. "There was no mention of any Rudy."

"He goes with me everywhere." Said Sara. "The lady must have forgotten to mention him, that's all."

Two huddled figures came out from beneath the stairs and stood before her, and Shayla saw that Sara was, in fact, the kitchen girl that Devon had given a coin to that morning. Rudy was the small boy who had been sweeping the bar earlier. A noise further down the hall caused the children to scuttle back into the gloom beneath the stairs.

"Quickly." Said Shayla. "Come in here." She opened the door wide to her room.

Once inside, Shayla closed the door quietly and then turned to face the two children. Sara stood awkwardly in the center of the room with Rudy, clutching her shift's ragged material. Shayla

155

groaned inwardly. Dealing with the children was the last thing she needed right now. The sun had set, and she knew that Devon would be waiting. Her first instincts were to send the children away, but the hope in their eyes and the memory of Sadie's harsh treatment stopped her.

"How long will it be before Sadie misses you? Shayla asked.

"Not until first light." Answered Sara, fear evident in her voice.

"Then stay hidden here, and I will return for you later." Said Shayla. "I have something to do first."

Shayla looked at the two dirty, bedraggled children. Sara's foot appeared swollen, and an angry red color spread from her toes to halfway up the leg.

"Your foot looks infected," Shayla said. "How long has it been like that?"

"More than a week, I think." Said Sara. "It doesn't affect me walking in any way." She lied hurriedly.

"No, I don't suppose it does." Said Shayla smiling, remembering how heavily the girl had limped earlier that morning. "I will take a look at that later. Get in the bed and stay quiet until I return. If you get caught through your foolishness, then I can't help you."

The two children nodded eagerly, and Shayla waited until they were beneath the threadbare cover on the bed before leaving the room. Shayla felt sure they would make no noise until she returned. Saressa had led Sara to her, but who this Liffy was, Shayla had yet to discover. Shayla had no idea how she would get the children out unnoticed either. She pushed these thoughts to the back of her mind and headed once more to the bar to meet Devon.

Devon was in his usual spot by the fireplace monitoring the customers for any sign of trouble. It was still early, and the bar was reasonably quiet. He spotted Shayla the moment she came through the doorway that led to the lower level rooms. He nodded in acknowledgment of the brief smile she flashed him. Shayla then paused to speak with Tanner before heading towards his side of the room. Devon assumed she must be paying for her room because she handed Tanner something that he quickly stuffed into a pocket in his shirt.

He had spoken with Tanner just a few moments before

Shayla had appeared. Devon had told Tanner that he had things to do this evening and might be back later. Even though Devon could not recall the last time he had taken a night off, Tanner had grumbled loudly. Ash could help out later if Tanner needed him. Devon was sure things would be quiet tonight anyway. It was mid-week, and there were no new ships expected in port for another two days. That was when there tended to be trouble. Sailors arriving at the port of Edenberry after long stretches at sea drank heavily and had enough money to do so.

"Let's go," Shayla said as she reached Devon. "I have another pressing matter to deal with later."

Tanner was surprised as he noticed them leave together, and then grinned as he realized why Devon had asked for the night off.

"Never thought I'd ever see a girl that would turn his head," Tanner said to himself. "That Shayla is a pretty little thing, but she's too quiet for my taste."

He laughed at the thought of Devon with Shayla. Tanner had wondered why the girl was hanging around for so long. His rooms were not the cheapest, nor were they the best in town.

"Devon is a bigger asset than I thought," Tanner said with a smile.

Motomo waited in the shelter of some thick bushes by the cave. A thick mist hung in the air blocking out the light from the moon. The fog also made the air, so still, he could hear the waves' crashing as they flung themselves on the rocks and boulders at the shoreline. Usually, Motomo wouldn't have been able to hear the waves so clearly this far up the cliff.

A quiet heavy rain had just begun, and it pattered on the ground in front of him. Motomo knew it wouldn't be too long before the water found its way through the thick tangle of branches and leaves that were currently providing cover. A flicker of light flashed high in the sky, followed instantly by a low rumble of thunder, and as if in response, the rain increased. Motomo shuddered as the first trickle of water ran over his back. It would take some time before his skin became wet because his fur was perfect for withstanding all the elements, including rain.

When Devon and Shayla approached the cave entrance, Motomo's hackles rose on his neck, and by instinct, he flattened his body to the floor. Motomo quietly sniffed the air in an attempt to learn what he could about the strangers. The girl's smell was strange; she carried the scent of another place as Raven did. The man smelt of the old, decayed bones that Motomo's pack sometimes scavenged for during the leanest months of winter. He shuddered involuntarily at the memory. Their scents were so strange and unfamiliar that he had to control his urge to growl.

Shayla found the concealed entrance to the cave and took a deep breath before entering. She was puzzled when the barrier stopped her. Shayla turned to Devon, a concerned look on her face.

"Something is stopping me from entering," Shayla said. "I am sure this is the entrance."

Shayla stepped back as Devon stepped forward to inspect the entrance. He ran a hand over what should have been the opening between the rocks and felt a tingle course through his fingers.

"A barrier spell protects the opening," Devon said.

"So, we cannot enter?" Asked Shayla.

Her heart sank at this revelation. It was raining so hard now that her heavy cloak clung to her body like a wet rag. The hood of her cloak was now flat to her head, causing more discomfort than protection against the rain.

"Well, if we can't get in the cave to shelter from this weather, then I am not waiting hours for Amani to show up," Shayla said.

"I cannot destroy a spell cast by another," said Devon. "But there may be another way in." He said with a smile.

"There is no other way in," said Shayla. The rain was making her irritable. "I checked thoroughly when I first found the cave."

Devon smiled again. "There is always another way," he said. "You forget that I lived with my people in catacombs and caves. We got to know rock structures very well. Wait here and let me see what I can do."

Shayla tried to protest, but Devon was already climbing the rocks that led up above the cave. She watched in awe at Devon's speed and agility. Shayla knew how slippery the rocks and boulders must be because of the rain, but Devon never faltered or lost his footing once. Finally, he disappeared from her view over the top of a ridge.

Devon kept close to a natural shelf of rock that jutted out

from the cliff's main wall. He concentrated and allowed the structure of the condensed mineral matter to give up its secrets. It had been many years since Devon used this skill. The Lunarians had survived because they listened to what the structure of their world had to tell them. Devon carefully tuned in to the sedimentary stone's vibrations as he felt his way along the cliff wall. If Devon could find a weakness, then he could persuade it to open.

Finally, he heard a distinct high-pitched hum coming from just above his left shoulder. Devon turned and faced the area that was betraying its weakness. He peered at the structure of the rock. Impatiently he threw back the sodden hood of his cloak that was obstructing his view. Devon smiled in satisfaction, ignoring the rain pounding on his face. A weakness in the rock appeared brighter to Devon's trained eye.

He positioned himself directly beneath the fault and pressed his body against the rock face. Devon stretched his arms upwards and outwards, placing the palm of each hand on either side of the weakened rock. He pressed a cheek against the rock, ignoring the discomfort of craggy contours digging into his face. Devon then closed his mind to everything except the slight humming sound coming from the rock. Slowly he willed time to move forward at the weakened portion between his hands. Devon encouraged the natural erosion process to speed up until he felt the rock begin to vibrate against his body. The cliff's infrastructure's natural erosion was hurrying towards its conclusion, which was another entrance to the cave.

Devon heard the rumble deep within the side of the cliff as the weakness eroded and finally crumbled, falling away from the outer structure. He sensed the shifting of larger pieces crashing down in the wake of a gushing stream of water that should have taken centuries in the ordinary course of events.

Devon began to lean his weight harder on the fissure that was now becoming visible between his hands. The whole cliff rumbled and shook more violently until finally there was a loud crack and Devon found himself tumbling in amongst the shifting rocks. He swiftly rolled to one side of the new opening to avoid the rush of water-charged rubble and boulders that exploded out from the confines of the cliff.

Shayla and Motomo heard the rumbling within the cliff. Shayla ran back to the clearing when a bolder narrowly missed her as it plummeted down from above. The ground shook as more boulders and rocks cascaded down. Shayla tried to locate Devon, but the rain stung her eyes as she searched for any movement on the mist clouded cliff.

More lightning forked its way to the sodden earth and for a brief moment lit up the side of the cliff towering before her, but it was too short for Shayla to see anything. A resounding crash of thunder startled her so much that she questioned if she should go back to the main track. The rain beat down on her as she stood anxiously waiting for some sign of Devon.

Motomo felt the vibration of the earth and pressed his body closer to the ground. His ears flattened in fear and anticipation as he watched Shayla run back into the clearing as the first rocks fell. He wished with all his heart that Amani would return with Twila and Raven soon.

"There it is done," Devon said.

He watched with satisfaction as the flow of water gradually returned to the gently destructive trickle that it once was. Devon stepped back to view his handiwork when the last rock and bolder had reached its final destination.

"Perfect," Devon said.

He had created an opening almost hidden from view behind a large shaft of rock. Cautiously he stepped forward, stumbling over loose stones, and peered into the newly created entrance. Devon could see a jagged path plunging steeply downwards into hidden depths of the cliff. Water ran down the inside of the opening, quickly covering his knee-length leather boots up to the ankle. Devon realized that he needed a light before venturing any further. He made his way back over the ridge and climbed back down the to where Shayla anxiously waited.

Shayla breathed a sigh of relief as Devon stepped out of the mist. She ran towards Devon, relieved at his safety.

"I was so worried when the rocks fell," Shayla said. "What happened? Did you find another entrance?"

The genuine concern in Shayla's voice touched Devon deeply.

"It has been many years since someone was concerned about my well-being," Devon said kindly. "Well, I have good news. The cave now has another entrance."

"Well, maybe we can get out of this rain when Amani arrives then." She said.

Shayla suddenly saw Devon's face stiffen in reaction to something behind her. She turned quickly and saw Amani, Twila, and a stranger walking towards them. At the same moment, a large wolf emerged from the bushes shaking the water from its fur. Shayla stepped backward when she saw the wolf, and a dagger was instantly in her hand. She stepped into the solid form of Devon behind her.

"Put your blade away," Devon said quietly in her ear. "The wolf has been there since we arrived. If he were not a friend, I would have dealt with him long ago."

"I wish you would have shared that knowledge," Shayla said. "I was down here by myself with it."

"Who is the warrior with them?" Asked Devon.

"I don't know," Shayla replied, reluctantly re-sheathing her dagger. "He looks like one of the warriors that are invading my home city, except even they are not that heavily armed."

"A warrior type indeed," Devon confirmed, keeping his voice low. "It appears that Amani has finally decided to end Ramos's meddling. Well, I hope for his sake, the warrior has more than his strength to offer."

Amani, Twila, and Raven stood before Shayla and Devon. Motomo was close to Twila and was very relieved to see her. He sensed the tension between the five people, and instead of showing his affection for Twila, he remained tense, waiting to see what would happen with the newcomers. The rain continued heavily, and it was Amani who finally spoke.

"We need to talk but not out here," Amani said. "We could have used the cave, but as you have probably realized already, Ramos has cast a barrier spell to prevent entry. Twila's hid her caravan nearby, and we can go there."

Twila and Raven nodded in agreement and started to leave the clearing.

"Wait," called out Shayla. "The cave now has a second entrance. Devon just discovered it, and we were about to investigate it when you arrived."

Amani, Twila, and Raven turned in surprise.

"I only saw one entrance," said Amani. "Show me this second entrance."

Devon walked towards the cave and climbed up the cliff face to reach the ledge high above. When he was on the ridge, Devon called down to Amani to follow.

Amani was not sure what to make of Devon. He had climbed the cliff face so swiftly, and his ashen complexion reminded Amani of a Dark One. However, Ramos had destroyed any of them that had escaped after closing the opening to the world of shadows. Amani had observed this world for some time after Ramos created the seal to make sure they were all gone. Their blood hunger forced them to slaughter indiscriminately, and the trail of bloodless corpses quickly betrayed their presence. Amani doubted that Devon had remained undetected for so long if he was indeed a Dark One. What concerned Amani was that if Devon was not a Dark One, then what was he?

Amani followed Devon up the cliff face to the ridge just as swiftly. The two of them peered down into the steep entrance.

"We have no light source," said Devon. "Maybe Twila's caravan will indeed be a better choice to shelter from the rain. Part of this entrance is still collecting water."

"Wait here." Said Amani as he stepped over the smaller pieces of rubble and climbed down into the darkness.

He stopped for a moment and concentrated briefly before holding his arm out in front of him, his fingers outstretched. A massive flood of green light instantly flowed from Amani's fingers. The green glow pushed its way into the hidden depths before him. Amani surveyed the steep twisting path, now adequately illuminated.

"A light spell," said Devon. "I'm impressed. You must teach me this spell, and I can share with you the magic I used to create this new opening."

"You know me?" Asked Amani, surprised.

"Yes, I know you." Replied Devon. "We will talk later. Now we have a light I will call for the others."

Amani nodded in agreement, still curious about Devon.

"Raven and Shayla may need help to reach this place, though," said Devon.

Getting everyone up to the new entrance of the cave removed some tension between them all. Motomo had found his own path to the ridge. No one was sure which way he chose, but the wolf reached the entrance long before Shayla had made it even halfway up the cliff.

Twila reached the ridge just as swiftly as Amani and Devon had. She was thrilled by the increase in her power since drinking Radon's blood. Twila watched as Shayla and Raven struggled to follow her and realized just how powerful she was becoming.

Raven, although powerfully built, discovered that the weight of his pack was hindering him in the treacherous climb. He was agile in battle, but his stocky build was not ideal for climbing. Raven was having problems finding a secure footing on the slippery rocks of the cliff's steep face too. Increasingly, Raven was becoming impatient with himself as he struggled his way up the top. Sweat ran in his eyes, blinding him for an instant, and Raven began to think he would not make it to the ridge. It crossed his mind how ironic it would be if his quest to avenge Haney ended before it began. Raven sadly remembered the mound far below him, where Amani had said that he had buried Haney.

"They can bury me right beside him," Raven said to himself. "I deserve nothing less after being stupid enough to attempt a climb like this, and in this weather."

Finally, Raven heaved his right arm over the edge of the ridge. He refused the offer of help from Amani, determined to finish the climb himself. What energy remained, Raven used it to pull the rest of his body onto the broad ledge. He slumped safely against the inner wall of the ridge, breathing heavily. Every muscle in his arms and legs screamed their protests at him.

Shayla was doing well until Raven had pulled himself over the ridge, showering her with rubble and dirt. She clung there for a few moments trying to blink away the dust from her eyes. Shayla had made sure to follow a different route up the cliff's side than Raven used to prevent being hit by falling debris. That hadn't helped her when he had reached the top, though.

Shayla started to climb again and eventually reached the ridge. She gratefully accepted help from Devon, who gripped her arms tightly and lifted her quickly onto the ledge. Shayla stood panting for breath rubbing the last of the dirt from her eyes.

"Now that I am up here," announced Shayla. "I will just have to live here."

Raven looked at her questioningly. "What do you mean, live here?" He said, dabbing at a bleeding gash in his leg.

"Well, there is no way I am going back down that cliff." She said.

Raven pondered on this statement for a moment and looked up at Shayla. She had a big grin on her face, and he smiled, suddenly realizing that Shayla was joking.

"Well, you may not have many visitors," he said. "I, for one, will not be visiting you."

Shayla laughed in response and offered her hand to help him up,

163

but he grinned and scrambled to his feet unaided.

"I don't know why you didn't use the path as I did," said Motomo. "It was a much easier way, and safer too."

Shayla stared at the wolf, surprised. "You can talk?" She asked.

"Yes, and I can find better ways to this ridge," said Motomo, his tongue lolling out of the side of his mouth that made him appear to be laughing.

Shayla grinned. "Well, I am making the trip back down with you then." She said.

"Me too," Raven muttered, still dabbing at the wound on his leg.

"This way," called Devon, leading them into the new entrance.

Raven chose to go down into the cave before Shayla and after Devon.

"If I slip, then at least I will not take you with me," he said, grinning. "I will just fall on Devon."

Shayla giggled, and Devon turned to look at Raven with a smile on his face.

"You had better not slip then," Devon said.

They all slowly made their way down the steep, narrow passage that led into the bowels of the cliff. The floor of loose rocks and rubble was wet and slick. Motomo was not having any trouble making his way down the passage, but everyone else was. Twila slipped once but was caught swiftly by Devon, who was close behind her. Raven heavily relied on the cold, wet walls on either side of them to prevent him from slipping. Shayla clung to one side of the wall as she carefully followed him.

As they descended further, the water beneath their feet got deeper. It was icy cold and quickly made Shayla's feet numb. Raven's boots were of better quality and kept the water out for longer, but his feet eventually grew numb too. The luminous green light adequately lit their way, but the rising water hid loose rock and boulders from view, making the passage even more dangerous.

Amani was leading the group and began to doubt that this passage led to the original cave. He continued to cast light spells as the path twisted and turned. Suddenly he stopped causing the others to stumble against each other in an attempt to stay upright.

"This appears to be a sheer drop." Said Amani.

"Let me look." Said Devon as he pushed to the front.

Amani was right. Where they stood, the water ran past them, falling freely like a small waterfall over the edge of what remained of the path.

"There must be a way down from here," said Devon. "I heard it sing to me. Can you cast another light spell just over to the left there?" Devon pointed down over the edge of the waterfall.

Amani nodded and cast the spell as far down and to his left that was possible from where they stood. As the green glow slowly illuminated the area beneath them, both Amani and Devon smiled. They could see a wide dry ledge that appeared to open out into a large cave just below them. It was steep but looked to be a relatively easy climb down, on the left side of the waterfall from where they all stood. A m a n i swiftly climbed down, and Motomo sure-footed followed him by leaping down to an out ridge of rock, and then down on to the ledge. Twila climbed down next as Raven and Shayla peered over the edge, watching her. It looked a little challenging but not as bad as the climb up the cliff had been.

"As long as you stay well to the left." Instructed Devon. "If you do fall, it will only be a short distance, and the ledge will stop you from falling down there." He nodded towards the waterfall.

Raven and Shayla looked down the waterfall and then across at the ledge.

"The ledge it is then," said Raven, his voice lacking confidence.

Shayla's eyes widened at the alternative.

Raven climbed down quickly enough, followed by Shayla, and they both sighed in relief as they reached the safety of the ledge. Devon dropped beside them in seconds.

They found themselves at the mouth of a cave, and Amani cast a light spell then led the way inside. Initially, Shayla and Amani were not sure if this was the correct cave or not.

"Here are the remains of the fire I made," Shayla said. "Well done, Devon, this is the cave."

Amani looked over at where Shayla was stood and then turned to the back of the cave where the key was. The back wall of the original cave now led to the waterfall. The niche where Haney had placed the key was gone. Amani groaned inwardly. The only way to locate the key now was to invoke its magic. If Amani did that, then Ramos would be here long before they found the key. Their best chance of defeating him was not here in this place.

Amani walked back to the waterfall and attempted to estimate how far it was to the bottom. The water flowed swiftly down into utter blackness. Amani knew that it must be a long way down because he could not hear the water hitting the ground below. They would have to defeat Ramos before they could retrieve the key. Amani was comforted by the fact that if they failed, Ramos would never find the key either. Ramos did not know how to use the key's magic, only Radon and himself did, so it was still safe for now.

Shayla and Twila had built a fire using the remains of wood and kindling that was still there. They sat close together around the rising flames in an attempt to dry off and get warm. Raven sat by the fire also, absent-mindedly stroking Motomo. Devon stood quietly by the old entrance, his face filled with concentration. Amani sat down by the fire, studying this strange group. He wasn't sure if they would be strong enough to deal with Ramos or not, but they would surely try.

Devon joined the rest of the group by the fire and closely studied Twila. He sensed that something was different about her since the first time they met.

"I think we should begin by explaining to the rest of the group what events have led to the situation we find ourselves in." Said Amani. "Twila, you should explain what happened to you first, for the benefit of Shayla and Devon. Then if you both are willing to assist us in the battle with Ramos, I can tell you how we can hopefully accomplish his destruction."

Twila nodded and told the group what had happened to her. As she spoke, Shayla and Raven felt their anger grow against Ramos and his callous treatment of Twila and Danior. Raven had not been too concerned about Twila until that is, he had watched over her with Amani as she lay in a deathlike state.

Shayla's eyes filled with tears when Twila spoke of her mother and father. When she heard of how Ramos tricked Danior, her anger grew. Shayla knew she had made the right decision to stay and help.

Devon shook his head grimly when he heard about Danior. From experience, he knew that the longer Danior stayed in the world of shadows, whatever goodness remained inside of him would eventually be destroyed by the darkness. Then he suddenly realized what was different about Twila since they last met. Her eyes were no longer blue. They were now golden in color and appeared to glow when Twila grew angry speaking about Ramos.

Devon leaned forward in interest as Twila described her encounter with Radon and mentioned that she had drunk his blood. He smiled across at Amani, who was quietly watching him.

"If she has drunk from a blood dragon," Devon said mentally to

Amani. "She might very well be capable of defeating Ramos."

Amani nodded in response. "She has yet to learn how to use it, though."

None of the others noticed this private exchange except Motomo, who listened with interest to all their thoughts.

When Twila had finished, they all sat in silence, deep in thought at what they had heard.

Amani invited Raven to speak next and flashed him a warning mentally not to talk about the key. Motomo caught the message and understood Amani's caution. Although they all knew of its existence, the key's safety relied on its anonymity, and only Amani and Raven knew of its real purpose.

Raven spoke only of his quest to avenge Haney's death, and Twila openly wept when she heard that Ramos had killed the old fiddle player. When he described how his mother died at the hand of another because she practiced the ancient faith of Ogham, Shayla's interest grew.

"Your mother worshipped Saressa?" Shayla asked with interest.

"Well, that is what Radon said the practice of Ogham meant," Raven answered.

Shayla nodded in agreement. "I too knew many that met their deaths because of their faithfulness to Saressa. They also used many different names for the faith to avoid detection and persecution for their beliefs."

Amani quietly spoke next. He briefly told the group about Radon and the creation of Vesta by Saressa. Shayla's eyes grew wide as Amani explained how Saressa had cast the Dark Ones into the world of shadows. Devon leaned in closer, listening intently. Amani explained about the blood lord Valeskas and his desire to use Ramos to find Vesta's entrance.

"If Ramos can access the power contained within the Dragon's Tear, he can release Valeskas." Said Amani.

Shayla realized that everyone was looking at her. Slowly Shayla spoke of how she came to be in this world, searching for a haven. Then she described her meeting with Amani in this cave and agreeing to help him.

"I am not sure how I can be of help against a powerful magic user who also has the strength of a blood drinker," said Shayla. "But, I willingly join you in the fight against him."

The others nodded at Shayla's statement. Then Shayla told the group about her dream vision of Saressa and the children that waited for her back at the inn.

"Saressa asked me to take Sara to Liffy," said Shayla. "The girl child is named Sara, but who Liffy is I have yet to discover. The children are not safe in my room, and I must get them out of there tonight."

"I know who Liffy is." Blurted Twila. "She is the wife of the tavern keeper Ned where Haney played the fiddle. That is where Danior found me. You spoke of an old black horse that had belonged to Haney. That would be Apple, the tavern keeper's horse. My father sold it to them years ago when we passed through there. They must have loaned it to Haney for the trip here in search of Amani.

"The horse will lead you back to the tavern. Ned, the tavern keeper, traveled to Edenberry for supplies on Apple until he started to use a local merchant named Fremont. Apple knows the way home. I will help you get the children out of the inn, and we can hide them in my caravan until it is light enough to travel. Buttergrove is four or five days from here, and the name of the tavern is the Traveler's Call."

Shayla nodded gratefully. "Thank you, Twila, this is very helpful."

"You can speak to Saressa?" Amani asked Shayla when Twila had finished speaking. "Radon has tried to speak with Saressa without success."

"Saressa speaks to me only in dream time," said Shayla. "She told me it is forbidden for her to come here." She suddenly remembered the shard of crystal. "Saressa asked me to give this to you."

Shayla retrieved the crystal from a pocket in her cloak.

"I thought when I first saw Saressa that it was just a dream and not a true vision. When I woke up, though, this was in my hand."

Shayla offered the crystal to Amani, who carefully took it from her.

Amani turned it over in his hand, inspecting it closely.

"Did Saressa tell you what I am to do with it?" Asked Amani.

"No," answered Shayla. "She said you would know."

"I will ask Radon about this," Amani said.

He held the crystal up to see it better in the limited light. Suddenly the crystal twisted violently in his hand, causing him to drop it. The crystal fell to the floor with a resounding clatter that echoed eerily around the cave. Amani was amazed it had not broken from the impact. He reached down to retrieve it, but the crystal shot across the floor and stopped at Devon's feet.

Devon reached down and picked up the crystal. It quivered slightly in his hand as he carefully turned it over, inspecting it. Devon concentrated on the crystal to see if it would sing to him, but he detected nothing.

Amani was puzzled by Saressa's message to Shayla. The crystal had chosen to go to Devon, but Amani felt there must be more to it than that. He concentrated on the crystal at the very moment that Devon did. Their minds met within the structure and joined for a moment, and the crystal suddenly began to emit a brilliant red light. Both Amani and Devon tried to pull their minds apart but remained locked within the innocent-looking crystal. A woman's voice gently pushed its way into their thoughts.

"This is the way you can defeat Ramos," Saressa said.

Both Devon and Amani saw the vision of a young woman in their minds, dressed in a flowing silvery white robe that reached her feet. Her waist-length silver hair flowed behind her in a breeze that neither of them could feel. A garland of braided silver flowers circled her head, and her face displayed extreme concern.

"I owe your people so much, Devon," said Saressa. "I cannot change my mistake from the past, but perhaps this small gift will help you stop Ramos. Amani, you have assisted Radon so faithfully in protecting the Dragon's Tear from falling into Valeskas's hands. This small gift is the only way I can help.

"I know you are forbidden to face Ramos in battle, but with your minds combined like this, the crystal can destroy spells cast by others, and the way to the world of shadows will be within your power."

Devon and Amani's minds suddenly parted, and the force of that release stunned both of them momentarily. The crystal exploded with a long beam of blinding white light from within itself. The blinding white power blasted its way across the cave and crashed into the barrier spell that Ramos had cast. Everyone watched in fascination as the white beam covered the wall. A green ripple appeared at the entrance as Ramos's barrier spell melted away under the crystal's intense force of power. The wave of green bled into the white until it destroyed the last remnants of the magic barrier. Suddenly the white beam disappeared, and the group sat there stunned.

Only Amani and Devon had seen the vision of Saressa, and their eyes met momentarily across the flickering fire. Motomo cautiously padded to the entrance of the cave and stepped outside. Twila grinned as she saw the wolf leave the cave only to return a second later.

"At least we don't have to leave the cave the way we entered," Raven said thankfully.

"I wasn't going that way back in any case," said Shayla with a grin.

CHAPTER THIRTEEN

Combined Forces

Devon inspected the shard of crystal. It had grown cold now and lay innocently in the palm of his hand. He looked over at Amani questioningly.

"Do I keep the crystal?" Devon asked.

"Well, it appears that Saressa wanted you to have it," answered Amani. "Saressa said that it would help in the battle against Ramos.

"Saressa spoke to you through the crystal before Ramos's barrier spell was destroyed?" Asked Shayla with surprise. They both nodded in response, and Shayla smiled.

As you have accepted Saressa's gift of the crystal, do I take it you agree to join us against Ramos?" Amani continued.

Devon looked around at the group before speaking. "I have questions before I answer that," Devon said.

"And we need to know more about you before we answer," Raven said before Amani had time to speak.

Devon looked at Raven with an amused expression. "I will tell you what you need to know, but only after you give me the same courtesy," Devon said.

"I told you everything you need to know about me," Raven answered, jumping to his feet.

"Sit down, warrior," said Devon. "I am not here to fight you."

Raven glared at Devon. "I will sit down when I am good and ready," said Raven. I do not take orders from you."

Devon grinned nastily at Raven and was about to get to his feet and face the obvious challenge when Amani suddenly stepped in between them.

"Enough of this," said Amani. "Devon, you are correct. There is something that Raven and I have not mentioned. Raven acted on my instructions not to speak of it."

Devon grinned in satisfaction, and the others looked at Amani questioningly.

"What is it?" Asked Twila, "and why have you not told us before this."

Raven slumped back down, still glaring at Devon, who smiled sweetly in response. Amani looked around at the group and thought carefully before replying to Twila's question.

"As you all know, there is a key that we came here to retrieve," said Amani. "It's called the Dragon's Key, and Haney brought it to me the night Ramos killed him. Haney was its keeper and would typically pass it on to one of his choosing when he could no longer protect it. If the key was in danger of being discovered or the keeper was in trouble, then the key's magic was invoked, enabling them to leave one world and enter another. Valeskas and Ramos knew of the key but never of its whereabouts.

"Ramos, unfortunately, detected the glimmer from the key as it brought Haney to this world when he had been injured severely in battle. He cast a spell to prevent the key from leaving this world, hoping that he would eventually find it. Radon and I decided that the key, once created, would destroy me if I ever touched it. The night Haney brought it to me, he hid the key in this cave, and I used magic to prevent its removal until I could bring a new keeper here. Raven will be the key's new keeper."

Amani looked around at the group waiting for a response.

"Can the key open anything else besides doors to other worlds?" Asked Shayla. "Ramos seems to have that power already to create openings to other worlds. He opened the one to the world of shadows, didn't he?"

"The key opens the doors to Vesta, and subsequently Radon." Said Amani. "If Ramos finds the key, he has access to Radon and, more importantly, the Dragons Tear power. Ramos will then have access to a force capable of releasing Valeskas from where Saressa imprisoned him within the world of shadows. If Valeskas ever gains his freedom, he will use the key to access all of the worlds and is powerful enough to destroy everything Saressa created. Ramos is seeking greater powers from Valeskas. He doesn't realize that demon is using him, and once free, he will have no further use for Ramos."

Devon was no longer smiling as Amani finished speaking. "Where is the key now?" Devon asked.

Amani waved his arm in the direction of the waterfall. "We sealed it in a niche at the back of the cave. When you created the second entrance, the key must have fallen with the wall back there. I assume it now lies at the bottom of the waterfall."

"Then we must retrieve it," Devon said urgently. "Valeskas must stay in the void."

Devon scrambled to his feet and headed for the waterfall.

"Wait, Devon," said Amani quickly. "The key is not exactly lost; it is hidden. If I invoke the key's magic to show itself, then Ramos will detect it and be on top of us before we can retrieve it. That is how Ramos found Haney. When we hid the key, it alerted him to its presence in this cave. When Ramos realized that he could not retrieve the key because of my spell, Ramos cast a spell of his own that prevented access to the cave. He planned that the next key keeper would have to seek him out to gain access to the key."

"So, how do you plan to stop Ramos and keep the key safe?" Asked Devon as he turned to face Amani. "Ramos has the skills of a blood drinker and can use powerful magic. More powerful, no doubt, because of Valeskas's assistance, as Shayla witnessed. As willing as this group you have gathered here is Amani, they need more than a will to fight to destroy him. Maybe you have the strength Amani, but I know that you are forbidden to destroy anyone. If this group fails, then Ramos can come here and retrieve the key at his leisure."

Everyone stared at Devon as he paced around the cave. Twila finally stood up and faced Devon.

"Some of us are not as innocent as we seem," Twila said. Her golden colored eyes glowed as she concentrated on Devon.

Devon felt powerful invisible bonds snake their way swiftly around his body, pinning his arms to his side. He then felt himself rising from the floor of the cave, and his feet were now two or three inches off the floor."

"Alright," Devon yelled. "Enough of this."

Twila waved her hand and, Devon collapsed in a heap on the floor. He was instantly on his feet, brushing the dust from his cloak.

"Impressive," said Devon with a grin on his face. "But not enough to defeat Ramos."

Raven was facing Devon with his sword drawn before Twila had returned to her place by the fire. He swung the heavy sword in a crisp slashing maneuver, and a bolt of brilliant lightning carved a deep gash in the rocky floor of the cave at Devon's feet. A slight wisp of smoke floated up before Devon's startled face.

Devon grinned appreciatively at their brief displays of strength. "I take it back, Amani, maybe you do have a chance against Ramos after all, and I will join you in the fight. The last thing I want is for Valeskas to be free again."

"Then, I think all of us would like to hear more about you," said Amani.

"And see if you have anything to offer other than a will to fight," mumbled Raven.

Devon smiled nastily at Raven. "I come from the world of shadows." Said Devon.

"A Dark One? Asked Twila, shocked at this revelation.

"No, not a Dark One," answered Devon abruptly. "My people are called Lunarian, named for the two moons that orbit our world. The world of shadows was a peaceful place before Saressa cast the Dark Ones amongst us. Worse still, she imprisoned their leader Valeskas deep within the core of our world. The Dark Ones hunted my people as their prey. They treated us like cattle to be used for their blood or destroyed us with magic wielded by the unskilled followers of Valeskas, in their efforts to free him.

"As time wore on, the few Lunarian survivors escaped to the inner catacombs, and they created a world for themselves that was safe from the Dark Ones. What loyal followers Valeskas did have in the early days are long gone now.

"My people eventually developed skills that allowed us to adapt to our new environment. But I grew weary of staying hidden and began tracking the Dark Ones. The concealment spells my people developed prevented the Dark Ones from discovering me amongst them. I destroyed all those that were unlucky enough to cross my path alone.

"When Ramos created the opening to this world, I followed the Dark One named Stefan. He was a leader of sorts, and when Stefan crossed to this world and met Ramos, I slipped past the two of them unnoticed. This world seemed the perfect place to bring what remained of my people, so once again, they could be free to walk in the moonlight, without fear. I wanted to be sure that this world was as peaceful as it appeared before I returned to lead them here. Unfortunately, before I could return, Ramos placed the seal preventing me."

Devon stopped talking, his back to the group. He walked towards the waterfall, and the others exchanged looks. Twila stood up and followed Devon. She found him leaning against the saturated wall watching the waterfall cascading past them. Twila gently laid her hand on Devon's arm.

"When we have defeated Ramos, I will help you return to collect your people," Twila said. "The blood dragon Radon has destroyed the darkness within my heart. His blood courses through my veins now and with it, the magical power of light that he possesses. I think we will be able to find another passage to your world Devon. We can combine our minds, our powers, and support you in this."

Devon turned to look at Twila, startled by her last words. He remembered what Saressa had said in the vision. Devon knew that Twila also had good reason to find another passage to the world of shadows. Danior was trapped there just as his people were.

"Then let us finish this with Ramos," Devon said gruffly.

Amani looked up as Twila and Devon returned to the group. "We must plan this carefully." He said. "Ramos lives in the mountains far to the north. It will take six or seven days to get there because of the caravan and the human limitations of Shayla and Raven."

"I must safely deliver the children, too," Shayla said quickly.

Amani nodded. "The inn is on the way to where Ramos is," he said. "Shayla and Devon should stay by the seal of the gateway because when we defeat Ramos, I feel sure the seal will be weakened or even destroyed. I cannot help you with Ramos, but Devon and I can close the gateway if the seal fails by using the crystal. Shayla is not equipped to deal Ramos but may manage to contact Saressa if we cannot close the gateway if it opens."

"What of Ramos?" Asked Raven. "Has he any weakness that will help us in this battle?"

Amani shook his head. "I don't know what his weaknesses are," he said. "When Ramos first placed the seal and returned to his mountain, we heard nothing of him until Twila went to him. Because he had remained in seclusion, Radon and I thought he had stopped meddling with the forces he could not control. We did not suspect that Ramos would become such a threat. We are not even sure how he controls the blood hunger. The night Ramos took Twila to the gateway must have been the first night he had drank blood since he originally placed the seal."

"I can help you discover Ramos's weaknesses." Blurted Devon. "The years I spent shadowing Dark Ones taught me everything about concealment. I have all the abilities of a Dark One but without the blood hunger. It will take me hours instead of days to reach Ramos. Let's meet up by the seal in seven days, and I will bring with me as much information about Ramos that I can find out."

"Agreed," said Amani. We will meet you seven nights from now at the site of the seal. Continue to keep your thoughts guarded, Ramos may sense the threat as you get closer to him."

Amani stood up and headed for the cave's entrance, as the group watched him leave. He stopped briefly to place his hand gently on Motomo's head.

"You can return to the pack now, my friend," Amani said. "Thank you for your help in all this."

Motomo shook his head. "I will return when we finish Ramos," Motomo said firmly into Amani's thoughts.

"Kamots would glow with pride at the courage in his son's heart, Motomo," Amani said and touched his forehead in respectful salutation.

Motomo watched Amani disappear into the thickening sea fog. The rain had finally stopped leaving the ground soggy and muddy. Motomo turned as one by one; the group joined him at the cave's entrance. Raven put out the last glowing embers of the fire before following them.

"I will wait at the caravan until you and Shayla have collected the children," Raven said to Twila. "Motomo can lead me to it."

"Agreed." Said Twila. "It should not take us long to collect the children, and the horse then we will meet you there. I can drive the caravan during the nights while you and Shayla sleep. During the day, I can sleep, and one of you can drive."

Twila, Shayla, and Devon headed back to Edenberry together. Devon had decided to collect his few processions and hand them over to Twila until they met at the seal. Devon knew he would not return to the inn again after tonight.

Motomo and Raven watched them disappear down the track, and

then they headed through the dripping wet bushes in the direction of Twila's caravan.

Raven decided that following a wolf was not an excellent choice. Size, for one thing, was a problem. Motomo led Raven on a trail that, at times, was impossible for him to follow. Raven finally stood and laughed at one of the thick thorn bushes that Motomo had just entered.

"I can't follow you though that one," said Raven. "You forget that your companion is human, my friend."

Motomo suddenly stopped when he heard Raven. Guiltily he turned around and returned to where Raven waited for him. Motomo saw the state of Raven, covered in mud all over, with pieces of twigs and foliage stuck to his clothing and hair. Streaks of blood amongst the dirt on Raven's legs, arms, and face betrayed scrapes and scratches from rocks and thorns.

"Forgive me for my thoughtlessness," said Motomo. "I will find a trail that will accommodate your size."

Raven grinned at the wolf's sad expression. "I would appreciate that," said Raven. "What chance will I stand against Ramos all cut up and bleeding like this before we even meet."

Motomo tongue lolled out of his mouth as he padded back towards Raven. "This way then," Motomo said. "The caravan is just over that ridge there, a much slower route I fear, but safer for a warrior such as you."

Raven roared with laughter at the touch of sarcasm he heard in Motomo's voice and as he followed him, threw a clod of soft mud at his disappearing form up the ridge. The soil slapped the rump of the wolf, and he yipped in surprise. Motomo caught the playfulness of Raven's gesture and leaped at him. The surprise attack caught Raven off guard, and he fell backward onto the muddy ground. He laughed and then scrambled after the wolf to retaliate, but Motomo was halfway up the path already.

"Come on, Warrior. I grow old waiting for you," called Motomo from the top of the ridge.

Raven groaned, trying to see the path that Motomo had taken. "I will show you a warrior, Motomo if I don't break a leg first," Raven added, laughing. "You do well to run from me, my friend."

Motomo howled gleefully in response, and in the far distance, members of his pack answered his call.

"And singing won't help you either," Raven said, grinning.

Devon and Twila heard Motomo's call, but Shayla was too

preoccupied with her plans to rescue the children to notice it.

"Sounds like Motomo and Raven are getting along well," Twila said, noting the joy in Motomo's call.

"Raven needs to be preparing for Ramos, not fooling around," commented Devon coldly.

"I don't understand your obvious growing dislike of Raven," said Twila. "He has a genuine desire to fight Ramos, and fears nothing for his safety."

"Well, his sort never does," said Devon.

"What do mean by 'his sort'?" Asked Shayla suddenly when she realized whom Devon and Twila were discussing.

"Raven is a mercenary," said Devon. "One who knows that his fighting skills are so good that people will pay for them. Well, we will see soon enough just how good Raven is."

"Well, no one is paying him this time," said Shayla. "He fights from the heart. If you are waiting to see him fail Devon, then expect disappointment."

"None of us must fail," said Twila hastily. "There is too much at stake."

The group grew silent as they approached the inn.

"How shall we get the children past Tanner without him seeing them?" Asked Shayla. "I can cast simple shadow spells, but they do not last very long. I doubt the children would even make it to the door before it wore off."

"Is there a window in your room? Twila asked.

Devon laughed coldly, "all the windows in the rented rooms are sealed shut," he said. "To prevent non-paying guests from entering or leaving. I can cast concealment spells on the children that will last long enough to get them out of the inn, and probably halfway to the caravan. As long as the children remain quiet, they will go undetected."

"Then I will go to my room and collect the children," said Shayla. "Devon, if you follow me to my room, Tanner will not be surprised as he saw us leave together earlier."

Devon grinned. "Yes, I am sure Tanner has been chuckling about that all night," he said. "I will cast the spells on the children, and you can get them out and meet Twila over there in that alley. Did you pay for the room already tonight?"

Shayla nodded. "Yes, I spoke with Tanner earlier and told him I would be leaving later," she said. "I paid up for the horse also so that

Tanner won't be chasing me for unpaid lodgings or stabling."

"Good," said Devon. "Then get the children out and let Twila take them outside of the town and wait there for you. That will give you the time to collect the horse. Ash is sometimes difficult to find, and I am not sure my concealment spell will last that long if he is napping somewhere. When you have the horse meet up with Twila."

Twila and Shayla nodded in agreement.

"What about you, Devon?" Asked Shayla. "Do we wait there for you while you collect your things and tell Tanner that you are leaving?"

"No.," said Devon. "After I have cast a spell on the children, the next time we meet will be at the seal. I am using a faster way of traveling, and I don't own much," Devon smiled at Shayla's questioning look. "Come, let's get the children out of here, the night is getting shorter."

Shayla and Devon entered the inn together, leaving Twila standing in the alley's shadows on the opposite side of the deserted street. The inn had no more than twenty patrons at tables or standing in groups around the room, Tanner noticed their arrival immediately, and a broad grin spread across his face. He wagged a finger mockingly at Devon and shook his head in disbelief.

"Ah, to be young again," Tanner said. "Not letting a little thunderstorm ruin the passion." Tanner laughed loudly at his joke.

Shayla inwardly groaned as she realized what Tanner was implying. Although their clothes were only damp now, both of them were still muddy and messy. As they walked past Tanner to Shayla's room, he poked Devon in his arm with his finger.

"Don't get mud all over the floors back there, or Sadie will have the skin off your hide in the morning," Tanner said.

"I would not be that foolish," said Devon. "That lady of yours can cause grown men to blubber like babes with that tongue of hers when she chooses. I don't dare invite her wrath."

"Ain't that the truth." Muttered Tanner.

Devon grinned at Shayla as they headed for her room. "Well, that was easy enough," he said.

"We're not out of here yet," said Shayla.

"That will be the easy part," said Devon, waiting for Shayla to unlock the door to her room.

When they first entered the room, Shayla thought the children had grown tired of waiting and left. She lit another lantern in the room as Devon walked over to the bed. Sara was disturbed by the light and bolted upright. Her eyes grew wide in fear and bewilderment when she saw Devon approaching her. He realized that Sara was about to cry out in alarm, and quickly Devon covered her mouth with his hand.

"Hush, I am here to help," whispered Devon. "Do you understand?"

Devon saw the recognition in Sara's eyes as she nodded her head. He removed his hand, and Sara smiled broadly at him.

"I must have fallen asleep, waiting for Shayla's return," Sara said. "Are we leaving now?" She shook the still sleeping Rudy.

The boy stirred groaning sleepily. His bleary eyes slowly focused on Sara.

"Is it time to get up?" Rudy groaned. "It's too early."

Shayla hurried around the room, gathering the rest of her things, as Devon helped the children.

"They are not dressed suitably for the outside," said Devon.

Shayla stopped what she was doing in horror. Devon was right; the children wore little more than rags. She looked at Devon, alarmed.

"What can we use to keep them warm?" Shayla asked. "I don't think I have anything that would fit."

"Wait here," Devon said. "I may have something."

Shayla was inspecting Sara's foot when Devon returned with two travel blankets and his belongings for Shayla to take with her. She was horrified to see just how red and swollen the girl's foot was. Devon slashed a hole in the center of each rug and pulled one of them over Rudy's head. The blanket reached the boy's feet, and Devon nodded his head in satisfaction. He turned to Sara and pulled the second rug over her head. The material only came to her knees, but it would help to keep her warm.

"I can't do anything about footwear, but the two of them can ride the horse," said Devon. "Maybe Twila can do something about their feet later."

"I'm worried about the girl's foot," said Shayla quietly, pulling Devon to one side. "It seems more swollen than it was earlier."

"Maybe Twila can help with that, too," said Devon. "Gypsies are known for their healing skills."

Shayla nodded in agreement, although still concerned about the appearance of Sara's foot.

Devon carefully explained to Sara and Rudy about the concealment spell that he was about to cast. Sara nodded, listening carefully to what Devon was telling them. Rudy moved closer to Sara, his eyes growing wide with fear.

"When I have cast the spell, the two of you hold hands so that you don't lose each other," Devon said. "Rudy, hold onto Shayla's cloak with your free hand. That way, Shayla knows where you are too. If you lose your grip, then make sure you follow Shayla out of the inn. Keep quiet at all times, if you speak or make any sound, others will hear you and find you."

The children nodded and held hands tightly as they waited for him to cast the spell. Devon looked over at Shayla, who acknowledged that she was ready. He concentrated and spread his arms wide before him. A black fog spewed from his outstretched fingers and covered the children's feet. Slowly it crept its way up their bodies until it shrouded them from head to foot. Devon dropped his arms, and the fog disappeared instantly. Shayla stared at where she knew the children were stood but could see nothing. She grinned at Devon.

"Can you see us?" Asked Sara timidly.

"No.," Shayla said, chuckling. "Come, Rudy, hold onto my robe. Take care not to brush up against anyone because they will feel you. Remember what Devon said. When we leave this room, don't speak again until we meet with Twila outside. She will take you both to the edge of town. I will meet you there later with the horse."

Shayla felt a slight tug at her cloak and smiled, knowing Rudy had understood what to do. Devon opened the door, and Shayla made her way back to the bar.

"I will see you at the seal," Devon said quietly.

"Take care, Devon," Shayla whispered back.

Shayla found Tanner in his usual spot by the bar. A big grin spread across his face as he noticed her.

"I am leaving tonight, Tanner," Shayla said. "Here is the key to my room. I will need Ash to have my horse ready within the hour."

Tanner was surprised at her statement but did not question it. "Well, you are all paid up, so I will send word to Ash about the horse." He said. "I hope we see you here again soon."

"Tell Ash I will meet him at the stables." Said Shayla.

Tanner nodded and waved to one of the serving girls. "Tell Ash to bring out the old black horse." He said.

The girl went in search of Ash at the same moment Shayla left the inn. Shayla breathed a sigh of relief when the door of the inn swung shut behind her. Twila stepped from the shadows when she saw Shayla.

"This is Twila," Shayla whispered. "She will take you both to the edge of town. I will meet you there in a little while."

Twila looked at Shayla. "Are they with you?" She asked.

"Yes," Shayla said, grinning. "Rudy, hold on to Twila's cloak now and follow her."

Twila felt a small tug at the side of her cloak and grinned. "I must get Devon to teach me this concealment spell. It works very well."

"The girl has an infected foot," Shayla said. "You may have to slow your pace a little so she can keep up."

"I can keep up," Sara whispered hurriedly.

Shayla flashed a worried look at Twila as she handed the bag with Devon's belongings. "Devon asked, we take this bag with us for him." Twila nodded.

"Come," Twila said gently. "Tell me if I'm going too fast."

Shayla smiled as she watched Twila slowly make her way down the street in the direction of the main road out of Edenberry. She then went around the back of the inn to the stables and stood waiting by the gate for Ash to bring out the horse.

Twila led the children to a thick clump of trees by the edge of the road into Edenberry. It was relatively dry beneath the trees, although the air was still damp and cold from the earlier storm. Twila found that she could see two small shadows by her side. Slowly the spell wore off and finally saw Sara and Rudy huddled together beneath the trees.

"I can finally see you," Twila said with a smile.

The two children looked at her and smiled back. Rudy was sniffing and shivering from the cold despite the rug that Devon had given him. Twila was immediately concerned about their appearance, but she knew that a fire was out of the question. Twila returned to the road again to watch for Shayla.

When Shayla eventually appeared riding the old black horse, Twila had been considering taking the children to the caravan alone. Shayla waved when Twila stepped out onto the road.

"Let's get the children to the caravan quickly," said Twila. "The boy is shivering with cold, and the girl looks sick. I can tend to her back at the caravan."

Shayla nodded as she nimbly jumped down from the horse.

Twila brought the children and helped them both onto the horse. "Hold on tight, and we will all be warm soon enough," said Twila.

Twila led the horse off the road and onto the almost hidden trail that led to her caravan. Shayla took one last glance up and down the road to make sure there was no one watching, then she followed them.

CHAPTER FOURTEEN

The Healing

Tanner's reaction when Devon had told him he was leaving was surprising. The tavern keeper's eyes grew bright with tears, his cheek flushed red, and his voice filled with emotion as he wished Devon well.

Tanner clutched Devon's arm, "you will always be welcome back here," he said firmly.

"Yes, of course, Tanner, and thank you," Devon said, smiling.

He stepped out of the inn into the damp night air, and as he made his way to the pier Devon doubted very much that he would ever return to Edenberry.

The waves slapped against the pier's support beams, spraying Devon as he strode along the damp sand. He headed for the drier sand that covered the rising dunes at the far end of the inlet. There was a steady wind blowing that whipped against his hair and cloak. Devon smiled. The wind was perfect. It had been a long time since he had used this skill, and Devon hoped there was enough time before the sunrise depleted his powers.

Devon chose a spot where the soft sand was deep enough to cover his boots. Concentrating, he willed himself to become one with the sand. Devon felt the grains of sand welcoming him amongst them as slowly his body crumbled into granules. He felt exhilarated as the wind caught his new body, whipping it into an unorganized cloud of sand. Devon grew accustomed to the new sensations coursing through him. He forced his sand body to form into a long powerful funnel cloud. The wind answered his call as he hovered for a moment above the dunes. Devon allowed the wind to propel him northwards as it combined with his power. Faster and faster, the wind carried Devon towards Ramos's mountain. The wind lifted and blew him above the low clouds that were blocking out the moon and stars. Devon welcomed the moon's rays as they filtered through his sand body. Particles of him sparkled in response to the moon's caress.

Devon traveled northwards away from Edenberry, and the heavy cloud cover became less until finally, he could make out the land structures far beneath him. The morning was fast approaching, and the last thing Devon wanted to do was be in Ramos's mountains when the sun rose. He decided to head for the base of Ramos's mountain and stay there during the daylight hours. After the sun had set tonight, he would find Ramos when his powers returned.

The land beneath Devon gradually changed from gently rolling hills and forests to sparse rocky ridges and scattered trees. The air grew colder as the snowy peak of what Devon presumed was Ramos's mountain loomed in the distance. Twila had described it as being the largest peak in the northern mountain range beyond the seal.

Devon studied the approaching mountainside in search of a suitable area to spend the daylight hours. He finally chose one of the broader ridges partway up the mountain. It was large enough to contain a cluster of hardy bushes and trees, their limbs contorted from the ravages over time by the wind and rain. A mountain stream rushed by the ledge. It's the source not visible in his range of view. He concentrated on the current of wind that was carrying him closer and closer to his destination. As the wind responded to Devon's will, he guided himself towards the ridge.

As the wind became a gentle breeze, his sand body cascaded gently down to join the sandy earth that covered the ridge. Moments later, Devon appeared to rise out of the ground as he returned to his old form. Devon closed his eyes and sucked the fresh sharp mountain air deeply into his lungs. He blinked the last of the sand from his eyes and stood for a moment staring out across the land. Devon understood why Ramos would choose this mountain as his home. You could see for miles. He could see the eastern sky growing lighter as dawn approached. Devon left the edge of the ridge in search of a suitable spot to conceal himself. He doubted that Ramos would detect his presence because his thoughts were secure, and as daylight approached, both their powers would fade. Twila had mentioned that

Ramos drank a potion to prevent this, but Devon decided that he was unlikely to use something like that daily.

Devon found a perfect spot, behind one of the larger bushes nestled in a sheltered area against the mountain face. He pushed back the sturdy limbs of the bush and forced his way forward until he reached the rocky wall of the mountain. Devon lay against the mountain wall and closed his eyes in concentration. Slowly he melded into the structure of the rock until he was no longer visible. Gratefully Devon relaxed as dawn approached, taking his strength with it. Devon felt secure knowing that he would remain undetected until the sun had set, and his powers returned. Then he could begin the task of studying Ramos.

Raven sliced more rabbit meat into long strips, then skewered them onto several small wooden rods. He had crafted them from little branches, stripped clean of their bark, and whittled each end into sharp points. When he was satisfied that the meat was secure on one end of a stick, he then pushed the other end of the rod into the ground beside the fire, the angle of which allowed the meat to dangle over the flames. As long as you closely watched the flesh, this method of cooking was quick and tasty. Raven had grown used to buying his food from villages or inns when he traveled. He cooked only to survive until he found someone willing to sell him food.

He replaced the cooked slices of meat with more raw pieces as Motomo watched with interest. By the side of Raven was a wooden bowl containing an ever-increasing stack of the cooked rabbit. Raven knew that Shayla and the children would be hungry by the time they reached the camp. With Motomo's help, they had brought back four rabbits. Then the wolf had left the campsite to hunt for his food. Raven guessed that Motomo had been successful because he had refused to accept any scraps of meat he had offered.

While Raven waited for the fresh slices of meat to cook, he brought out his cards. Thoughtfully he shuffled them before placing the pack before him. He decided to look a little further into his future this time by using a different spread. The two-card draw only showed him current conditions and what may occur in the next day or two. Raven was very curious to see just what the next few days may hold. He turned over the first card and placed it centrally in front of him. It was the spider card again. Raven nodded in recognition of what the card signified. It was the pact that they had all just made to combine forces

185

to destroy Ramos. The position of this first card represented the present circumstances. Raven turned over seven more cards one after the other and placed them in an arch around the picture of the spider in its web.

He positioned the cards from left to right. When all seven cards were before him, Raven studied the cards before him. The first of the seven cards that Raven placed represented the past. It was a painting of the moon. He interpreted this card to mean shadows and secrets, and this was true. He had kept his true feelings hidden all his life, and he found it very difficult to trust anyone because of that. A mercenary lifestyle makes it very difficult to develop real friendships. Raven saw in the card his lonely existence before following Amani. He still didn't trust any of his new companions yet though, especially Devon.

The second card represented what had led to the current circumstances. The painting on this card was of a lightning storm. It indicated the death of his past and the dawn of a positive cycle of events. He felt this was an excellent card to draw, and he had made the right decision to follow Amani and leave his past life behind. The third card indicated the general outlook for the future. On it was a painting of a large tree struck by lightning, flames rising from its limbs. Raven smiled when he saw this card. He had turned this card over many times before a battle. He recognized this card to be the enemy or the challenge they were all about to face. Like the tree that had been hit by lightning, Ramos was about to be attacked, and hopefully destroyed.

Motomo, who had been watching what Raven was doing, had grown curious. He came closer to Raven to see what was on the cards in front of him. Raven quickly removed the cooked pieces of rabbit, adding them to the ever-increasing pile in the bowl. He noticed that Motomo was studying the cards.

"They speak of the future," Raven said. Motomo looked puzzled.

"I cannot hear them speak," Motomo said.

Raven smiled. "They speak with images that show me what may happen," he said. "See the spider on the web that represents the pact we all made earlier to defeat Ramos. The cards that arch around it give me clues about what will likely happen in the next few days, and the idea of the outcome, good or not so good."

Motomo looked at the cards as Raven explained about the moon's pictures, the storm, and the tree struck by lightning.

"The position of this card," said Raven. "Speaks of tactics I should use in battle. The picture is a squirrel. A squirrel prepares for winter by storing its food in advance, and by doing so, he is prepared to survive the season's challenge. I have seen the squirrel card in my spreads many times before battle. It tells me to prepare well and be ready for the worst of the battle."

Motomo listened thoughtfully to what Raven was telling him.

"You are a warrior Raven," Motomo said. "The squirrel card is not necessary."

Raven laughed at Motomo's statement. "You are right, my friend. But a warrior of any worth always prepares for battle."

"The next card shows a butterfly," said Motomo. "What does the butterfly card tell you?"

Raven smiled as he looked at the painting of the butterfly. "The position of this card tells me that I am about to go through major changes, just as a butterfly does when it emerges from the cocoon. I am to prepare for a new life."

Motomo looked at the card. "This is a good card, then?" He asked.

"Yes." Said Raven.

"What does the next card tell you, Raven?" Motomo asked.

Raven looked at the next card. Its position spoke of the challenges to be faced. It was a picture of a fox, and Raven was not happy to see it. The acrid smell of burning meat caught his attention, and quickly he removed the scorched flesh. Motomo waited patiently for Raven to explain about the picture of the fox. He didn't care for foxes.

Raven turned his attention back to the cards. "The position of this card speaks of challenges to be faced," said Raven. "Because this card is a fox, to me, it speaks of cunning and deceit. We need to be very alert, my friend. Someone may not be as they seem, and I am not sure if this person is one of our group or not."

"What do you mean?" Asked Motomo. "Does the card tell you of another?"

"It may just represent Ramos," said Raven.

Motomo looked at the card. "Everyone has their thoughts in shadows to prevent Ramos from capturing them and being warned of our coming," Motomo said. "What they don't realize is that I can still hear their thoughts. I can only hear the upper level because the rest is in shadows, but maybe it will help to discover who the fox is if he is indeed one of our group."

Raven nodded thoughtfully. He looked at the last card, and his mood brightened a little. "This card shows the outcome of our battle, my friend," said Raven.

Motomo looked at the picture of a star, shining brightly amidst the inky black sky that surrounded it.

"The star card is a good omen," said Raven. "It is perhaps not the best card to see in this position, but it tells me that the future is bright. The star gives me hope, but our victory will not be easy."

"But, victory is possible?" Asked Motomo.

"Victory is always possible when you know your enemy," Raven said. "Our problem is that although we thought Ramos was the only enemy, there may be another that we do not know about yet. But the cards have warned us, and now we have an advantage."

Motomo nodded. "I know in my heart the traitor is not Twila." He said.

"I agree," said Raven. "That leaves Devon and Shayla."

"I sense your dislike of Devon," said Motomo. "But I find it hard to believe he would betray us to Ramos. When Devon spoke of his people, the pain was immense. I felt it."

Raven gathered up the cards and returned them to their leather pouch.

"Well, unless there is another enemy out there that we are not aware of," he said. "My choice would be Devon."

Motomo silently disagreed with him.

Raven was poking out baked potatoes from within the ashes of the fire when Motomo alerted him to Twila and Shayla's return. The wolf left to greet them as Raven retrieved the last potato. He hoped that Twila would not be mad at him for using them, but Motomo had assured him it would not matter to her. The potatoes and other vegetables stored beneath the caravan had lain there unused since Motomo joined Twila.

Twila leading an old black horse, entered the camp, closely followed by Shayla and Motomo. Raven walked towards them when he noticed the two children, draped in blankets, clinging to the horse and each other. When they secured the horse to a tree, Raven plucked a small boy from its back and carried him to the fire. He could feel the cold scrawny frame of Rudy through the thick travel rug that covered him. Raven carefully set the boy down by the fire, instructing him to eat, before returning for the girl still clinging to the horse. Rudy needed no further prompting when he saw the strips of roasted meat in a large bowl. Before Raven reached the horse to collect Sara, Rudy's mouth was stuffed full of the delicious crispy rabbit.

Raven held his arms out for Sara, and sluggishly she slipped from the horse. He scooped her up and carried her to the fire. Sara's body's heat surprised him, and Raven looked more closely at the girl's face. Unlike Rudy, who was pale from lack of sunlight, Sara's cheeks glowed red, and her eyes bright from a fever. Raven carefully placed Sara by the side of Rudy, noticing her swollen lower leg and foot. The angry red glow betrayed the infection that was no doubt causing the fever. Sara shook her head at the offer of food and instead asked for water. Twila pushed a mug of it into Sara's hand.

Raven pulled Twila to one side, and Shayla joined them.

"The girl is very sick," he said. "Infected wounds like that can poison the blood enough to kill a grown man, let alone a child. I can see the mark where the infection hasn't reached yet. If the infection persists in the wound, her leg may need to come off to save her life."

Shayla's eyes filled with tears at Raven's bluntness.

"There must be something we can do for her other than that," she said.

"Let me try something my mother taught me first," said Twila. "I need to find the ingredients for a fever tea too. If I fail to stop the infection, then to save her life, Raven is correct, we will have to remove the leg."

Shayla nodded hopefully. "Tell me how I can help."

"Come with me then, and I will show you how to make both the tea and the salve for the wound," said Twila. "Raven can keep an eye on her until we return."

Raven watched Twila and Shayla leave the camp before joining the children by the fire. Sara was so sick with the fever that he was afraid she would fall over. The mug was empty and had slipped from her hands. Quickly he retrieved a bedroll from his pack and spread it on the ground by the fire, but not close enough to be at risk from sparks off the burning wood. He picked up Sara and placed her gently on the bedroll and covered her with his travel rug. Sara smiled weakly at him and closed her eyes and quickly fell into a restless sleep.

Raven sat at Sara's head, watching her breathing. He felt so helpless, which was an emotion unusual for him. Awkwardly he gently stroked away the girl's plastered hair from off her forehead, and the heat from Sara's skin burned his fingertips. Rudy left his place by the fire, both his hands filled with rabbit meat and sat by Raven's side.

"Sara isn't going to die, is she, sir?" Rudy said fearfully. "You can help her, right?"

He looked down at the small boy's earnest face and struggled to reply. Raven was not used to changing the truth to protect the feelings of others. Raven dealt with death in the same manner all warriors did, bluntly and without emotion.

"Twila and Shayla have gone for the herbs necessary to help Sara," Raven said.

He was hoping that Rudy had not detected the doubt in his voice. Mentally he spoke with Motomo, who sat by the fire, smelling the poison emitting from Sara's pores. His pack avoided the flesh from a prey smelling of decay unless they were starving.

"Motomo, my friend, find Twila and tell her to hurry," said Raven, mentally. "This girl will not last the night if she doesn't do something soon. We need to break this fever quickly."

Motomo stood up and, without replying, ran off into the woods after Twila and Shayla.

Rudy munched the strips of meat and went back to the fire for one of the potatoes. He juggled it in his hands to stop it from burning him, as he returned to sit beside Raven. Despite the potato's heat, Rudy pushed back the blackened skin to reveal the soft, cooked flesh beneath.

"Here," said Raven. "Add a little of this salt. It makes it taste better." Raven handed the boy his pouch of sea salt that he always carried.

Rudy nodded appreciatively. "Ma Sadie just gave us slops from the kitchens," he said. "This is the best food I have ever tasted."

Raven's heart lurched at Rudy's words. He clearly remembered how hard it was when his mother had died, leaving him alone. At least he had been old enough to hunt and prepare his food. It was fundamental, but at least it wasn't the leftovers from someone else's meal. He rubbed his hand roughly over Rudy's tousled hair.

"Well, you had better get used to the change of food," Raven said. "There is more where that came from, and if you like, I can show you how to hunt and cook it."

Rudy nodded eagerly. "You will show me?" He asked excitedly.

Raven smiled. "Later, when you have rested, I will teach you how to hunt."

Twila and Shayla burst into the camp with Motomo close on their heels.

"How is she?" Asked Twila.

Raven mentally warned her to say nothing out loud because of the boy.

"She grows hotter," he said to her mentally so the boy couldn't hear. "You need to stop the infection from the leg quickly. It is poisoning her blood, causing her fever to rise. Already she is restless. I have seen infected battle wounds kill in this manner. When the fever rises like this, it is followed swiftly by death."

"Take her into my caravan and then watch the boy," said Twila. "I will do all I can." She mentally added so Rudy could not hear her.

Raven carried Sara into Twila's caravan, closely followed by Shayla. He placed her on one of the four sleeping cots that doubled as benches or storage shelves when not being used. Raven left Sara with Shayla and returned to the fire where Rudy sat watching Twila pounding leaves and herbs in a wooden bowl with a large rounded stick. A pot now dangled over the fire, suspended from a frame that Twila had positioned.

"How did Sara hurt her leg?" Twila asked Rudy.

The boy's eyes grew wide at this question. He turned to look at the caravan before answering.

"If I tell you what happened," said Rudy. "You won't tell Sara I told, will you?"

"No, I won't tell her," said Twila. "If I knew more about what started the infection, it might help me stop it, do you understand?"

Rudy hesitated for a moment and took one last look at the caravan before speaking.

"Ma Sadie sent Sara down into the cellar because of me." Rudy said. "I had spilled a pail of milk when I was carrying it out to the kitchen. Ma Sadie came after me with her stick, and Sara tried to stop her."

Rudy sniffed and ran the back of his hand quickly across his face so Twila would not see the tears. He quickly learned how to hold his tears because Ma Sadie would take a stick to him for crying.

"So did Ma Sadie hurt Sara's leg?" Asked Twila, trying to keep the anger out of her voice.

"No," said Rudy. "Ma Sadie locked Sara in the cellar all night to punish her. There are rats in the cellar. I've seen them. Sara told me one had bitten her foot while she was sleeping. She was afraid to tell Ma Sadie because she would get mad."

"When did the rat bite her?" Asked Twila.

"I forget," said Rudy. "About three or four days ago, I think."

"So, Sara didn't clean the wound?" Asked Twila.

"She washed it in water," said Rudy. "But she wouldn't tell Ma Sadie. When her foot got red and swollen, she covered it in flour so no one could see. It must have hurt bad, though, because I could hear her sobbing when she thought I was sleeping."

"Do you know when she started with the fever?" Asked Twila.

"It must have happened two nights ago because she started saying things in her sleep. Lin, the other kitchen girl, threw a mug at her because she woke her up. That was the night Sara saw the lady."

"What lady?" Asked Twila.

"Sara said the lady spoke to her and said we must find Shayla, who would take us to a better life," said Rudy. "Sara said the lady told her we would find Shayla on the first floor if we waited beneath the stairs. To tell you the truth, Miss, I thought it was just the fever talking. But she told the truth, didn't she?" A broad smile crossed Rudy's face.

Twila smiled. "Yes, she did," Twila said. "Did Sara cover her foot with flour before you both went to find Shayla?"

Rudy nodded. "Sara thought Shayla wouldn't take us to the lady if she knew about her foot," he said. "The flour must have washed off in the rain because Raven saw it. You won't take us back there, will you?" Rudy's face grew worried.

"No," said Twila loudly. "You will not be going back there, ever."

Rudy's broad smile returned. "Will Shayla be angry when she finds out that Sara fooled her?" He asked, his face growing somber again.

"Shayla is too worried about Sara to be angry," answered Twila. "Why did Lin not come with you?"

"Lin is to marry Ash, Ma Sadie's son," answered Rudy. "Sara didn't dare tell her that we were going anywhere. Lin would have told Ma Sadie." A visible shudder ran through Rudy's small body.

Raven came out of the caravan and joined them by the fire. His face displayed no emotion until he met Rudy's anxious eyes, and then he smiled for the boy's sake.

"When the water begins to bubble, bring it to me," Twila said to Raven.

Raven nodded and watched her as she went up the steps of the caravan.

"Here," Twila said to Shayla, handing her the bowl and stick. "I need to find the medicine bag my mother gave me before I left. She didn't realize that I would no longer need such things. I almost gave it back to her. The boy told me everything. It was a rat bite that became infected."

Shayla watched Twila open a large leather pouch and spilled out its contents on the floor in front of her.

"I swear her foot did not look this red last night." Said Shayla.

"She covered it in flour to hide the redness," said Twila. "The boy said that Sara was afraid you would not take them if her foot looked infected."

Shayla's eyes filled with tears. "I would have taken them anyway," she said.

Twila nodded her agreement as she threw some dried roots and flower heads into the bowl that Shayla was holding, naming them as she did so. Shayla recognized them but knew them by other names. She crushed each addition to the bowl as Twila spread out strips of linen on the floor. Twila took the cloth cover off a small wooden bowl that had been in the medicine pouch. She scraped out a handful of the salve and smeared it onto the strips of linen.

"We create this from fish oil, garlic, and soap-weed," Twila said. She took the bowl from Shayla and dumped half the contents on top of the salve. "The rest of this can be mixed with the water when it is boiling to make the tea," she said. "Pull back the rugs from Sara's leg so I can wrap this around it."

Shayla pulled back the rugs and gasped when she saw how deeply infected Sara's foot, and now her leg was. Shayla turned to Twila with tears in her eyes.

"Are we too late?" Shayla whispered.

Twila frowned when she saw the red and swollen lower leg in the light from the lantern above the cot. Carefully she wrapped Sara's foot and leg with the salve coated strips of linen. Shayla supported Sara's leg as Twila wrapped it, biting her lip every time the young girl groaned. When Twila had finished wrapping it, Shayla gently lowered Sara's leg onto the bed.

"I am pressing carefully on the wrappings now to warm them," said Twila. "My mother told me that this activates the herbs in the salve. While I do this, go and see if the water is boiling for the tea."

Shayla nodded and grabbed the bowl containing the last of the mixture. Twila concentrated on her hands as she gently massaged every inch of the wrappings, not immediately noticing her hands' increasing temperature because of the heat from Sara's fever. Twila finally realized that her hands were burning hot and she looked down at them puzzled. Her hands appeared to be golden in color, glowing with a bright yellow light starting to illuminate the whole caravan. Shayla came back into the van carefully carrying the steaming hot tea, and almost dropped it when she saw Twila.

193

A golden glow emitted from Twila's hands spreading beyond her fingers and over the dressings covering Sara's leg. The girl groaned and grew restless as the golden glow spread over her leg. Twila finally removed her hands, and slowly the light disappeared.

Sara's eyes fluttered open. "The pain has gone," she said gratefully. "Thank you."

"Here, sip this," Twila said, taking the bowl from Shayla. She scooped a small amount of the tea into a small mug from a shelf above the cot where Sara lay.

Shayla moved behind Sara to help support her as she greedily sipped the bitter smelling brew. Sara still felt hot to Shayla's touch, and she exchanged concerned glances with Twila over the girl's head. When the mug was empty, Shayla lowered Sara back on the bed. The girl immediately fell into a deep sleep. Her breathing seemed more comfortable, but Shayla was still concerned.

"What did you do to her leg?" Shayla asked as she helped Twila return all the items into the medicine bag.

Twila stopped what she was doing and faced Shayla.

"I don't know what I did," she said. "I was concentrating on warming the dressing to activate the salve, and it just happened."

"She seems to be breathing better, but the fever still rages through her body," said Shayla. "I cannot see through the dressings, but she said the pain was gone. Do you think she will live because of what you did?"

Twila shook her head slowly, "morning fast approaches, and I must sleep. When the sun sets, we will remove the dressings and see if there is any improvement.

"If she lives that long," muttered Shayla. She remembered clearly how the leg looked before they wrapped it in dressings.

"I believe she will live," said Twila touching Sara's cheek. "She is much cooler already.

Shayla gently felt Sara's forehead and then smiled at Twila. "Well, whatever you did seems to be working. I agree. She is much cooler now. I will give Raven and Rudy the good news."

Rudy had fallen asleep in Raven's lap when Shayla and Twila came out of the caravan. Raven's left leg had gone dead from holding it still to prevent waking the boy.

"How is she?" Asked Raven softly to avoid waking Rudy, carefully shifting his weight to restore his leg's circulation.

"She is doing much better," said Shayla relieved. "I don't

know what Twila did, but it seems to be working."

Twila grinned at Raven. "Let me carry the boy inside," she said. "We need to make plans to break camp and head to the seal."

Raven nodded and gratefully stretched his leg when Twila picked up the boy and carried him effortlessly into the caravan.

"What did she do?" Raven asked Shayla.

"I am not sure." She answered. "Twila made a salve dressing from the things we collected and what she had in a medicine bag that her mother had given her. When I returned after making the tea, a golden glow came from her hands as she held Sara's leg. In no time at all, the girl seemed better."

Raven nodded. "I think Radon's blood has given Twila more powers than she realizes," he said. "I just hope the girl makes it. Rudy will take it very hard if she dies. He was telling me that she has cared for him like a mother."

"Then, I hope Saressa has chosen well for their next home," said Shayla. "If not, then when all this is over, I shall take them back with me."

Twila joined them by the fire. "Sara is even cooler now," she said. "I think she will recover."

Shayla inspected the cooked meat strips and baked potatoes in the bowls. She tried some of the meat and found it to be delicious. Shayla realized just how hungry she was. Raven smiled as he handed her the salt. Shayla frowned for a moment and then realized it was for the potatoes, and she scraped off the ashes and dust from the skin.

"Well, I would have normally covered them in leaves before burying them in the ashes," said Shayla, taking a bite out of the potato. "But it tastes delicious."

Raven grinned. "I am just sorry Twila is not interested in tasting my cooking."

Twila laughed. "Well, unfortunately, I can only breathe in the delicious aroma," she said.

"You don't know what you are missing," laughed Shayla, grabbing more strips of meat.

"The sun is starting to rise, and I must sleep," said Twila. "I will sleep in the caravan with the children, and the two of you will have to break camp for me. Raven, if you come with me, I can show you quickly how to harness my horse to the caravan."

Raven nodded and followed Twila, listening to her

instructions; he had never cared much for horses. He didn't trust them. As the sky lightened in response to the rising sun, Twila returned to the caravan to sleep.

It took Raven and Shayla more than an hour to attach Twila's horse to the caravan and successfully move out of the campsite. Apple, the old black horse, was secured at the rear of the van and would follow behind. Reed, the horse that would pull the caravan, seemed to know how inexperienced his new handlers were and grew difficult when Raven attempted to place the harness. Raven was hot and irritable when he finally flicked the Reins to get the horse to move forward. He breathed a sigh of relief when the caravan slowly moved onward as the horse responded to the reins' feel.

"Never did like horses," grumbled Raven, as they started their journey to meet up with Devon.

CHAPTER FIFTEEN

Daybreak

The horse's hooves' rhythmic clop and the caravan's gentle swaying were lulling Raven to sleep. The road to follow was the last thing that Motomo showed him before falling asleep at his feet. Raven had sent Shayla into the caravan to sleep once they were on the open road so that he could sleep in the afternoon. Judging by the position of the sun, it was approaching noon. However, Raven was not sure if the sun in this world behaved in the same way as it had in his world. If it did, then Shayla could take his place whenever he decided to wake her up.

The journey so far had been uneventful. Raven had seen very few travelers on the road. They appeared to be mostly traders taking their goods to Edenberry. He had seen a man and a boy leading three horses earlier in the morning. The man called out a greeting to Raven as they passed each other on the road. Raven had pondered whether to buy one of the horses. If they planned the travel day and night in this manner, then the extra horse would allow Twila's horse to rest. He knew little about horses, but the old black horse that Shayla was returning, did not look capable of pulling the caravan. Raven had gold and had verified with Twila that he could use it in this world. If he could have just gotten Twila's horse to stop then, Raven would have purchased one from the man.

He had managed to get Twila's horse onto the main road, with a lot of help from Shayla and Motomo, but that was it. Raven thought the horse would probably continue whether he was there or not. He had tried pulling on the reins to stop the horse, and that hadn't worked. Raven had finally jumped down from the caravan and ran to the horse to stop him. That maneuver had cost him the indignity of falling flat on his face because the van was moving faster than he expected. Raven then had no choice but to run to catch the horse up. He began shouting at the horse until he realized that might cause it to run faster and possibly leave him behind, or worse, cause the animal to buck and tip the caravan over. Raven heard the laughter from the man and boy in the distance and knew he was the cause of it.

Shayla climbed beside him and held out her hands for the reins. "You get some rest now," she told Raven. "How do I control where the horse goes?"

"He goes where he wants," replied Raven, "whether you are here are not."

Shayla looked puzzled. "Well, how do you stop him then?" She asked.

Raven laughed. "We should have asked Twila for instructions before the sun rose," he said.

Shayla gently pulled the reins back to test what the horse would do. The horse slowed down in response to the command, and Raven stared at Shayla in amazement. She grinned broadly at him.

"Well, that wasn't hard," said Shayla.

"Then try getting him to stop," said Raven.

Shayla pulled the reins back more firmly this time, calling out to the horse. The horse slowed to a walk and then finally stopped, quietly snorting as he waited for another command or release from the harness.

Raven didn't trust himself to speak. He turned away from Shayla's grinning face and went into the caravan to sleep. The van started to move again as the horse trotted forward at Shayla's command. Despite his irritation at Shayla's skill with the horse, he wrapped a rug around himself and quickly fell asleep on the creaking floor of the moving caravan.

Devon stood on the edge of the ledge, looking across the landscape far below him. The sun had just set, and the horizon still glowed with the blood-red trail of its wake. He felt his strength returning as the red glow slowly disappeared. Devon turned and looked up the mountain to assess how far it was to the top. He hesitated only briefly and then began the climb up to the top.

Devon reached the edge of what he thought was another large ledge. Effortlessly he heaved himself up and saw the small house built into the side of the final peak of the mountain, as Twila had described it. A rosy glow from the windows of the house beckoned enticingly, almost as if Devon was an expected guest. He crouched behind a pile of boulders as he familiarized himself with the area around the house. Devon saw that Ramos had cultivated a garden around the house, and plants flourished in organized rows. He couldn't see what the plants were, though, because of the low light and his distance away from them. Devon assumed they provided some of the ingredients Ramos needed to create his spells. He knew that Ramos was a blood drinker and would have no need for a regular food source.

Devon noticed the shadows spreading beyond the light from within the small house, and he slowly smiled as an idea came to him. He hadn't decided beforehand on how he was going to remain hidden from Ramos. Devon had just assumed he would determine what strategy to use once he reached the area where Ramos lived. Quickly Devon cast a concealment spell over himself and then quietly headed for the shadows edging the pools of light from the windows. A concealment spell could have kept him hidden for as long as he continued to cast it. The problem with a concealment spell was that there was always the danger of it wearing off too soon, and then Devon would be openly visible to Ramos. So, he had decided to do something else.

Devon stopped walking when he reached the shadows just outside one of the areas of light. He concentrated and started to meld with the various sized shadows cast by the light from Ramos's house. Devon paused for a moment while he grew accustomed to the strange sensations of this new body. When the peculiar lightheaded feeling had dissipated, Devon oozed himself around the perimeter of the light and headed towards Ramos's house. He was careful to stay as one with the shadows to prevent detection. If Devon remained cautious, Ramos would not detect his presence.

Devon felt a slight tug as the delicate fabric of his shadow host released him, and seconds later, he was pouring his way underneath the door of Ramos's house.

Raven woke up suddenly when he felt a light touch on his shoulder. Instantly he was ready to defend himself but then stopped when he saw the startled eyes of Rudy.

"Never creep up on a man while he's sleeping, lad," Raven said. "It could mean your head. Better to call out his name if the situation allows it. If you cannot call his name, then make sure you are well away from his grasp before you try anything else."

Rudy nodded quickly, his eyes still wide with fear. Raven grinned at him.

"So, what was important enough to almost lose your life for then? Raven asked him.

"Twila sent me to fetch you," said Rudy. "She says the sun is down, and you need to eat what Shayla made for us before we break camp again."

Raven nodded and followed the boy out of the caravan. Until the boy had spoken, he hadn't even realized that they were no longer moving. When they stepped out of the van, the first thing he saw was Sara walking towards them without even a suggestion of a limp. She grinned at Raven as she approached him.

"Rudy was right about you," said Sara. "You do look like a warrior. I am sorry I caused so much trouble earlier. I am completely well now, and I helped Shayla cook dinner."

"Then lead me to it," said Raven. "I will not be much of a warrior in battle if I don't eat."

Sara laughed and ran towards the campfire, where Shayla and Twila were deep in conversation.

"We need another horse," said Twila to Raven as he sat beside the fire. "My horse will not hold out for long if we don't get a second horse to relieve him regularly. The old black horse would not be strong enough to pull the caravan."

Raven nodded in agreement as he heaped a delicious smelling stew from a large cooking pot suspended over the glowing fire, into a large wooden bowl handed to him by Sara. He quickly ate while listening to Twila and Shayla discussing the purchase of another horse. The last thing that he wanted to become involved in was dealing with another horse. Shayla smiled over at him, making him feel that she was reading his thoughts about another horse. He also chose not to mention the earlier event when he had tried to stop the horse to purchase another one.

"Some things are best left unsaid," he thought.

"Motomo tells me that there is a group of Gypsies two miles east from here," said Twila. "When you have eaten Raven, go with Shayla to purchase a horse from them. If you show them this, they will give you a fair price for the horse." Twila handed him a small, round wooden token.

Raven took it from her and inspected it in the flickering firelight. There were circular symbols burnt into the wood. "What do the symbols mean?" Raven asked Twila.

"It is my clan token," Twila said. "We often make them for traders and merchants who treat us fairly. A Gypsy clan token guarantees them fair prices in return. You must go without me because they will know me and would see what I have become." Twila's eyes betrayed the pain in her heart at this last statement.

Raven nodded sympathetically and resumed eating. He noticed that Rudy had crept beside him and was quietly studying his every move. Rudy still wore the rags that he had arrived in, and Sara looked no better.

"Will this Gypsy group sell us some better clothing for the children?" Raven asked Twila.

"Yes, they will sell anything available that is over their needs, but I don't have the funds to pay for clothing in addition to a horse," Twila said. "Shayla and I will make something for them as we travel."

"I have gold," Raven said. "Gold is acceptable in this world, too, isn't it?"

Twila nodded. "Then, make sure you bring them some footwear," she said. "That Sadie woman kept them shoeless to prevent their escape. I would like to meet her one day." Twila's golden eyes flashed dangerously, causing a shudder to run down Raven's spine.

Shayla was surprised by Raven's genuine concern for the children. His overall appearance was a formidable fighter, but there was a gentle side to him, grudgingly showing itself since the children's arrival. Rudy was always by his side, asking questions only a child would dare to ask, and not once had Raven lost patience with the boy. As she heard Raven discussing the purchase of clothing for the children, something also stirred within her heart. Quickly Shayla turned her attention back to Twila, fearful that Raven would see something in her eyes that she was not ready to admit to yet. Shayla was angry at herself for allowing Raven to creep into her heart this way. Especially now that there was so much to accomplish.

Raven and Shayla left the camp searching for the Gypsies, led by Motomo, who declared that he could show them the swiftest route. Raven was silently hoping that Shayla would deal with any horse they may bring back with them. He noticed that she seemed thoughtful as they concentrated on following Motomo, and he wondered if perhaps she was a little fearful of thieves or worse, being out in the forest so late in the evening.

"You have nothing to fear with me here," said Raven. "If anyone approaches, Motomo will warn us in plenty of time, and I can swiftly deal with thieves looking to relieve us of our gold."

Shayla stopped and turned to him in response. "I fear nothing," Shayla said. "My appearance may give the impression of a helpless female, but I am perfectly capable of taking even a man your size down."

Raven smiled to himself at her words. "I have offended you," Raven said carefully. "The women of my world tend to stay home with their families. They would be fearful of thieves if they were out so late in the forest. You seemed thoughtful, and I assumed, apparently incorrectly, that you were concerned for your safety. I have been employed many times by concerned husbands to escort their wives and daughters on long journeys."

Shayla felt foolish at her sudden outburst of anger and was even more confused by her sensitivity where Raven was concerned.

"Well, I am not like the ladies you escorted in your world," Shayla said sharply. "I can look after myself."

"Please accept my apology," Raven said, bowing his head to her. "I have no doubts you will be a powerful ally by my side in battle if someone attacks us."

Motomo, suddenly realizing that the two of them were no longer following him, returned to hear Shayla's angry words. He sensed the attraction between them.

"Humans are not very different from wolves, after all," Motomo thought. "Aggression between a male and female is always the first indication of attraction."

Shayla noticed Motomo patiently waiting for them.

"Come," Shayla said. "We are wasting time." She strode purposely into the forest, leaving Raven and Motomo to follow her hastily.

"Women." Mumbled Raven under his breath to Motomo.

The wolf replied with a low rumble deep within his throat. To Raven, it sounded almost like a distorted chuckle. Raven laughed in response.

"Just be glad she does not use her teeth like a female wolf," Motomo said mentally. "You would be nursing your wounds for days."

Raven laughed as the two of them hurried after Shayla.

Devon carefully oozed across the floor, shadows inside Ramos's house. Initially, he was concerned that someone could easily detect his movements in such a small room, but no one was in there. Devon was afraid to search mentally for Ramos because it would weaken the guard on his thoughts. He was not sure just how strong Ramos's power was yet, and Devon was using great caution until he knew more about him.

Devon spent some time carefully searching the room. He slipped along the single shelf above the fireplace, carefully peering into the variety of bottles and jars. Although they all had some kind of cover, none of them contained anything. The fireplace grate included the remnants of a long-dead fire, and Devon saw woodworm feeding on logs that had been carefully stacked by the side of the hearth. Devon would have assumed the house abandoned if it were not for the two lanterns that brightly lit up the room until he turned and saw the formidable bolts on the outer door and window shutters, only securable from the inside.

Satisfied there was nothing of interest in this room, Devon headed for the door at the rear. He knew from Twila's description that this must lead to the cavern. Carefully Devon slipped beneath the door and found himself in a narrow, dimly lit passage. Lanterns that were secured high on the damp, craggy walls alarmingly flickered as if threatening to go out at any moment. Devon felt a cold breeze immediately when all of his shadow body was in the passage. He thought that the draft within the passageway was a little odd. Devon was relieved, though, that there were many shadows for him to hide amongst if Ramos suddenly appeared.

The passage was unexpected too. Twila had described the house as being built around the mouth of a cavern. She had not spoken of a passageway leading from the house into the cavern. Devon wondered if Ramos had drugged her with the wine she said she drank, or perhaps he had cast a confusion spell to prevent her finding the cavern should Twila ever return without his knowledge.

Devon concentrated on the song from within the vast mountain structure. He pressed his shadow body against the passage's left wall and listened carefully to its high-pitched sounds. Devon stayed there for some time, listening carefully, becoming familiar with the complexity of the inner passageways and secrets of what lay hidden before him. Devon smiled grimly but was finally satisfied that he would not become lost on his journey to Ramos.

The mountain rock voices spoke of many passages and caverns that ran for miles deep down into its core. Ramos would no doubt believe that he was safe from detection here. To anyone other than a Lunarian, he probably was.

Devon finally began the journey down the first of many passageways, his shadow body caressing the left wall's rough surface. For an instant, he was homesick for his Lunaria caverns, but Devon cleared his thoughts of such foolishness and concentrated on finding Ramos.

Motomo stopped suddenly, causing Shayla to almost fall over him in the gloom beyond Raven's lantern.

"What is it?" Said Shayla; her dagger was instantly ready.

"I can go no further because the dogs and horses will sense me," said Motomo. "Continue on this track, and you will find them."

"Well, you could have stopped a little less dramatically," said Shayla, re-sheathing the dagger.

Raven started to laugh but instantly stopped when Shayla glared at him. Motomo looked surprised by Shayla's outburst and was going to reply but decided against it.

"And hold that lantern higher," Shayla said to Raven.

Raven flashed a grin at Motomo as he hurried after Shayla.

"Whatever you have done to that girl," Motomo said mentally to Raven. "You need to repair the damage quickly."

"I have no idea what has gotten into her," Raven replied mentally to Motomo. "But, I'm finding it to be very amusing."

Motomo shook his head as he settled down to wait for their return. Humans were very puzzling creatures. It was perfectly evident that Shayla was significantly attracted to Raven and mad at herself for being so. Raven could not see it, and he was not even sure whether Shayla realized how obvious it was. Motomo decided it would be interesting to watch the situation develop. He felt a wave of sympathy for Raven, who had no idea what was wrong with Shayla. Motomo decided that although Raven was an accomplished fighter, he knew very little about female behavior.

Raven and Shayla reached the camp very shortly after leaving Motomo. Three barking dogs circled them, heralding their entrance into the campsite.

"Quiet," a male voice commanded the dogs.

In response to the voice, all three dogs lay flat to the floor in front of Raven and Shayla. Although they had stopped barking, all three dogs continued to growl a warning.

Two men walked towards Raven and Shayla, each of them armed with large sticks. Raven fought with the urge to draw his sword as Shayla gently touched his arm to warn him not to.

"State your business or leave our camp," said the older man.

"We require a good horse," said Raven. "We were directed to your camp, and instructed to show you this to ensure we get a fair deal."

The older man took the wooden token from Raven and inspected the carvings. He passed it to the younger man as he led the way to the center of the camp.

"So, you are a friend of Stavos's group, are you? Asked the younger man as he handed the token back to Raven.

"Yes," lied Raven without hesitation. "A fine man."

"Pity about young Twila, though," said the young man, eyeing Raven curiously.

"Enough," said the older man. "We do not speak the name of the banished, and you know that. He flashed a glance of disapproval at the young man.

What kind of horse are you looking for?" He asked Raven.

"We need a second horse to pull our cart," said Shayla quickly, noticing the dilemma in Raven's face in response to the horse question. "We are taking two children who have found themselves homeless to relatives in the north. Their parents perished in a fire, and we offered to help them. They lost everything except what is on their backs, and we hoped you might sell us some clothes and shoes also."

"Bring Daybreak and let him inspect her, Morry," said the older man. "And then wake up your mother and tell her to come here."

Morry handed Raven the end of Daybreak's rope harness before going to wake his mother. Raven held onto the rope as Morry's father skillfully pushed Daybreaks lips back to prove that she was only two years old. Raven nodded, attempting to show knowledge that he did not have about how horses' teeth indicate their age. Daybreak tolerated the man's hands in her mouth very well, just quietly snorting when released. Morry's father continued to display the features of Daybreak that constituted a good horse. He grabbed each of her legs and upturned the hoof so that Raven could see that the shoes were secure. Raven obligingly ran his hands down each of Daybreak's legs at Morry's father's suggestion. He had no idea what he was doing, and the legs felt okay to him.

Daybreak had become interested in Raven as he clutched the rope just waiting for the Gypsy to discover his lack of horse knowledge. The horse pushed Raven with her nose curiously. Raven turned quickly, expecting the horse to sink those enormous teeth that he had just been shown, into his shoulder.

"Looks like Daybreak has taken a fancy to her new master." Morry's father said with a salesman smile.

Raven just nodded as he kept his eyes on Daybreak's actions. The horse's gentle eyes stared back into his suspicious ones. Daybreak seemed to know of Raven's lack of horse knowledge and had decided not to act on it. Raven awkwardly petted Daybreak's muzzle that appeared to seal this sudden bond between them.

Shayla had been talking with Morry's mother about the sizes of clothing that she needed for the children. The gypsy woman returned to the caravan more than once, before Shayla was satisfied. Then she returned to where Raven stood with Daybreak, and all that was left to do was decide on a price.

Raven wanted to hand the horse's rope to Shayla quickly so he could pay the price and be out of this camp. He deposited several coins into the eager hand of Morry's father, who peered at them carefully. Morry's father bit down on one of the odd-looking coins and then nodded satisfied as he inspected them once more.

Shayla inwardly groaned when she saw how many Raven had given Morry's father. This amount of gold would likely draw attention that they did not need.

Morry's father quickly pocketed the coins and smiled broadly at Raven.

"It's been nice doing business with you," Morry's father said. "I wish you both well on your journey."

Raven nodded and led the way out of the camp. Shayla saw the way Morry was staring at them both as she turned to follow Raven.

"The young one is suspicious of us," Shayla whispered to Raven as they left the camp. "You aroused his suspicion by the number of coins you gave. Gypsies like to barter."

"I paid a fair price, and we have no time for bartering." Raven snapped.

Shayla slung the children's sack of clothes over Daybreak's shoulders and followed Raven back into the forest. Daybreak seemed determined to push her nose curiously against Raven whenever she got close to him.

"I think this horse has taken a liking to you," said Shayla finally.

"I think you are not in control of the horse," said Raven, patting Daybreak's head again.

"Then, you hold her," snapped Shayla flinging the rope at Raven. "And I will watch our backs for signs of that young Gypsy."

Raven grabbed for the rope in surprise, and he patted Daybreak's head gently. "I am in trouble again," he whispered in the horse's ear.

As they reached the spot where Motomo waited for them, Daybreak grew skittish. Raven patted her gently. Motomo was surprised by Raven's actions.

"I thought you didn't care for horses, Raven," Motomo said, his tongue lolling out of his mouth in a wolf grin.

Raven grinned at him. "She is the only female that likes me at the moment," he said.

"Then let me speak to her, and she will no longer fear me," said Motomo. He concentrated on the horse as he mentally introduced himself. To his surprise, Daybreak answered him.

"You are a wolf," Daybreak said to Motomo. "Why should I trust a wolf?"

Motomo was surprised. "You understand me?" He asked. "No other horse I have been around understood my voice and so I usually just suggest to them that they ignore me. My friend Amani taught me how to do that."

"I hear lots of voices," said Daybreak. "I answer, but they don't take the time to listen to me. The human named Raven speaks to me, and I answer, but he cannot hear me. Can you teach him to hear me, as Amani taught you the power of suggestion? I have been waiting for Raven to come for me."

"You knew of him?" Asked Motomo.

"I know of many things," said Daybreak. "I know that the young Gypsy named Morry is following us. He has gathered four of his cousins and plans to surround and attack us."

"When does he plan to do this?" Asked Motomo. "And how could you know this?"

"He told me," said Daybreak. "When he brought me before Raven, Morry was upset by a token that Raven had with him. Morry told me that it was the one only Twila could have had. He was to be married to Twila, but something bad happened to her on the road. She was banished and then disappeared. Morry thinks that Raven was the cause of Twila's downfall."

"But that is not true," said Motomo. "Raven is not from here, Twila's banishment was not because of any human."

"Yes, I know," said Daybreak. "And I tried to warn Raven, but he cannot understand me."

"Raven," said Motomo. "Daybreak has been trying to warn you of an ambush. The Gypsy named Morry thinks that you must have attacked Twila, causing her banishment. He believes this because you carry her family token. Morry is the one that Twila should have married before Ramos destroyed all that for her. He has gathered others to help and plans to ambush you."

Raven frowned at Motomo's revelation. He patted Daybreak's neck. "Thank you, my friend," he said.

"He probably seeks more of that gold you are so willing to throw away," Shayla said when he told her what Motomo had revealed to him.

"It was Twila's token that drew the suspicion, not the gold," said Motomo quickly in Raven's defense.

"We can defend ourselves against them easily," said Raven quickly. "I doubt that Twila wants any of the Gypsies killed on her behalf, though. Motomo, you must run ahead and bring Twila back with you. She needs to speak with this Morry, despite the pain it will cause her. If they attack us before you return with Twila, then I cannot guarantee their safety."

Motomo saw the cold gaze of a warrior in Raven's eyes at this statement. Shayla felt the attraction for Raven bursting into new flames within her heart, and she fought weakly against it.

"I will return with Twila swiftly," said Motomo. "Try not to slay the world while I am gone."

Raven smiled as Motomo disappeared into the forest. "Well, let us go to meet our attackers," he said calmly. "When they attack, we fight back to back."

Shayla nodded in agreement.

"You stay out of their way," said Raven to Daybreak. "Shayla and I can deal with the attackers, so keep yourself safe."

Shayla looked at Raven in surprise at the apparent complement of her fighting skills. "Then let's do it," she said, grinning.

Raven grinned back. For once, he seemed to have said the right thing to her. He tugged gently at Daybreak's rope to encourage her forward as the three of them headed back to their camp.

Daybreak pushed once more against Raven, hoping he would now listen to her. But he just kept walking. The horse followed obligingly, wondering what he would think when she chose to stay and fight by his side.

"He knows little of horses," Daybreak thought to herself, "otherwise he would have ordered me to his back in battle. I will show him what a horse can do with swift kicks and bites."

Daybreak listened to Shayla, arguing to herself mentally about the growing love for Raven within her heart. She then listened to Raven as he planned for the upcoming battle. Daybreak realized that Raven found Shayla intriguing, but there was no love for her in his heart.

"Raven's match is not in this world," Daybreak thought knowingly, "and he will not meet her for some time yet."

Daybreak continued to follow her two new companions. She felt sorry for Shayla's heart, but most of all, Daybreak wondered how she knew all this. Daybreak just knew things and didn't know why.

CHAPTER SIXTEEN

The Cavern

Devon decided that he should head for the core of the inner mountain. The song that the mountain sang to him was different when it told him of the center. Devon felt that if Ramos were not there, he would spread out his search to include each of the many passages and caves that the mountain sang of on the way back up to the entrance.

The initial passage that Devon was traveling in began to descend steeply. As it did so, the breeze became more robust, causing the passageway's temperature to be even colder. The first passage crossed through a second passage. The wind blew wildly in this second passage, loudly roaring as it hurried on to its unknown destination. There were no lights in this passage, but the walls glowed with a greenish hue that provided enough light for Devon to see the thick sheets of ice covering the floor. The water that had trickled down the walls from the roof was pure ice, too, frozen in time on its journey back to the sea.

He was surprised by the ice passage's appearance and would have liked to investigate it further, but Devon wanted to find Ramos first. Devon peered down his passageway and realized that it seemed to end just after crossing the ice passage. Devon slid across the ice passage as he continued forward. The closer he got to what looked to be the end of the entrance passage, the more his curiosity grew. The mountain song had not indicated that this passage ended so abruptly. When Raven reached the end of it, he found himself on the edge of what appeared to be a sheer drop. The sheet of rock that hung down across the passage effectively hid the edge of this decline. If anyone came down the passageway, they would assume that it ended here and go back to the ice passage.

Devon lay flat on the floor and peered down into the gloom before him. He saw that steps carved out of the rock face about ten feet below him. Devon slipped beneath the sheet of rock and over the edge. He clung for a moment with his fingertips before dropping down onto the first step. Devon realized that it would not be easy for a human to reach this first step, but it was possible. He looked carefully at this new passage and was surprised to see a shallow staircase carved from the rock just ahead that led downward. The light that the torches, positioned on many of the steps, gave off adequately lit the way.

He began the long climb down the staircase, carefully staying close to the left wall. The step passage held another nasty surprise for intruders, and he saw them when he reached the fifth step. Large black rats scuttled across the stair he was on. There were five of them all the size of dogs. Devon pressed against the wall as they hurried past him up the steps. One of them stopped at his feet and sniffed the air curiously. Its bright black eyes searched for a source of what must have been Devon's scent. The rat was so close that Devon could see the sharp yellow teeth in its partially open mouth. It gave off a rancid odor that Devon associated with sickness and death.

The rat finally scuttled after the others, following them up the steps and into another hole near the entrance. Devon breathed a sigh of relief.

"I must warn the others to watch out for those," Devon thought, "they are like no rats I have ever seen before."

Devon continued down the steps, staying close to the wall. The passage twisted and turned deeper down towards the core of the mountain. He began to think the steps would never end when the path became narrower. As it did so, Devon found himself on the last stair. The sandy floor before him sloped gently down towards a natural arch in the rock face. Torches on either side of the arch flickered gently, casting dancing shadows across the sandy floor. Devon pressed against the left wall as he made his way to the archway, finally slipping beneath it, and found himself in a short passage that led out into an enormous cavern, the largest that Devon had ever seen.

He stepped through the archway pressing himself against the wall of the cavern, avoiding the light from a torch above his head. Devon stood motionless for a few moments as his eyes took in his new surroundings.   Glistening Stalactites and stalagmites gave the impression of many pillars and corridors spreading out before him. Devon smiled as he realized these would provide him many shadows to travel amongst undetected. He also realized that it made his search for Ramos a little more complicated.

Devon listened to the mountain's song for a few moments to get his bearings.   The base of the structure was still beneath him, and he doubted that the way down would be in the center of this cavern, but he decided to go forward anyway.   Devon continued to memorize every path he took so he could draw a map for the others later.

"They could be down here for years." Devon thought. "And still not find Ramos without my help."

Devon continued forward, slipping from shadow to shadow, on the meandering path created by the looming stalagmites. An oppressive silence filled the cavern, broken occasionally by the resounding drip of the mineral-rich water.   The drops came from a stalactite, growing down from high above him, and onto a slowly developing stalagmite on the rock floor.   Devon wished he could just use his power to sense Ramos, but that would mean instant detection. He fought the natural urge to use his intuition skills as he continued forward.   It made him uncomfortable not having the advantage of sensing others before they were aware of him.   He assumed Ramos was alone down here, except for the rats, but he still felt uneasy.

The path Devon was following opened abruptly into a circular area that had a strange circle of stalagmites in the center.   The space between him and the center was clear of shadows, and that concerned him.   He had not seen Ramos yet, so Devon finally decided to run across the shadowless path that led to the center. Just as he was about to run, something caught his eye on his right. Devon melded closely with the shadows that currently hid him and waited for whatever might be there to show itself.

Devon held back, carefully controlling his breathing to avoid detection, but he saw nothing, and after a few minutes, began to think that he had made a mistake. Suddenly a shadow spread unnaturally across the floor from his right. It headed towards the center like Devon was planning to do. He watched incredulously as the shadow reached the center and melded with the shadows within the circle of stalagmites. He knew of no other race capable of adopting a shadow body except the Lunarians.

"Could this be Ramos?" Thought Devon puzzled, "or did another

Lunarian cross into this world and became trapped in the same way I was?"

Devon waited until convinced that there was no further movement within the circle of stalagmites. Then he ran across the shadowless path leading to the center. Quickly Devon melded with the shadows on reaching the strange ring of stalagmites. He scanned the shadows around him but saw nothing, and the center of the circle of stalagmites held another surprise for Devon, as a low human-made wall of rocks lay before him.

Staying within the shadows, Devon carefully circled the wall's edge in the center, studying it. He saw an opening in the wall and what appeared to be more steps leading down. Satisfied that there was no one else within this circle, Devon then headed for the opening in the wall. Pressing into the shadows, he found himself on the first of many more steps of rock leading downwards. These steps were much narrower than the others had been, and there was very little light. Devon could see no movement in the gloom below him. Satisfied that he was alone, Devon slowly began the long descent downwards to the mountain's core.

Daybreak attempted to warn Shayla and Raven that Morry was up ahead, but they did not hear her. Shayla noticed a hesitation in the horse's step and realized that there was something wrong. She patted Daybreak's neck gently to reassure her that they knew what lay ahead. Raven glanced over at Shayla and gave her a brief nod, warning her to be ready. A dagger dropped into her hand from its sheath. Shayla prepared to get this over with realized as they stepped into a small clearing, that this was the perfect place for an ambush.

Morry stepped into the clearing blocking the way forward. Three other men stepped into position at the right, left, and rear of Shayla, Raven, and Daybreak.

"Let us pass," said Raven coldly. "We have no further business with you."

"But, we have further business with you," said Morry, taking a step towards Raven.

"Then state your business, and we can be on our way," said Raven.

"I want you to tell me where you got the Gypsy token from?" Said Morry.

"A Gypsy friend gave it to us," said Shayla, "given with the promise

213

of fair trade with any Gypsy group. We gave more than a fair price for the horse and clothing, and now you plan to attack us?"

"Your woman needs to know her place," said Morry to Raven. "You should take your hand to her more often, speaking out like that when men are doing business."

Shayla's rush of anger at Morry's words flew with her dagger, nicking the top of his ear and ending up embedded in a tree behind him. Morry clapped a hand to his injured ear, and Raven inwardly groaned as he saw the blood trickling through the Gypsy's fingers. All thoughts of ending this confrontation peacefully were destroyed by Shayla's attack.

"I will speak when I chose to," said Shayla to Morry, another dagger already in her hand. "I belong to no man, and no man tells me when I can and cannot speak. Now get out of our way."

Morry stepped towards Shayla, drawing his knife as he did so. The other Gypsies took his lead and rushed forward. One slammed his broad wooden club across the back of Shayla, sending her sprawling on her face at Morry's feet. Daybreak dealt swiftly with Shayla's attacker with one well-placed kick to the head with her hoof. The Gypsy flew across the clearing and lay unconscious in some bushes behind her. Shayla was only stunned momentarily and quickly rolled away from Morry's foot as he aimed a kick at her gut. She swiftly threw her second dagger at him, the low angle of her aim caused it to fall short of the intended target, and it ended up buried deep into his thigh.

The resulting spasm in the assaulted muscle in his thigh created enough pain to cause Morry to drop to the knees groaning. That was the opportunity Daybreak needed as she sent Morry sprawling with a resounding kick to his head. Shayla saw that Morry was no longer a threat and looked over at Raven, dealing with the remaining two Gypsies. Surprisingly Shayla noticed that Raven had not drawn his sword. She retrieved the dagger from Morry's thigh and wiped it hastily on the grass. The blood flow increased as she removed it, but there was no movement from him.

Shayla glanced over at Raven and saw him block an intended blow to his head with one of the Gypsy's clubs. She was about to get to her feet and deal with the second Gypsy when Raven's next actions startled her. It happened so swiftly that Shayla could barely believe her eyes. Raven blocked the blow from the club and grabbed the center of it. He rammed the club's handle into his attacker's face with a swift movement even though the Gypsy still held it. At the same time, he dealt with the first Gypsy, with a resounding sidekick at the second Gypsy's groin. The result of these two swift actions by Raven was terrific. The first Gypsy's face exploded with blood as he fell backward, spraying it everywhere. He lay there moaning as Raven turned to the second Gypsy, who was dry heaving with pain as he rolled around, clutching his groin. Raven grinned over at Shayla, who winked at him in return.

"Take a hand to you more often?" Laughed Raven thinking back to Morry's suggestion that started this. "Not me."

Shayla tore two strips of cloth from Morry's shirt and wrapped his thigh to staunch blood flow from the wound. Raven retrieved Shayla's second dagger from the tree and handed it to her, then headed towards Daybreak, who stood snorting and stomping her feet.

"Thank you, my friend," said Raven, patting her gently on the neck. "You are a good ally to have in battle."

Daybreak snorted in pleasure at Raven's compliment and pushed her wet nose into his face. She just wished he could understand her.

"Well, I will teach him," said Motomo as he ran into the clearing. "I see we arrived too late to help."

Twila stepped into the clearing and looked around at the scene. She recognized Morry instantly and hurried across to where Shayla was still trying to stop the bleeding.

"I can't get it to stop," said Shayla anxiously. "It must have been because of the angle of my throw. I didn't mean to hurt him this badly, but when he spoke of hitting women to keep them in their place, I lost my temper."

Twila frowned at Shayla's words. "He spoke of hitting women?" She asked.

"Well, he suggested to Raven that he should take his hand to me because I spoke without an invite," said Shayla. "I should not have lost my temper, though."

"I was promised to him in marriage until I met Ramos," said Twila. "I wonder if he would have raised his hand to me?"

"Well, he would not have raised it more than once to me," Shayla snarled.

Twila placed her hand over the wound and closed her eyes. The now-familiar warmth flowed down her arm and into her fingertips. Morry's thigh glowed in the golden flow pouring from Twila's fingertips, and he struggled slightly as consciousness returned to him.

The blood stopped flowing from the wound, and to Shayla's amazement, bright red granulation tissue developed before her eyes. Shayla knew it should have been days before Morry's injury showed this evidence of healing, and she looked at Twila, who still had her eyes closed in concentration. When Shayla returned her attention to Morry's wound, it was just a bright pink scar betraying recent healing. Twila removed her hand and sighed deeply as the golden glow around Morry's healed wound dissipated. Morry suddenly woke up and scrambled backward away from the two women. As he got to his feet, Morry suddenly recognized Twila.

"Twila?" Morry said. "Is that you?"

Twila nodded, "yes, Morry, it is." She said.

"So, I was right then," Morry said, looking over at Raven. "You are the one that raped my woman and took her for your own."

Raven looked up, surprised at Morry's accusation. He had dragged the three other injured Gypsies together and stood over them to prevent their escape.

"I hope you are ready to take those words back," said Raven. "Just before I slice you in two."

"Stop this," said Twila. "Raven is helping me. He is not the cause of all this."

Morry turned back to Twila. This time he studied her closely. Her paleness almost glowed in the dim light from their lanterns. Twila's eyes were golden instead of the unusual blue that Morry remembered.

"What happened to you?" Asked Morry stepping backward away from her. "What have you become?"

"That no longer matters," said Twila sadly. "What does matter is we find the one responsible and destroy him. Raven and Shayla are helping me."

"Your father's group sent word of your banishment because a man raped you," said Morry. "They say that your father appears now to have forgotten he ever had a child. Your mother grows old before their eyes."

Tears trickled down Twila's face as Morry spoke of her parents. "They would not speak of me," she said. "I am banished."

"Amani made them forget they ever had you," whispered Motomo into Twila's mind. "He told me he did it because they were so sad when you left."

"I didn't know," Twila said to Motomo mentally. "I didn't

know." She repeated sadly.

"Then I was wrong about you," said Morry to Raven. "And I apologize, but when you turned up with Twila's personal token at the camp, I thought you must have been the one to cause her banishment. I sought only to avenge her."

Shayla had wandered over to Raven because Twila's tears made her uncomfortable. She checked the other Gypsies and found them to be more embarrassed than hurt. They sat nervously, looking first at Motomo and then Raven. Not one of them would have dared an attempt to escape.

Suddenly the bushes to Ravens right parted as Sara and Rudy ran into the clearing. Raven groaned inwardly again. He never had to deal with complications such as these before. If it was not an unpredictable woman, the children and the horses did just as they pleased. Life was much less complicated as a mercenary because you had enemies and allies, both of which behaved as expected.

"What are you doing here?" Said Raven to Sara and Rudy swiftly. "Don't you realize just how dangerous it is out here on your own?" Raven tried to be stern, but it convinced no one.

"Twila said Gypsies ambushed you, and we just had to come and help," Rudy said breathlessly. "Did you kill anyone?"

Shayla rushed forward and took the children's hands, pulling them behind Raven and Daybreak.

"Is that the new horse?" Asked Rudy excitedly. "What's its name?"

"Hush," whispered Sara urgently. "We're in enough trouble as it is."

"My name is Daybreak," said Daybreak, pushing her nose into Rudy's face. "What is yours?"

"I'm called Rudy," answered Rudy, surprised. "You can talk?"

"Yes, I can talk," answered Daybreak. "Unfortunately, not everyone can understand me."

"I can understand you," said Rudy patting Daybreak's nose. "Sara, the horse talks," he whispered, turning to Sara."

"Will you hush?" Said Sara. "They'll think you are mad. Horses can't talk."

Rudy grew silent as he patted Daybreak's nose gently.

"Not everyone can understand me," said Daybreak gently. "Speak to me with your mind and not your mouth."

Rudy's eyes grew wide, and he quickly looked at Sara, who was watching Twila and Morry. He almost giggled but thankfully stopped himself. "Sara can't understand you, can she?" Said Rudy, mentally.

"No, she can't," replied Daybreak.

Rudy almost squealed with glee when he realized Daybreak had heard him.

"You can hear me?" He asked mentally.

"Yes," answered Daybreak. "But we will keep it our secret. Not everyone will believe you."

Rudy grinned and nodded, patting Daybreak on the nose. "Yes, our secret," he agreed.

Morry looked over at the children when he heard their voices. "Who do the children belong to?" He asked Twila.

Twila explained about the children as the two of them walked back towards where Raven and Shayla stood. Raven nodded at the other three Gypsies to indicate they could get to their feet. They needed no further encouragement and were on their feet instantly. Raven kept his eyes on them while Shayla pushed the children to the rear of them both, in case of further trouble. Curiously Morry made his way to Rudy and gently grabbed the boy beneath the chin forcing his face upwards to view his face better in the light.

"This boy has Gypsy in him," he said to Twila, who was observing him.

"Get your hands off the boy," demanded Raven dangerously.

Twila placed her hand reassuringly on Raven's arm. "We don't know anything about the children," she said to Morry. "They came to Shayla and begged her to help them escape from the inn where she was staying. They had been sold to the innkeeper, probably by their parents."

Morry looked at Sara and then back to Rudy. "Look at the color of his skin. It is dark, like a Gypsy. Do you remember your mother, boy?"

Rudy shook his head slowly. "I don't remember my father, either," he said tearfully. "I wanted Raven to be my father and teach me to fight like him. But I don't think he wants to be my father," he added sadly.

"Your father needs a son," Morry said to Twila, "and your mother needs a child to love. That is what the word is from your father's group. Would you like that boy to live with Twila's parents?" He asked Rudy.

Rudy smiled broadly. "Yes," he nodded eagerly. "And when I am older, Raven can teach me how to fight. Isn't that right?" Rudy said to Raven.

"Wait," said Twila. "How can I just hand the boy over like that? No one would accept him as a leader if anything happened to my father. My parents may not accept the boy at all."

"Your father is highly respected," said Morry. "If he took the boy as his own, no one would question his inheritance. You don't think he would be the first leader that took another child on as his own. Talk has it that another in your group offered their son to him when you disappeared. Your father refused because he knew the pain it would cause the boy's mother. This boy has no mother. You would be doing him a favor."

"You could suggest to them that he is their son," whispered Motomo into Twila's mind. "You received the power of Radon, and surely you have much the same power as Amani has with that skill now."

"Is this what you want?" Twila asked Rudy. "To live as the son of a Gypsy leader and one day inherit that leadership?"

Rudy looked around at Sara and Raven. "Can Sara and Raven come too?" He asked.

"No," answered Twila. "But you will no doubt see them again one day."

Sara's eyes filled with tears, but she nodded encouragingly at Rudy. "This journey is supposed to be only mine, Rudy, but I couldn't leave you with Ma Sadie. I just had to bring you with me. Just think of me now and then."

Raven couldn't trust himself to speak, and he just patted Rudy's shoulder reassuringly. He nodded in agreement when the boy asked that Raven teach him fighting skills when he was older.

"Then it is settled then," said Twila. "Where is my group now?" She asked Morry.

"Two days north from here," Morry said. "They are traveling south now for the summer gathering."

Twila nodded, painfully realizing that she would have soon been married.

"I ask then that none of you ever speak of this meeting or the boy's origin," she said to Morry and the other Gypsies.

"I swear no one will speak of this again," answered Morry. "That goes for all of us."

The three other Gypsies mumbled their agreement to this pact, swearing to pledge their silence about the boy and Twila.

"Then I will take the boy to my father," said Twila. "And he shall be with him before the summer gathering. I just ask one more thing before we go our separate ways."

"Then, ask it," said Morry. "I owe you that much."

"Don't ever raise a hand to your new wife," said Twila firmly. "Or we may meet again sooner than planned.

"I wish you success," said Morry, nodding to Raven. "If I can help destroy the one who took my betrothed from me, find my group. Anything we have to offer is yours."

Twila watched Morry and the other Gypsies leave the clearing before turning to Rudy.

"My parents will treat you well," said Twila. "But you must never speak of me or the others here. No one would understand or even believe you. Now, are you sure this is what you want?"

"Yes," said Rudy. "And Daybreak thinks so too."

Twila smiled. "Well, let's get back to our caravan, and when Motomo has found where your new family's camp is, I will make plans to take you there."

Motomo instantly ran into the bushes heading north in search of Twila's group. Raven lifted Sara and Rudy onto the back of Daybreak to make the journey back to camp swifter.

"So, you can understand Daybreak, too, can you, Rudy?" Raven asked.

"Yes," answered Rudy.

"Then, before you leave us," said Raven smiling. "You had better teach me how to understand her too."

"Just listen to her," said Rudy. "That is what I do. I just listen to her."

Raven grinned as he took Daybreak's rein and led her gently forward. "I think it will take more than that," he said with a smile.

CHAPTER SEVENTEEN

An Ally

By the time he finally reached the bottom of the steps that led to the mountain's core, Devon's body ached from pressing himself so closely against the wall. He slipped through yet another arched entrance and found himself in a cavern that was perhaps half the size of the first one. What was different about this cavern, though, was the massive fire in the center. There were no flames from the fire, just a deep red glow from the fossilized wood used for fuel. Rocks had been positioned around the fire pit to contain it. A single whisper of smoke from the red-hot coals trailed its way up to the roof of the cavern.

Devon's eyes followed the smoke's lazy journey upward until it reached the top of the cavern. He noticed that the smoke gathered there for a few moments, before making its way across the roof and then finally it disappeared through a jagged gash in the rock wall. Devon assumed the smoke would eventually find its way to the surface. He judged this had to be a frequently used fireplace and natural chimney from the amount of ash around the fire pit, and the black soot smears on the cavern roof above him.

Around the fire pit, there stood roughly made benches and large wooden tables. The tables, piled high with large books that appeared to be bound in leather, and in some cases, an actual animal skin with the fur still attached. Amongst the books, various wooden bowls, jars crafted from clay, urns, and dark glass bottles also sat on the tables. Some had what looked to be a large wooden spoon handle resting on the rim. Many of them had carvings that possibly were magical in nature.

He looked around the edge of the almost circular cavern. He could make out five openings, including the one in which he entered. He headed for the closest one to him on his right and found himself in a horrid smelling cave that led nowhere. There were plants and roots carefully tied at their bases, hanging from hooks driven into the cave walls. Row upon row of bottles and jars lined the natural shelves of rock jutting out from the cave's floor and walls. A stone slab fashioned into a table from what had once been the beginning of a majestic stalagmite. On the table were more wooden mixing bowls and a lantern, the light from which showed the many dark stains ingrained into the surface. Although the lantern cast more than an adequate pool of light on the table, the rest of the cave was in shadows.

Devon hesitated a moment, searching the shadows for signs of any movement. Then he headed for one of the storage shelves and carefully peeled back the cover on the closest jar. It was half-filled with a thick dark liquid. Devon sniffed at it and was instantly sorry that he had. An overpowering smell of rotting meat assaulted his nose, making his eyes and throat burn. He closed the cover quickly, gasping for fresher air.

He left the storage room, satisfied that there was nothing of use to him there, and headed for the next opening. As he reached the threshold of the entrance, he heard a noise from within. Devon pressed himself against the wall and listened carefully; he detected sounds of movements inside. The sounds grew more distant until Devon could no longer hear anything. Quickly he slipped into the cave and stood motionless amongst the shadows by the entrance. As his eyes adjusted to the gloom, Devon realized that this was, in fact, another passage. He was about to move when he heard something approaching in his direction from further down the passageway. Devon stood rigid as the sounds grew closer until finally, a figure appeared in front of him from out of the gloom. As the figure stepped into the dim light from the one flickering torch, he saw a woman.

The woman walked in a strange shuffling way, dragging one leg behind her. Her long, straw-colored hair was wildly tangled, and a ragged ribbon was precariously dangling, clinging on to the last few strands that prevented it dropping, forgotten, into the dust. The rags of what appeared to have been a well-made traveling dress hung from her strangely drooped shoulders. The woman held her arms stiffly by her side as she walked. She stopped and appeared to be listening for something. Her head cocked on one side. Suddenly she turned, and for a moment, her strangely glazed eyes seemed to stare directly at Devon. He held his breath, studying the woman's face. It was a pretty face but smeared with dust, and Devon could see a greenish pallor beneath the grime. She slowly started moving again, shuffling towards him. Devon, convinced now that the woman had sensed him, waited to see what would happen next. Surprisingly she turned back towards the exit, shuffled past him, and left the passage.

Devon, relieved that she had not discovered him, took a deep breath in and immediately smelt the stench of decay that the woman had left behind her. However, before he could move, she returned, carrying a large jar and shuffled her way back down the passage. Devon started to follow her when a voice close to his ear stopped him.

"A tragic creature, don't you agree?" Whispered a male voice into his ear.

He spun around quickly and found himself face to face with the shadow figure he had seen earlier.

"Alive but not alive. Dead, but not dead," said the shadow. "But forgive me, I have not introduced myself. I am Rowan, and it appears we are on a similar quest."

Devon was not familiar with that name, and although his features were not distinguishable in his shadow form, he felt sure he must be a Lunarian. He had not heard of or encountered any other race able to become one with the shadows.

"Are you a Lunarian?" Devon asked.

"What else could I be?" Replied Rowan. "Are you going to give me the same courtesy that I gave you and tell me your name?"

"I am Devon," he replied. "I am of the Tolarist clan. My father is Elan."

"Elan is a legend amongst the Lunarians," said Rowan, impressed. "He fought bravely in the battle of Silverna. I feel honored to meet his lost son."

"Was Silverna lost?" Asked Devon slowly.

"No, Silverna is one of the last cities that the Lunarians still hold," replied Rowan. "Thanks to the unselfish sacrifice that your father made."

"My father is dead?" Asked Devon slowly.

"No, not physically dead," replied Rowan. "But your mother's death destroyed his spirit, and they say that the only thing keeping him alive is the belief that you will return to his fireside."

Rowan's revelation about his mother's death crashed into Devon's senses like a bolt of lightning. The red-hot pain of loss coursed through his body, changing into anger as it pumped its way from his heart into his veins.

"The history tomes speak of you, Devon," continued Rowan. "As the first Lunarian to fight back against the dark invaders. Many felt you must be dead. It honors me to meet such a hero."

"Well, you seem to know everything about me," said Devon coldly, wishing he could ask more about his mother's death but deciding against it. "However, I do not recognize your name."

"Forgive me," said Rowan. "I belong to the Foleema clan. My father was Jute, and my mother is Eleesta."

"I know of Eleesta," Devon said thoughtfully. "She was but a child when I last saw her."

"You have been gone for many years," said Rowan. "I know of you only because of the tomes."

Devon thought for a moment before speaking. "I have much to ask you, but this is not the place," he said. "The woman may return at any moment. Let us go back to the huge cavern above this one and see how we can help each other in all this."

Devon led the way back to the stairs leading to the cavern above. He was deep in thought as Rowan followed closely behind him.

Twila stood waiting while Rudy said goodbye to the rest of the group. His eyes were bright with unshed tears by the time he got to Raven, who had kneeled before the boy, so they were on the same level.

"This is for you," said Raven fighting with an unusual choking sensation in his throat that was affecting his speech. "It belonged to a man who was like a father to me. Twila tells me that her father can teach you to play it."

Rudy clutched the top of the sack that held Haney's fiddle. Tears were spilling out beneath his dark lashes now, and he sniffed as Raven's gentle thumbs brushed them away before grabbing the boy and hugging him tightly.

"I wanted you to teach me how to become a fighter," said Rudy.

"Here, this for you too," said Raven, handing him a flat

wooden sword. "This was my first weapon. Start with this, and then when you are older, I will come to see how you are doing."

"Really?" Asked Rudy, a broad grin pushing away the tears. "And you will help me become a warrior like you?"

"I will find you," promised Raven. "And if you still want to be a warrior, then I will teach you."

"When will you come?" Asked Rudy. "You won't forget, will you?" He added anxiously.

Raven ruffled the boy's dark hair. "I will come when the time is right," he said. "I promise. His death only breaks a warrior's word."

Rudy nodded solemnly and hugged Raven once more before running to Twila. She lifted him on to her back after securing the sack and sword to her waist and told him to hang on tightly.

"I will be running swiftly," said Twila. "Don't be afraid. It will be fun."

Rudy nodded as he wrapped his legs around Twila's waist and laced his fingers around her neck.

"I'm ready," giggled Rudy. "Bye, everyone, until we meet again."

"I think you may have chosen the next keeper of the key already," said Daybreak into Raven's mind.

Raven whipped around to see who had spoken. Shayla was comforting Sara, and Motomo had left with Twila.

"You heard me," Daybreak said excitedly. "The love for the boy broke down the barrier."

Raven found the high-pitched whisper in his mind disturbing, especially as the voice knew of his half-formed plans for Rudy. He looked over at Daybreak, who was watching him intently.

"Yes, it is I," said Daybreak, snorting suddenly and pawing the ground before her. "Your stubborn warrior mind had better get used to it. We have much to accomplish together."

Raven shook his head, grinning in disbelief. "I really need a drink," he thought.

Devon followed Rowan into a small empty cave that led off the upper cavern.

"I use this place when the sun goes down," said Rowan. "Ramos stays in the lower levels during the day."

"How did you cross into this world?" Asked Devon, sitting down in the corner of the cave. "Is the way still open?"

"I crossed the seal undetected when the dark one Stefan crossed," said Rowan. "Before I could cross back, Ramos had replaced the seal. So, now I am trapped as you are."

Devon nodded. Twila had spoken of the seal briefly failing before Ramos had the chance to replace it.

"So why did you cross into this world?" Devon asked.

"I came to find a way for our people to be free of the Dark Ones, just as the tomes say you did," said Rowan. "When I realized I could not leave this world, I followed Ramos here to see if I could find a way to cross back."

"Then, you have observed Ramos closely during your time here?" Said Devon.

"Every chance I get," said Rowan. "Ramos feels secure in this place, and so far, he has not sensed me."

"Then, you can save me some time," said Devon. "I came here to study Ramos for his weaknesses. You seem to have been doing that already."

Rowan nodded. "Ramos grows more dangerous each day. Maybe we can stop him," said Rowan. "It would be an honor to join you in the fight against him."

Devon and Rowan spoke together for the rest of the night. Rowan told Devon that Ramos was preparing for something, but he had not discovered what it was yet. Devon was not sure why but decided not to tell Rowan everything. He spoke of Twila and Raven but did not mention Amani and Radon. When Devon talked about the key, Rowan leaned forward, listening with great interest.

"Ramos spoke of a key," said Rowan. "I think he plans to release Valeskas by using this key, is this possible? Where is it now?"

"I know of the key's existence only, not what its purpose is. The key was lost when I created another opening in the cave where the last keeper hid it," said Devon.

"Then, it is still retrievable?" Rowan asked, hopefully.

"I don't know," said Devon.

He was beginning to think that Rowan showed an unusual interest in the key, and he grew more cautious.

"Well, Ramos must be expecting a fight because he has been preparing many spells since I followed him here," said Rowan.

"What kind of spells?" Asked Devon.

"I don't know," said Rowan. "All I do know is that he invokes that monster Valeskas now when he is creating one, and he is the one guiding Ramos on how to make it."

"How can Valeskas's body be trapped in Lunaria, and yet he speaks in this world?" Asked Devon.

"I don't know," said Rowan. "I wish I knew. Ramos has only recently discovered how to invoke him here."

"What manner of thing was that woman we saw earlier?" Asked Devon.

"Ramos thinks of himself as a necromancer," said Rowan. "I think she was one of his first attempts at raising the dead to serve him. He brought her from another world. She was a follower of Saressa that Ramos tracked down and arranged to have killed. Then he raised her from death and brought her here, thinking that the woman's connection with Saressa could help him release Valeskas. "Unfortunately, Ramos was inexperienced then, and the woman was not dead long enough. She ended up being a half-dead and half-alive creature that serves Ramos only because he drugs her wine and casts control spells on her. When I first arrived, I planned to release her, but that would have alerted Ramos to my presence."

"You have learned a lot by just observing Ramos so far," said Devon, trying to keep the suspicion out of his voice.

"It wasn't hard," said Rowan. "Ramos and Valeskas speak to each other orally. I don't believe they can mentally communicate because Valeskas's body is not in this place. The girl speaks too when the drug or spell begins to wear off. I almost let her see me when I first arrived but decided against it."

"I don't understand how Ramos managed to cross into another world besides ours," said Devon. "Ramos was forced to close the gateway to our world with a seal because he couldn't close it any other way. Where is the gateway to the woman's world?"

"That is not clear either," said Rowan. "Since I have been here, the only things I have learned is what has been openly discussed by Ramos or from the ramblings of the woman. There was talk of a crystal on one occasion, and I know it has some connection with the woman. Ramos threatened to destroy the woman once when the spells and drugs were wearing off. I remember she told him that if he destroyed her, then the crystal would be useless. I have not seen this crystal, so I have not discovered what that conversation meant."

"I need to take information back to the others on the best

strategies to use against Ramos," said Devon.

"Then, I hope they are magic users," said Rowan. "That is the only way to defeat him. Ramos gathers and raises more of the dead that he plans to use to protect him if someone comes to attack him. He raises them with dark magic so that light magic will be the most effective against them. From his conversations with Valeskas, I have learned that he expects someone to come here to attempt to defeat him very soon."

"Where are his dead slaves now?" Asked Devon. "I have seen no one on my way down here."

"Ramos began searching for graves to provide for his dead army when he returned to this cavern a few days ago." Said Rowan. "He leaves each night at sunset and returns before dawn, with a sack of bones. The woman glues the bones together with some dreadful smelling paste while he is gone. There are at least ten now," said Rowan.

"The odd thing is Ramos hasn't raised any yet. I know he has prepared a potion to cast the spell, though, because he spoke of it with Valeskas, but it was not clear when he plans to do it. The woman has them all laid out in a row around the bottom cavern. Ramos seems to search out the bones of dead warriors specifically because also he brings all of their broken or rusty weapons and armor buried with them."

"How can these dead slaves be destroyed?" Asked Devon thoughtfully.

"What I hear from the woman's constant ramblings," said Rowan. "If you remove the head from the bodies, it destroys their unnatural life force. She talks to the bones as she glues them together. If the pieces don't match up or won't stay in place, she threatens to remove their heads."

A noise from the large cavern caused Rowan to hold his hand up to Devon in a warning gesture. The two of them slid to the entrance of the cave. They remained motionless as they peered amongst the stalagmites and stalactites for the source of the noise. A cloaked figure came into view dragging a large misshapen sack behind him. Irritably he pushed back the hood of his cloak as the load became caught between rocks. Devon recognized Ramos instantly. There had been no visible change in his appearance since Devon had first seen him all those years ago when he had first crossed into this world.

Ramos muttered angrily to himself as he tugged at the

sack to release it. Once loose, he grabbed the bag and slung it over his shoulder, bending slightly to even up the load. A large cloud of dust spewed from the sack, hanging in the air momentarily, before disappearing in the gloom of the cavern. Ramos headed towards the center and then vanished amongst the stalagmites' circle that hid the lower levels' entrance.

When they were sure that Ramos was far below them, Devon and Rowan relaxed and continued to speak quietly together.

"Dawn must be approaching," said Rowan. "He always returns just before dawn."

"It looks like he is still building his army then," said Devon. "An army of the dead."

Devon and Rowan felt their powers begin to drain, and despite the fact they could not see the sunrise, both of them knew that it was morning.

"Tonight, when the sun goes down," said Devon, melding into the shadows of the cave. "I want to see this army Ramos has made for myself."

"And so, you shall," said Rowan.

Twila stood just outside her father's camp, holding Rudy tightly by the hand. Motomo had led them most of the way here but stopped before the dogs caught his scent.

"I will make it so that my parents believe that you are their child," whispered Twila. "The rest of the Gypsies will know that you are a stranger but will treat you as my father's son. Only you will know the truth Rudy, so tell no one."

Rudy nodded his eyes wide with apprehension. "It will be our secret," he said. "And I can keep secrets. Just ask Sara."

Twila smiled at him. "Are you ready, then?" She asked.

He nodded eagerly, clutching the wooden sword and sack in one hand, and gripping Twila's tightly in the other.

Twila concentrated on the dogs that lay by the dying embers of the fire. She crept into their minds and placed the suggestion to ignore her but recognize Rudy as a friend. Twila stepped into the clearing of the campsite, and the dog's heads lifted and seeing Rudy, they lazily trotted up to him. Rudy grinned up at Twila, and she released his hand so he could pet the dogs. They sniffed and licked his hand and face in welcome before returning to their spots by the fire.

Twila led Rudy to the caravan steps and concentrated as she crept her way into her father's mind. The sadness she sensed there clutched her heart, and for a moment, Twila fought with her tears. Rudy slipped his hand in hers as if he felt her pain.

She pushed the suggestion that Rudy was his son into her father's memories and was glad when she sensed his sorrow dissipate. Her father's mind grew calm, and plans for his son developed like a dream as Twila felt the last drop of misery evaporate.

Twila then concentrated on her mother and felt the same sorrow and despair. She took a deep breath and placed the false memory of Rudy into her mother's mind. The effect was just as pleasing to her as Twila felt the depressed and hopeless sensations that filled her mother's mind vanish in an instant. She lingered for a few moments before leaving her mother's mind. There was something else troubling her mother that was still on her mind. Twila knew her mother was very concerned about something, but she was unable to define it.

"Come," Twila whispered to Rudy. "It is done. Be very quiet, and you can get in what was once my bed. There is very little time before dawn, so if you close your eyes and fall asleep when you open them again, you will begin your new life."

Rudy nodded and suddenly hugged Twila clumsily. "I will be a good son and look after your mother for you," he said. "I know your mother is sick in here," he said, pointing to his heart. "I felt it when you went in her mind. Can you not heal her like you healed Sara's foot?"

"You can enter people's minds and sense things?" Asked Twila, astonished. "I didn't feel you."

"I am gentle," said Rudy. "Gentle like the touch of a butterfly wing. I thought everyone could do it, but Sara said it was strange, and I shouldn't tell anyone about it."

"You have the Gypsy gift of intuition," said Twila. "Morry was right. You do have Gypsy in you. Can you see what is wrong with my mother's heart?"

"The blood gets stuck," said Rudy, frowning deeply. "It causes her pain. I don't know the word for it, but the medicine she brews doesn't help it for long."

"Then let us go inside, and I will see what I can do," said Twila.

"Can I tell my new mother of my gift?" Asked Rudy.

"Yes," said Twila smiling. "and she will understand it. Your new mother also has the gift."

Rudy grinned broadly and followed quietly behind Twila as they entered the caravan. Twila painfully noted that they had removed all evidence of her life there. Her old bed was still neatly made, and she pulled back the blanket, and Rudy scrambled underneath it. He closely observed as Twila showed him the storage area to store his sword and sack that Rudy had clutched so tightly. Twila kissed him on the forehead as she pulled the blanket up to his chin.

"Heal my mother before you leave, won't you?" Rudy mouthed silently.

Twila nodded and crept to her mother's bed. She was shocked by Netta's appearance. Her hair was much grayer than she remembered, and her face betrayed the constant pain that her heart was now causing. Netta's breathing was shallow, and there was a bluish tinge to her lips that Twila had never seen before. She knelt by the side of her mother's bed and concentrated. Carefully Twila positioned her hand over Netta's chest. The now-familiar burning sensation rushed to her fingertips, and a golden glow enveloped Netta's chest. Twila sensed the irregular heartbeat that pulsed back into her fingertips. She concentrated harder, and it felt as if her fingers were rushing through the blood vessels of her mother's body, heading towards the heart. Twila felt the fatty plaques' resistance reducing the blood flow to her mother's heart muscle and causing the pain. The burning sensation in her fingers increased as the fatty plaques melted away, allowing the blood to flow without restriction. Twila instantly felt the change in her mother's heartbeat. It faltered for a moment, and then the rhythm gradually became normal.

She removed her hand and sat for a moment, looking at the face of Netta. She saw the color returning to Netta's pale cheeks, the blue-tinged lips becoming pink before her eyes. Twila looked over at Rudy, who was sitting up in his bed watching her closely. Rudy grinned at her when he sensed what Twila had accomplished.

"You healed her," Rudy mouthed silently. "I can sense it."

"I know," Twila mouthed silently back to him. "Now, I can leave."

Rudy nodded and settled back down in his new bed. Twila blew him a kiss, and he blew one in return. She carefully crept out of the caravan and headed back into the woods to meet Motomo.

Motomo waited anxiously, watching the gray light of dawn creeping through the trees' leaves and branches. Twila was suddenly beside him, and he jumped up, relieved. Instantly he noticed that she appeared even paler than usual.

"Did it go well?" Asked Motomo, running hard to keep up with her as she ran through the woods.

"Yes," she answered. "We must hurry and catch up to the others, dawn approaches."

Motomo heard the strain in Twila's voice and realized that seeing her parents again must have been painful. He followed closely behind her and asked her no more questions.

Raven had found that Daybreak was a much more willing horse. The only problem was that although she did what he asked, Daybreak complained about it. Trying to harness her to the caravan went smoothly enough. Daybreak even instructed him on what strap went where. Once Raven had the van back on the road, Daybreak had begun to speak to him. Not only did she speak to him, but Daybreak also complained about everything.

"I don't mind pulling this caravan," said Daybreak. "But I just want to point out that I am much more intelligent than the other two horses."

He grinned and sympathized with Daybreak. "We are all making sacrifices to destroy Ramos," he said.

Shayla and Sara giggled together like children at Raven's responses to Daybreak. Neither of them could hear what the horse was saying, but Raven's patient responses and expressions were amusing. He hadn't yet learned that he could just think his words to Daybreak, so he spoke them aloud. But they were both enjoying the one-sided conversation too much to tell Raven that yet.

"They are foolish animals you have with you," continued Daybreak. "I have tried to engage them in conversation and explain to them that I feel they are much more suited to pulling this caravan than I am. But they don't hear me."

"Well, the old black horse would probably drop dead in its tracks," Raven patiently pointed out, "If it tried to pull this caravan. I think you are doing a wonderful job. Look how fast we are going."

"I hope you are not suggesting that I am perfect for such menial tasks," said Daybreak. "That strap is rubbing into my shoulder too. I hope you are planning on wrapping something around it before it tears my flesh."

"I would not dream of suggesting you are nothing but a workhorse," said Raven. "I will see to it personally to pad the offending strap at first light."

Shayla and Sara had laughed themselves into exhaustion.

"Come," said Shayla to Sara. "We must sleep before Raven destroys us with laughter.

Sara giggled again and gave Raven a quick hug. "Thank you, Raven, for cheering me up."

Raven was surprised by all the laughter and even more surprised by Sara's last statement. He just wanted to keep Daybreak pulling the caravan in the right direction until Shayla took over.

Raven noticed that the night sky was turning gray as dawn approached, and concern that Twila and Motomo had still not returned washed over him. He pushed the lingering thoughts of Rudy out of his mind because the warrior in Raven knew that he could not allow anything to cloud his concentration and judgment now that a battle was imminent.

He absentmindedly listened to Daybreak now because, despite all her complaints, she was pulling the caravan quickly. As the sky grew lighter, Daybreak stopped complaining for a moment to comment on how Twila should be returning soon. Raven soothed Daybreak's concerns by assuring her that Twila would return in time.

"Oh." Blurted Daybreak. "Here is that wolf again."

Raven grinned as Motomo leaped beside him on the caravan. Twila was moments behind him.

"Just in time," said Raven. "You cut it close."

Twila laughed. "Yes, Motomo has been worrying about me too. I see that you are making perfect time, Raven. We should reach the tavern this evening, and once Sara is safe, we can head for the seal."

"Thank Daybreak," said Raven grinning. "She is pulling the caravan swiftly without a thought for her comfort."

"Well, in that case," said Twila. "Thank you, Daybreak."

Motomo was confused. Daybreak was now complaining about the added weight and how the uneven road caused unnecessary wear on her new shoes.

"But," began Motomo, before he was stopped by Raven's hand on his head.

"I'll explain it all later," said Raven grinning at Motomo's confused look.

"I must go and rest now," said Twila. "Tomorrow night, we should reach the seal and then wait for Devon's return."

Twila went back into the sleeping portion of her caravan. She was careful not to disturb the sleeping forms of Shayla and Sara. As Twila lay down in her bed, and the sunrise drained her powers, her unshed tears began to flow. By the time she fell asleep, Twila's hatred of Ramos had developed into a screaming rage. The sleeping faces of her father and mother followed Twila into her dreams. Only there now could she return to the life that Ramos had taken from her.

CHAPTER EIGHTEEN

The Cave of Light

Devon's strength returned as he saw Ramos heading towards the upper caverns, presumably on another search for more recruits for his macabre army. He and Rowan waited until they were both sure that Ramos left the caves before making their way to the lower levels. Rowan led the way back to the passage where Devon had first seen the woman. They both hesitated briefly, listening carefully. Rowan was satisfied that nothing lay ahead in the passageway and beckoned silently for Devon to follow him.

The passage was unexpectedly shorter than it had looked to Devon, perhaps because the height of it gradually reduced, giving a false impression of length. Rowan stopped when they drew close to the end of the passage. He pressed himself close to the wall and slipped around the entrance of yet another large cavern. Devon followed him and found himself inside the lowest level of the mountain. Torches that were positioned high on the walls brightly lit the area. There were no stalactites or stalagmites in this area as there were in the cavern above, so although they could see if anyone entered it, they had no shadows to hide amongst if they did.

There were only three exits from this cavern, and one of those led to the passage by which they had just entered. Rowan pointed to the opening to their left.

"That is where the Woman sleeps," whispered Rowan. "The opening directly ahead leads to Ramos's cave."

Rowan led the way to where the woman slept and carefully peered around the corner.

"She isn't here," whispered Rowan. "She must be in Ramos's cave, putting together what he brought back this morning."

Devon looked into the woman's cave. It was barely more than a natural recess of the main cavern. There was a shelf of rock on the right of the entrance, roughly fashioned into a bed. It had what looked to be a straw-stuffed mattress, with a sleeping rug neatly folded at the bottom. In the center of the cave was a small glowing fire. The fuel was of the same fossilized wood that he had seen burning in the first cavern. On the left side of the cave was a roughly made wooden table with the remnants of some kind of stew in a misshapen wooden bowl. There was a clay pitcher beside the bowl and an overturned mug. The liquid had spilled from the cup, and a dark stain spread across the table. The wine had flowed across the table until it reached the edge and now quietly dripped onto the floor into a small developing puddle.

"It's the drugged wine," said Rowan noticing Devon's interest. "If Ramos doesn't watch her, then she doesn't drink it."

The only other thing in the small cave was another shelf of rock that, from its position near to the table, it served as a bench. Devon also saw a shackle attached to a long chain, the end of which was a stake, driven into the rock.

"Ramos chains the woman when he leaves for longer periods," said Rowan in response to Devon's puzzled look. "I told you the woman was his first attempt at raising someone from death. The woman is not completely under his control."

Devon followed Rowan to the opening that led to Ramos's cave. He was puzzled by the half-eaten meal on the table.

"I thought you said the woman was dead?" Devon said. "Why would a dead person need food?"

"I didn't say she was dead exactly," said Rowan. "And I didn't say she was alive. Whatever it is that Ramos turned her into, the creature needs to eat and drink. That is why Ramos knows she will eventually drink the drugged wine. She has nothing else to quench her thirst."

Devon's dislike of Ramos grew as he realized that the woman was little more than a prisoner in these lower levels.

"You'd think he'd just put her out of her misery," muttered Devon.

"I think he needs her for something," said Rowan. "I just haven't discovered what it is yet."

Rowan slipped quickly into Ramos's cave and pressed himself to the wall. Devon followed and found himself finally at the core of the mountain and was surprised at the massive cave structure. There were natural shelves of rock around the walls, all the way up to the curved roof. Many more jars and pots filled the racks. A large slab of rock that looked like a table dominated the northern portion of the cave. The table seemed to be where Ramos created his spells, and strange symbols decorated the wall above it. A wide strip of linen decorated with more symbols covered the top of it. A carved wooden bowl and knife strategically positioned in the table's center, with a thick half-burned candle placed between them.

Torches on either side of the symbols on the wall behind the table flickered strangely. Devon looked up to see what was affecting their flames. He saw that the roof of the cave above the table was an open shaft. Devon was very curious to see how far up into the mountain the crevice went. He was about to move forward when Devon suddenly noticed the woman sitting on the floor in the middle of the cave.

The woman sat amongst a small pile of bones that were spilling out of a sack. Devon assumed it was the one that Ramos had been carrying earlier. She was grabbing the bones, which in most cases still had pieces of rotting flesh and clothing attached, and was sorting them into three separate piles.

"Three today," the woman sang. "Three more bodies to be stuck up with glue. I am Soleon, and it's such a pleasure to meet you."

Soleon screeched with laughter as she grabbed the hand of a dismembered arm and shook it in mock greeting. Chunks of earth and rotted flesh flew across the cave, causing clouds of sandy dust to rise when the pieces landed on the floor. She threw the arm onto one of the small piles of bones, laughing insanely.

Rowan slipped along the wall until he drew level with Soleon, and Devon swiftly followed. Rowan pointed to the floor in front of Soleon, and Devon saw the two neat rows of bodies. There were ten of them just as Rowan had said. They lay close together, each dressed in a long shift of sacking material. They had leather breastplate armor, and each one had a weapon in one hand and a wooden shield in the other. The dead soldiers lay on their backs, legs together, and arms by their sides. Some of the soldiers had varying amounts of flesh and hair still attached to their bodies. The rest of them were nothing but yellowed bones, their grinning skull heads covered with leather hoods. Swords seemed to be the most dominant weapon. Six of the soldiers had them in their hands. Three of them had wooden clubs, and one of the bodies held a medium-sized spear. The air in the cave was sickeningly stale and mixed with the smell of decay. It was making it difficult for Devon to concentrate on anything else.

Devon followed Rowan carefully until the two of them reached the far end of the cave. They stood beneath the open shaft, and Devon peered up into total darkness. He knew it was impossible to see where the aperture ended without climbing up into it. In his shadow body, that would be an easy task.

"Have you searched up there?" Devon mouthed silently to Rowan.

Rowan shook his head.

Devon looked over at Soleon. She was mumbling to herself as the three piles of body parts and bones grew larger around her. He turned his back on her and pressed himself against the wall. Devon then climbed up the wall to the roof of the cave. He edged himself into the shaft and began to climb up into the darkness. Instantly Devon became aware of the crisp fresh air blowing down the shaft. He continued to climb blindly, and as the fissure became wider, his fingers discovered a ledge. Devon scrambled over the edge and saw a gray light filtering through from a large hole up ahead. It illuminated the narrow tunnel that he now found himself in, but as Devon could not stand up in the tunnel, he crawled on his hands and knees towards the light. As Devon left the tunnel, he was startled by the bright light that greeted him. Blinking rapidly to encourage his eyes to adjust, he quickly looked around to be sure that he was alone, and he was.

The cavern of light was the most incredible place that Devon had ever seen. The walls sparkled with flashes of white light, and when Devon examined them more closely, he found them composed of a naturally formed crystal rock. He looked around the cavern center and saw that the floor had clumps of the crystal rock set in two uniformed rows, which created a pathway between them. Devon followed the path and found himself at a well-constructed, human-made, bridge of stone that crossed a tranquil lake of blue water. He found the color of the water startling. Devon, accustomed to seeing everything by moonlight, found that the light from the crystals all around him was bright enough to mimic the sun. He started to go over the bridge, but an unseen barrier prevented him. Devon carefully touched the air in front of him and saw a distinct shimmer in the view beyond. A barrier spell was blocking his passage and disappointed, he turned and went back towards the tunnel's entrance.

Devon realized that Rowan had not followed him and suddenly became suspicious. There was something about Rowan that he didn't trust. Devon became aware of a burning sensation on his right leg at the start of his climb back into the tunnel. Alarmed, he carefully touched the place that was burning. Devon felt the heat and was startled to see a red glow piercing the darkness of his shadow leg. Quickly he concentrated and returned to his natural form. The red light grew brighter, and Devon promptly dug into the pocket of his cloak. His fingers burned as they touched Saressa's crystal. Devon pulled it out of his pocket and held it for a moment in his open palm. The heat from the crystal finally forced Devon to place it on the floor in front of him.

The effect of this action was stunning. The red glow from Saressa's crystal flowed across the floor like a large pool of blood. Each clump of crystal on either side of the path to the bridge grew bright with the red glow. Devon watched as Saressa's crystal clattered across the floor of the cave, ending up against the wall. Then the red light from Saressa's crystal began to fade until it returned to its normal appearance. Devon stared at it for a moment and went over to retrieve it. As he bent over to pick up the crystal, a bright flash of light emitted from it, almost blinding him. The pure white light spread up the wall of crystal and pulsed momentarily. Devon shielded his eyes and looked at the portion of the wall that Saressa's crystal was illuminating. The bright light disappeared suddenly, and everything returned to normal. He carefully touched the wall and found no resistance to his touch. Devon pushed a little harder, and his hand disappeared into the crystal wall. Surprised, he pulled his hand back again and stared at what appeared to be solid rock. He noticed that although this portion of the rock initially seemed impenetrable, it shimmered if you looked carefully enough.

Devon picked up Saressa's crystal and put it back in his pocket. He tentatively pushed his hand into the wall, and this time Devon did not pull it back. A strange shudder passed through his body as Devon thrust himself through the crystal door. Devon smiled when he realized that it had brought him to the small cave he had slept during the daylight hours. He turned and looked at the wall, through which he had just walked, only a slight shimmer betrayed the crystal door. Devon walked back through the wall and was once again in the cave of light. The clumps of crystal still glowed red, and Devon once more followed the path to the bridge. He touched the air in front of him and discovered the barrier was gone. Devon crossed the stone bridge to the other side and walked beneath an archway of sparkling crystal. He found himself at the entrance of another tunnel, but this one was high enough to stand and walk normally through.

The light in the tunnel grew dimmer as Devon got farther away from the crystal's light. There were no torches to illuminate this tunnel, and finally, Devon had to feel his way forward by touching the wall on his right side. A rumbling noise in the far distance grew louder as he advanced. Devon began to feel a vibration through the wall under his touch and wondered about turning back. However, curiosity drove him towards the increasing noise, and he saw that the tunnel was growing lighter up ahead.

When Devon reached the end of the tunnel, he found himself on a circular ridge of rock around the edge of a cave floor. He jumped down onto damp sand at the bottom and walked towards a wide opening at the far end of the cave. The crashing waves grew louder as Devon grew closer to it. Ragged fingers of frothy gray seawater ran towards his feet and then quickly pulled back again as the force of the wave receded. Devon stepped out of the cave and found himself on a moonlit sandy beach.

"This is the way Twila and Raven can enter Ramos's mountain without being detected," Devon thought to himself. "It's perfect."

He smiled as he watched the silver-tipped waves rushing towards the beach. The moon was directly above him, and Devon had a clear view of the cliffs that he recognized as the lower portion of Ramos's mountain.

"Ramos is not as secure as he thought." Devon smiled, "thank you, Saressa, for pointing out the way."

Devon reluctantly left the moonlit beach and headed back into the cave. The crystals on either side of the path still glowed red as Devon headed for the crystal door and back into the cave where he had slept. Devon, currently in human form, needed to change back into shadows. He looked around and chose a good collection of them beneath a torch and quickly melded with them. Devon entered Ramos's cave and saw Rowan stood beneath the shaft that he had climbed up. Soleon was still in the middle of the room, mumbling to herself as she worked on one of the three piles of bones and body parts. She was constructing another recruit for Ramos's army. The grinning skull head was in position already. Soleon was carefully placing the torso in position as

Devon slipped along the wall to where Rowan stood.

"Well, here's another shadow spy of Ramos," blurted Soleon. "I only thought there was one, and now there are two."

Devon froze when he heard Soleon's words. He looked over at Rowan, who was slowly shaking his head.

"You're very silent, shadow spy number two," Soleon laughed, "I suppose you have come to see what happened to your friend. Well, he enjoyed my company so much that he decided to stay."

Soleon screeched in laughter as she waved her hand in Devon's direction. A bright yellow bolt of light hit him squarely in the chest, and Devon could not move. His body securely held against the cave wall, and although he tried to break loose, nothing worked.

"Now, you are a prisoner like me." Soleon screeched.

Twila and Motomo watched Shayla, Raven, and Sara leave for the village. Sara was riding on Apple and turned around one last time to wave as they disappeared into the forest. Twila had camped as close to the town as she could without using the same spot her parents always used. There were too many memories of her past life in that place.

"I hope Sara is happy with her new life," Twila said to Motomo.

Motomo agreed as he followed Twila, who was heading towards the seal.

"I have to see if Danior still waits for me at the seal," said Twila. "It seems so long since we left here that I am afraid he will have given up hope."

Twila took a deep breath when she reached the seal. She wanted so badly to hear Danior, and although she concentrated intensely, Twila heard nothing. She turned to Motomo in tears, shaking her head in disbelief.

"I cannot hear him," said Twila. "There is nothing."

"Perhaps you can only hear him when he is close to the gateway," said Motomo. "It may be too dangerous for him to remain there constantly."

"Yes, perhaps you are right," said Twila, hopefully. "I just wish there was at least a small trace of him, so I would know that he was safe."

She gave up and walked away from the seal and sat for some time watching the moonlit water. The silver-tipped ripples danced cheerfully before her, but Twila did not notice their beauty. She was thinking back to the last time she had sat in this place with Danior.

"I will return to the camp Twila," Motomo said quietly, "and let the others know that you will be back later."

He turned and ran back in the direction of the camp. Twila watched him leave without any comment.

Shayla stepped inside the Traveler's Call and looked for the tavern keeper. It only took her a few moments to identify him amongst the crowd. He was laughing loudly with a group of patrons, a large club in his hand. Shayla immediately noticed that this tavern's patrons were utterly different from those in the Black Wolf Inn. Most of them dressed like farmers with rough woven shifts, worn over thick woolen leggings. Their rugged weather-scorched faces bloomed healthily beneath shocks of sun-bleached hair, or in some cases, a wide-brimmed hat of woven reeds. The whole atmosphere of the tavern was cheerful and utterly different. Shayla felt sure that Sara would be safe here.

"I need to speak to your wife, Liffy," said Shayla to Ned when she caught his attention.

Ned looked at the unusually dressed young woman. She was a stranger to him and yet was asking for his wife by name. A sense of foreboding rushed through him. Haney should have been back by now, and both he and Liffy felt convinced something must have happened to him.

"What do you want with my wife?" Asked Ned. "She is busy back there and will not be of even temper if I bring her out on a whim of a young stranger. State your business with her before I decide if it's worth risking a tongue-lashing, or if it can wait until we are closed for the night."

"It cannot wait, sir," said Shayla firmly. "I must see your wife. I have something for her."

Ned saw the sincerity and urgency in the face of Shayla, and he grew more disturbed.

"Wait here," said Ned. "I will bring her to you. "

Ned made his way around the bar and headed for the kitchen. He instructed the server to give the strange girl a drink.

"Maybe she is just looking for a job," Ned thought to himself, unconvincingly. "Then, I will be in trouble for wasting Liffy's time."

Ned entered the kitchen and found his wife rushing around the kitchen, preparing the bread for tomorrow, and serving up dinner orders. Liffy's face was even more flushed than usual, beads of sweat evident on her forehead, wisps of hair escaping from her cap. A rush of affection ran through Ned as he saw how hard his wife was working to keep their business successful. He hoped that the strange girl in the bar was not bringing bad news. Liffy would be heartbroken.

"There is a girl in the bar," said Ned. "Asking for you by name. The girl didn't state her business, but if she is asking for a job, I think we should take her on to help you in the kitchen."

Liffy stopped in her tracks at Ned's last statement. She looked at her husband's face and knew he was concerned about something. Liffy had been asking for help in the kitchen for months. She found it very curious that he should suddenly suggest they hire this stranger to help her.

"What?" Liffy said. "You are finally giving me the help I have been asking for because a strange girl appears in the bar asking for me by name? I suppose she's pretty then?"

Ned grabbed his wife in an awkward but genuine hug. "There will never be anyone but you, Liff," Ned said truthfully. "You know how much I love you."

Liffy sniffed haughtily but knew that Ned was speaking the truth. In all the years they had been together, he had never given her any cause to suspect Ned as unfaithful.

"Well, then," said Liffy. "Let's see what she wants with me."

Liffy hurriedly wiped her hands on the big apron she wore, adjusted her cap, causing more wisps of hair to escape, and bustled through the door into the bar. Ned smiled fondly at his wife as he followed her.

Ned pointed out Shayla to his wife, and Liffy went around the bar to speak with her.

"Are you Liffy?" Asked Shayla, as the tavern keeper's wife approached her.

"Yes," said Liffy. "State your business with me quickly. I have work to do."

"I need you to come outside with me for a minute," said Shayla carefully. "I have something that Saressa sent for you. I also am returning something that is yours."

The effect on Liffy by the mention of Saressa's name was alarming. Her flushed face lost all its color instantly, and Liffy gripped the bar for support. Shayla grew concerned.

"Are you alright?" Shayla asked.

"How do you know about Saressa?" Whispered Liffy. "Her name is long forgotten here."

"Saressa is rewarding your faithfulness by answering your prayers," said Shayla. "Come."

Shayla headed for the door of the tavern, and Liffy hurried behind her, waving Ned away who was about to follow them.

"I will deal with this," said Liffy to Ned over her shoulder as she followed Shayla. "Just give me a minute."

Ned watched, concerned as Liffy and Shayla left the inn. He had never seen his wife so visibly shocked. He had not been close enough to hear their conversation, but whatever the girl had said to Liffy must have been bad news.

Raven helped Sara off Apple when he saw Shayla leave the tavern. Sara stood anxiously as Shayla and, who she assumed was Liffy, approached them. She squeezed Raven's hand for support.

"Your new mother looks to be a nice lady," Raven whispered to her.

Sara nodded, hopefully. "Saressa said she would be," she said quietly.

Shayla had briefly told Liffy about Sara as they left the tavern. Liffy had tears in her eyes and love in her heart the second she saw Sara. Although the clothing they had bought for her to replace her rags were of decent quality, nothing could hide the years of neglect and abuse she had endured. Liffy picked up Sara in her plump arms and gently hugged her.

"Bless you, Saressa," Liffy said silently, tears running down her cheeks. "For sending me this child."

Sara, not used to hugs, was initially stiff in Liffy's arms. The warm, comfortable feeling of being in Liffy's arms, however, melted the little girl's discomfort, and Sara found herself clinging on tightly, never wanting this feeling to end. Liffy could feel just how thin Sara was, and anger rushed through her. She had wanted a child of her own for so long, and it was incomprehensible to her that someone could mistreat a child in this way.

"What's your name, child?" Asked Liffy gently.

"Sara," said Sara hesitantly. "But you can change it if it doesn't please you."

Sara's words cut through Liffy's heart. "Sara is a wonderful name," said Liffy, her voice was breaking with emotion. "Unless you don't care for it yourself, I wouldn't dream of changing your name for another."

Sara smiled broadly. "I like my name," she said. "I think my real mother gave it to me because it has been my name for as long as I remember."

"Then it's settled then," said Liffy. "Let's get you inside and start putting some meat on those bones of yours."

Sara giggled. "I can help you in the kitchen," she said.

"Only if you want to," said Liffy firmly.

Shayla and Raven grinned at each other as Liffy carried Sara quickly towards the inn. Sara would be safe here. Raven suddenly remembered the horse.

"Wait, ma'am," Raven called after her. "There is one other thing.

Liffy turned back and, for the first time, saw her horse Apple. So wrapped up with Sara, Liffy had not noticed the horse. Her stomach churned as she stood, looking at Apple.

"Where is Haney?" Liffy asked slowly. "He isn't hurt, is he?"

"No." Answered Shayla, quickly grabbing Raven's arm. "Haney isn't hurt, but he cannot return here."

Liffy looked at Shayla, knowing that this was a lie. Sara hugged Liffy's neck tightly, sensing her distress.

"You can no longer hurt when you are dead, can you?" Asked Liffy, pain evident in her voice.

Shayla dropped her head sadly.

"Haney was a father to me," said Raven. "I will avenge his death."

Liffy's tears flowed once more, but this time they were tears of sorrow.

"Bring Apple around the back of the tavern, and I will get my husband Ned to let you through the gate." Said Liffy. "Let us discuss how we can be of help to you. Haney was like a father to me too."

Raven nodded as he grabbed Apple's reins. He noticed Shayla's tears and clumsily put his arm around her shoulders.

"She had to know," Raven said gently. "As painful as it was, she deserved to know the truth."

Shayla nodded silently. "I just didn't want to destroy her happiness," she thought to herself.

Raven and Shayla waited silently for Ned to open the gate. Apple knew this was home because he grew restless, snorting, and stamping his feet. Raven struggled with the reins until Shayla finally took them from him.

"You are not good with horses at all, are you?" She said.

"No," said Raven abruptly.

Shayla grinned in response, patting Apple's flank to settle him.

Apple rushed through the gate the moment Ned opened it for them. Shayla let him go as Ned stood to one side to allow the horse into the yard.

"I want to thank you for bringing Sara," Ned said huskily. "You will always be welcome here. Anything I have is yours for the asking."

Raven and Shayla nodded. "Seeing Liffy's happiness with Sara was everything we needed," Shayla said.

Raven and Shayla turned to leave, but Ned called them back.

"Hold on a moment," Ned said. "Liffy is preparing some food for your journey."

As Ned finished speaking, Liffy and Sara ran into view from the rear door of the inn.

"Wait," shouted Sara. "I want to say goodbye." She ran up to Shayla and hugged her tightly. "Thank you for helping Rudy and me," Sara said tearfully. "Without you, we would never have escaped Ma Sadie's place." Shayla nodded, hugging Sara back.

Sara turned to Raven and hugged him too. He stroked her hair gently in response. "Be brave little one," said Raven. "These seem good people. I feel sure that you will be happy here."

Liffy pushed a huge sack into Shayla's arms. "Sara tells me you have very little food for your journey," said Liffy. "The warrior there needs good home cooking to give him the strength in the battles to come." Shayla tried to protest, but Liffy was not listening. "What's your name, warrior?" Said Liffy to Raven.

"Raven," he answered. "That was the name Haney gave me."

Liffy nodded knowingly. "Then, this is for you, Raven," she said, handing him a small pouch. "Haney once told me that this was for the one named Raven if anything happened to him."

Raven took the bag from Liffy's trembling hand.

"You avenge his death for us," said Liffy firmly. "Do you hear?"

Raven nodded nervously, gripping the soft leather pouch.

"To my death," Raven said solemnly.

Liffy nodded satisfied and holding Sara's hand tightly, the two of them headed back to the tavern. Ned touched his forehead in a gesture of respect as he closed the gate.

Shayla looked at Raven curiously. "What did she give you?" Shayla asked.

"I don't know," said Raven. "And it's too dark here to find out."

Raven started walking quickly in the caravan's direction, forcing Shayla to run after him to keep up.

CHAPTER NINETEEN

The Spy

Raven hadn't spoken a word to Shayla throughout the return trip back to their camp. Shayla was struggling to keep up with him and had begged him to slow down on more than one occasion. She saw a resolved expression on his face and realized that Raven had his mind on the upcoming battle now that the children were safe. His eyes had also grown colder from the moment Liffy had given him something of Haney's.

Motomo was waiting for their return at the campsite. He immediately sensed the anger and pain in Raven's mind.

"Did it go well?" Motomo asked Shayla silently, deciding not to ask Raven.

"Yes," answered Shayla. "Liffy was thrilled with Sara. The girl will be happy there."

Motomo nodded and looked over at Raven, who opened his packs and pulled out armor pieces and small hand weapons. He was spreading them out and carefully inspecting each piece.

"What is wrong with Raven?" Asked Motomo, carefully blocking his thoughts as he spoke silently with Shayla.

"I am not sure," Shayla silently replied. "Liffy gave him something of Haney's that he had left with her to give to him. How Haney knew that Raven would come to this world was surprising. He has not looked at what Liffy gave him or spoken to me since."

"His loss is recent, and Liffy has reopened wounds that had not even begun to heal," said Motomo. "His hatred for Ramos and desire for revenge will be his downfall if accompanied by anger, though."

Raven, now occupied sharpening the blade of a sturdy battle-ax, with a flat stone that he had carefully unwrapped from a piece of soft leather.

"Has Devon returned yet?" Raven asked suddenly.

Motomo and Shayla turned in surprise when Raven spoke. There was no anger in his voice; there was no emotion evident in the tone at all.

"Twila waits at the seal for him," answered Motomo. "She doubts he will meet us there yet because we made good time getting here by using the extra horse and little-known gypsy paths."

"You had better get some rest then," Raven instructed Shayla.

Shayla nodded and shrugged her shoulders at Motomo. Both of them felt that the Raven they had come to know seemed gone for the time being. Only the warrior was left now, preparing for battle.

Twila sensed Amani before she saw him. The still night air had slightly quivered as he crossed into this world. Reluctantly Twila turned to watch him approach. The moonlit water was soothing to her.

"Has Devon returned yet?" Asked Amani as he sat beside her.

She shook her head. "No, not yet, but we are here earlier than planned," said Twila.

Amani quietly studied her. "This is a place of bad memories for you," he said quietly. "We should have chosen somewhere else to meet."

Twila shook her head. "It is not the memories that are my concern," she said. "I can no longer sense Danior. I have been here hours now, and he is not on the other side of the seal. Do you think Stefan and the others destroyed him?"

Amani saw the tears well up in her eyes as she turned to him, and he felt helpless. The world on the other side of the seal was inaccessible to him. He finally put his arm around her, and silently they sat waiting for Devon together.

Shayla had grown tired of Raven's silence and went into the caravan to sleep. Motomo wandered off to hunt for his supper. Now that he was finally alone, Raven sat close to the campfire and carefully opened the small leather pouch that Liffy had given him.

His hands were trembling as he pulled out carefully folded pieces of linen paper. Raven straightened the linen paper and leaned closer to the light from the fire to read the words. Haney's hand had written it, and Raven recognized the writing. Haney had written many lessons for him when he was younger. Raven remembered how he had grown impatient with Haney because all he had wanted to do was learn how to fight, not read, and write.

"In the event of my death, I have instructed Liffy to give this letter and pendant only to you, Raven." The letter began. "Liffy asked me how she would know you. I told her to look for a noble warrior who would strike fear into the hearts of his enemies and turn the heads of the ladies."

Raven smiled at Haney's words and realized just how much he missed him.

"I am not sure why I feel compelled to write this to you," the letter continued, "you are in another place, and the hate in your eyes the last time I saw you should be more than enough for me to know that this note will never find it's way into your hands."

Raven put the letter down for a moment. Haney's voice burst from the linen paper, and Raven's eyes stung with tears of regret. He breathed deeply to control his emotions and continued to read.

"When you chose to join your friends as a mercenary, I feared for your life. I knew that the death of your mother was the driving force behind all of your actions. To find your mother's murderer was the edge that you needed to become a reckless but skillful warrior. When you finally left, I heard the tales of your drinking and wild antics with the group that you joined; I had to do something. It took me over a year to find the village of your birth, and even longer to find the site of your mother's grave."

A cold shiver of excitement ran down Raven's spine at these words. He reread them carefully before turning the paper over and reading the rest of the letter.

"I thought perhaps I could discover the name of your mother's murderer. At the very least, I thought I could bring you something of hers to ease your pain of her loss. I had hoped, above all, to stop the self-destructive path that you were determined to follow.

"When I arrived at the village, I spoke with everyone who would give me the time of day. Eventually, I discovered where your mother was buried but informed that her grave soon after she died, had been desecrated. The only thing left to mark it was a simple wooden carving bearing her name. An older woman in the village told me that she had found the grave destroyed when she came to take you in after your mother's death. She searched for you but to no avail. When the woman saw the small wooden marker cast to one side amongst the destroyed grave's rubble, she wept tears for you.

"The woman restored the grave and replaced the marker in case you ever returned. She thought you had suffered enough by the loss of your mother, without also having to witness a grave robber's handiwork. The woman told me that your mother's body was missing from the grave. I found this difficult to believe, and it pains me to tell you this, but I dug down into the grave, and the woman had spoken the truth; there was no sign of a body.

"I tried to make sense of this and thought that the years had reclaimed your mother's body, turning her back into the earth where surely, we all have our beginning. I suspected the woman was telling me a story that was nothing more than a village tale created to frighten children into good behavior. When I suggested that the passage of time had caused the body to return to the earth, the woman told me that they prepared the body well for burial. Your mother's healing skills were much respected. So, the people of the village pooled their resources to pay for it. The woman spoke of special rituals after death and assured me that your mother received a full priestess's burial. Preservatives had been used that should have maintained the body indefinitely."

Raven clutched the paper in anger. It was bad enough to witness his mother slain before his eyes but to defile her grave was unthinkable. Raven hesitated to read the rest of the letter. Anger consumed his rational thoughts, and knew he had to control it. Finally, his curiosity overcame the rage, and he opened up the second piece of linen paper.

"I questioned the woman further," continued the letter. "I thought at least she would know something about the man who ended your mother's life, but the woman knew nothing. The woman did eventually tell me that she was keeping something for you. I insisted that the woman show me what it was, ensuring her that I would find a way to place it into your hands.

"She finally gave me a pendant that belonged to your mother. The woman had found it buried in the earth as she restored the grave. When she had given me your mother's necklace, the woman made me swear that I would bury it deep in the earth if I could not find you. I gave Liffy the same instructions. I honestly wished that I would be the one to provide you with this pendant, but if you are reading this, then it was not meant to be.

"I hope it can help destroy some of those demons that your mother's death has forced you to carry. I also wanted to pass on a role of great importance to you, that I have grown too old to perform, but it seems that our paths were destined never to cross again. I can no longer hope that the role would eventually be yours, and so when the time comes, I will leave in search of the one that can help me. If you read this letter and receive the pendant, I have won my last battle, and I can rest peacefully. Know this one last thing Raven, I loved you as a son."

Raven sat, staring at the letter for a moment after he had finished reading it. Carefully he folded it and tucked Haney's note into a pocket beneath his shirt. Raven picked up the leather pouch that Liffy had given him and felt around inside it. His fingers touched a cold metal object, and he carefully brought it out. Raven inspected the pendant closely. The sight of it stirred deeply buried memories within him. His mother had worn it continuously around her neck; he remembered it.

The shape of the pendant was an intricately carved symbol of a tree fashioned in gold. Encrusted into the center of the tree's trunk was a crystal. The crystal's clarity captured the firelight with a dazzling display of red and amber hues, imprisoning them deep within its center. Raven traced his finger along the tree pendant's branches, marveling at the tiny but detailed leaves of gold adorning them. The braided leather cord that the tree pendant dangled from appeared relatively new, and he suspected that Haney must have replaced it.

Raven turned the pendant carefully first one way and then another. The changes in position caused the crystal to capture the firelight from various angles and produce bursts of different colors. Although it was many years since he last saw the pendant, Raven was still fascinated by it. Memories of his mother flooded his mind, and Raven found them strangely comforting. Reluctantly he started to put the pendant back into the leather pouch when Daybreak's voice suddenly nudged its way into his mind.

"You should wear the pendant," said Daybreak gently, "it holds the magic of your mother. I can sense it."

Raven looked up, startled as Daybreak walked towards him. He realized that the horse must have been listening to his thoughts, and this initially irritated him. Daybreak pushed her muzzle gently into his shoulder to reinforce her words. Raven found he could not be angry at the horse. He patted Daybreak gently as she continued to gaze at him through her soft, milky brown eyes, which peered out from beneath the long and shaggy, almost white mane.

"Please wear it," Daybreak said. "I can feel the magic within its heart."

Raven smiled and put the pendant around his neck, dropping it down beneath his shirt to hide it from view. The cold metal of the tree pendant nestled comfortably against his chest, as if it had always been there.

Devon had grown tired of trying to reason with Soleon, and Rowan had not said a word to help. Soleon had ignored Devon's pleas to be released, and at times she either laughed hysterically in response or threw something at him that missed and hit the wall before it fell to the floor.

The final insult was a skull from one of the piles of bones that Soleon had before her. The head came flying through the air and hit Devon squarely in his chest. It bounced back towards Soleon and then dropped to the floor before rolling across the cave towards Rowan. The impact of the fall broke several already crumbling teeth, scattering pieces everywhere. When the skull finally stopped moving, Devon noticed with disgust that the jaw was hanging in a comical grin.

"Ramos will not be pleased that you are destroying his army before they even have a chance to fight on his behalf," Devon warned her coldly.

Soleon uncontrollably giggled when she saw the skull's jaw. She got up stiffly and went to retrieve the damaged head.

"I suppose you will report all this to your master Ramos, shadow spy," she said to Devon.

"I am tired of telling you that I am here to spy on Ramos, not to spy on you." Devon snarled. "Your foolishness is preventing me from stopping him."

Soleon seemed preoccupied with the broken jaw of the skull. It dangled precariously from what remained of the muscles and tendons that had secured it in life.

"You are lying to me," Soleon said suddenly. "He speaks with Ramos all the time." She pointed a dirt-encrusted finger in the direction of Rowan. "Ask him." Said Soleon, and dropped the damaged skull amongst the rest of the bones that belonged to that particular body.

Devon went cold when Soleon said this. As crazy as she was, Devon felt Soleon spoke the truth. He looked across at Rowan, held with the same binding spell that also trapped him.

Rowan shook his head wildly in Devon's direction.

"The woman is mad," Rowan said. "You can't believe her rantings. Just look at her. Picking through bones like some starved animal, then gluing them together to create yet another macabre addition to Ramos's army. You believe her words over mine?"

Devon was surprised by Rowan's sudden outburst. Soleon had been rambling for hours about both of them. Devon found it strange that Rowan had finally reacted to her taunting.

"What words do you refer to?" Said Devon. "You have been silent through all of her tauntings."

Rowan didn't answer. Devon saw him renew his struggle against the invisible bonds. He looked over to where Soleon had calmly recommenced the reconstruction of the first body. Devon, convinced now that Soleon had spoken the truth. Rowan was a shadow spy that Soleon had accused them both of being. This revelation answered the question of why Rowan had stayed within these caverns so long. He was with Ramos, not against him.

"I think the woman speaks the truth," said Devon. "For whatever reasons you have, deep within that black heart of yours, I think you truly are what she says you are."

Soleon tilted her head at these words and looked over at Devon. The arm that she had been working on dangled forgotten in her hand. She stood up and walked towards Devon, stopping suddenly in front of him. The usual flat, emotionless expression on her face lifted for a moment as she studied Devon.

"You are not here to help Ramos release Valeskas from his banishment, like the other shadow?' Asked Soleon. For a moment, the madness left her eyes.

"No," said Devon firmly. "I am here to discover how to stop him in his quest."

Soleon laughed coldly. "One shadow man can't stop him," she sneered. "He has grown too powerful for that. Since Ramos learned how to invoke Valeskas, his spells have become more powerful. Valeskas has taught Ramos magic he could have only dreamed of discovering. Ancient, forgotten spells, which should have stayed that way, are once more being cast.

"Ramos should have been stopped long before this. You should have destroyed Ramos before the first shadow man arrived. He was the one who told him how to invoke Valeskas. Go ahead and ask him," she finished.

Devon was stunned by Soleon's outburst. He was also deeply concerned about her revelations of Ramos's ability to invoke Valeskas. The most shocking thing was her accusation that it was Rowan who had helped Ramos to invoke Valeskas. Devon found it difficult to believe that a Lunarian would want Valeskas to escape his prison. The Dark Ones had destroyed their people, forced them to live in hiding underground, no longer able to bask in the moonlight as their ancestors had.

"Does the woman speak the truth?" Asked Devon slowly. "You, who dare call yourself a Lunarian, did you show Ramos how to invoke Valeskas?"

Rowan did not answer. He was desperately trying to send out a warning to Ramos mentally until he realized that Soleon's binding spell was not only holding him physically; it was also preventing him from mentally projecting his thoughts.

Devon took Rowan's silence to be an affirmation that Soleon had spoken the truth.

"Why?" Asked Devon. "Why would you want to help Ramos release Valeskas? It would be the end of our people."

"I was not about to destroy our people, you fool," said Rowan angrily. "I had planned to trap Valeskas here in this world, and all of his dark brood. Then our world would be free of them. We could once more come to the surface where we belong. Freedom was what I planned for our people, not their destruction."

"You cannot condemn the people of this world in that way," said Devon quietly. "Valeskas is safely imprisoned in our world. He must remain there, and his Dark Ones should be destroyed, not cast once more into another innocent world. I intend to find my way back to our world and end the Dark One's reign after the destruction of Ramos."

Soleon waved her hand, and Devon dropped to the floor, suddenly released from his invisible bonds. He instantly returned to his usual body and stood towering over Soleon.

"Now, what do you plan to do?" Asked Soleon tauntingly. "You are not strong enough to destroy Ramos by yourself. I would help you, but I know very few spells.

"Ramos drugs me or casts spells to keep me under his control. I did not drink the wine last evening, and when Ramos returns, he will know it. The shadow there will tell him, or he will see it in my actions. You need others if you are to succeed in this plan of yours."

Devon beckoned Soleon to follow him to the level above, where the doorway to her freedom lay. He felt no malice towards her for holding him prisoner. Soleon began to follow him when the ragged blue bow finally escaped its last hold on her hair. It fell to the ground, and she looked at it, puzzled as if seeing it for the first time. She picked it up and placed it carefully on one of the piles of bones.

"Wait," Soleon said suddenly.

Devon stopped and turned around just in time to see Soleon wave her hand in Rowan's direction. When he realized that she was releasing Rowan, it was too late. Devon watched in horror as Rowan dropped to his knees as the magic bonds dissipated. He ran towards them the instant the spell was removed, returning to his usual body as he did so.

Devon pushed Soleon to one side as he braced himself for his attack. Rowan slammed into Devon. The impact of which forced the two of them into the cave wall, falling to the floor. Devon felt his breath forced from his lungs on impact with the wall; he defensively reacted as he felt Rowan's hands grabbing his head and pushing it backward.

Rowan's face was inches from Devon's, his fangs already in position as he fought first to extend then bite his intended victim's neck. Devon realizing what Rowan's intentions were, forced both his hands up between them, and with every bit of strength, he had slammed both his fists into the face of Rowan. The force of the double-handed blow threw Rowan backward, causing him to relinquish his hold on Devon's head.

Soleon howled with delight at this maneuver, clapping her hands excitedly. Devon dived after Rowan, taking both of them to the floor again. They rolled around, scattering bones everywhere, as they grappled for dominance.

Devon tore into Rowan's right shoulder, dragging out a large chunk of flesh with his teeth, narrowly missing a major blood vessel. Rowan screamed in pain and anger as he grabbed for the nearest weapon and slammed it into the side of Devon's head. The skull shattered harmlessly against Devon's shoulder. Soleon screamed in horror when she saw the head destroyed. She hurried forward, picking up the pieces, totally ignoring now what was going on around her.

Rowan's anger at realizing it was a skull that he had grabbed and not a bolder drove him into a wild frenzy. He lashed out at Devon's face with what remained of the head. A deep jagged wound instantly reopened the old scar on Devon's left cheek. The initial numb sensation from the injury in Devon's cheek changed to a blazing trail of fire that ran along the whole length of the cut, as his nerve endings recovered from the assault.

Devon grabbed Rowan's wrist to prevent another attack with the remnants of the skull. He was on top of Rowan at this point and had the advantage. Devon slammed Rowan's arm on to the ground, in an attempt to release his grip on the weapon of bone. There was a crunching snap as the bones in Rowan's lower arm hit a bolder on the cave's floor. Rowan howled in pain and slammed his left fist into Devon's face, and at the same moment, used the force of his body to pitch Devon sideways, causing him to plunge into another pile of bones.

Soleon wailed at them to stop as she frantically ran around the room, picking up the scattered bones.

"You're jumbling them all up," Soleon sobbed. "I will never get them straight again."

Devon scrambled to his feet as Rowan threw himself at him. This time Devon had time to plant a sidekick squarely in the stomach of Rowan. There was so much force behind the kick, Rowan flew backward through the air and hit the cave wall. His head smashed into the rock, and the impact caused his skull to burst open in an explosion of blood.

Rowan slid down the wall ending up in a crumpled broken heap on the floor. Devon prepared himself for another attack, but there was no movement from Rowan. He walked towards him, irritably wiping the blood from his face, which caused another flash of pain from the wound. Before he managed to reach Rowan, Soleon got there first. She grabbed Rowan by the head, and before Devon could stop her, Soleon snapped his neck with a resounding crack and then pushed his body to one side.

"I told you to stop fighting," said Soleon sternly. "You've jumbled them all up."

Devon stopped in his tracks, stunned. He watched Soleon drag the body of Rowan across the floor, a glistening trail of blood marking his passage. Soleon carefully placed him at the start of a new row of soldiers, yanking at the broken arm to make it lie straight. She struggled briefly, trying to straighten Rowan's head, but it fell to one side at an odd angle, each time Soleon released her grip.

"Fetch me those two large rocks over there," demanded Soleon. "I need them to hold this head in position."

Devon retrieved the rocks for Soleon without question. He was stunned and somewhat saddened by her behavior. Ramos had driven her to madness, and despite the brief periods of sanity, Devon suspected that Soleon was beyond any help he could offer her.

"There." Announced Soleon, wiping the blood and gore from her hands on the rag of a dress she wore. "Now, for the rest of them."

Devon shook his head sadly as he watched Soleon bury all the traces of blood with the sand from the floor of the cave. Soleon began constructing the next body from one of the piles of bones, carefully positioning the pieces by Rowan's side. Suddenly she stopped and turned towards Devon.

"You were going to show me something," said Soleon. "I forgot. Show me quickly because I have work to do here."

Soleon got up and stood waiting for Devon. He hesitated for a moment, but then he decided to still show her the doorway despite her inconsistent mental stability. She followed Devon silently, always staying a few paces behind him. Staying behind him like that made Devon feel uncomfortable, especially after seeing the speed and strength she had displayed when she broke Rowan's neck.

They reached the cave containing the hidden door, and Devon stood before it. "There is a doorway here," he said. We can enter together, or you can watch me go through it, then follow me."

Soleon pushed past Devon and studied the wall in front of her. "I can't see the door," she said bluntly. "Show me the door."

Devon pushed his hand through the door, and Soleon squealed with delight when it seemed to disappear. She hesitatingly touched the wall and found no resistance. Devon smiled and nodded at her questioning look.

"This can be your escape from here," said Devon, walking through the invisible doorway that led to the crystal cave.

He waited for a few moments, watching Soleon's fingertips tremble on his side of the door. Eventually, Soleon burst through the door. Its lack of resistance caught her off guard, and she would have fallen flat on her face if Devon hadn't caught her. Soleon cried out as the bright light assaulted her eyes. She covered them with her hands, groaning.

"Your eyes will get used to the light," Devon said gently. "It is a cave of crystal, and you will like it once you see it."

Soleon eyes slowly adjusted to the bright light, and she smiled like a child as she saw just how amazing it was. Her reaction tore into Devon's heart.

"It is so pretty," Soleon sobbed. "I have never seen anything like it. Well, maybe I did see something like it once, but it was somewhere else, and I can't remember."

She ran from one crystal wall to another crystal wall, gently touching the sparkling shards of crystal that flashed and sparkled with unimaginable colors.

"I have something else to show you," said Devon. "Follow me."

Soleon looked puzzled for a moment when she heard Devon's voice. She stared at him oddly as if seeing him for the first time. Then recognition suddenly spread across her face, and then she followed him down the path lined with the red crystals.

Devon led her to the moonlit beach he had discovered earlier. She said nothing as she looked out across the silver-tipped waves.

"This is your way to freedom," said Devon. "You can leave here and come with me now." Soleon didn't respond, and he became concerned. "I know this is a lot for you to comprehend or even believe, but come with me now, and you will be free of Ramos.

She finally turned to Devon, and in the light from the moon, he saw the trails of tears coursing down her dirt-streaked cheeks.

"I can't come with you," said Soleon quietly, "I cannot leave Ramos."

Devon was stunned by these words. "What do you mean you can't leave Ramos?" He asked. "I can take you with me right now."

She shook her head slowly. "I can't leave him because he made me. I am dead, I think."

Devon wasn't sure how to respond to this. He remembered that Rowan had said she was alive but not alive, dead but not dead.

"Thank you for showing me this beautiful secret," she said, "I can come here again, can't I?"

Devon nodded sadly. "Yes, but I just wish I could have given you your freedom," he said.

"When you destroy Ramos, you will," she smiled.

"Well, I came here to learn what his weaknesses are," he said, "and there are others who wait for my return. Each one of them has their reasons to destroy Ramos, and I am returning with nothing to help them accomplish that."

Soleon was silent for a moment, and then suddenly, she smiled broadly.

"You need to stop the binding spell," she said excitedly. "Ramos's army can be destroyed easily by a skilled swordsman. Remove the heads, and that renders them harmless. Use protection spells of light against Ramos' dark magic but remember to prevent him from casting the binding spell; that is the most important. You will never get a fair chance in the battle if he casts that on you."

Devon nodded in agreement. "If it is like the spell that you cast, then I was rendered useless by it," he said.

"I have something to protect against it," she said suddenly, "I had forgotten about it." Soleon started feeling around her neck, searching for something. "I know it was here," she said. "Where is it? Do you think I dropped it?" Soleon became more and more distressed and started tearing at her clothes, searching for it.

Devon finally placed his hand on her shoulder. "Stop searching, Soleon," he said gently. "You are just distressing yourself. The information you have given me already will help us to destroy Ramos."

She stopped and looked up at Devon. "Destroy Ramos, and you will give me my freedom," she reaffirmed, "and when the time comes, I will help you if I can."

Devon nodded. "Two of the others who are coming to destroy Ramos are powerful," he said. "One is a warrior, and the other is a magic user with spells of light as strong as Ramos's dark magic."

"I will watch for them," said Soleon. "I must go now. Dawn approaches, and he will return."

Devon watched her as she returned to the crystal cave. He smiled when she stopped to drink the water that rushed down the side of the cliff from the mountain top. She turned to wave goodbye before disappearing into the cave.

He looked up at the waning moon and realized it was too late for him to meet the others at the seal before sunrise. He decided to wait just long enough for Soleon to find her way back to the doorway, and then he would return to the crystal cave to sleep. Devon realized that he was taking very little information back to the others, but he hoped what he was bringing would be enough to help them destroy Ramos.

CHAPTER TWENTY

Ramos

Ramos dropped the sack he was carrying containing more warrior bones, by the side of Soleon. She ignored it and continued to work on the second warrior from the last load. Ramos glanced at his growing army of soldiers as he headed for the rear of the cave. His eyes narrowed for a moment, and then he turned to Soleon.

"What happened to Rowan?" He asked.

"He jumbled them up," Soleon said. "Look what he did to this one's head." Soleon picked up a piece of the shattered skull from the final pile of bones and held it up for his inspection. "I was just going to replace the head with Rowan's," she said, "but it wouldn't come off, so I had to use all of him."

Ramos shrugged his shoulders indifferently at this revelation and then continued down to the rear of the cave. He removed something from a pocket beneath his cloak and held it up into the torches' light. It was a large black crystal shard, and Ramos placed it carefully on the cloth-covered table. He ran his finger over the edges of the crystal for a moment, inspecting it, looking for any signs of damage. Ramos was becoming increasingly concerned each time the crystal key gave him access to Soleon's world. If the shard lost its power on the wrong side of the door, that would trap him there.

He glanced across at Soleon, who was now trying to piece together the shattered skull. Ramos realized that he had been fortunate to find her. Without Soleon's unique power with crystal, he would not have been able to leave her world. However, it was unfortunate that without the exact ingredients needed for the spell to

260

raise her after death, the result had been disastrous.

Soleon was not the servant she was supposed to be, and in fact, her actions were very unpredictable. Ramos had quickly discovered that she still needed food to allow her to function. She would eat anything that came to hand if he did not provide food for her. Soleon had eaten many rare ingredients for his spells before he had realized that feeding her prevented that.

When he had first raised Soleon from death, she had recharged his damaged crystal key, and that had enabled him to cross back into this world.

Ramos looked again at his crystal key, convinced that there must be more shards like it within this mountain somewhere. He had found this one jammed into the rock above his head, just inside the shaft. Ramos had searched every inch of this roof, including as far as he could reach into the shaft, but found nothing.

He began combining powders from several leather pouches and poured a dark liquid from one of many large jars on the shelf into a wooden bowl. It irritated him that he had to rely on this damaged shard so heavily, to enter the other world. The crystal key only gave him access to Soleon's world, though, which was very frustrating. Ramos also recognized that he was responsible for the crystal's limitations because when he had first found the shard, he had immediately sensed the power within it. He invoked it, and the crystal opened a doorway into Soleon's world. Ramos had used the key many times initially, convinced that there must be new and powerful magic to be discovered there. Perhaps if he had used caution, opening doors to another world would not have damaged it.

Over time he had learned all about Soleon's world by visiting its villages and listening to the loose tongues of old women or the drunken ramblings of old men. Ramos learned all about Saressa's innocent world and about its invasion by Dra's army of Dark Ones. He had been fascinated with the stories of blood-drinking night creatures. Ramos also heard how the people of Soleon's world became warriors in an attempt to protect themselves.

The Dark Ones had suddenly disappeared, at the same time as their goddess Saressa. The people assumed that she had abandoned them, and everyone was forbidden even to speak her name. Only a few of Saressa's most faithful worshipped in secret and continued to practice her magic.

Occasionally some of these faithful followers were discovered and slain for their beliefs. Many betrayed by a loose tongue, or because of the promise of gold for information. Saressa's faithful were methodically hunted down and destroyed by self-declared leaders of the new provinces. They were fearful that Saressa would return to regain their self-claimed lands and turn them back over to her followers. The leaders also believed that continuing to practice the earth magic of Saressa would attract the war god Dra's attention, and he would send the Dark Ones back into their world.

Ramos discovered that Saressa's earth magic eventually became known as Ogham. This change of name hid the truth of what they believed in from the province leaders. There had been very few believers left who practiced it when he had first discovered Soleon's world, and it had taken him a long time to find Soleon. Ramos initially had been interested in learning more about the Dark Ones, and not the Ogham magic. That was until he heard tales about earth magic being used with crystals to create doorways into other worlds.

He slowly shook his head as he remembered his excitement at discovering the Ogham followers could use crystal magic.

"What a fool I was," Ramos thought, adding more dark liquid to the evil-smelling potion that he was creating. "I should have been more patient, researched the Ogham crystal magic more carefully. I knew the ingredients were not quite right for the crystal spell that I used, but I was too impatient to think that it would matter."

His fascination with necromancy and dark magic had started in his childhood when he had first discovered that he possessed the Gypsy gift. Ramos worked hard to develop it. Much harder than any other gypsy born with the power did. The simple protection spells and the ability to enter another's thoughts were not enough for him. There was no one to teach him any new magic either, so he had worked at creating different spells on his own.

Ramos smiled as he remembered how simple those first spells were, but so very satisfying to him when they were successful. If it had not been for the night that he had spent searching for a particular spell ingredient, Ramos doubted that his magic would have progressed very much further.

He remembered that he had been having problems with a shadow spell. He had used it effectively once before, to relieve traders of a few gold coins. Ramos realized that the ingredients' consistency was critical in producing the desired results as his skill had grown. When he had first created the shadow spell, Ramos used the wing from a particular night moth. He had tried other things but could not reproduce the magic successfully without it.

By the time he had found the correct moth species, it was well after midnight, and as he was making his way home, a large black bird had flown down into the clearing in front of him. He had quickly hidden amongst the bushes, initially intending to capture the bird. Its plumage was so dark that he thought it might make the shadow spell work even better than a moth wing.

Carefully he had readied his slingshot waiting for the best angle to kill the bird effectively, then he had almost cried out in surprise when the bird had suddenly grown in size and began to change form. A few moments later, to Ramos's amazement, what was once a bird had become a man right in front of his eyes.

Ramos stopped mixing his potion for a moment as he remembered his encounter with the Shapeshifter. It had been that moment when he saw the bird become a man that had changed his life forever. Ramos hadn't known about Shapeshifters then. Naively Ramos assumed he was witnessing a powerful magic display and thought initially that the man could be the teacher he had been searching for. It could mean that there would be no more groping around in the mysteries of magic alone. Ramos decided to ask this man for his help and was ready to step into the clearing to talk with him when something even more astounding happened.

The man had placed both his hands on a nearby tree and bowed his head in concentration. Ramos had watched with interest, waiting for what he knew must be an even greater display of the magic that could soon be his. He had listened carefully but heard no chanting. Ramos saw no powders or ingredients to use for a spell, but he could see that there was something in one of the man's hands.

A brilliant white glow began to emit from what appeared to be a long-jagged piece of rock that the man held. As Ramos watched breathlessly, the tree and the man became one. He felt the air shudder around him, and then the bright light faded and finally vanished, and the man had disappeared. For a few moments, Ramos had just stood there stunned, attempting to make sense of what had happened. He had cautiously stepped from the bushes, fearful that at any moment the man would reappear, but he hadn't done.

Ramos added another powder to the wooden bowl and smiled at the foolishness of his younger self. For months he had returned to that same spot where the man had disappeared, hoping to see him reappear. Ramos had cursed himself for not speaking out to the Shapeshifter quickly before it was too late. Although he never did find out who the man was, the event had shown him what he could himself perhaps achieve.

After that incident, his spell concoctions became even more bizarre and reckless. When he had attempted to raise a dead horse they had owned, his younger brother had then gone to their father and complained about him.

The attempt to raise that horse had failed miserably. Unfortunately, the horse had staggered to its feet and then immediately burst into eerie black flames before exploding into a million particles of dust. Ramos's brother, unfortunately, had witnessed the whole thing.

Ramos suspected that his brother must have been monitoring his magic experiments for some time before the horse disaster, to gather evidence of his dark magic to present to their father. His brother had wanted to become the group's leader after their father's death, and Ramos had been in his way. The story of the horse sealed his fate with the Gypsies, and they banished him forever.

Ramos laughed out loud at the memory of his brother's smug expression when his father banished him.

Soleon looked up, puzzled at Ramos's laughter, and grinned lopsidedly in response.

"My brother did me a great favor that day." Ramos thought to himself. "I found my way here."

He had not been that happy initially, though, cast out from his home with nothing but what was on his back. It had been months before he finally discovered the abandoned shack at the top of a mountain, and even longer to find the hidden caverns beneath it.

His spells had been improving, and there were more successes than failures. He had craved to reproduce what he had seen the Shapeshifter do, though, and he had started to experiment with pieces of different types of rocks, but nothing produced the desired effect.

When he had finally found that piece of crystal, he had been at the point of giving up. The first time he had managed to create a door with the crystal, he could scarcely believe it. He quickly wrote down the spell combination that had worked before he crossed cautiously into Soleon's world. Although he had later discovered his crystal could only open one door, it had been enough to satisfy him. Until he had heard about the Dark Ones and their banishment to another place,

Ramos had not even considered that there could be more worlds accessible to him. Because of his experiments, he opened a new door with the crystal that had almost destroyed him and ruined all his plans to become more powerful.

Ramos remembered how he had decided to open a door into the world where Saressa had banished the Dark Ones after he had first heard of them. He had cast a spell on the crystal, intending to create a key that would give him access to that world. Unfortunately, something went badly wrong, and instead of a door, the crystal created a great rift between their world and his.

To make matters worse, when the rift had opened, it had also damaged the crystal. He had only intended observing the Dark Ones and inviting them to exchange spells with him, but what had happened was almost a disaster for him. He had been attacked and nearly killed, but one of their leaders, Stefan, had intervened, and initially, Ramos thought he had saved him. However, he had quickly realized that Stefan had not saved him. He was using his leader's rank status to claim him to satisfy his blood hunger. Luckily, Ramos had managed to reason with Stefan asking him to spare his life with the promise of providing entry into his world.

Stefan had agreed, but had drained him of blood to the edge of his death anyway and then revived him as a Dark One. As agreed, in return for not killing him, Ramos had led Stefan and his blood-crazed followers into his world, and they had arrived here like a pack of mad dogs.

He picked up the crystal and inspected it again. A flash of anger coursed through him at the sight of its now flawed center.

"I was too reckless," Ramos thought to himself. "This time, it will go differently. I have learned patience."

Ramos clearly remembered how quickly the blood hunger had affected him after his revival. It was some time before he thought of anything except satisfying the constant, unrelenting desire for blood. He had learned no new powers or magic from Stefan; the only thing he had gained was immortality.

The havoc that the dark ones had caused in his world after he initially created the rift went unnoticed by Ramos. The blood hunger consumed him too much to concern himself with what was going on around him. Despite his blood-crazed thoughts, he eventually managed to create a potion that satisfied his hunger, and he no longer needed to hunt nightly for prey.

By mixing potions, he had also discovered a way to retain his strength during daylight hours. Unfortunately, when he did drink the potion that stopped the effect of daylight, his blood hunger returned.

When the Dark One's invasion of his world had started to impact his search for the Shapeshifter, by their indiscriminate creation of Half Deads, he decided to develop a spell that would close the rift. However, to create it had required blood from an innocent Gypsy girl born with the gift, mixed with his own. He had also carefully chipped off small pieces of his now damaged crystal, ground them to a powder, and added it to the spell potion.

Ramos had decided to ask the Gypsies to help him get rid of Stefan and his blood drinkers. He knew that the Gypsy leaders were so desperate to rid their world of Dark Ones that they would agree to help.

Ironically it was his brother's child who had provided the blood. Her Gypsy gift was the strongest he found amongst them. Dark Ones had attacked two of the Gypsies, who came to help him when he had sealed the rift. One Gypsy became fatally injured, and he had no choice but to break his neck so that he would not return as a Half Dead. He had then decided to revive the other one with his blood, in the same way that Stefan had revived him. He had decided to use him as a guardian of the newly sealed rift. Ramos had then also created a spell that prevented his Gatekeeper Danior from feeding on this side of the seal. He wanted no more dealings with Dark Ones.

When Ramos had rid his world the blood drinkers, he had then concentrated on his obsession with finding and entering new worlds in search of more powerful magic. He had decided to return once more to Soleon's world and spend the time necessary searching for another key. He had been sure that the Shapeshifter must have crossed into Soleon's world with one, and if so, then he was determined to find him and his key.

Ramos had spent over two years in Soleon's world, searching for information that could lead him to the Shapeshifter. He didn't find anyone with stories of a Shapeshifter, but he had discovered the existence of something far more intriguing.

He had traveled to a small hamlet to seek out a blacksmith. Ramos had been directed there by an old farmer. With the help of a never-ending flow of ale provided by his gold, the old farmer gossiped like a woman. Ramos had found the old blacksmith easily, and his tongue loosened quickly with ale. What the blacksmith had told him was precisely the type of information that Ramos had been seeking.

He had spoken of a strange pendant that had been kept safely by his wife's mother. The blacksmith had told Ramos that he had once suffered a bad year with very little work, and he had secretly searched his mother-in-law's room, looking for a box that his wife had mentioned one time she kept under her bed. He was desperate for money and thought that she might have gold hidden in that box. He had found very few coins in the box, though, but the blacksmith had borrowed it, intending to repay her when he was able.

The blacksmith told Ramos that by accident, he discovered a secret compartment in the box. There was a hidden catch that had opened it, and inside the bottom section was a pendant in the shape of a strange beast. The blacksmith had attempted to remove the trinket so he could examine it more closely, but a peculiar thing had happened. As he had touched the pendant, it began to glow, and it generated heat so intense that it had burned his hand badly. He had pointed to his palm upon his right hand so that Ramos could see the scar from the burn.

"These hands can tolerate temperatures that you cannot imagine," the blacksmith had told him, "but I had to drop it."

Ramos's interest had grown at the blacksmith's story, and he had continued to buy him ale, hoping to find out more about the pendant.

"I also felt something else before the heat forced me to drop the pendant," the blacksmith had continued hesitantly.

Ramos had felt like beating the story out of him, but he had learned to be patient.

"What did you feel?" Ramos had asked carefully.

The blacksmith had grinned and looked embarrassed. "If I tell you that," he had said, "you will think me a drunken fool."

Ramos had smiled kindly at him, encouraging him to continue. "No, I would not think you are a fool. I have witnessed and heard many strange things while on my travels," he had said, ordering another ale for him.

The blacksmith had looked around carefully, afraid of being overheard. He had leaned closer to Ramos over the table, his face flushed from the effects of the ale.

"When I touched the pendant," he had almost whispered, "I felt the room begin to shake beneath my feet. My hand was on fire, but for a moment I was unable to let the pendant drop. Then I saw something," he had said looking around once more to make sure that no one could hear him.

The blacksmith had stopped to drink deeply from his mug, and then he clumsily slammed it down on the table. Ramos had immediately signaled for a refill.

"What did you see?" Ramos had prompted when the blacksmith appeared reluctant to continue.

The blacksmith had looked uncertain for a moment, and then he had continued, but more slowly.

"The room I was standing in changed suddenly and became another place," he had said so quietly that Ramos had to lean forward to hear him.

"I turned around and saw pillars of gold that seemed to go on forever. Then I heard something behind me. When I turned, I saw a beast like the one on the pendant, running towards me. They say that fear can freeze a man to the spot, but I never believed it until then.

"The beast was almost upon me, and I just stood there shaking like a leaf from head to foot, unable to move. It stopped in front of me, and I stared up into the beast's partially open mouth, there was row upon row of teeth. It was the height of ten houses piled on top of each other, and I just waited for those teeth to tear me in two. The beast lowered its massive head until its golden eyes were level with my face.

"I waited for death, as its hot breath washed over me, and then the beast had spoken, telling me that I was not the keeper of the key. It commanded me to release the pendant, and the next time he found me in his domain, I would pay for it with my life.

"I looked down and saw smoke pouring from my burning hand that caused me to drop the pendant, and then suddenly I was back in my mother-in-law's room again. The secret compartment in the box was closed, and I never opened it again."

He had been breathing heavily by the time he had finished his story.

Ramos had been stunned by what the blacksmith had told him. He was unsure what the blacksmith had seen, but he had been confident that he had spoken truthfully. Ramos had forced himself not to appear too excited and had asked calmly to see the pendant. The blacksmith had shaken his head and explained that his mother-in-law had died some years ago, and when he and his wife had cleared out her room, the box's hidden compartment was empty.

Ramos had questioned the blacksmith further and had learned that a boy they had brought up as their own had left shortly after his mother-in-law's death, and they had not seen him since. Ramos had assumed that he must have found and then left with the pendant. So determined to find that pendant and its keeper that the creature had spoken of, Ramos planned to use a spell to seek them out. That was when he had found out just how damaged his crystal was when he had tried to use it to return home. It had failed him, and he found himself searching for someone who still practiced Ogham, so this person could hopefully repair it.

Ramos had eventually found Soleon, who had managed to repair his crystal and then decided that she had to stay with him, in case the crystal ever failed again. She had refused every offer of riches that Ramos had offered her. Ramos had gotten so irritated with her refusals that he decided to kill her so he could control her.

He had just been about to kill her but then had stopped himself when it had occurred to him that she may become a Dark One if he did. So, instead, he had searched the seediest taverns for a mercenary who would kill for a price, with no questions asked.

In Soleon's world, there had been many such individuals to be bought, if you looked in the right places. He had hastily gathered the ingredients for his revive spell while he waited for the mercenary to return for the rest of his money after she was dead.

Although Soleon wasn't precisely what he had expected after he had revived her, she could be somewhat controlled and was able to repair his crystal when necessary.

When Ramos had returned home with Soleon, he spent many hours creating a spell that would allow him to detect the pendant key next time the keeper used it. Ramos initially had taken Soleon with him every time he used the crystal; he had been so afraid it would fail him again. Over time, however, he discovered that the crystal remained stable for four or five times before needing repair, so he had left Soleon behind.

He had waited impatiently for the keeper to use the pendant key so that his spell could detect it, but nothing had happened. Ramos had continued to search for someone else who may know of the massive beast or the pendant, but he had found no one else.

Ramos had grown tired of Soleon's world, but he had been afraid that the keeper would use the pendant key in his absence, and his spell to detect it wouldn't work from his world. He had then decided to attract the pendant key into his world by creating another spell type. After he had cast it, Ramos had spent less and less time in Soleon's world.

His long wait finally rewarded when the keeper used the pendant key, and Ramos had felt it enter his world. He had searched the area where he was sure it had entered Sheukhawn but found nothing. Ramos had then created another spell that prevented the pendant key from leaving Sheukhawn. It was then just a matter of time before the keeper used the pendant key again, and he had sworn that next time he would find it.

Ramos slammed his fist down on the table in front of him, causing Soleon to look briefly in his direction.

"I am so close to the key," he growled, "and still, it evades me."

Soleon smiled a crooked smile as she added finishing touches to the last warrior, and then picked up the new sack and began pulling out more bones and body parts.

Ramos had been intrigued initially but later became angry when Twila had arrived to tell him the seal was failing. Ramos hadn't thought that the seal would fail when Netta became older. He had not seen that possibility when he had initially created the spell.

However, this time, he had made sure that the seal would remain intact this time by killing her and then allowing Danior to revive her with his blood. Ramos had not intended to create another Dark One but had felt that he could deal with Twila if she became a problem.

He hadn't cared for the way Twila and Danior behaved around each other, either. That had been another complication that he had not wanted to have to manage. He recognized that Danior was no longer needed to guard the new seal now that there was not a chance it would fail, and so he had decided to trap him on the other side of it.

Ramos still clearly remembered the taste of Twila's blood, and he savored it in his mind. Even increasing the ingredients in his spell that prevented him from being consumed once more by the blood hunger had not removed that memory.

The failure of the seal seemed to have heralded a series of events that had surprised him. The first thing that had happened when he had returned to his mountain was that he had discovered Rowan. Ramos glanced over at the body of Rowan. His neck was at an odd angle, despite the two rocks that Soleon must have placed on either side of his head to support it.

Rowan had told him many things, some of which he knew already. He had, however, told him the whole story of how the Dark Ones had been banished to his world by Saressa. Rowan had also told him about Valeskas, which was much more interesting, and Ramos's desire to possess the pendant key grew even more desperate.

Initially, Ramos had thought that the pendant key might open Valeska's prison, and he envisioned the power that would be bestowed on him from the grateful blood lord once released. He hadn't told Rowan about the pendant key but had said to him that he would release Valeskas.

Rowan was anxious to help and had told him that many had tried to release him and had failed. He had also provided him with enough information about Valeskas for Ramos to create a spell that had successfully invoked the blood lord.

The first time he had gotten the spell right, he had come face to face with a smoke image of Valeskas, who at first had been barely able to speak to him. He had then realized that this blood lord was, in fact, a dragon when its smoke body had appeared in the cave.

Valeskas had been elated by this temporary freedom, and he had told Ramos about another dragon named Radon. Valeskas had convinced Ramos after they had discussed the pendant he was seeking, that it could open the door to Radon, and more importantly, an immense source of power.

Valeskas believed that Saressa had tricked the other dragons into allowing themselves to become a part of a sphere known as the Dragon's Tear. It was the most significant source of power imaginable. He had told Ramos that The Dragon's Tear was the only thing powerful enough to release him from his prison. Valeskas had spoken angrily of Radon being chosen by Saressa to guard the Dragon's Tear, and he had promised Ramos that if he could release him, then the Dragon's Tear would be all his.

Ramos had voiced his concerns about the power needed to destroy Radon and take the Dragon's Tear. Valeskas had assured Ramos that now he could invoke him, he would teach him the most potent spells in existence. The blood lord was more impatient than Ramos had been while waiting for the keeper to use the pendant key again, but neither of them could do anything until it was.

When Ramos had first felt a small glimmer from the pendant key, he was afraid it had been his imagination. He had just returned after drinking Twila's blood and had thought that her blood might have caused some kind of hallucination. He hadn't told Valeskas about the glimmer and had left in search of the pendant key without his help.

Ramos had arrived moments too late to prevent it from being hidden by a concealment spell. The old key keeper had made him furious when he found out what had happened to it. Ramos had also been shocked seeing the man who had kept the pendant key hidden from him for so long. It was not a man of great magic as he had expected it to be, but just an old fool who had been smart enough to keep it hidden from him by choosing not to use it.

He had destroyed the old key keeper without another thought, and then he had returned to his mountain with a sense of dread knowing that now he had to tell Valeskas.

Ramos would have preferred not to invoke the blood lord, but he hadn't yet taught him the spells needed to destroy Radon. So, he had no other choice but to tell him he had missed another chance to find the key, and he had braced himself for Valeska's wrath.

Surprisingly the blood lord had been pleased by Ramos's news.

"Go to the cave where the pendant key is hidden," Valeskas commanded, "together we will cast a spell and stop the pendant key from being removed."

Ramos had returned to the cave and noticed immediately a freshly dug grave. He had been alarmed initially, thinking that the same person had also retrieved the pendant key. Ramos, however, sensed the key, magically hidden, and still inside the cave.

He had invoked Valeskas inside the cave, and together they cast a barrier spell that effectively prevented anyone from retrieving the pendant key. He knew that someone would be coming soon to find him, and he planned to be ready for them when they arrived.

Valeskas had agreed with him and had instructed him to begin preparing an army of the undead. Ramos was reluctant to raise anyone from the dead again, after the disasters with the horse, and then Soleon. Valeskas assured him that if they cast the spells together to raise them, nothing could go wrong.

Ramos had followed the blood lord's instruction to collect only the warrior's bodies for his army, but there were no warriors in Sheukhawn. The people here lived peacefully. There were no wars or disputes between villages or self-claimed leaders who declared war on other territories, and the Gypsies held their private council to deal with their problems.

Thieves were perhaps the most significant problem or petty

squabbles between neighbors. There was an occasional murder in the seedier back-alleys, but nothing that couldn't be swiftly dealt with by the villagers themselves.

The only place that Ramos knew where there would be warriors was Soleon's world. Collecting the warrior bodies was not the problem; Ramos was more concerned that his crystal key would fail again.

He looked at the three rows of warrior bodies that Soleon had carefully constructed. Valeskas had said that it would be a younger warrior who would come to collect the pendant key.

His army of dead warriors was to be the first line of Ramos's defense. His spells would be the second, enhanced by Valeskas's assistance. Ramos thought it sounded a little too easy, and he still remembered the Shapeshifter and his magic. He felt that whoever came to collect the key would not come alone, and he wondered if the Shapeshifter would be with them. He liked that idea; he wanted to meet that Shapeshifter.

Ramos began chanting the words to his spell, and Soleon's head jerked up as she recognized it. She scuttled backward, never taking her eyes off him until she reached the darkest corner of the cave. She clawed at her neck in search of something, but there was nothing there.

Soleon saw the plume of smoke heralding Valeskas's arrival, and she buried her face into her dirt-encrusted hands, no longer willing to look.

CHAPTER TWENTY-ONE

The Gift

Shayla watched silently as Raven expertly strapped his padded leather breastplate over a woven chain mail shirt. He secured a pair of leather armlets to his wrists and elbows before putting on his cloak. Raven then carefully wrapped his chain mail hood, helmet, and padded leather thigh plates, creating a small bundle that he secured carefully to Daybreak's back.

When Raven flipped his cloak back to make final adjustments to the position of his sword, Shayla shuddered, suddenly thankful that she was not the enemy. Raven's whole demeanor was different, now that the battle with Ramos was imminent. His face was expressionless, yet his eyes were always moving, searching the shadows, ready for the unexpected. He moved with confidence. His shoulders pulled back, head erect, the fingers on his right hand were never far from the handle of his sword.

She had no doubts that Raven was preparing to fight to the death against Ramos, and it would be an honorable death, a warrior's death. Her eyes suddenly filled with tears, and she swallowed hard in an attempt to remove the lump that had developed in her throat. Shayla quickly turned her head away so Raven would not see her foolishness. She was relieved to be staying behind with Amani and Devon to monitor the seal because Shayla knew it would be unbearable for her to observe it should Raven die in battle.

As the last burning red glow of the setting sun dropped behind the trees, Twila stepped from the caravan. She immediately noticed Raven's partial armor but chose to say nothing. Her appearance was the signal to leave, and the three of them left the camp in silence, heading towards the seal. Twila was leading Fen, and Raven led Daybreak. Motomo trailed behind the group sensing the tension, and like Daybreak, he also chose to remain silent.

Amani was waiting when the solemn group arrived. There was no sign of Devon. Raven was about to suggest that they just head for Ramos's mountain and not wait for Devon but held his tongue when Amani pulled Twila to one side.

"There is something different about the seal," said Amani quietly to Twila, "It seems more complex, stronger somehow. Maybe that is the reason you can no longer sense Danior."

Twila immediately hurried across to the seal and placed both her hands on the rocky mound's rough surface. She closed her eyes and concentrated, mentally searching the intricate fabric of the seal's invisible barrier. Twila had been so concerned with mentally reaching Danior yesterday that she had missed these subtle changes in the seal's structure.

"You're right," she agreed, "there is another element to the seal that was not there before. Do you think Ramos has returned and added another element to it?"

As Amani shook his head at her suggestion, Twila suddenly realized what could have caused the change.

"I must have done it," she said, "I never thought it could affect the seal, but it has."

"What did you do that affected the seal?" Amani asked curiously.

Twila looked at him guiltily for a moment before replying. "I healed my mother's heart," Twila whispered hoarsely. "I didn't think that making her well again would replenish my mother's portion of the seal, and now look what has happened. I have trapped Danior even more securely in that place filled with those blood-crazed Dark Ones."

Amani nodded thoughtfully. "Yes, I agree with you," he said, "that is what has happened. You have made your mother strong again and replenished her essence within the seal's structure."

Twila suddenly burst into tears and would have collapsed to her knees, had Amani not caught her and held her close to him.

"Then I have destroyed what chance we had to rescue Danior," she sobbed.

Amani continued to hold her silently, and his anger grew. He logically analyzed the consequences of this new change to the seal's structure. Amani suddenly decided to ask Radon if he would reverse the spell that prevented him from killing, perhaps just long enough to be useful in this fight against Ramos.

"I don't know what we can do about Danior yet," he said, stroking Twila's hair absent-mindedly, "but what I do know is that you have helped improve our chances of defeating Ramos."

Twila lifted her head and looked up at Amani, hopefully. "Really?" She asked. "How?"

"Unless you and Ramos are both destroyed, then the seal cannot fail, because your mother's essence will maintain one half of it," he said firmly. "We can destroy Ramos, and your essence will maintain the other half.

"So, no one needs to stay behind and watch the seal then," she asked, "we can all go to Ramos's mountain together."

Amani nodded in agreement as he continued to hold Twila gently. He felt the tension in her body gradually fade, and she seemed reluctant to pull away from his arms.

Raven and Shayla had curiously watched everything that had transpired between Amani and Twila. They were too far away to hear the discussion between them, but it was clear how upset Twila was. Before either of them could comment on the events, a sudden gust of wind blasted into their faces. It caused Raven's cloak to flap angrily behind him, and Shayla shivered from its icy touch.

The wind whipped up particles of dust and sand from amongst the lush green grass covering the ground. The particles swirled wildly into a rapidly growing dust cloud before their eyes. Raven drew his sword as Shayla readied one of her daggers. Amani and Twila ran back to help Raven and Twila, as they saw the enormous black mass growing between them.

Devon's form gradually emerged amongst the swirling dust cloud, and as suddenly as it had arrived, the wind just as suddenly died. The particles of dust and sand fell silently onto the ground around them, in a shower of black and golden rain. Devon brushed the last of the dust from his cloak and smiled at the surprised expressions around him.

"I have always found it to be the fastest way to travel," he smiled.

"It was almost your last trip," snapped Raven, re-sheathing his sword.

* * *

Ramos grabbed Soleon by the arm and dragged her with him as he almost ran up the stairs to the second level. Soleon's face was a mask of puzzled fear as she struggled to keep up with him, desperately trying to prevent herself from losing her footing and being dragged the rest of the way. When they reached the second level, Ramos hurled her to the floor and pointed at a set of footprints tracked across the cavern center.

"Someone else has been here," Ramos said, his voice echoing eerily around the cavern. "Look, these footprints are different from ours and Rowan's. Who else has been here?"

Soleon covered her ears to prevent Ramos's shouts from reaching them. Using a child's logic that if she couldn't hear him, then she couldn't answer him, Soleon huddled against his legs.

"Well?" Ramos commanded. "Who else was here?" He looked down at the tragic figure at his feet.

She looked at the footprints as if seeing them for the first time, and then suddenly remembered Something. Soleon's fractured memories danced around in her mind as she tried to remember. She almost had the answer for him, but his voice was too loud. It crashed into her mind-destroying everything but one half-formed broken memory.

"A shadow made them," said Soleon thoughtfully. "At least I think it did."

Her words drove Ramos into another frenzy of rage, and he kicked out at Soleon impatiently, sending her sprawling across the cavern floor. She wailed loudly in response.

"I just told you Rowan did not make them," snarled Ramos, "you must have seen who made these footprints. Who are you protecting?"

Soleon scrambled to her knees and began rocking backward and forwards, mumbling quietly to herself. Ramos realized that this was getting him nowhere. In another flash of anger, he lashed out with his fist, and with such force, hurling Soleon across the cavern. She ended up in a crumpled heap against a pile of fallen boulders.

Ramos stormed over to where Soleon lay and then stopped. He saw that she was motionless, her neck at an odd angle as it rested against a large rock.

"Oh, how convenient," he raged, "she's dead, and there are still the warrior bodies to prepare." He turned on his heel exacerbated, leaving her body where it was and stormed back down to his cave below.

Ramos had been about to use his key after Soleon repaired it when he had noticed the footprints. Soleon had stubbornly refused to follow him up to the cavern to look at them, and that convinced him she was protecting the intruder. Now that he had killed her, he would have to wait until sunset tomorrow before she would rise again.

He had discovered that unique fact after killing her in an attempt to rectify the initially failed resurrection. Ramos had killed Soleon many times and in many different ways to see if it fixed the problem controlling her. He had used magic, physical blows, decapitation, and even fire, in attempts to kill and restore a more serene and controllable version of her. Nothing had worked. Ramos would rise each evening when the sun went down, and she would be there, precisely the same, and with no evidence of the previous night's attack.

He decided against leaving tonight to search for more warrior bodies; instead, he wanted to speak with Valeskas. The footprints had changed things. Someone had discovered his cave, and he needed to know who. He felt confident though that this uninvited guest and the pendant key had a connection, and if so, then maybe now was time to raise his army.

The group had listened with great interest to Devon's description of the events that had occurred inside Ramos's mountain, and Raven was ready to set out immediately.

"Wait," Amani commanded, stopping Raven in his tracks. "Something has happened to change the properties of the seal. It has another element now that will maintain the seal's strength, even if we destroy Ramos. Therefore, no one needs to stay behind as planned to deal with any attempts to cross into this world. From what Devon has just told us, everyone's skills and powers are critical in stopping this monster."

"Are you sure about this?" Asked Devon.

"Yes," Amani firmly responded.

"Then let us get this over with," Raven said impatiently, "the longer we wait, the larger Ramos's army grows."

Raven grabbed Daybreak's reins and led her towards the forest.

"Do you think that the one named Rowan was the friend that was not a friend, shown to you in those cards of yours?" Asked Motomo.

"I hope so," answered Raven slowly.

Shayla approached Devon, offering to apply a salve to the angry red wound on his face, but he waved her away.

"I do not need a salve," he said, "but thanks for the offer," he quickly added when he noticed Shayla's injured look.

"Well, it looks like it needs something to take the anger out of it," she said, "just let me know if you feel a fire in it."

"I will," smiled Devon, watching her as she turned and followed Raven into the forest.

Devon paused briefly before following her, and he looked questioningly at Amani and Twila. "Are you coming?" he asked.

"I must first speak with Radon," replied Amani, "I will meet you tomorrow when the sun has set."

"Meet us where?" asked Devon.

"On the beach by the cave that you found." Answered Amani.

"You will not be able to find it so easily," said Devon, "portions of Ramos's mountain surround it. It is well hidden."

"I will find it," said Amani firmly.

Devon smiled and shrugged his shoulders. "Then I wish you luck," he said before following Raven and Shayla into the forest.

Twila hurried after Shayla with Fen. She handed the horse's reigns to Shayla.

"You will need to take care of him," she said, "Devon and I will have to leave you and Raven when dawn approaches, and then catch you both up when the sun sets."

Shayla nodded, took the reins, and continued to follow the others through the forest.

Twila waited until Shayla was out of sight before returning to the clearing. Amani had his back to her, but she knew he was aware of her presence.

"I thought you were unable to join us in the battle against Ramos," Twila said softly, "won't you be destroying yourself?

"The only one who ends up destroyed, little one, is Ramos," he responded firmly, "I will see to it." Twila looked at him, puzzled but chose to say nothing. She suddenly hugged him impulsively and hurried after the others, leaving Amani alone.

He watched her leave until the dark shadows of the forest seemed to swallow her up. A wave of loneliness washed over him; the clearing around the seal seemed suddenly very empty. Over the years, Amani had grown accustomed to being alone, and this new sensation surprised him. Without another thought, he pressed his crystal key against a large oak tree to open a doorway to Vesta to speak with Radon.

Ramos stopped chanting as Valeskas's smoke body began to take form. The gray and white plume of smoke rose above Ramos as it poured from the small wooden bowl set on the table before him. Ramos had witnessed it often but still found it disturbing, from the innocent billowing smoke cloud, the unmistakable shape of the banished blood dragon took form.

Valeskas's big head formed first, followed quickly by a large portion of his body. Ramos watched quietly as the glowing red eyes of Valeskas appeared amongst the smoke. The mouth of the dragon opened and closed soundlessly, rows of sharp smoke teeth becoming visible. It took a few more moments before the talons on Valeskas's front feet clawed at the empty air in an attempt to drag himself further out of the bowl. Ramos knew from experience that attempting to climb out was useless; he had only ever managed to evoke Valeskas's body's upper portion.

"Is it time to raise our warriors?" Asked Valeskas in his strange whispering voice.

Ramos nodded slowly in response, grimacing a little at the red-flecked smoke bubbling from Valeskas's mouth as if it was blood.

"Then let's waste no more time," said Valeskas eagerly, "bring the ingredients for the spell here, and together we will raise our army."

"Someone has been here," said Ramos carefully, "but I was unable to discover who it was."

Valeskas brought his face close to Ramos's. "Did the Lunarian Rowan see the intruder?" He asked.

Ramos fought the urge to turn his head away from Valeskas. "Rowan's dead." He said, pointing to the body outstretched on the floor.

Valeskas stretched himself across the cave floor until only a sliver of smoke held him captive within the wooden bowl. He hovered over Rowan for a moment before returning to face Ramos. "Did the half-dead see who killed the Lunarian?" Asked Valeskas.

"I think she did," said Ramos, "and unfortunately, I killed her in a fit of anger at her stupidity when I was questioning her earlier, so now we will have to wait until tomorrow, when she will rise again, to question her further."

Valeskas hovered thoughtfully before Ramos for a moment. "Well, let's ask the Lunarian what happened then?" He said.

"He has a broken neck," said Ramos, "he is useless to us now except in battle."

Valeskas roared with laughter that sounded like an older man's wheeze at this statement, causing red froth of smoke to fly everywhere. Ramos drew back involuntarily to avoid it but knew there was no need. Valeskas was only a visual representation of him crafted from the smoke. He could see, and Ramos could see him, but he could not touch or be touched.

"What is so funny?" Asked Ramos, a little irritated, "he may have even been killed by the intruder."

"He is Lunarian," stated Valeskas, "if we raise him, Rowan will be as he was, but controlled by you."

Ramos looked at Valeskas suspiciously. The last thing he needed right now was another half-dead mistake following him around for eternity.

"Did you also retrieve the old key keeper, as I suggested?" Asked Valeskas, slowly hovering above each of the bodies in turn.

"I brought him back with me this morning," said Ramos, as he gathered the ingredients for the raising spell.

He glanced at the grotesque faces of his army, and in response, their hollowed eye sockets seem to gaze back at him in silent accusation.

"I don't see him there," said Ramos, turning his back on them, "his body must be still in that sack over there, waiting for Soleon to prepare it." Ramos indicated to the sack with a jerk of his head.

Valeskas mouth parted in a distorted grin as a slight breeze blew through his smoke face, distorting the image for a moment. "Then open the sack," said Valeskas, "I long to see this elusive key-keeper."

"I don't have time for that now," snapped Ramos, "Soleon can do it later."

He could sense Valeskas hovering above him but continued to mash the ingredients together in a large bowl in front of him.

"Then make the time." Valeskas persisted somewhat threateningly.

Ramos hesitated for a moment before abandoning his

potion. Sighing impatiently, he went over to the sack and dumped out the last two bodies on the floor, one of which was Haney's. He pushed the jumble of limbs around with his foot until he separated Haney from the other body.

"That's him," snapped Ramos, going back to his potion.

Valeskas hovered above Haney, peering at him closely.

"I don't know why you had me dig that one up," grumbled Ramos, "he looks too frail to put up much of a fight. There were no weapons buried with him either."

"We will create a special spell for this one," said Valeskas mysteriously, "I never intended him to be a part of the army."

Ramos turned in surprise at this. "Then what exactly do you intend to do with him?" He asked.

"He can retrieve the key for us," Valeskas said slowly with a tooth-filled smile.

Radon looked down at Amani sadly. He had known that one day Amani would choose to be free from the constraints necessary to serve the Dragon's Tear.

"You know that when I remove the spell of destruction, said Radon slowly and carefully, "you can no longer return here?"

Amani nodded. "It hurts me greatly to know that I can no longer come here, but I must sacrifice our friendship so I can assist in the destruction of Ramos," he said.

Radon nodded and took a deep breath before beginning the spell to free Amani.

"I know that you have not made this decision lightly," he said wistfully, "I will miss you, old friend."

The blood dragon began to chant the words of the reversal spell. His deep melodious voice rumbled like thunder, and winds began to gust around Amani, tugging at his hair, causing his cloak to flap wildly around him.

A bright yellow glow appeared around his feet, and they disappeared as the light progressed up his legs and quickly enveloped all of Amani's body. His vision became blocked by the bright yellow light, and as he closed his eyes, a brief moment of indecision flashed through him then replaced instantly with the distraught image of Twila. He held himself stiffly as the yellow glow turned a luminous green as the ability to cast effective and destructive spells returned to him.

"I have removed it," said Radon sadly, "now you must leave this place."

Amani slowly opened his eyes again at Radon's words and looked deeply into the dragon's golden eyes.

"I understand," he said, "but know that I would never attempt to use the Dragon's Tear power. Only you have that right, and only if Saressa commands it."

He walked towards the Dragon's Tear as Radon silently watched. Amani looked up at the sphere, lost in thought for a moment. Silvery flashes of light exploded periodically amongst the swirling red mist within its mysterious depths.

"Whatever happens, and for as long as I am able," said Amani firmly, "I will continue to do whatever I can to protect the Dragon's Tear. Your people sacrificed themselves to save everything that was, is, and will be. I could no longer stand by and watch Ramos's attempts to destroy everything."

Radon sighed deeply. His hot, smoky breath pushed its way to Amani, caressing him like an old friend.

"Your sacrifice has been just as great as my brothers were," he said.

Amani shook his head slowly but said nothing in response, he then turned away, and with one final glance at Radon, headed for the hall of pillars.

As he reached the massive archway, Amani heard a resounding crash. He turned swiftly in response to the sound but was not quick enough to avoid the impact of an enormous bolt of light crashing into his chest.

The incredible force of the bolt hurled him backward into one of the carved pillars, pinning him helplessly against it. His eyes wide with surprise, Amani saw that the light, the force of which was pulsing against his chest and effectively holding him captive, was emitting from the center of the Dragon's Tear. The light was bright to his eyes, and the crushing pressure on his chest was making it difficult to breathe. Amani closed his eyes against it, and the last image he saw was of Radon rushing towards him, his enormous tail swishing up the golden dust that covered the floor in its wake.

He opened his eyes again briefly and saw the blood dragon's massive head looming over him, blocking out his view of the billions of stars above them.

"Amani," called out a female voice faintly.

Amani was puzzled for a moment. He could see nothing, just

impenetrable darkness. The voice called his name again, and he struggled with his senses, trying to remember where he was.

Slowly, consciousness stirred from deep within him, pushing him closer and closer to a gray light that gradually appeared before him. As the gray light grew brighter, it changed into an ivory-colored mist, and he began to remember what had happened. He realized that his eyes were still tightly closed, and cautiously he opened them.

"Welcome, Amani," said the female figure hovering before him.

Swirls of delicate silver fabric fluttered about her in the gentle breezes that fanned Amani to full wakefulness. Her long, pale yellow hair danced with her robe. The cascades of perfectly spiraled curls flowed around her, tangling, then untangling themselves as if in some kind of wild dance. The paleness of her skin glowed in stark contrast against the blood-red mist surrounding her.

"I am Saressa." She said softly.

Amani had scrambled to his feet but dropped to his knees when she said her name. He bowed his head, which caused his long white hair to drape around his face like a hood. Amani longed to gaze at Saressa's beautiful features again, but he was afraid to raise his head.

"I am dead then?" he asked.

Saressa laughed. "No, not dead," she said.

The sound of her laughter gave Amani the courage to raise his head and study his strange new surroundings. He wondered for a moment if this was the dream time that Shayla had mentioned.

"No, Amani, this is not dream time, either," said Saressa, reading his thoughts. "The dragon's souls called to me from here within the Tear."

Amani gasped when he realized that this place was the inside of the Dragon's Tear.

"The essence of the dragon's souls brought you here for me," she said, "this is a safe place for me to speak with you without breaking my pact with Dra."

Amani looked around him curiously. He saw only a deep red fog as far as his eyes could see. His lower legs submerged in it, and although it appeared to have no substance, the fog supported his knees gently as he knelt before Saressa.

He looked up above him and saw nothing but the same red fog. Amani noticed that at times portions of the mist began to gather into swirling half-formed figures, each fading before becoming a recognizable form.

"I don't understand why Radon's brothers brought me here," he finally said, puzzled. "I asked Radon to remove the spell that prevented me from destroying anything within your worlds. Good or Bad. Ramos has gone too far, and we must kill him.

"I see no other way but to help the girl Twila and the others in their attempt to destroy him, because with Valeskas helping him, he may now be too powerful even with my help. If Radon's brothers intend to keep me here, then Ramos will no doubt succeed in releasing Valeskas."

Saressa smiled at his words. "The dragons have brought you here because they want to gift you something," she said, "it is all they able to do to help you stop Ramos. They tell me that they sense Valeskas calling to them, mocking them. He tells them that Ramos has discovered a way to release him from his frozen prison."

"That is why there is no time to lose," urged Amani, "I implore you, Saressa, ask the dragons to release me. The others are on their way to fight Ramos as we speak. They will need what help I can give if they are to succeed."

Saressa nodded. "Then accept this gift that the dragons bestow on you, Amani. Become their champion."

A blinding red flash exploded around Amani, followed by a burning sensation that started in his feet then legs until it gradually flowed through his whole body. Alarmed, he looked down at himself and found that the red fog appeared to be swallowing him up. The mist was already up to his chest, obscuring everything below that in impenetrable redness. Amani looked back at Saressa in sudden alarm.

"Don't be afraid, Amani," she smiled, "The dragons sacrificed themselves to protect my worlds from Dra's mischief. This gift of power you are about to receive will allow their strength to become yours when needed. Not only should you now be able to destroy Ramos, but the dragons have also decided that the constant threat from Valeskas needs to end.

"Radon's brothers ask if you are willing to accept this gift."

"Yes," Amani responded firmly. "If it takes an eternity, I will spend that time hunting Valeskas and his followers until they are all destroyed."

"Then let it be so," she said.

Amani gasped as the burning sensation grew into an intense searing heat within him. A groan involuntarily escaped his lips as he fought to stop himself screaming out in pain. He could no longer see Saressa through the thick red fog that now covered his eyes.

Amani slumped forward and blindly lay face down, cushioned by the spongy texture of the red fog that supported him. Voices crept into his mind as the fire within him started to fade. He tried to make sense of the jumbled mess of words rushing into his head.

"Individual voices slowly began to emerge, and Amani sensed their urgent tone, but the language was unknown to him. He finally clasped his hands to his ears in a useless attempt to block them out.

"Stop," he groaned mentally, "this is too much. I cannot understand you." The voices instantly stopped and were replaced by total silence. Amani sighed gratefully. "Thank you," he said as he slowly opened his eyes and saw Radon's massive head looming over him.

"Thank you for what?" Asked Radon, puzzled. "I have done nothing. You brought yourself back from wherever that blast of light took you."

Amani quickly sat up and looked around. He was back in Vesta with Radon. Saressa was gone, and the Dragon's Tear sat innocently in the claw of the golden dragon statue. He became aware of searing pain in his chest, it felt on fire, and he was just about to touch it with his hand carefully when Radon stopped him.

"Your chest," Radon gasped. "Look at it."

Amani staggered over to one of the gold pillars and struggled to see his reflection in the torchlight.

The front of his shirt was in shreds. He carefully tore away the remnants from his chest, wincing as the pain increased with this movement. As the remainder of his shirt fell to the floor, Amani saw what Radon had seen. In the center of his chest was the image of a dragon, branded deeply into the flesh. The dragon was a perfect copy of the golden statue that held the Dragon's Tear, and as he peered at the reflection of his chest, he noticed that this flesh copy of the golden dragon also had a sphere aloft in its claw. He slowly smiled as he gently traced his fingers around the edges of the dragon brand on his chest. It marked the blood dragon's gift of power to him, and now Amani was even more anxious to meet up with the others and end Ramos.

CHAPTER TWENTY-TWO

Undead Warriors

Daybreak tensed every muscle in her body, trying desperately not to move under the pressure of Raven's third attempt at climbing onto her back. The last two tries had been hilarious disasters. He took a running jump up onto Daybreak's back on the first attempt, but lost his balance and slid off, ending up flat on his face in the mud by her feet. The event had taken her by surprise, and she had snickered in her horse laughter when she saw Raven's face covered in mud. Her laughter instantly stopped when he had angrily scrambled to his feet and grabbed the reins for another attempt. Daybreak tried to help by edging towards a rocky bank at the side of the path, thinking it would make the mount less difficult for him, but he would have none of it.

"If you keep moving around," he grumbled, "I will never get up there."

She tried to reason with him, but the sight of his mud-streaked, angry face set her off laughing again. Daybreak forced herself to turn it into a snort, hoping that Raven wouldn't realize that she was laughing.

For the second attempt, the position was wrong for both the horse and potential rider, so it made no difference whether Daybreak stood still or not. It failed once again. Raven did not allow enough play in the reins to give him the freedom to maneuver. He yanked on them, causing her head to jerk to the left. Daybreak followed his unintentional signal, as trained, and she promptly turned to her left. This maneuver caused her body to move away from Raven as he began to mount, and he ended up half on the horse, and half off. Frantically he hopped on the foot that was now barely touching the ground, desperately trying to follow the rest of his body that was now moving left on the back of Daybreak.

Raven eventually lost his footing and came crashing down in a tangled mess between her legs. Daybreak felt like she would explode with laughter after this second attempt. He scrambled to his feet again, slapping the mud and grass off his clothes before turning to face Daybreak.

"This isn't going to work if you keep moving," Raven spat.

Tears trickled out the corners of Daybreak's eyes, and she sucked in a deep breath of air in an attempt to control her laughter. His features instantly softened as he became concerned when he noticed the tears and labored breathing.

"Have I injured you?" Raven asked, gently patting her neck.

Daybreak could control herself no longer, and a loud snort of laughter, followed by a burst of high-pitched snickers, blasted its way out of her aching jaws. The alarm on Raven's face fueled Daybreak's laughter as she bowed her head, trying to catch a breath between snorts.

"You were right," Daybreak finally said between snorts. "You are no horseman."

Raven's look of concern changed to flushed anger as he realized that Daybreak was laughing at him.

"That's right," he snapped, flinging her reins to the ground, "and it was not my idea to ride you; I was content to walk."

Daybreak's laughter instantly stopped when Raven stormed down the trail after the others.

"Wait," called Daybreak, trotting after him, "the others were right; you need to ride so that you are well-rested when we reach Ramos's mountain."

"I have walked, in fact, even ran to many battles," called Raven over his shoulder, "it has never affected my performance so far."

"This will be no ordinary battle," Daybreak cautioned. "Shayla rides Fen so she will not be exhausted, Devon and Twila have unlimited strength while the sun is down. They need you to be at your best for this battle, or you will fail to defeat Ramos."

Raven slowed his pace as Daybreak's words edged their

way through his anger. Daybreak grew encouraged when she saw this and nudged him gently in the back.

"I am sorry I laughed at you," she said gently, "can we try again?"

Raven abruptly stopped causing Daybreak to almost trample over him. She backed up hopefully and positioned herself against the rocky bank that edged the moss-covered trail.

He turned to face her, and with a sharp intake of breath, he strode towards her. The voice of his old teacher flowed into his thoughts. He could hear the admonishing tone that Haney would use when his young student lost his patience with a tricky maneuver. Raven smiled sadly at this sudden flash of memory. He stood for a moment analyzing Daybreak's position and height. He grinned as he noticed the horse was holding herself rigid. Her eyes avoided his as she patiently waited for another of his clumsy attempts to mount her.

"I suppose my last attempts were amusing," he acknowledged, "and if we keep the details between ourselves, I would appreciate it."

Daybreak turned to face him. "Many things remain between a horse, and it's human friend," she said firmly, "it's the code of my kind."

Raven chuckled and patted her neck, "then see to it that you do not break it," he said, "now hold still while I will try this again."

With Daybreak's encouragement, he was upon her back within moments. She felt him wobble slightly but knew by the fierce grip of his knees in her ribs that he would not fall this time. Daybreak slowly began to walk down the path after the others. Raven held himself rigid in concentration at staying on her back. The horse smiled to herself as she recognized these unmistakable signs of a new rider. She knew from experience that he would eventually relax a little, and that would be her cue to begin the task of teaching him how to ride a horse properly.

"If I don't teach him to relax and become one with my movements," she thought, "his muscles will be too stiff for him to be of any help at all when they meet Ramos."

When the two of them caught up with the others, he looked more at ease on her back. Twila glanced at him and noticed that his feet were not in the customized pockets at the edges of Daybreak's riding blanket. Not suspecting that he was a novice, Twila just assumed that he was unaccustomed to this Gypsy adaptation, designed to take the pressure off the rider's thighs.

"Here," she said, pushing one of Raven's feet firmly into the pocket.

"It takes the strain off the legs. You'll only find it in a Gypsy blanket, so you probably weren't aware of its purpose. There is another one on the other side," she said.

This sudden movement almost unseated Raven, but somehow he managed to keep his balance. He pushed his other foot into the remaining pocket and instantly felt the difference.

"Thanks," he called after Twila as she vanished from his sight.

"The pockets help," said Shayla, "my legs were beginning to cramp already until Twila pointed them out to me. Even on horses, we can't keep up with Twila and Devon's pace, but at least the ride is more comfortable now."

He felt much safer with his feet securely in the pockets, and when Daybreak felt him relax, she began to speed up, closing the gap between her and Fen.

Ramos became aware of the pulsating heartbeat sound that grew louder and more intense as he completed the words to the resurrection spell. The sound matched the excited pounding of his heartbeat as he watched the thick plume of red smoke pour from the bowl containing his spell ingredients and flow slowly across the floor of the cavern. It gradually started to cover his collection of dead warriors. The pulsating beat grew louder and louder, as the final body disappeared beneath the glowing red smoke.

"Now," screeched Valeskas attempting to get Ramos to hear him over the massive sound of the heartbeat, "add the last ingredient now."

He needed no further prompting; the pounding heartbeat now so loud that the whole cavern was vibrating. Pots and jars toppled down from the many shelves around the walls, crashing to the floor, spilling their precious ingredients into greasy colorful messes. He pulled the stopper out of the small leather flask that he was clutching tightly in his hand. Quickly Ramos poured out some of the thick black liquid into the bowl that was still billowing out red smoke. He raised his arms and began to chant without even pausing to replace the stopper of the flask that was still in his hand.

Suddenly there was absolute silence. Ramos's ears were still ringing as he turned to look at the rapidly disappearing smoke across the floor of the cavern. One by one, the warriors became visible again. Valeskas hovered above their bodies, the smoke threads that restrained him grew thinner and thinner as he struggled against them.

Ramos waited breathlessly for some indication that the spell had worked. A minute went by and then another. Impatiently he replaced the stopper in his flask and tucked it back into a pocket in his robe.

"It didn't work," Ramos stated finally.

"Quiet," hissed Valeskas, "you need to learn some patience."

"Patience?" Ramos retorted. "Someone or something has discovered this place and will return with others, and you speak of patience?"

Before Valeskas could respond to this comment, a loud clatter caused them both to turn in the direction of the sound. Ramos smiled as one by one; the bodies of his warriors slowly began to move. Valeskas hovered above them, monitoring their progress.

The Lunarian woke suddenly from his sleep of death. He scrambled unsteadily to his feet, and then immediately clutched at his throat, his eyes wildly looked around the cavern until he saw Ramos. Rowan lurched towards him, and Ramos quickly waved his hand, sending a yellow blast of light in defense. Instantly the Lunarian was flung backward, crashing through the slowly rising warriors, scattering bodies, weapons, and armor in his wake.

Rowan lay stunned for a moment but then scrambled to his feet again and faced Ramos. He started to move towards him again, but when he saw Ramos raise his hand, the Lunarian decided against it.

As his thoughts cleared, Rowan realized that it was Ramos before him and not Devon. The Lunarian's last recollection was of his fight with Devon, and now he was confused. Rowan saw Valeskas looming above him and tried to speak, but no sound came out of his mouth. He pushed his thoughts out to Ramos, trying to explain the attack on him.

Ramos attempted to make sense of Rowan's confused thoughts, and the only clear one was of the fight with another Lunarian.

"There is another Lunarian in this world?" Ramos asked him.

Rowan nodded frantically in response. Ramos tried again to make sense of Rowan's thoughts, but it was like looking into a muddy stream.

"Did the Lunarian cross into this world with you?" He asked irritably.

Rowan shook his head and began mouthing words in an attempt to get Ramos to understand him. Ramos was in no mood to even try and work out what Rowan was trying to say. He turned angrily to Valeskas, who was hovering thoughtfully above them.

"Why can't he speak?' He snapped.

Valeskas shook his head slowly. "I am not sure," he answered slowly, "possibly Soleon lost a piece of his neck when she assembled him."

"What about the confusion within his mind?" Asked Ramos, "his thoughts are coming through to me all mixed up. Will it clear? I need to know about the other Lunarian."

"I don't know that either," responded Valeskas, "I have never encountered a resurrected Lunarian before."

Ramos was about to question this further, but the writhing warriors on the floor distracted him. Life was returning now to the macabre figures. They rose to their feet in unison, staggering and swaying on their broken and decaying legs. Most of their heads were at alarming angles with their shoulders. How they remained attached to their bodies at all was surprising to Ramos. Arms, or what was identifiable as arms, dangled uselessly by the warrior's sides.

Rowan was horrified at the realization that Ramos had resurrected him, but he slumped to the floor in fascinated disgust when he saw the rising warriors. Ramos turned to Valeskas, once again beside himself with anger.

"What is this? Ramos screeched. "They will not be able to fight. Look at them." he gestured with his hand in the direction of the slowly stirring warriors.

"Patience," Valeskas said calmly. "Have some patience."

Amani's sudden appearance on the track in front of them startled Fen. Shayla quickly reacted and managed to prevent the horse from rearing up and throwing her off. Daybreak had already sensed Amani's presence before he had shown himself, so she did not react as Fen had. She had been about to tell Raven that he was waiting for them, but Amani stepped out onto the track before the horse had time to say anything.

Raven looked on in admiration at Shayla's skill at controlling the panicked horse. He was more than grateful to Daybreak for her calm reaction to Amani's sudden appearance, and he patted her neck appreciatively.

"Thank you, my friend," he said, knowing for sure that he would have fallen to the ground.

The last few hours of riding Daybreak had not improved his horse handling skills anywhere close to Shayla's.

"I am sorry I startled Fen," apologized Amani, "I should have spoken to the horse so she would know I was here."

Shayla grinned at him in response, her cheeks flushed from the brief struggle to control Fen. "Well, I hope you remember next time," she said, "I was already beginning to doze a little and had I been asleep already, you would have had to chase after Fen."

Raven looked at Amani closely in the limited light. He sensed something was different about him but could not define what it was.

"I sense it too." Agreed Daybreak.

Amani suggested that they should stop to rest and feed the horses. "We should use this opportunity to plan our attack on Ramos," he said, as Twila and Devon rejoined them.

Raven got off Daybreak far more graciously than he had gotten on and was thankful. He ached all over but had to admit they had traveled much farther than if he had stayed on foot.

When the group settled, Amani then shared that he could join them in the fight with Ramos. The others looked around at each other, puzzled at this revelation. However, Amani chose not to share the details with them, and none of the group asked for any. Twila decided to ask Amani later what had changed things. Radon must have removed the spell that prevented him from destroying Ramos, and she was curious as to why he removed it.

At the prompting of Amani, Devon described every detail he could remember about his visit to Ramos's mountain. He even drew a reasonably detailed map on a piece of linen paper, provided by Twila, so that Shayla and Raven could find the concealed entrance when dawn forced him to sleep. Raven took the map and studied it carefully, then passed it to Shayla.

"You should arrive at the shore before the sun goes down," said Devon, "we can all meet there tomorrow. If you are not there at that time, we will follow the trail backward until we find you."

Amani glanced at the map Shayla was holding and quickly familiarized himself with the most significant landmarks indicated on it.

"I will go ahead of you," he said, "just to make sure that nothing is waiting for our arrival that the sunrise doesn't affect."

"I agree with you," said Twila quickly. "We couldn't help if you run into a trap while the sun is up. I know from experience that Ramos has a potion that allows him to function while the sun is up."

Raven silently wondered if Amani was suspicious of Devon's allegiance with the group like he was. Devon caught Raven's unguarded thoughts, and the Lunarian grew angry.

"Guard your thoughts, warrior," Devon snarled at him, "Ramos will destroy us all before we even reach his mountain if you don't control them."

Raven was startled by this outburst and was then immediately embarrassed by his blunder.

"It will not happen again," he retorted defensively, "but if Amani is indeed unsure of your loyalty in this, then I agree with his decision to go on ahead. You may indeed be leading us into a trap."

"And what would I gain from that," said Devon, turning to Amani.

"Exactly." Said Amani, stepping in between Raven and Devon. "Stop this nonsense, Raven. Devon wants Ramos destroyed just as much as the rest of us. He needs to return to Lunaria and find his father."

Now it was Devon's turn to be surprised, and he faced Amani curiously. "What do you know of my father?" He asked.

Amani suddenly realized that he could not answer Devon's question, and neither could he explain the rhythmic pounding that reminded him of a heartbeat coming from the direction of Ramos's mountain. He initially assumed that everyone could hear it, but when none of the others commented on it, Amani realized that it had increased his senses when the blood dragons marked him.

Amani knew about Devon's decision to find a way back to his father, but not by reading his thoughts. Devon guarded his thoughts very well. Amani just knew this to be a fact. He thought that Devon had told him earlier, but that was not the case. Amani realized that he had to tell the others something about the changes he was going through. They all needed to be as one in this fight against Ramos.

"I just knew about your father without being told," Amani said slowly, "I asked Radon to remove the spell that prevented me from being a danger to the Dragon's Tear so that I could fight with you all against Ramos. Somehow removing the magic has increased my senses. You guard your thoughts well, Devon, and he is correct. Raven, you need to block your thoughts, especially as we are getting closer to Ramos.

"The real reason that I have decided to go on ahead to Ramos's mountain is not that I suspect your loyalties. I am sensing something from there that none of you can hear. I want to see if I can learn anything else that can assist us."

The others looked around at each other, nodding in silent agreement at Amani's plan. Anything he could discover could potentially help them.

Ramos's excitement grew as he watched the changes transpiring in the grotesque group of warriors before him. Slowly, their rotting remains were regenerating, and extremities realigned, clothing restoring itself to new. As each warrior's rejuvenation finished, it searched out its weapon and armor. As the warrior retrieved its weapons and armor, the same regeneration took place, and each item became restored to pristine condition.

He surveyed the expressionless army stood before him. Their uniformed sightless gaze made him a little uncomfortable. What flesh was visible from beneath their variety of battle dress and uniforms was pale, with a blue-tinged hue.

The most startling and alarming aspect of this army of dead warriors was their eyes or lack of them. A dark blood-red bulging mass now filled the eye sockets. Ramos disappointedly assumed that they were unable to see through this abomination for eyes.

He walked along the front line of his army and found that they either heard the sound of his feet or could indeed see his movement because all heads instantly turned in his direction. Ramos slowly smiled at their responsiveness.

"You need to place them strategically," instructed Valeskas, hovering above each of the warriors in turn.

Ramos nodded in agreement as he beckoned to six of the closest warriors.

"Follow me," he commanded.

The six warriors closely followed Ramos as he led them back to the surface of the mountain. Ramos positioned the first two in the vast cavern filled with stalagmites and stalactites. The next two, he ordered to guard the grand stairway that led to the lower levels. He placed the final two in the first cavern at the rear of the cabin.

Each time Ramos positioned his warriors, he commanded them to attack anything unless he ordered otherwise. The Warriors responded in the same toneless way to each of his commands.

"We serve you, Dark Lord," the warriors chanted into Ramos's mind.

Ramos smiled appreciatively at this response. He was also very pleased and somewhat relieved at the success of their resurrection. Now he had slaves to do his bidding. Ramos just wished that there had been time to gather more of them. He planned to use the warriors to find more bodies for his army, but that would have to wait until after they had destroyed whoever it was that had breached his mountain.

When Ramos returned to his cave, he decided that he found the last three warriors too disturbing to remain there. He took them up to the next level, where Soleon still lay in a heap against one of the walls. Valeskas laughed scornfully at Ramos when he sensed his discomfort.

"They are your servants," laughed Valeskas mockingly, "you are foolish to be unnerved by their presence. Why you are as squeamish as that mute over there." Valeskas pointed a smoke claw in Rowan's direction, who was still cowering in the farthest corner of the cavern.

"Quiet." Snapped Ramos. "I have potions to replace, and the warriors will be in my way."

"Oh, is that how it is? Mocked Valeskas, "then I will speak of it no further." He bobbed tauntingly in front of Ramos, who chose to ignore him.

"What I want to know is this?" Questioned Ramos. "What use to me is the Lunarian in all this? He can't speak, so therefore unable to tell us who was here. He does not appear to be under my control either. I can only hope he is not as unpredictable as Soleon is."

Valeskas studied Rowan closely. "We will just have to wait and see, I suppose," he said thoughtfully.

"You mean you don't know how the Lunarian will behave either?" Snarled Ramos, slamming down a pitcher of dark liquid that he been about to pour into a wooden bowl.

"No," answered Valeskas simply, "it should be interesting to find out, though, don't you agree?"

Ramos angrily turned back to the potion he was compiling; the last thing he needed right now was another unknown element in all of this.

Rowan decided he had heard enough and unsteadily scrambled to his feet. Quickly he bolted for the exit of the cave. When he reached the entrance to the cavern above, the last three warriors stopped him. They stood motionlessly, observing the Lunarian. Rowan finally leaned against the wall of the cavern expecting to be attacked at any second.

Ramos groaned when he saw Rowan run for the exit of the cave. "Now, I will have to waste time trying to find him," he said, then stopped as suddenly a clear picture of Rowan appeared in his mind.

He recognized the place as being the cavern above him. He could even see the slumped body of Soleon to the far right of Rowan.

"We destroy him, Dark Lord?" The toneless voices of the warriors drifted into Ramos's mind.

"No," replied Ramos. "But do not let him leave the cavern."

"We serve you, Dark Lord," responded the warriors in unison, and instantly the image in Ramos's mind vanished.

Valeskas had seen the image too and pushed his smoke face close to Ramos's.

"Better than expected?" Valeskas taunted.

Ramos smiled broadly in response. "Better even than that," he said.

Valeskas's features suddenly started to lose form slightly. Wisps of his smoke head drifted upwards, disappearing when they reached the roof of the cavern. Ramos frowned as more and more of Valeskas was dissipating. The smoke demon had a look of surprise on what was left of his face, as the trail of smoke that confined him to the wooden bowl grew shorter and shorter, dragging him backward.

"What is it?" Asked Ramos, puzzled. "The spell can't be wearing off already, surely?"

Valeskas's mouth no longer had enough sustenance to form words, so he answered Ramos's question directly into his mind.

"Something is coming," Valeskas said weakly into Ramos's thoughts, "I sense a blood dragon's presence."

"But that is impossible," said Ramos quickly. "You told me that they were as trapped and powerless as yourself unless released."

Ramos felt a cold shiver of realization pour down his spine at his statement. "Has someone released them?" Asked Ramos slowly.

"No, that is impossible," replied Valeskas, "that honor should be ours."

Ramos chose not to respond to Valeskas's statement. He thoughtfully watched as Valeskas grew smaller and smaller until the little wooden bowl seemed to swallow him up.

"I will think about this new development," said Valeskas. "Sunrise approaches, and I doubt there will be an attack until nightfall. Summon me then, and the greatest of powers will be yours."

Ramos watched as the last of Valeskas disappeared in a final wisp of smoke. An uncommon sense of foreboding washed over him, and as he shrugged it off, he said a small prayer up to Dra asking for his assistance in whatever he and Valeskas were about to face.

Amani found Devon's entrance to Ramos's mountain quite quickly. He circled high in the air above the small beach that was completely cut off by water on three sides and the vast mountain to its rear. Devon had been right; this was indeed the perfect way to reach Ramos

297

quickly, giving them the best opportunity of surprise.

He flapped his raven wings and aimed towards the beach, the cold air rushing through his feathers invoked the familiar pleasure of flight. He landed accurately to one side of the cave's entrance and immediately changed into his human form.

Amani looked across the dark water as it lapped against the shore. Devon had not mentioned how the others would cross from the mainland, and Amani pondered on this apparent oversight. It would not be a problem for him, but the others would not find it easy to cross. He finally turned in the direction of the cave's entrance, and then without hesitation, he strode purposely towards it. He would worry about getting the others across later. First, he wanted to see if this entrance gave them any kind of advantage.

As Amani entered the cave, a warm sensation began to develop in the center of his chest, where the blood dragon's mark was still tender against his shirt. He crossed the small bridge leading to the glowing spires of crystals that formed the passage to the cave wall's hidden entrance. The warm sensation grew to a throbbing heat in his chest and became almost unbearable as Amani reached the crystals. He dropped to his knees as a flood of feelings and visions filled his mind.

One by one, Amani relived the life and death of each blood dragon that had given himself to Saressa and the Dragon's Tear. He fell facedown and writhed in pain from their memories, seeing everything as clearly as if they had been his own memories.

As the last memory faded, Amani weakly raised his head, and he felt a rush of power course through him. The crystal spires seemed to pulse in rhythm with the power coursing through him. A thick red mist began to form around him, and he was alarmed when he realized that it was coming from his own body.

Amani watched as the red mist traveled from crystal spire to crystal spire, surrounding it briefly before going on to the next.

"Gateways," said a voice within his mind, "The only place you cannot reach from here is Vesta."

"Is this the correct place to enter Ramos's caves unnoticed?" Amani asked the red mist.

The mist had returned to surround Amani as he asked the question. Slowly it changed direction and disappeared from Amani's view beyond the crystal gateways. He hurried after it and found the mist swirling around a portion of rock at the rear of the cave.

"Here," said the voice, "this is the entrance."

Amani peered through the mist and initially saw nothing but a rock wall. "I see no entrance," said Amani, "but Devon spoke of one. Is there truly an entrance here, or are we being led into a trap?"

In response to the last question, the cave wall became transparent, and he could see a small cave on the other side. Cautiously Amani touched the now visible entrance and found no resistance.

"Devon spoke the truth about the hidden entrance," said the voice, "you will have to discover for yourself if he is leading you into a trap."

The red mist surrounded Amani once again and then disappeared. He stepped into the small cave, and instantly a shudder of foreboding coursed through him. Amani sensed a powerful evil force filling the air. He thought about investigating further, but the voice in his head stopped him.

"Dawn approaches," cautioned the voice, "now is not the time for this."

Amani didn't hesitate; he turned around and went back the way he had come. Gratefully he breathed in the crisp ocean air as he stood on the beach. This time he noticed that the beach looked to be inaccessible to boats. A sizable shallow bank of rock just offshore looked deadly enough to tear up any vessel attempting to leave the ocean's main channel.

He could see the majestic waves crashing against the rocks. Once over the barrier, the waves ran weakly towards the beach, where Amani stood watching their progress. He pondered again on the problem facing the group when they tried to cross this stretch of water. He looked to his right, where the land was closest, and the place where Devon had directed everyone to meet tonight.

Amani agreed with him; this looked to be the only place where the others would have a chance to cross the water safely. The sky began to turn gray, heralding the sun's arrival, and satisfied that Devon had spoken the truth so far, he changed into the form of the Raven and flew towards land. He headed for the closest tree so that he could return to Vesta and meet with his old friend, perhaps for the last time.

CHAPTER TWENTY-THREE

The Ice Path

Raven rechecked the map to ensure that this was the place they were to meet the others after the sun had set. Gratefully he climbed down from Daybreak's back. Shayla saw Raven's action as confirmation that they had reached their destination and jumped down from Fen. The sun was low in the sky, but there was at least another two hours before nightfall. While he carefully explored the immediate area, Shayla prepared a fire.

The air had gradually grown colder the closer they got to the foot of Ramos's mountain. Ice laced the small stream's outer edges that, according to the map, was their final landmark before reaching the meeting place. She planned to collect water at the creek to boil for their tea after Raven had determined it was safe to light a fire.

"There is nothing for miles around here," Raven said when he returned. "Except for this mountain and a beach down there." He waved his hand to indicate where the beach was.

"And Ramos?" Questioned Shayla as she expertly generated a bright spark from her two firestones as she clashed them together.

"I saw no one," he confirmed as he watched Shayla encouraging the reluctant smolder into a bright flame.

She fed more of the long-dead foliage that she had collected while he was scouting out the area into the glowing heart of the immature fire, gently blowing on it occasionally to encourage its growth. When the fire was strong enough to consume twigs and then finally branches without threatening to go out, Shayla rested back on her heels for a moment relishing its still meager warmth. Raven had previously started their fires and commended Shayla on the skilled way in which she had quickly made this one.

"If you tend the fire until it takes hold," she instructed, "I will fetch water from that stream we saw. I need a hot drink to get rid of this travel dust."

Raven jumped to his feet instantly. "You watch the fire," he said, "I need to move around and get rid of this stiffness in my muscles. I will fetch the water."

Shayla grinned at his response and began to remove the items she needed from her pack to assemble them some kind of quick supper.

"There is something about fires and cooking that always seems deemed to a woman's responsibility," she thought, and Raven caught her thought. "Just be quick about it then," Shayla taunted, "this taste of road dust is ruining my appetite."

Raven laughed as he headed back to the stream.

The cold wind tugged at his senses as he left the scanty shelter of trees and bushes that seemed to huddle against the bottom of the mountain. He clambered over rocks and boulders that once had been a part of this majestic mountain towering above him.

A single snowflake and then another danced before him, carried by the increasing wind. The outer edge of the stream was now a thickening sheet of ice. It cracked beneath his weight as Raven filled two flasks with water. He looked up at the stream's source and saw large icicles hanging down like razor-sharp fangs from the edges of rock that the water was gushing over. Raven was surprised that the stream was turning to ice because it was flowing quite fast. More snowflakes fell, and he decided that hot tea was a good idea.

After they had eaten, Raven quickly created a rough but efficient shelter for the horses. The trees' tops already bowed from the years of savage coastal storms that blew through without resistance. So, it was a reasonably simple task to pull them lower, attach them to the rocks, and create a windbreaker for Daybreak and Fen. It was the perfect spot for them.

Shayla had positioned her fire in a well-sheltered position too, and while they waited for nightfall, she fell asleep. He was unable to sleep; he never could just before a battle. He did rest though, slumped comfortably against a tree, his blanket pulled around him, watching the flickering flames from the fire grow brighter as the sky grew darker.

It wasn't just the impending battle that was on his mind. Raven had gone down to the beach while Shayla was preparing their meal. Although he wasn't sure exactly where the cave was that Devon had spoken of, Raven knew that it must involve crossing the water.

His eyes had carefully searched the cliffs around this beach and saw nothing in the rock face that appeared to be a cave. He followed the beach around the cliffs that formed the mountain's very base until the sea prevented him from going any further. There were two other small sandy areas farther around the coastline, but he couldn't see anything else from where he had stood, the waves lapping at his feet.

Raven doubted that the other beaches could be reached by boat either. There was a rocky barrier running from the cliff into the water for as far as he could see. Maybe if you sailed far enough out then, you could get around this natural barrier. Raven frowned as he studied the map again and wondered once more about Devon's allegiance.

"Why would Devon lead us to this place when it's obvious that the only other person that could cross this water easily is Amani," he thought suspiciously. "Has he joined Ramos against us?"

Shayla had not asked about his search for the cave, and he chose not to offer any information. He just hoped the sun would go down quickly so they could get on with this. The final hours before a battle always made him restless, and what made it worse this time was the lack of a structured battle plan, and now apparently a planned route to the cave. Raven was also becoming irritated about having to mask his thoughts carefully. That was taking more of his concentration than he had the patience to give.

Motomo wandered quietly into the camp as the final glow of day gave way to nightfall. He drew close to the fire, and steam began to rise from him as the snow on his fur melted. The wolf gazed thoughtfully into the flames. He had spent the day with his family and had realized that he no longer belonged amongst them.

Raven sensed the wolf's mood and patted his damp fur kindly. "What is it?" He asked Motomo.

The wolf pulled his eyes away from the flames as he answered. "I am wondering what to do after all this is over," he said, "I no longer belong with my kind, and Twila spoke of traveling with Devon to find Danior. There are not many people who would invite a wolf to their campfire."

"I am stuck in the same dilemma," Raven smiled. "We will travel as outcasts together. That is with your agreement, of course."

Motomo's features brightened instantly. "It would please me greatly," he said.

"If you two outcasts have no other plans than to sit by campfires," blurted Shayla, "you can return with me. I will need all the help I can get."

Raven looked at Motomo questioningly. "How say you, friend?" He asked the wolf. "If we come out of this battle alive, should we go to Shayla's world and help her cause?"

Motomo nodded. "It would be an honor to serve Saressa," he answered solemnly.

Twila and Devon seemed to appear from nowhere and startled the other three. Raven scowled across at Devon. He was very anxious to hear how the Lunarian planned to get them safely across the water to reach this cave of his.

Amani arrived as Shayla was reluctantly dousing the fire. She had thought to leave it burning for the horse's sake, but Devon stated that they should take them to the shelter of the cave. Raven was about to ask Devon how he proposed to get any of them over the water when Amani asked the question for him.

"I found the cave and the secret entrance into the mountain," Amani said, "but what I didn't find was any way to reach the cave from this side of the mountain.

"There is nothing but water and rock shelves between us and the cave; only you and I can reach it easily, Devon. I found no trees that I can use as gates to transport them across either, so how do I plan to get everyone over there".

Devon looked stunned for a moment as he realized the truth of Amani's words. The others watched Devon curiously, except for Raven, who was enjoying the Lunarian's obvious discomfort.

"You are correct," said Devon slowly, a smile beginning to form on his lips, "I had not taken into consideration the limitations of the others. Luckily this cold weather has saved us from having to go up the mountain. It is so cold tonight that the edges of the spring we just passed are now frozen."

"How will that help us?" Raven snapped sarcastically. "You certainly can't be implying that the sea is about to freeze also, or are you?

"No, not implying," responded Devon confidently, "I know the sea will freeze."

"How?" Asked Amani quickly, waving his hand at Raven to quiet him.

"Break camp and then follow me," said Devon as he headed down to the beach.

Raven shrugged his shoulders and grabbed Daybreak's reins. "This is a waste of time." He grumbled, heading for the beach.

Shayla doused the fire with the tea's remnants, hastily packed up her blanket, and reached for Fen's reins, then followed after Raven.

Amani secretly agreed with Raven but chose to say nothing as he followed the others after Devon.

Soleon squealed with delight when she saw the three resurrected warriors. They were the first things Soleon saw as she woke, again restored to her cursed state after the sun had set.

Ramos scowled as he saw his mistake rise once more like nothing had happened the previous night. Surprisingly the warriors ignored Soleon, and Ramos could only presume that they recognized her as one of their own. That hadn't been the case with Rowan, who was sitting solemnly in a far corner of the cave.

"The others?" Soleon questioned him. "Where are the others?"

Ramos pointed wearily upwards to indicate their positions on the higher levels, and she immediately searched for them. He watched her go and then headed down to the lowest level to prepare the spell to invoke Valeskas. Ramos resolved that when this was all over, he would use his new powers to discover a way to destroy Soleon permanently.

The solemn group stood silently, waiting at the edge of the water. It was evident to all of them that crossing the sea to reach the cave looked impossible. Devon ignored them as he began searching around the cliffs that formed the bottom of the mountain. He finally disappeared over a ledge, and the others looked at each other in surprise.

"I wish he would hurry up," muttered Shayla finally, her teeth chattering, "I am about to freeze to death stood here."

Devon reappeared suddenly and stumbled his way down to the beach. He carefully carried something wrapped in his cloak. Devon went to the water's edge closest to the shoreline that they needed to cross and carefully placed his burden on the sand. As the others watched curiously, Devon unwrapped large chunks of ice that he had brought from the frozen edges of the stream.

"Sorry, it took so long," said Devon. "I felt sure there would have been ice much closer than this pile was. Devon got to his feet and put on his sodden cloak before turning to the others.

"Now watch this," he said, smiling.

Raven impatiently held his tongue against saying how ridiculous this all was, and he watched with the others as Devon had requested. What happened next sent a shudder down his spine. He watched in astonishment as Devon slowly lost height, and within a few moments, melded into the ice piles from the stream.

Devon smiled to himself as he heard a gasp of surprise from the group as he slowly changed into ice crystals. The first part was easy; what he planned to do next, however, needed his full concentration. Slowly Devon pushed himself along the edge of the sea as it lapped against the cliff wall leading to the next beach. His touch turned the water before him into ice as he snaked his way forward.

Seawater did not easily become ice, but it froze quite quickly because of the cold night and Devon's powers. Slowly he made his way across to the next beach, leaving a path of ice in his wake. He stretched out his body of ice as far as possible in front of him, thrilling at the sensation of the seawater surrendering to his cold touch. Devon stayed close to the cliff face, so his ice path was stable enough to allow the others to walk on it.

The craggy rocks that would have destroyed a boat or severely injured a swimmer were now becoming support structures to stabilize his creation. Devon reached the next beach swiftly and efficiently. He remained in an ice form so that he could maintain power over his temporary creation. Devon knew that if he changed back to human form now, the ice would likely submit to the seawater beneath it and melt before the others could cross.

Twila and Amani saw the sheet of ice that was Devon arrive on the next beach. One half of him was on the beach; the rest of him was indistinguishable within the path of ice that he had created. Amani knew that Devon could not call them mentally, being so close to Ramos. He also realized that as long as the Lunarian remained as one with some portion of the ice path he had created, it would stay frozen.

"Come," he said to the others. "We can cross now."

Amani stepped onto the path and found to his surprise that it was very sturdy. He began to walk towards where Devon was waiting, and Shayla unhesitatingly followed him.

Twila spoke quietly with Fen before stepping onto the path. Fen allowed Twila to lead her onto the ice path. The water was lapping against her feet, but she showed no indication of fear. Motomo followed them but was panting nervously. The young wolf reasoned that at least he would be able to swim back to the shore if the ice path melted beneath him.

Raven watched grimly as the others meandered their way across the surface of the water. Daybreak nudged him gently from behind.

"It looks safe," Daybreak said unconvincingly, "I will wait for your return beneath the trees back at the camp."

Raven laughed at her words. "My thoughts exactly," he said, "but look, Fen is not nervous, see how she follows Twila."

"Fen thinks she is walking through a meadow," snorted Daybreak. "Twila suggested it to her." "Come," said Raven more calmly than he felt, "I will make sure you are safe. If the ice path breaks, I promise to get you back to shore."

Daybreak briefly resisted as Raven took her reins, but she followed him to the edge of the path. He took a deep breath and peered across the water to where the others were more than halfway to their destination already. He looked down at his feet and found that the shimmering ice path was more than wide enough for himself and Daybreak to walk side by side.

Raven placed one foot on the ice and felt it sink slightly under the weight, but the ice was strong enough to hold him. When both his feet were firmly on the path, Daybreak felt calmer. Together they slowly followed the others along the ice path towards the next beach.

At times, the path turned towards the open sea when the cliff's ragged edges barred their way. Neither Raven nor Daybreak felt comfortable walking away from land. He breathed a sigh of relief as the beach grew slowly closer to them. The snow was increasing, it built up on top of the path beneath them, and it blinded his view of the others up ahead, but it was also helping him see where the ice trail turned next.

At times he felt the ice crack warningly beneath his feet, and both of them would stop moving for a brief moment, expecting to fall into the water at any second. It was impossible to move fast because following the path's course took all his concentration, but when they neared the beach, Raven desperately fought against the urge to run the last few yards.

"How do we get back?" Asked Daybreak breathlessly as the beach drew closer.

"Let's just get there first," answered Raven nervously, "but I don't think we will be coming back this way."

The moment Raven and Daybreak were safely on the beach, Devon pulled himself out of the freezing cold water and found that changing from ice to his human form was extremely uncomfortable. As his upper body took shape, pulling itself out of the rapidly melting pool of his lower ice body, he became acutely aware of the cold. His clothes, soaked and icy cold, caused him to shiver violently as his body attempted to generate heat within itself.

"Quickly," he said, his teeth chattering from cold, "let's get into the shelter of the cave before I freeze again."

Twila handed Devon his travel pack to change into dry clothes when they were all inside the cave. Devon gratefully took it from her with shaking hands.

"Thank you for bringing this over," he said appreciatively, "I didn't realize that shifting into ice would be so uncomfortable."

Twila didn't answer him as she walked towards the bridge that led to the high crystals.

"Isn't it everything I said it was?" Asked Devon as he struggled to release himself from the clinging wet material that his clothes had become.

"It's wonderful," breathed Twila.

Shayla walked across the bridge and instantly knew that she had seen this place before. Everything was so familiar to her. "I know this place," she said with surprise, "Saressa showed it to me in my dream time. This cave is the place I am supposed to bring her persecuted followers."

Amani turned to her with interest in this statement. Shayla strolled between the crystals trying to remember the exact words Saressa used when she had shown her this place.

"This was to be the passage to freedom for her followers," Shayla said, "these crystals are gates leading to her worlds, but the color is wrong. I remember them as being of the deepest blue, not red like this."

The others had gathered closer with interest as she spoke of the crystal gates.

"The gates are red because of Ramos," Amani said quietly, "when we have destroyed him, Saressa will open the way to her worlds."

"And then her true followers can cross safely into this world," finished Shayla. "Yes, that is what Saressa said.

There will be a chosen one to lead her faithful to a new haven in each of her worlds, where they can be free from persecution. In my world, there are lands beyond the eastern mountains, where wars have raged between villages for many years. Up until recently, the easterners have never ventured into the peaceful western regions. Our army fought the occasional easterner's group, trying to invade us, and turned them back to their lands.

The soldiers have few skills or weapons other than their strength and courage to keep the east at bay. The mountain ranges have also been a natural barrier against invasion. Until recently, that is. They say that a warlord has emerged amongst them. He is organizing the easterners into armies that are slowly defeating everything in their path.

Just before I came here, two of Saressa's priests arrived at my Uncle's inn. One was severely injured and later died. We hid the other one in the wine cellar, not knowing what else to do with him. He told us that they were from Highcrest, a village at the foot of the eastern mountains. The priest spoke of Saressa's followers being dragged from their homes and slaughtered in front of the other villagers.

The night he arrived, Saressa first appeared to me in my dream time and showed me this place. I am not the chosen one to lead her followers, but she asked me to help. Saressa told me that Dra is behind the invasion. He is once again trying to destroy what she has created. She directed the priest to our inn because he will build the haven."

"Where did you cross into this world?" Asked Amani curiously. "Is there another gateway besides this one?"

"I am not sure how I got here," Shayla answered, "after I agreed to help, Saressa returned to me the following night, and when I woke up, I was by the cave where we first met. I wasn't even sure how I was to return to my world. I just trusted that when the time came, Saressa would show it to me.

"I initially thought the cave where the key is hidden was the one that Saressa had shown to me, but I was wrong. This cave is the place. It will become the path to freedom for her followers."

"Once the gateways are open," remarked Twila quietly, "will it also open the way for the likes of Stefan, or even the warlord's army?"

No one answered her question because none of them knew the answer. Everyone's attention turned to the crystals, and the realization that this statement could be true washed over them. As if in response, the deep red glow within each of the crystals began to pulse rhythmically, Amani felt the dragon scar on his chest grow warmer, but this time, he knew that the blood dragons were warning him.

"Ramos awaits our arrival," he said quietly.

"Then, let's not disappoint him," said Raven pulling his pack down from Daybreak's back to retrieve the rest of his armor and weapons.

Ramos combined the ingredients that he needed to invoke Valeskas. However, this time, he planned to use a portion of the combined blood from Twila's and his own in the spell. Valeskas had told him that this was necessary now that it appeared someone had discovered his caverns. Ramos wasn't sure what effect using the combination of their blood would achieve, but he did as Valeskas had instructed.   H   e measured a small portion of the blood mixture and then carefully replaced the stopper tightly.   Ramos rocked the flask gently in an attempt to judge how much of the liquid was left.   He had thought about bringing the Gypsy girl back here to be at his side to help him fight the intruder, but the notion had occurred to him too late.

The flask was only a quarter full now, and Ramos would soon have to seek out another innocent with the gift. Twila's blood was useless to him now that the darkness tainted it.

Soleon had lost interest in the undead warriors, and she wandered down to the cavern where Ramos began the spell to invoke Valeskas. She watched curiously for a moment as the first wisps of red smoke began to pour out of the wooden bowl.   Then Soleon suddenly remembered that she had to do something but didn't know what it was.

The thought danced beyond her reach in her mind as she tried to concentrate on it. Soleon was sure that she had to look for someone or something and then gave up trying. She watched, briefly fascinated with the spectacle of Valeskas's appearance, but it didn't hold her interest for long and wandered off back up to the next level. She was hungry and knew from experience that Ramos had probably forgotten to bring food for her.   Soleon vaguely remembered that there was another source of food around here somewhere.

"If I could just remember where it is," Soleon said to herself.

She headed towards the small cave off from the larger one

where Ramos typically left her food.

"I think it is in here," she said to herself.

Soleon entered the small cave and found that Ramos had indeed forgotten to bring food. Soleon wailed miserably at the sight of her empty plate lying on the floor. She bent down and turned it over, thinking that some of her last meal may still lie beneath the plate. Soleon wailed again when there was nothing left; the rats had finished it for her.

Angrily she picked up the plate and flung it at the wall of the cave. Soleon waited for the satisfying crash as it hit the wall, but it didn't hit the wall; the plate went right through it and disappeared. She slowly smiled. "Now, I remember." Soleon laughed crazily.

Rowan watched as Soleon entered the small cave. He was growing restless, confined to the cavern. Clearly, Rowan remembered his fight with Devon but had decided not to speak of it to Ramos. It must have ended in his death, and because of Ramos, he was now little more than the rest of the abominations that were cursed to remain here forever.

He had tried to leave the cavern and escape to the upper levels, but Ramos's warriors blocked the steps before he even made a move in that direction. Rowan would have screamed in frustration, but his voice had not returned. Carefully he began testing the warrior's interest in his movements. They only seemed interested when Rowan made a move towards the steps leading to the upper levels. If he moved in the direction of the lowest level, the warriors did nothing.

They didn't move either when he started to follow Soleon into the small cave. Rowan decided he preferred the half-dead's company instead of being under the scrutiny of these silent dead warriors. Their eyes were beginning to make Rowan's skin crawl. What was making things even worse for him was a painful gnawing sensation that was increasing, deep within the pit of his stomach.

It had taken a little while for him to recognize what the sensation was. Initially, he had hoped it was an indication that death was blissfully coming to put an end to his awful situation. Gradually, however, he realized what the growing sensation was. It was hunger. Rowan was not hungry for food like Soleon though, he was hungry for blood, and it became unbearable.

The Lunarian smiled at the memory of the scurrying rats he had seen earlier. He had watched them enter Soleon's small cave where they were accustomed to finding the food that Ramos occasionally brought for the half-dead.

"At least rats have blood running through their veins," he thought to himself, trying to ignore the blood hunger, "nothing else in this place has."

Rowan slipped into the small cave behind Soleon. He heard her wailing as the Lunarian approached the entrance. As Rowan stepped into the gloom, he stopped in amazement. Unaware of his presence behind her, Soleon had walked towards the cave's rear wall and disappeared.

Ramos watched with interest as Valeskas's now-familiar form took shape. There was something different about the blood dragon's usual smoke body. When Valeskas was complete, another transformation took place. In the same fashion, as the dead warrior's bones were miraculously enveloped in new tissue, making them whole again, Valeskas's smoke body became flesh.

Eventually, the dragon stood towering above Ramos, in the full splendor of his natural form. His body's color was of the same blue-tinged gray that the dead warrior's skin tone was. However, his eyes blazed with a fiery red intelligence, unlike the unseeing gaze of the warrior's eyes.

Valeskas stretched his scale tipped wings, deliciously savoring the sensations that only one
without a body of sustenance for so long could appreciate. His wingspan was so great that it almost brushed the sides of the cavern. The dragon's height blocked the light from many of the torches, plunging parts of the cavern into shadow.

Ramos ran his hand over a portion of Valeskas's scaly leg. "Did I finally release you? He asked with interest. "Does this mean you are free from your exile?"

"Sadly, no," answered Valeskas. "I can go no further than I could go before, and I can only remain until the spell loses its power. We need much stronger magic than this to release me permanently. What it does mean, however, is you will no longer be alone to fight the intruders, and I sense they are close."

Amani turned swiftly as the plate hit his shoulder and clattered down onto the stone floor. The noise echoed around the cave, stunning everyone into silence.

Raven was the first to react and ran forward to where Amani absent-mindedly rubbed his shoulder as he stared at the secret entrance to the mountain.

"It came right through the wall there," said Twila quietly, "I suppose that is the entrance that you and Devon spoke of Amani?"

Amani nodded, still watching the wall. Devon rushed to Raven and Amani's side as they waited to see who, if anyone, would follow the plate.

Daybreak, Motomo, and Fen were on the opposite side of the bridge. The loud noise had reached their ears, and Fen nervously stomped at the sandy ground beneath her feet. Daybreak, sensing Fen's alarm, leaned against her comfortingly. She understood that they were at a safe distance away from the noise across the bridge, and she wanted to make sure that Fen knew it too.

Raven readied his sword when a dirt-encrusted arm pushed its way through the wall, followed by the strangest creature he had ever seen.

"That's the half-dead I told you about," muttered Devon. "She is unpredictable, so take care."

"Shadow!" Said Soleon happily when she saw Devon. "Did you bring me food?"

Devon cautiously approached her. "Has Ramos gone to collect more warriors?" He asked.

"No," she replied. "I have many friends now. Are these your friends?" Soleon wandered around the group, grinning foolishly at them. "Did they bring me food?" She asked, hopefully.

"I'll get you something," Shayla said when none of the others offered.

Soleon happily screeched when Shayla handed her a large chunk of bread and cheese.

"It's not much, I'm afraid," apologized Shayla as Soleon scuttled to a corner of the cave and began tearing at the bread, then cramming larges pieces of it into her mouth.

What should we do with her?" Asked Twila sadly.

Shayla approached Soleon and placed a mug of water by her side, afraid that the half-dead would choke on the stale, dry bread. Soleon looked up at her, pieces of bread and cheese hanging from her mouth, desperately trying to eat all of the food before the rats came and took it. She nodded in thanks to Shayla and immediately went back to her meal.

Rowan touched the wall of the cave where he had seen Soleon disappear. He smiled when the tips of his fingers vanished. A loud screech from Soleon caused him to pull back his hand, undecided for a moment, whether to follow her or not. Rowan realized that there was someone else on the other side of the wall, too, because he could hear other voices. Not only the sound of conversations, but a smell of blood was also drifting towards him through the wall, filling him with a blinding blood hunger that was now impossible to ignore.

He managed to control the urge to go smashing through the wall to satisfy this hunger. Instead, Rowan returned to the closest pool of light from a torch and melded himself with the shadows edging the light. Changing into his shadow body hadn't stopped Ramos's warriors from detecting him earlier, but knew it could fool Soleon if he used caution. Rowan felt it was worth the risk of detection if he could discover who was with her because they had the blood he craved.

CHAPTER TWENTY-FOUR

A Revelation

Rowan timed his entrance into the crystal cave perfectly. Soleon was spluttering and coughing as she choked on the food that Shayla had given to her. The disturbing noises that she was making caused everyone's heads to turn in her direction. Rowan used this distraction to his advantage and quickly slipped unnoticed into the crystal cave. He slithered swiftly to the closest shadows and became one with them. Rowan then took his time to assess his new surroundings and the group of strangers he found there.

He recognized Devon instantly, and a flash of rage rushed through him. It took all the restraint he possessed to stop himself from charging at him and tearing into his throat. Rowan knew how stupid that action would have been because he wasn't sure yet who the others in this group were or what kind of powers they may possess. It would, however, have been very satisfying just to sink his teeth into Devon's throat.

Rowan realized he vastly outnumbered, but the blood hunger within him intensified and washed out his caution. One by one, he quickly studied the strangers to locate the safest victim to attack. The girl stood by Soleon looked to be the easiest target, and her blood was human. Rowan could almost hear it rushing deliciously through her veins. He also discovered that the only other human amongst the group was the muscular warrior who possessed an extremely lethal-looking sword. Rowan knew the human warrior if attacked, would remove his head in an instant. He needed to satisfy his hunger and build his strength up first. The other man and girl in the group did not have human blood running through their veins, and although Rowan was curious about them, his blood hunger was currently his most significant concern.

Rowan watched his chosen prey eagerly. By the group's conversation, it was evident that they were about to seek out Ramos. His excitement grew at the group's suggestion that Shayla should stay behind with the half-dead. As their conversation grew more heated, he was losing patience. Shayla currently was too close to the others for him to attack.

"I grow tired of this," he thought angrily and decided suddenly to escape from Ramos's mountain. He knew that there would be many easy victims beyond this prison of rock. Rowan peered across the bridge, ready to make his escape when something else caught his attention.

"Horses," Rowan thought happily, "horses with pure living blood running through them. I shall quench this blood hunger before I leave here after all."

Daybreak was munching on the grain that Shayla had put out for the two horses. Fen had calmed down quickly with Daybreak's encouragement, and the food helped the process. It seemed to her that their area of the cave was growing darker, she looked up from her meal to see if one of the torches had gone out, but all were still blazing. Daybreak looked across the bridge to where the others had gathered amongst the crystals. Everyone was masking their thoughts, making it difficult for the horse to follow their conversation, and she was too far away for her to hear them.

Fen became restless again, and Daybreak grew irritable. They had traveled a long way, and Daybreak planned to enjoy this rest after she had eaten. Motomo approached her from the far corner of the cave where he had been observing the others. Daybreak immediately assumed that it was the wolf's approach that was unnerving Fen this time.

"You would think that Fen would know you by now, Motomo," Daybreak said into his thoughts.

Motomo sniffed the air as Daybreak nuzzled against Fen, attempting to calm her once more. Fen stopped moving, and Daybreak was about to return to her grain when Motomo interrupted her.

"What is wrong with Fen?" Asked Motomo, alarmed. "Her eyes are clouded."

Daybreak stepped quickly away from the other horse and saw that Motomo was right; something was wrong with Fen.

Motomo sniffed around Fen's legs, and surprisingly the horse did not react. He was trying to detect the pungent odor that a sickness produced, but it was not there. Motomo slowly began to smell something other than an illness. The wolf could smell blood.

"I smell blood," said Motomo, puzzled. "Was Fen injured crossing the water?"

Daybreak shook her head. "I don't think so," she answered, "there doesn't seem to be any wounds, but look at her neck. It's twitching."

Motomo came around to the right side of Fen. Daybreak was correct. Fen's neck was twitching. The wolf peered up at Fen, trying to get a better look at her neck. Shadows draped the horse's neck so he couldn't see it clearly, but the smell of blood became overpowering to him.

"She must have a wound on her neck," he said., "I can't see because of the light here. Can you get her to move into the light from that torch there? It would make it easier to see the wound?"

Daybreak attempted to push Fen out of the shadows, but the horse resisted rigidly. "Fen won't move," she said, now becoming alarmed, "what is casting that shadow? Has a torch gone out? And look at the twitching in her neck now. It's becoming worse."

Motomo's hackles suddenly rose on his neck. "It is not Fen's neck that is twitching," he growled deeply, "it's the shadow."

Daybreak backed away from Fen, snorting in alarm as she saw the unmistakable shape of a figure begin to emerge from the shadows across the right side of Fen.

"Raven." Shrieked Daybreak into his thoughts, "Come quickly, something is attacking Fen."

Rowan had found his attack on Fen to be easy. The wolf and the other horse had not detected him. Rowan had initially been concerned that the wolf may smell him and sound the alarm before he could attack the horse. But he had quickly realized that the wolf could not sense him in his shadow body. Rowan had planned only to drink enough of Fen's blood to take the edge of his hunger. However, the remarkably exquisite sensations that coursed through him with each frantic gulp of Fen's blood made it difficult to keep his thoughts focused on anything else. He was in almost the same trance-like state as his victim was, and because of that, the Lunarian began to change back to his human form without realizing it.

Raven went charging back across the bridge in answer to Daybreak's cry. "Quick, it's the horses," he yelled to the others as he ran.

Devon followed Raven's lead with Amani close behind. As the three of them reached Daybreak and Fen, they were just in time to see Motomo tearing into the shoulder of what appeared to be half a man and half a shadow.

"It's Rowan," said Devon incredulously, "but I saw the half-dead snap his neck."

Rowan shook the upper portion of his body in an attempt to loosen the ferocious grip of Motomo's teeth, but the action just caused the wolf to clamp down his jaws even tighter. When his shadow legs returned to human again, he attempted to run towards the cave's exit but stumbled and fell to his knees.

The fall allowed Motomo to sink his teeth even further into his shoulder. Rowan gasped out a silent scream as a white-hot flash of pain coursed down his arm as the nerve fibers in the shoulder tore apart. Motomo's position made it difficult for Rowan to get a good enough hold on his attacker to free himself. He clawed frantically with his uninjured arm to get a hold of some part of the wolf. Rowan finally grabbed a good portion of Motomo's coat and yanked hard enough to pull himself free. Waves of nausea coursed through Rowan as he flung Motomo to one side, feeling the flesh and sinew rip from his shoulder.

Only after the wolf hit the floor did he finally unlock his jaws. Quickly Motomo shook his head to remove the remaining pieces of Rowan's shoulder from his mouth before attacking again. Rowan had gotten to his feet and ran towards the exit of the cave but stopped when he saw that Amani and Twila were blocking it. Frantically he turned back towards the bridge but found Devon and Raven running towards him. Motomo was crouched, ready to attack should Rowan make the slightest move towards the exit.

Rowan turned first one way and then the other, desperately searching for a way out. The others circled Rowan as Shayla ran to look at Fen. No one noticed that Soleon, who had been watching the whole event, got up and wandered back inside the mountain.

"I must tell my friends that Rowan is trying to escape," she muttered to herself. "Ramos wouldn't like that at all. We all have to stay here."

Ramos frowned as he sensed Daybreak's warning to Raven. Valeskas heard it too and sighed with satisfaction, freedom would soon be his, and the first thing he planned to do was rid himself of this useless necromancer. There was just one task left that Valeskas needed Ramos for, and then the dragon would get rid of him. Valeskas could exchange places with him at any time, now that his smoke body was flesh, but only Ramos could retrieve the key that he needed.

"Patience," cautioned Valeskas, "the intruder's approach."

Ramos nodded. He was listening carefully for any more stray thoughts, but there was only silence. He finally gave up, and with Valeskas's instruction, he began mixing the ingredients for one final spell that would permanently release the dragon. There was just one item missing before the magic was complete, and it was soon to be within their grasp.

Raven dragged Rowan to his knees and pulled his head back by the hair to expose the vulnerable area of the Lunarian's throat, and firmly pressed the point of his sword into the soft flesh. A trickle of blood betrayed the wound that the pressure of Raven's sword was causing with its razor-sharp edge.

"Just one false move," snarled Raven, "and I will have your head." Rowan stiffened beneath Raven's grasp but made no move to escape.

Devon approached curiously. "What happened back there?" He asked Rowan. "I saw the half-dead behead you. Our healing skills cannot restore life if we lose our heads." Rowan opened his mouth to reply, and Raven pressed his sword deeper into his throat in response.

"Release your hold on him, Raven," said Amani, "he cannot answer with your sword at his throat."

Raven tightened his hold once more on Rowan's hair as a warning before releasing him as Amani had requested, and Rowan clutched at the small puncture wound in his neck immediately. His other arm hung uselessly at his side, but Rowan appeared ready to leap at Raven.

"Try it," taunted Raven, "when I slay someone, they stay dead."

Amani stepped between the two of them and faced Rowan. Now that he was closer to the Lunarian, he could see the odd-looking blue tinge to his skin color.

"Answer Devon's question," commanded Amani quietly, "or I will allow Raven to finish what he started."

Rowan silently looked up at Amani and slowly shook his head. The hunger for blood was returning, probably in response to the gushing wound in his shoulder. Rowan knew that the injury could not heal itself until after the sun rose, and he had slept. Rowan also realized that his current situation was bleak, and suddenly he wanted an end to this.

He leaped at Amani, ramming into him with such force that it caused him to fall backward. Amani was taken by surprise at the sudden attack, and Rowan briefly had the advantage. The Lunarian scrambled on top of Amani, and as he raised his head briefly just before tearing into his flesh, Rowan saw a bright flash out of the corner of his eye.

Rowan's head flew through the air, raining down blood over the surprised group. Raven kicked the now lifeless body off of Amani and offered his hand to help him up from the floor.

"He wasn't to be trusted," said Raven in reply to Amani's stunned expression, "we have more than enough to deal with as it is."

A sudden screech filled the air, and everyone turned to see the distraught figure of Soleon. Rowan's severed head had come to rest at her feet.

"You shouldn't have done that," she said hysterically, "now you have made my friends angry."

Two figures appeared from the shadows on the crystal side of the bridge. The undead warriors briefly stopped when they reached Soleon and looked down at Rowan's severed head at her feet. Then slowly, they began walking purposely towards the bridge.

"My friends have called to the others," yelled Soleon, "they are coming down from the higher levels. You must leave here and leave quickly."

"And so finally it begins," Raven said calmly, tightening the grip on his sword, "Shayla, get those horses out of here, and do it quickly."

Shayla pulled at Fen's reins and led the unsteady horse down the tunnel leading towards the cave entrance. Daybreak nudged Fen from behind to hurry along the process. Shayla left the two of them just inside the opening so they would be out of the wind, then returned moments later with their food and water.

"Make sure Fen drinks plenty of this," said Shayla to Daybreak. "She has lost a lot of blood. It will help."

Daybreak didn't need to encourage Fen to do anything. The moment Fen saw the water, she lowered her head into the wooden bucket and drank deeply. Daybreak watched Shayla run back down the tunnel.

"This is going to be a long night." She thought.

Raven waited for the warrior that faced him to make his move. Amani had positioned himself in front of the second one. Twila and Devon moved closer, ready to assist as necessary. Motomo crouched amongst the shadows in one corner of the cave. From his position, he could leap to the assistance of any of them within seconds. Shayla positioned herself well behind the others. She was the weakest of the group and knew to stay back. Shayla was no coward, though, and already had a dagger ready in each of her hands.

The two warriors slowly turned their heads in unison, observing each member of the group in turn. Their eyes sent shivers down everyone's spine as they rested briefly on each one of them.

"What are they doing?" Whispered Twila.

"They are reporting what they see to their master," said Amani coldly, "these abominations are his first line of defense."

"How many are there, Devon?" Asked Raven, firmly keeping his eyes fixed on the warrior, stood before him."

"Not many," answered Devon, "nine, I think. Remember that you can only stop them if you remove the head."

"That will not be a problem," snarled Raven, "I grow tired of this waiting."

Raven swung his sword, aiming for the warrior's neck, and instantly the warrior raised its shield, deflecting the blow. The clash of metal echoed eerily around the cave as the warrior swiped at Raven's head with the spiked metal ball attached to a thick chain and secured to a wooden handle. Raven dodged the blow swiftly, feeling the rush of air on his cheek as the spiked ball missed its target.

The warrior instantly swung the ball again at Raven, and in response, he dropped to the ground and rolled to change his position. Raven immediately drove his sword into the warrior's unprotected side, and it staggered briefly before resuming its attack. As the warrior raised its arm to attack again, Raven thrust his sword upwards. The open wound in the warrior's side was rapidly healing as Raven's blade found its target. Raven pushed his sword forcibly into the throat of the warrior as he dodged another blow from the spiked ball. The sword almost severed the dead warrior's head but not entirely; he could see the black gaping wound in the neck. Surprisingly there was no blood, but a sudden stench of decay filled the air.

As Raven battled with the first warrior, the second one attacked Amani. This warrior held a curved sword in each hand and fought with a scissor-like action that made it challenging to block easily. Amani swiftly avoided one blade, but the second slashed open a good portion of his left arm. As the warrior raised its swords a second time, Amani waved his hand and blasted him backward with a fireball of light. The warrior jumped back up to his feet and marched towards him to attack again.

However, the distance between them this time allowed Amani to duck beneath the blades. He got behind his attacker by rolling out of his way on the ground. He jumped up to his feet again, swiftly grabbed the warrior's head from behind, and snapped his neck. The warrior dropped his swords with a loud clatter, and Devon grabbed for one. As Amani released the warrior, allowing him to fall to the floor, Devon beheaded him with its sword, kicking the severed head away from the body.

At almost the same moment, the first warrior lost his head to Raven's sword. The wound to the warrior's throat had caused its head to hang lopsidedly from the portion of its spine that remained intact. The warrior had difficulty aiming its weapon accurately at Raven and so was slain quite easily by a resounding blow on the side of its head. Raven's impact was so powerful it knocked the undead warrior's head from its shoulders. Its body staggered for a moment and then collapsed in a heap at Raven's feet.

"More warriors are coming," shouted Shayla suddenly as she saw them approaching.

Everyone looked across the bridge and saw three more warriors running towards them. Soleon was right behind them, carrying the head of Rowan by its hair.

"I told you my friends would be angry," said Soleon sadly, "they won't listen to me anymore."

Amani grabbed the second curved sword and waited for the next three warriors to reach them.

Raven quickly defeated the third warrior. Its weapon was a spear, which was not the correct choice for close attacks. As the undead warrior lunged the spear at Raven, he nimbly moved to one side. The warrior stumbled forward, and as he did so, Raven swung his sword hitting the creature's throat squarely and cleanly removed the head. He then quickly turned to face the fourth warrior while Amani and Devon circled the fifth. Both of these warriors fought with swords and shields.

Raven found his opponent to be the toughest one yet. It was taking every ounce of his fighting skills just to defend himself against the blows.

"Use your powers." Yelled Twila when she saw how strong Raven's opponent was.

"No time," Raven yelled, wincing in pain as the warrior's sword slashed a deep wound into his thigh.

Twila waved her hand in the undead warrior's direction. A flash of bright golden light left her fingers, hit the warrior in the chest, and held him there.

"Quickly, Raven," she yelled. "Finish him. The spell won't hold him for long."

Raven sliced his sword through the air the moment Twila's spell gave him the advantage, and as the fourth warrior's head left its neck, both the body and head dropped instantly to the floor at his feet.

Amani and Devon were using the same tactic to destroy the fifth warrior. Amani cast a restrain spell, and Devon promptly sliced off its head.

"These things are getting tougher," commented Raven, inspecting the gash in his leg. "Thanks, Twila, for your help, but I was wearing the creature down.

Twila grinned at Raven's attempt to make light of what had been a very tough fight. "Well, I am sorry to have ended it so quickly for you then," she laughed, casting a healing spell on his wound.

Soleon wandered up to Raven and moaned when she saw the slain warrior at his feet.

"He was the biggest one," she said miserably, "it took me a long time to piece him together. Now, look at him. You have to stop this."

She swung around and waved her hand in Raven's direction. A yellow flash flew from her fingers and hit Raven in the chest. He stepped back in surprise, raising his sword instantly. Soleon started to drag the warrior towards the bridge when she suddenly noticed that her spell did not have the desired effect. The center of Raven's chest started to glow brightly as her binding spell hit him. Then there was a

shower of yellow sparks as her magic dissipated. Soleon dropped the
warrior's body and walked up to Raven, staring at the fading glow that
had been her spell. She grabbed the neck of his shirt, ripping it away
from his chest. Raven was stunned by her behavior. He raised his
sword but couldn't bring himself to strike her with it. Instead, he
grabbed Soleon by the wrist with his other hand to stop her from
clawing at his shirt.

"What are you doing, woman?" He asked, astonished at her strange
behavior.

She suddenly saw the pendant that hung around his neck and
slowly raised her head. Raven saw her eyes searching his face as he
held her arm firmly. There was something in those eyes that sparked a
memory deep within him, but he couldn't recall what it was.

"Eashar?" Asked Soleon slowly. "Is that you? You finally
came for me? She suddenly smiled widely. Ramos told me you were
long dead, but I knew he was lying." Soleon leaned against Raven's
chest, hugging him with her free arm. The acrid stench of dirt and
decay was overpowering, and he fought against a sudden wave of
nausea.

"You are mistaken," Raven said kindly. "I am not Eashar."

Soleon pushed away from him and searched his face
again. "But you wear my pendant," she said firmly. "Who else could
you be but my husband?"

"Again, you are mistaken," said Raven, as another half-
formed memory rushed into mind. "This belonged to my mother."

"Jian?" Asked Soleon suddenly, her eyes lighting up with
hope. "Is your name Jian?"

Raven's stomach suddenly lurched at the sound of his
given name. The last time he had heard, it was when his mother died
before his eyes. It had been the last words on her lips. Raven was
speechless as waves of emotion coursed through him as the last
memories of his mother burst into his heart.

"What trickery is this?" Raven finally said, his voice filled
with emotion.

The tattered blue dress that Soleon wore reminded him of
one that his mother was wearing when the village buried her. The
memories that Raven had locked away for so long flooded his mind
with the last painful images he had of her. Soleon wept as she reached
up to wipe the tears away that had painfully formed and then spilled
out to run down his cheeks.

"Ramos will pay for what he has done to you," Raven snarled, the lump of emotion in his throat, making it hard to breathe and swallow.

"Destroy him for me, Jian, and I will be free," she whispered, "I cannot be one with the earth until someone breaks Ramos's spell."

Raven hugged his mother, and she clung to him in response.

"Use caution, Jian," Soleon whispered. "Valeskas grows stronger within Ramos's blackened heart."

Raven released his hold on Soleon and strode purposefully towards the bridge. "I will destroy them both." He snarled.

"Wait." Cautioned Amani.

"I have waited long enough," snapped Raven striding between the crystal spires.

Amani stepped in front of Raven, effectively blocking his entrance into the mountain. His unnatural speed allowed him to catch Raven up before he reached the access to the caves beyond.

"We need to be together for this," said Amani firmly, clearly seeing the pain and anger in Raven's eyes. "Otherwise, you are just sacrificing yourself."

Raven did not reply and made a move to go around Amani. Twila and Devon joined Amani, and he stared at the three of them angrily.

"If you are not ready to fight with me, then get out of my way, all of you," he said.

"Please listen to reason, Raven," Twila pleaded. "I, too, have been badly hurt by Ramos. I want to destroy him so badly that every fiber screams out for it, but Amani's right. We can only succeed if we all fight together. You have every right to be angry but look at your mother now, Raven. Already she has forgotten who you are."

Raven looked back across the bridge at his mother. Twila was right Soleon was dragging the now decaying body of the last undead warrior over the bridge towards them. Pieces were falling off, but she ignored that and pulled what remained of it past the four of them and through the mountain entrance.

"Remember your mother as she was," said Amani firmly, "not what she has become."

"And most of all, don't trust her." Devon cautioned. "The control that Ramos has over her is unpredictable."

"Even if she doesn't realize it," responded Raven, his voice breaking with emotion, "she does not deserve to be treated worse than an animal."

"And if we fight together, then we can end her suffering," said

Amani firmly.

Raven didn't answer as the undead warrior's legs disappeared through the hidden entrance, dragged by his mother, but he knew they spoke the truth.

"Where are the rest of the warriors?" Asked Shayla as she and Motomo joined the group. "I thought you said there were nine of them?"

Shayla stood by the side of Raven and quietly squeezed his hand. He looked down at her and smiled appreciatively at her gesture of support, and he squeezed her hand back in response.

"There must be others still inside," answered Devon. "I don't know the exact number. We should use caution and expect to meet them on the path to Ramos's cave."

The crystal in Devon's pocket suddenly grew warmer. Initially, it was so subtle that he thought that it was his imagination. He took it out and saw that it was glowing brightly in the palm of his hand.

"The crystal," Devon said.

The others turned to look as the crystal pulsated a brilliant white light, so bright that it burned their eyes. The crystal rose above Devon's hand and hovered there briefly. The next instant, it flew through the air and crashed into the drawn sword in Raven's hand, shattering it into a thousand pieces on impact. Everyone was stunned as they watched the tiny shards of the destroyed crystal rain down onto the floor around their feet.

"Look at Raven's sword," said Motomo, alarmed.

All eyes turned to look at the sword. It was glowing with the same brilliance that the crystal had. Slowly the light grew dimmer and dimmer until all that remained was a faint glow in the center of his sword. A few moments later, even that was gone.

"I think Saressa means for you to take the final blow," commented Amani. "A gift to you to avenge your mother's fate."

Soleon dragged the few pieces that were left of the warrior down to the lowest level. She was puzzled when the cave was empty. Dropping her burden, she began to search through each level, looking for Ramos. Soleon became more agitated, the closer she got to the surface of the mountain. It was forbidden to go to the upper levels, and until now, Soleon had had no reason to disobey Ramos. She wanted to find the location of the other warriors too. Soleon couldn't understand why they had not responded to the calls for assistance from the destroyed ones, either.

She eventually reached the final steps leading to the surface. A warrior stood to attention on either side of the entrance that led to the steps. They turned their heads to watch as she approached them. Soleon went up to the warrior on the left and slammed her fist hard into his chest. He looked down at his attacker, saw that it was Soleon, and did not retaliate.

"You didn't come when they called to you," she snarled. "They are destroyed."

"We are to guard these steps, Lady." The undead warriors said in unison.

Soleon was satisfied with that explanation and headed back in the direction of the lower levels. Then she remembered what else she had to do. Slowly Soleon climbed the steps that led to the final level. Large rats scurried past her as she made her way up.

The rat's squeaked obscenities at the half-dead for intruding on their territory, and they jostled against her. She angrily attempted to capture one as they ran boldly between her legs as if to trip her up, but they were too fast.

Soleon did manage to kick one of them finally, and with such force, it flew through the air, landing on one of the lower steps with a resounding slap. She shrieked with laughter at the motionless body of the rat. Two other rats quickly attacked their slain brother, growling and squealing as they wrestled over the prize. Soleon watched delightedly for a few moments before losing interest and resumed her climb to the surface.

Devon led the others into the mountain. Everyone had agreed that Motomo should stay behind with the horses. The wolf watched as, one by one, the group disappeared through the wall before he headed back over the bridge. Now that the immediate danger was over, Motomo had decided to bring the horses back into the cave where it was warmer. His heart was heavy with the knowledge that he could not help his friends beyond this point.

Ramos turned as Soleon entered the cavern from the tunnel of wind. The half-dead went first to one of his warriors and then the other. Finally, she approached him.

"They are coming, I think," Soleon said.

"Yes, we know," said Ramos impatiently.

"They killed my friends," she moaned.

"Get down to the lower levels," snapped Ramos, swiping at her with his hand. "You will be in my way up here."

Soleon fell to the floor and wailed loudly, although Ramos had barely touched her. Then her sobs changed to screeches of insane laughter. "They will kill you," she laughed hysterically, "and you too," she said, pointing at Valeskas.

Valeskas bent low to the ground, causing Soleon to squirm out of his way. "We wait for them patiently half-dead,' he boomed.

She stared at the dragon and saw the fire blazing in his eyes. "You are of the flesh," she stated incredulously.

"Yes," replied Valeskas, raising his head again, "and soon, I shall be free to leave this place."

Devon was puzzled when they found the lower levels deserted. "Ramos must be waiting for us in the higher levels," he said.

"I don't recognize any of this," said Twila looking around them.

"Those are the steps that lead to the upper levels," said Devon pointing in that direction. "Ramos could be anywhere."

"Then, let's find him," Raven said as a cold calm resolve once more settled over him and headed for the steps leading up to the next level.

CHAPTER TWENTY-FIVE

The Battle

Soleon wandered back down the steps, aiming kicks at the rats that she disturbed as she went. She wasn't lucky enough to catch any this time, though; they were staying well away from her feet. The undead warriors turned to look at her as she passed them, but Soleon took no notice. Halfway down to the next level, she found herself face to face with Devon. The half-dead screeched loudly and ran back up the steps to alert the warriors.

"Quick," Amani said, "stop her."

The group hurried up the narrow steps to catch Soleon, but it was too late. When they spilled out into the cavern at the top of the steps, the two warriors were waiting for them.

Devon was hit fully in the face by a large wooden club that one of the warriors was wielding. The impact sent him sprawling across the floor, bleeding profusely from his nose and mouth. As he staggered to his feet, the warrior swung at him again, hitting him on the shoulder, knocking him sideways. The warrior raised his club again, ready to bring it down, smashing it onto his head when Twila cast a binding spell. The warrior stopped in its tracks, momentarily unable to move, which allowed Devon to roll sideways out of danger.

"Give me that sword," Twila yelled urgently, "before the spell wears off."

Devon jumped to his feet in a rage, ignoring Twila's request for his sword. He raised the curved sword and quickly slammed the sharp blade into the warrior's neck, removing its head instantly. Devon wiped a hand across his mouth and nose to remove some of the blood and watched with satisfaction as the warrior's body dropped in a crumpled heap at his feet.

"Are you alright, Devon?" Asked Twila, alarmed by the open wounds on his face.

"I'm fine," Devon answered, spitting out a broken tooth and more blood. "I just won't be looking my best when we meet Ramos."

Raven and Amani were still battling with the second warrior, as Twila used a healing spell on Devon's face. Amani raised his hand to cast a fireball spell, but the warrior quickly flicked a long leather whip encircling his arm. Immediately the warrior yanked the whip and dragged Amani to his knees. The warrior then swiftly lunged at Amani with his second weapon, a lethal-looking trident. Amani managed to roll away from the three sharp prongs, and they missed his left side by inches.

That maneuver avoided impaling him on the trident but caused his right arm to become even more entangled by the whip. He had no time to attempt another spell before the warrior lunged at him again with the trident.

This time Amani was not fast enough to avoid it, and one of the three prongs buried itself into the muscle of his upper left arm. The warrior twisted his weapon and yanked it loose, effectively tearing out a large portion of Amani's flesh with it. Despite the excruciating pain as the undead warrior fought to free its weapon, Amani turned it to his advantage. He managed to get a good hold on the whip's tongue and instantly yanked it hard, catching the warrior off guard.

The warrior fell forward, losing its grip on the trident. The trident skidded across the cavern floor, narrowly missing Raven as he ran to assist Amani. The warrior's face was now inches from his; the putrid breath was assaulting his senses. Waves of pain and nausea from his wound, plus the smell of this living corpse he was battling, washed over Amani.

He mustered every bit of strength left to grab the head of the warrior with both of his hands. With one quick twist, Amani heard the satisfying sound of bones snapping as he broke the warrior's neck. Amani flung the limp body to one side, and Raven swiftly removed its head with his sword.

Twila knelt beside Amani as he was untangling himself from the whip's tongue. She was about to begin healing the wound on his arm but saw that there was no need. The injury was rapidly healing by itself, and Twila watched fascinated. She looked questioningly at him as he got to his feet. He just smiled in reply, and Twila chose not to question it further.

Soleon, when she saw two more of her friends, the warriors, were slain, was mortified. She had been about to run back up to Ramos to announce their deaths but then remembered that he had ordered her down to the lower areas. Soleon watched the group as they started to climb the final steps and suddenly ignored Ramos's order. Cautiously she followed them as they made their way up to the last level.

The last two warriors were positioned just inside the cavern where Ramos and Valeskas waited impatiently for the attack. They suddenly stiffened, their heads turned in the direction of the passage leading to the lower levels.

"They come, Dark Lord," the warriors said in unison and immediately marched out of the cavern.

Ramos watched them leave before turning to Valeskas. "They are destroying the warriors very swiftly," he remarked, "especially after all that trouble it took to create them. They have not been much assistance, have they?"

"That is where you are wrong," answered Valeskas, "your slaves have served their purpose admirably. They were never powerful enough to stop the intruders, but they will have no doubt taken a toll on their energy."

"What do you know of these intruders?" Asked Ramos suspiciously.

"I know there is one amongst them who is emitting a great power," responded Valeskas, "I can sense him getting closer and closer."

"Should I prepare any more spells?" Asked Ramos, the first hint of uncertainty in his voice.

"No," answered Valeskas, "he will not be strong enough to defeat me, despite Saressa's help."

"Saressa?" Questioned Ramos. "How can she be involved in this? You told me that she was forbidden to return to this world, or Dra would also be permitted to return."

Valeskas laughed, the sound of which rumbled around the

cavern, "Saressa has not returned to this world," he said. "But she has found a way to meddle in matters here with her limited powers." Valeskas turned to Ramos smiling nastily, rows upon rows of sharp teeth glinting in the torchlight, "and Dra is retaliating in the same devious way."

Devon cautioned the group when they reached the top of the final staircase by holding up his right hand to stop them.

"The end of this passage is narrow, and only one person at a time can get through it," he said. "The final tunnel leads to the largest cavern, and it is the only place left that we haven't searched. He must be waiting for us there. I think we can assume that some of his undead warriors are there to guard it, so we need to watch for them."

"Then I will lead from this point forward," said Amani pushing his way to the front, "you don't need to come any further than this, Shayla, if you don't want to, but it is your choice."

"I have come this far," responded Shayla quickly, "I intend going the rest of the way."

Devon and Raven jostled each other to be next in line behind Amani, and Devon won. Raven scowled at the Lunarian's back but chose to say nothing. Twila positioned herself behind Raven, leaving Shayla to bring up the rear as they headed down the narrow tunnel to the wind passage.

Amani and Devon were waiting for the others to exit the tunnel before heading for the cavern. When the first of the last two warriors suddenly appeared at the entrance of their intended route and ran towards them. Amani reacted first by running out to meet one of the warriors, so there was some space to fight.

What Amani hadn't realized was that the floor was, in fact, a sheet of ice because of the freezing blasts of cold wind that blew through the passage. His feet skidded on the ice, propelling him uncontrollably towards the warrior. Unable to stop himself, he crashed into the warrior, and the two of them ended up on the floor in a tangled mess.

Devon carefully went to help Amani, yelling out a warning about the icy floor to Raven, who had just exited the tunnel.

Amani was desperately trying to free himself from the warrior's vice-like grip around his throat. The two of them rolled and slid around on the floor. Because they were locked together in battle, neither noticed that they were sliding down a gradient. They ended up in an unlit portion of the passage. The freezing wind that was howling past Amani and the warrior increased the farther away from Devon they got.

Devon was still trying to catch them up to help Amani without slipping on the ice himself, but they were moving away from him too quickly. He felt the wind increase in intensity as it blasted against his face like the sting of a thousand insects. Devon was also having difficulty locating where they were now because the last torch was far behind him now, and the roar of the wind made it impossible to hear them.

Twila hurried after Devon just before the final warrior came running towards Raven. He raised his sword, ready for the attack, and found himself looking directly into the face of Haney. Raven hesitated for an instant, and that was all the undead body of Haney needed.

Haney swung at Raven's chest, and although he reacted quickly by jumping backward, it was not fast enough. The sword sliced through Raven's armor and into the flesh of his abdomen. It was not deep enough to cause any internal damage, but it distracted Raven long enough to give Haney the advantage. Blood flowed through Raven's fingers as he clutched the wound with one hand and attempted to fight off his attacker with the other.

Shayla didn't hesitate when she saw Raven's dilemma as she stepped out of the tunnel. Quickly she dropped a dagger into each of her hands and almost in the same instant threw them with absolute accuracy into the grotesque eyes of Haney's body.

Haney's body stopped the attack on Raven, dropped its sword, and clutched at the daggers to remove them. Shayla sprinted forward to retrieve the sword, and Raven swung at Haney's body with such force that it was sliced in two at the waist and fell to the ground. Shayla immediately removed its head with Haney's sword and then retrieved her daggers.

"Thanks," muttered Raven, his voice breaking with emotion, "when I saw it was Haney, it threw me off guard. Ramos has defiled not only my mother's grave but also the final resting place of the greatest warrior I have ever known. A man who was like a father to me." He fell to his knees in a mixture of emotion and pain from his wound.

Shayla looked at the now decaying remains of the last warrior and realized how upset Raven was. She dropped on her knees in front of him. Shayla then wrapped her arms around him as if he was a child. At first, Raven resisted but then put both his arms around her, and the two of them clung to each other silently.

Twila was momentarily in a dilemma when she heard Raven fighting behind her. Devon was up ahead of her with Amani, and Twila momentarily thought that she should probably go back to assist him. Then Twila remembered that Shayla had been close behind her. Shayla could help him if he needed it.

The passage ahead of her was so dark that she could see nothing. Twila could hear Devon calling out to Amani but only muffled grunts, and scuffling sounds came back. Twila cast a light spell, and as it illuminated the passage, she saw that Amani was rolling around on the floor with an undead warrior, frantically trying to free himself of its hands around his throat. As Twila got closer, she cast another light spell to illuminate the area better and saw with horror that Amani and the warrior were right on the edge of a Ravine.

"Watch out," Devon called out to Amani when Twila's spell finally provided enough light for him to see what was going on, "there's a sheer drop just behind you."

Amani grimly smiled when he heard this, and with one almighty effort, he launched himself backward into the ravine pulling the warrior down with him. The ground skidded away beneath him as Amani felt himself falling. He could see Twila and Devon's concerned faces peering down at him from the edge of the ravine as he fell.

The undead warrior suddenly released its grip on his throat when it realized its dilemma. Amani, now free, rolled over in the air pushing the warrior to one side as the two of them tumbled down into the dark void below. The warrior crashed against the rocks below him, as Amani became the raven, and with a graceful flap of his wings, he flew back up to where Twila and Devon anxiously waited.

Twila grinned with relief when a raven fluttered up from the depths of the ravine.

"What happened to the warrior?" Asked Devon, "did you remove the head?"

Amani returned to human form and shook his head in

reply. "The warrior smashed against the rocks down there, but the head remains intact. I doubt it can climb its way back up here quickly; it was a long way down. Even if it tried, all this will be over by then because when we have destroyed Ramos, it will destroy everything he created."

Twila leaned over the edge of the ravine, peering into the darkness. She could see nothing. Her ears strained to pick up the slightest sound, but all Twila could hear was the rushing water far below. Twila had to agree with Amani. If the warrior did manage to climb back up, it would be too late, no matter which way the battle went with Ramos.

Soleon quietly giggled as she passed the dead rats lying on the final steps to the upper levels. Soleon decided that she liked this group of strangers. They were getting rid of the things that she hated the most.

When Soleon heard their voices growing closer, she cautiously looked around the small exit of the passage and saw them just up in front of her. Soleon curiously watched as they made their way across to the final cavern where she knew that Ramos and Valeskas were waiting for their arrival.

"I am sorry that Ramos will destroy them," she mumbled sadly, "they are very good at killing the rats."

Amani led the way into the cavern with the others close behind him. "Welcome, intruders," Ramos said coldly. I have someone here who wishes to meet you."

Valeskas loomed from the shadows, his eyes blazing with pleasure as he focused on his intended victims. Shayla gasped in horror but stood her ground as more of Valeskas became visible, towering above them.

"What is this?" Said Twila to Amani quietly, "he is of flesh. Are we too late?"

"He may be of flesh, but he is not yet free," Amani replied, suddenly aware of increasing warmth in the center of his chest. "You deal with Ramos. Leave this evil abomination to me."

Movement caught Raven's eye, and he looked in that direction, his hand tightening its grip on his sword. As Valeskas slowly advanced towards the group, Amani seemed to grow in size. A brilliant red glow began to pulse around him, and as Raven and the others watched in amazement, Amani slowly changed into a dragon.

The martyred brothers' spirits became one, using Amani as their vessel to wreak vengeance on their traitor brother. When the transformation was complete, the red dragon raised its massive head and faced the advancing Valeskas.

"What trickery is this?" Valeskas screeched. "You are forbidden to leave the Tear."

"Just as you are forbidden to leave the void," replied the red dragon, his voice sounding melodious from the many dragons that created him.

Valeskas roared angrily in response. The sound crashed against the cavern walls with a deafening velocity. He leaped at the red dragon tearing into it with his teeth and talons. The group scattered out of the way of the battling dragons, leaping for safety as their massive tails lashed from side to side, crushing boulders and rocks and spreading the pieces everywhere.

"Quickly," yelled Raven to the others, trying to make himself heard above the din, "if we destroy Ramos, then we destroy the dragon."

Ramos stood to one side, watching the battling dragons in growing amazement. He could sense that his quest for more power was almost at an end, and the excitement within him grew. It was too soon to determine which dragon would be the victor, but Ramos saw with satisfaction that Valeskas was not bleeding from any of his wounds. However, the red dragon had several long-jagged injuries on its chest and neck, caused by the talons of Valeskas, and they were now bleeding profusely.

"Ramos," snarled Raven rushing towards the necromancer.

Ramos turned irritably at the sound of his name, not wishing to miss the fight between the dragons, and saw Raven, Twila, and Devon rushing towards him. Almost absent-mindedly, he waved a hand in their direction, casting a binding spell before turning back to watch the dragons.

Twila and Devon stopped instantly, secured by their invisible bonds. However, Raven was not affected by the spell due to the protection from his mother's pendant.

"You will have to do better than that," Raven snarled.

Ramos turned in surprise when he heard this and found himself face to face with Raven. A sudden rush of foreboding ran down his spine. It was the first time Ramos realized that was a chance that he could lose this fight. He turned and ran towards the table where the ingredients for his spells lay.

"The warrior has some kind of protection," Ramos said mentally to Valeskas.

"Then deal with him," Valeskas roared. He had discovered that his opponent, the red dragon, was tougher to fight than anticipated.

Ramos managed to dart out of the way as Valeskas's tail slammed down between himself and Raven in an attempt to slow down the latter's pursuit. He grabbed the ingredients for his most powerful spell, a lightning bolt. Ramos had decided against preparing it earlier because its components were rare, but that didn't matter now.

Raven, now forced to back up into a small recess in the cavern to avoid Valeskas's tail, became trapped. It effectively protected Ramos from his attack. As the red dragon saw Raven's dilemma, he attempted to push Valeskas away from where he had trapped the warrior. Raven frantically tried to time his escape as Valeskas's tail swished from side to side, but it moved too fast. Just a glancing blow would kill him instantly.

Devon and Twila struggled against their bonds, but both knew it was futile. Twila saw that Raven had got himself trapped because of the battling dragons and was now unable to get to Ramos. She looked over to where Ramos was working feverously with his flasks and jars. Twila realized that Ramos was creating a spell of some kind, just in the same way he had the last time they were in this cavern. She watched his hand gestures and could see his lips moving, chanting a spell, the words of which was impossible to hear over the roaring of the two dragons.

"Is there nothing we can do?" Twila screamed at Devon.

He suddenly remembered Soleon. Ramos created her so she should be able to remove a spell cast by him. He managed to turn and saw that Shayla was still at the cavern entrance, undecided what to do. "Shayla," he yelled urgently to her, "find the half-dead. She can release us from this spell."

Shayla nodded and sprinted out of the cavern in search of Soleon. It crossed her mind that she may not be able to get her to understand what was needed, but it was worth a try.

The red dragon tore into the icy cold flesh of Valeskas

with its rows of razor-sharp teeth. Each mouthful of flesh instantly evaporated into the real smoke body of Valeskas. The wounds that the red dragon caused left holes that did not bleed, and they healed instantly with the same blue-tinged flesh that the undead warriors had.

Valeskas was not winning the battle because the red dragon had forced him to the ground. As he thrashed his immense body to break free from the red dragon's assault, Valeskas effectively trapped Raven in a small recess.

The red dragon knew of Raven's dilemma and was also aware of the binding spell that held Devon and Twila. They could not move out of their way if Valeskas broke free from his grasp and rammed into them.

Valeskas was in such a rage that he noticed none of this and did not realize the red dragon had started to drive the two of them towards Ramos with its strength. The red dragon knew that eventually, Valeskas would begin to lose his power as Ramos's spell gradually wore off, and all the red dragon could hope for was that he could maintain his hold on him until then.

It didn't take Shayla long to find Soleon; she was already heading towards the cavern where the battle was. The half-dead carried a battle-ax that the warrior had discarded when it fell down the ravine. Shayla stopped in her tracks, trying to assess if the half-dead meant to attack her with it. Soleon, however, just happily smiled when she saw Shayla.

"Ah, it is the killer of rats," greeted Soleon happily, "I hate the rats."

"I need your help Soleon," Shayla said urgently, "a binding spell has trapped my friends. Can you help by removing it for me?"

Soleon looked puzzled for a moment, and then a look of terror crossed her face, "I cannot do that," she whispered fearfully "it would make Ramos angry."

Shayla thought frantically for a moment wondering how to persuade Soleon to remove the spell. She just had to find something to say to her that would make her want to defy Ramos.

"Your son is trapped in there too," she said suddenly, "you remember your son Jian, don't you? He came to save you, but the dragons are fighting, and now he is trapped."

Soleon's face softened for a moment, and Shayla noticed

that her eyes cleared as she slowly recognized her son's name. "Show me where my son is," she said firmly, "he is just a child and too young to be involved in all this."

Shayla was surprised by this response but did not correct her belief that Raven was still a child, "follow me then," she commanded and turned to run back towards the cavern.

As they approached the entrance, Shayla stopped when she found the way blocked by the ravine warrior. She readied her daggers as he started to run towards her and planned to blind it like the other warrior. It was on her before Shayla had the chance to throw them. The warrior no longer had a weapon, so it slammed its fist into the side of her head, knocking her off her feet sideways, and she landed heavily on the floor.

He grabbed the now stunned Shayla by the throat, dragging her up to her feet. Its fingers of ice surrounded Shayla's throat, tightening them until she could no longer breathe. Her knees buckled as she fought frantically to release its grip on her throat to catch her breath, but Shayla was not strong enough. Her lungs were burning from a lack of oxygen, and she started to lose consciousness. Suddenly the tortuous hold on her throat was gone, and Shayla fell to the floor on her knees, coughing and gasping for air.

"Hurry up," said Soleon urgently, "take me to Jian." Shayla looked up at Soleon in surprise.

"The warrior," she gasped.

Soleon smiled and held up the head of the fallen warrior. "I had to stop him hurting you," she said, "he wouldn't listen to me, and you need to take me to my son."

"Thank you," Shayla said hoarsely, "you just saved my life."

Devon breathed a sigh of relief when he saw Soleon enter the cavern, still carrying the battle-ax in one hand and the head of the warrior by the hair in her other hand. He strained to turn his head in her direction, fighting against the resistance of Ramos's spell.

"Quickly Soleon," he yelled, "release us."

Soleon promptly dropped the head and waved her now free hand in Devon and Twila's direction, but her eyes fixed on the dragons. Immediately on release, both Devon and Twila ran to the rear of the cavern.

Their release gave the red dragon the space to wrestle Valeskas away from Raven and, more importantly, towards Ramos.

On noticing that they had started to move away from him slowly, Raven edged his way forward to escape from the recess that trapped him.

Ramos's spell was almost complete, and he raised his arms, ready to use it against the two that were already trapped by his magic. The necromancer hesitated a moment when he suddenly recognized Twila. It didn't cause him concern that she was here, or even why. What did concern him, however, was what to do about the seal if he destroyed her.

He looked over at the dragons as they fought and saw with satisfaction that the red dragon seemed to be retreating away from Valeskas as it backed up in his direction. The new power that Valeskas promised him was almost his, and he wouldn't need the Gypsy girl then. If the seal failed, he would have his own magic to replace it.

"And if we lose the fight," he laughed, "then let the victor deal with the seal and what comes through it."

He chanted the final words of the spell as he lifted his arms. The moment he was about to release the magic, Soleon freed his captives.

"No," he screamed in anger as he watched Twila and Devon dart out of sight, "I will obliterate you this time, you meddling abomination."

He closed his eyes in concentration before releasing his magic. He watched with satisfaction as lightning bolts arced from each of his open palms then coming together in front of his face. The sound of their joining was like a clap of thunder, immediately followed by a brilliant silvery blue flash of light that shot across the cavern, slamming into the chest of Soleon.

Brilliant blue flames began to erupt as her clothing and flesh burned from the lightning bolt. Raven saw the attack, and rage exploded within him just as powerful as the magic unleashed on his mother. Within moments a pile of gray dust lay where Soleon had been, and Raven launched himself towards Ramos.

Ramos was concentrating on producing another lightning spell when Raven reached him and rammed his sword up to the hilt, in the center of his chest. The necromancer's eyes flew open in surprise, and he staggered back across the stone table, knocking over the jars and flasks that held his precious ingredients. He clutched the handle of the sword and attempted to pull it out but failed.

The white glow that had emanated from the blade when the crystal had smashed into it earlier returned. The light it produced quickly surrounded Ramos as he franticly tried to remove the sword. Suddenly his body rose into the air, and he flew across the cavern, smashing into the wall and burst into a shower of brilliant red sparks. There was a moment of silence, broken only by the clatter of Raven's sword as it fell to the ground.

Raven was stunned by Ramos's disappearance. Cautiously he picked up the sword expecting him to reappear at any moment. A sudden deafening silence filled the cavern, and Raven turned quickly to see why noise from the fight between the dragons had ceased. The red dragon was towering over the fallen Valeskas, and slowly he returned to the shape of Amani.

Devon, Twila, and Shayla gathered around Valeskas cautiously as he lay on his side, breathing heavily. An increasing rhythmic sound suddenly broke the silence. Raven slowly joined the others as the pounding beat, which he now determined was Valeskas's heartbeat, increased in volume. The sound grew louder and louder until it boomed within the cavern. An audible gasp of air suddenly escaped Valeskas's jaws.

"This is not over," gasped Valeskas, "it will never be over until I am free."

The heartbeat stopped suddenly, and he started to lose his flesh form. He seemed to meld into the cavern floor until finally, just a long wisp of smoke remained where the dragon had lain moments earlier. The smoke slowly receded into an innocent-looking wooden bowl that stood upon a flat rock close to where Ramos had been when he had disappeared.

Raven followed the smoke, his sword still drawn, until it disappeared into the thick dark liquid at the bottom of the bowl. He turned back to look at the rest of the group as Amani returned to his proper form.

"What happened?" Asked Raven.

"You defeated them," Amani replied, smiling. "When Saressa's power of light within your sword destroyed Ramos, it also destroyed the spell invoking Valeskas. He cannot remain in this place without someone to use as a vessel for his evil."

Raven turned back to look at the wall where Ramos had disappeared. "I am not so sure that I destroyed Ramos," he said slowly, "he just seemed to disappear."

Motomo and Daybreak exchanged glances nervously when they heard a rhythmic pounding that grew louder and louder. The sound echoed eerily around the cave and vibrated the floor, causing Fen to snort nervously. Daybreak nudged the horse to calm her.

"What do you think that is?" She asked alarmed. "It almost sounds like a heartbeat."

"I think that's what it is," Motomo replied thoughtfully.

The heartbeat began to lose its rhythm, and the final beat shook the whole cave. The silence that followed was just as alarming.

"Look across the bridge," said Daybreak walking forward curiously.

Motomo looked and saw a glowing green light amidst the crystal spheres. He crossed the bridge cautiously, leading the way, his ears upright, alert for the slightest sound. Daybreak followed behind him and saw that the green glow was beginning to shape itself. They both stopped for a moment and watched as the light transformed into the figure of a woman.

"Saressa," gasped Motomo when he recognized her and dropped down onto his belly in a gesture of respect.

"Then, the battle is over," said Daybreak thankfully as she kneeled on her front legs, also in a gesture of respect.

"Motomo," commanded Saressa gently, indicating that he could rise. "Bring my heroes to me." She laid her hand on his back. Motomo felt a slight tingling sensation where she touched him, and he turned on his heels immediately and ran in the direction of the entrance into the mountain.

Motomo met the others as they were wearily making their way back down through the levels. Their pace was much swifter coming down because they knew there was nothing left to fear. As they passed by the trail of slain warriors, Twila noticed that they all had become gray dust just as Soleon had done. Raven was desperately trying not to see this dust because it was an unwelcome reminder of his mother and Haney.

When they saw Motomo running towards them, panting heavily, the group stopped in surprise. Raven drew his sword, waiting to see what was chasing the wolf.

"What's wrong?" Asked Amani when the breathless wolf reached them.

"Saressa waits for you all below," Motomo panted.

"Then we must not keep her waiting," Amani smiled.

CHAPTER TWENTY-SIX

Separate Journeys

Daybreak turned in surprise when she heard Fen trotting across the wooden bridge behind her. Fen walked right up to the shimmering light that held the essence of Saressa without any sign of fear. Saressa smiled gently and touched Fen on her nose. The horse's nostrils flared briefly, but as the healing power from Saressa's fingers flowed through her, she relaxed.

"Fen needs to be strong for her next journey," said Saressa. "There is still work for you both to do."

"I will gladly serve you, Saressa," replied Daybreak, as she too received Saressa's touch on her nose. "I am not sure that Fen knows anything about all this, though."

"She knows in her own way of understanding things," smiled Saressa.

Motomo came running into the cave, closely followed by Amani, Twila, and Devon. Raven and Shayla arrived soon afterward and joined the others grouped around the vision of Saressa, and all went to their knees in respect.

"You have done well to rid this world of Ramos," Saressa said. "I believe I know how Valeskas managed to reach Ramos in this world. Dra is behind all of this. He gave Ramos a small taste of his dark power without breaking his pact not to enter this world. Dra must have appeared to him, in the same way as I appear before you now. I am not physically in this world, so I am not breaking my pact either, but I can release small amounts of power using crystals. Dra no doubt promised Ramos great powers if he assisted him to free Valeskas from the void.

"The rift that Ramos created between here and Lunaria was no accident, although Dra led Ramos to believe it was. He needed to infect Ramos with his dark gift, so Valeskas could then begin to use him in his bid for freedom. When Dra first gave Valeskas his dark heritage, anyone he infected is still currently under his influence. Except for the dragons.

"When I first discovered what Dra had done to these gentle beasts, I called them to me. All but Valeskas answered my call. One by one, the dragons allowed me to destroy the evil that was coursing through their veins before Dra could completely control them. As each one gave their life, I captured the soul of that dragon, and from their combined souls, I created the Dragon's Tear.

"The Dragon's Tear is the most powerful source of magic in all worlds. Only Dra would dare to try and access this power then use it against me. He uses Valeskas to find it because Dra agreed never to enter Vesta, which houses the Dragon's Tear."

"Why would an evil God agree to do anything?" Asked Devon.

"Dra had no choice but to agree," replied Saressa. "I turned over many of my worlds to him when he defeated me, and in return, he agreed never to enter Vesta. That is why I placed the Dragon's Tear there. Gods and goddesses do not break war treaties."

"But it hasn't stopped Dra from getting someone else from entering Vesta on his behalf, though, has it?" Said Amani angrily.

"Unfortunately, that is correct," said Saressa sadly. "I suspected in the beginning that Dra would do something to try and get his hands on the Dragon's Tear, so I tried to make sure that would never happen. There was only one of my dragons that, although bitten, had not drunk blood after Valeskas turned him, and he has guarded the Dragon's Tear for me.

"Radon sacrificed his freedom to stay within Vesta to guard it, and I gave him as many powerful abilities as I am capable of bestowing. Dra's powers, however, are more substantial than mine. I fear that if Valeskas ever gains access to Vesta, then what is now good will become evil. Valeskas will be free from the void, and Dra will cause chaos amongst the heavens again. He will be the most powerful amongst the gods and goddesses, and also the evilest.

"You have defeated Valeskas this time, but unless destroyed, I know Dra will continue to use him. Valeskas is the only one who can enter Vesta because I called to him from there. I invited him there, and that spell to welcome him cannot be broken. If he finds Vesta, then the fight is over."

"Why did you choose my world to send Valeskas and his minions?" Asked Devon quietly.

"That was a mistake, Devon," Saressa answered sadly, "I was creating Lunaria when I lost to Dra. I had completed half of the world, and two suns blessed it with light. The other half remained in the darkness waiting for me to bring light to it also.

"I had only just begun to create the seas and the rivers and had not even started on life forms. I thought the world was without any life form when I gave it to Dra. I had to send Valeskas and everyone he infected to a place where innocents would no longer be terrified by their evil. When I learned that Lunaria had evolved in my absence, it was too late, and there was nothing I could do.

"That world belongs to Dra, and I was and still am, unable to go there and repair what I have done. My heart will be heavy until they are gone from your world, and I will help you to do this as much as I can. If you destroy Valeskas, that will rid Lunaria of the Dark Ones, and peace can return to your people Devon.   "Dra never showed any true interest in your world; he just wanted it because I created it. He also has no interest in creating any worlds, like the rest of the gods and goddesses; he just causes chaos and wars amongst the worlds we create and also their inhabitants."

"Then we will find Valeskas and destroy him," said Amani firmly. "Can we use the rift that Ramos created to enter Lunaria?"

"When you destroyed Ramos, the rift between this world and Lunaria was closed forever," answered Saressa. "I will open another gateway for you using these crystals." She waved her hand in the direction of the crystal spheres around them.

"Unfortunately, I will have to close the gateway after you have entered it. I cannot risk the Dark Ones finding another entrance into this world," explained Saressa.

"So, once we enter Lunaria, we cannot return here?" Questioned Twila.

"The gateway will shatter once entered," confirmed Saressa. "All I can offer to you as a way to leave Lunaria are crystal keys that can only work after Valeskas's destruction. While he lives, then whoever agrees to go to Lunaria cannot leave."

"I will return to Lunaria," Devon stated firmly, "that is my world, and my father needs me. I am determined to find a way to destroy Valeskas even if I die trying."

"I too will go to Lunaria," Amani stated, "the blood dragons have wished it."

Saressa smiled at him. "And they have chosen their champion very well, Amani," she said, "you have been Radon's most faithful ally all these years, and I thank you for your service to me."

Twila was thoughtful for a moment. Her life changed irreversibly the moment she met Danior. There was nothing left for her here in this world now.

"I will go to Lunaria also," Twila finally said, "I made a promise to Danior."

"It may be too late to save him from the darkness," cautioned Saressa quietly.

"There must be a way to remove the evil within him like Radon destroyed the darkness in me," Twila said thoughtfully, "and if I fail to remove it, then I will destroy him along with the rest of them because of my love for him."

Saressa smiled at the group of volunteers on their knees before her.

"Then rise, and I will give to each of you a crystal key that will return you to this place if you choose to use it after the destruction of Valeskas," she said, waving her hand in the direction of one of the crystal spheres.

A green mist covered one of the crystals, and it glowed brightly for a moment, then suddenly it exploded into a million pieces that fell to the ground in a glittering shower of dust. When the green mist cleared, the group saw an archway of rock, and lying on the floor before it was three crystal shards.

Amani approached the archway and saw a dark sky filled with billions of twinkling stars. A mountain range, brightly lit by moonlight, stretched out before him for as far as his eyes could see.

"Welcome to Lunaria," said Devon coming up alongside Amani and saw what lay beyond the archway, "this is my world."

Twila joined them and gasped in awe at the many stars. Amani reached down to pick up the crystal keys. He handed one to Twila and one to Devon and kept the third one.

"It looks beautiful, Devon," said Shayla breathlessly, stepping up beside them. "I wish I could come with you."

"Unfortunately, you must return to your world," said

Saressa, "the armies from the east are advancing on your village. You must bring my followers here to this world where they can live in peace and protect them until the priestess that I have chosen for them arrives. I will open the gateway for you."

Saressa waved her arm again, and another of the crystal spheres exploded into dust, revealing another archway of rock.

Everyone looked into the archway curiously but could only see a long passage with flaming torches secured to its walls.

"This gateway must remain open," said Saressa, "the hidden entrance is in the cellar of your uncle's inn Shayla. The Dragon key that Raven holds will open the passage for my followers. That way, there is no danger of the easterners discovering this entrance and finding their way into this world."

"How will I find your priestess?" Asked Shayla.

"She will find you," Saressa replied.

Shayla nodded and then looked around at the others. "It is time I returned home," she said. "If the easterners have entered my village already, I must quickly bring the priest here before they discover him. I have hidden him in my uncle's cellar."

"I don't hold the Dragon key," said Raven quickly, "It is somewhere in the cave where Haney placed it."

"The key has its own magic Raven," responded Saressa, "call to it."

Raven was a little surprised by this suggestion. "How do I do that? He asked.

"Will it to come to you in here," Saressa said, pointing to her head.

He looked unconvinced, but he closed his eyes and thought of the key that Haney had planned to pass on to him. As Raven had never seen it but knew it as the Dragon key, he assumed, carved in the shape of one.

"Come to me," he thought, feeling a little foolish, "Come to me now." He commanded, this time with more conviction.

A sudden gasp from the others caused him to open his eyes. Raven gasped too, as he saw a blue ball of swirling light, slowly making its way towards them from the direction of the cave that they had used to enter the mountain from the beach.

The blue ball of light came over the bridge and paused for a moment, as if in thought. It started to move again and stopped in front of Raven, and in response, he held out his hand. It hovered above his hand briefly and then settled onto his palm. The blue orb of light burst like a soap bubble, and a key, the shape of a dragon, dropped into his hand.

Amani smiled and nodded in Saressa's direction as he watched this.

"I will guard this with my life," said Raven, tracing his fingers over the exquisite features of the Dragon key, just as Haney had done as a boy. He put the leather cord that was still attached to the key around his neck and tucked it beneath his shirt, where it nestled comfortably against his chest.

"My blessings go with all of you," said Saressa.

The group watched as Saressa's image flickered briefly, then she disappeared.

Shayla turned to Twila and hugged her tightly. "I hope you find Danior," she said softly. Twila's eyes filled with tears at this. "And I wish you well with your fight against the easterners," she responded.

"Maybe we will all meet up again someday," Shayla said quickly, fighting back her tears.

Raven nodded at Devon and Amani, individually grasping their right arm in a goodbye gesture. "Good fortune to you both," he said. "I wish I could be with you when you destroy Valeskas."

"If we are successful, I will find a way of letting you know," said Amani firmly.

"Then I know our paths will cross again," said Raven with conviction.

"It is time to go," Amani called out to Twila, who was hugging Motomo goodbye.

"Goodbye, my friend," Twila whispered into the wolf's ear before joining Amani and Devon, "I will miss you the most."

Devon entered the archway to Lunaria first, closely followed by Amani and then Twila. As she stepped over the threshold, the rock structure around the entrance began to rumble. The top portion of the arch crumbled and fell to the ground. Within a few moments, the only thing left of the gate was an innocent pile of rubble on the cave floor.

"Do you think they will find and destroy Valeskas?" Asked Shayla as she grabbed Fen's reins and led her towards the remaining archway.

"I hope so," Raven replied as he grabbed Daybreak's reins and followed Shayla.

Motomo gazed sadly at the pile of rubble from the first archway for a moment before following the others into Shayla's world.